DAVID PAYNE is the author of *Confessions of a Taoist on Wall Street* (winner of the Houghton Mifflin Literary Fellowship Award), *Early from the Dance*, and *Ruin Creek*. He lives in North Carolina.

GRAVESEND
LIGHT

A NOVEL

DAVID PAYNE

A PLUME BOOK

PLUME
Published by the Penguin Group
Penguin Putnam Inc., 375 Hudson Street, New York, New York 10014, U.S.A.
Penguin Books Ltd, 27 Wrights Lane, London W8 5TZ, England
Penguin Books Australia Ltd, Ringwood, Victoria, Australia
Penguin Books Canada Ltd, 10 Alcorn Avenue, Toronto, Ontario, Canada M4V 3B2
Penguin Books (N.Z.) Ltd, 182–190 Wairau Road, Auckland 10, New Zealand

Penguin Books Ltd, Registered Offices: Harmondsworth, Middlesex, England

Published by Plume, a member of Penguin Putnam Inc.
This is an authorized reprint of a hardcover edition published by Doubleday. For
information address Doubleday, A Division of Random House, 1540 Broadway,
New York, New York 10036.

First Plume Printing, August 2001
10 9 8 7 6 5 4 3 2 1

Grateful acknowledgment is made for permission to reprint:

"You Can't Be Too Strong." Written by Graham Parker. Copyright © 1979,
ELLISCLAN, LTD. (PRS)/Administered by BUG. All Rights Reserved.
Used by Permission.

 REGISTERED TRADEMARK—MARCA REGISTRADA

The Library of Congress has catalogued the hardcover edition as follows:

Payne, David (William David)
Gravesend light : a novel / by David Payne.—1st ed.
p. cm.
ISBN 0-385-47338-9 (hc.)
ISBN 0-452-28262-4 (pbk.)
1. Outer Banks (N.C.)—Fiction.   I. Title.
PS3566.A9366 G7 2000
813'.54—dc21   99–089408

Printed in the United States of America
Set in Simoncini Garamond
Original hardcover design by Fritz Metsch

BOOKS ARE AVAILABLE AT QUANTITY DISCOUNTS WHEN USED TO PROMOTE PRODUCTS OR
SERVICES. FOR INFORMATION PLEASE WRITE TO PREMIUM MARKETING DIVISION, PENGUIN
PUTNAM INC., 375 HUDSON STREET, NEW YORK, NEW YORK 10014.

TO GRACE,
a-boundin'

Diabla Rosa, Monkey Toes, starer
at ceilings, may Xena, the Tigress
of the Euphrates, and all the Amazon nations
heed your pterodactyl cry and come
to aid you in your cause

[The anthropologist's] personal relationship to his object of study is, perhaps more than for any other scientist, inevitably problematic . . . All ethnography is part philosophy, and a good deal of the rest is confession.

—CLIFFORD GEERTZ,
The Interpretation of Cultures

When that which drew from out the boundless deep
Turns again home . . .
—TENNYSON,
"Crossing the Bar"

Gravesend Light

Prologue

Cracking the hawser like a sluggish whip, Joe Madden shook off the row of icicles that had formed like murderous tinsel overnight and leaped aboard, his steps ringing on the steel deck plate of the already moving boat. Above him in the bow, Jubal Ames, in aviator glasses, red hair stiff as a wire brush, loomed through the tinted Lexan windows of the wheelhouse. As the captain nudged her from reverse to forward, the corroded stack kicked back a croupy cough of diesel-scented smoke, her old Cat engine dropping an octave into a black-lunged *basso profundo*. The wake she boiled washed through the barnacle-encrusted pilings, stirring filleted skeletons and beer labels from the bottom of the Gut. A soft breeze stirred Joe's hair, the cutwater releasing smells of oxygen and something else fundamentally nameless and marine.

As the *Father's Price* gained headway, Joe took up a position in the stern, gazing aft at the world he was rapidly leaving behind. Day had climbed out of the idling Wagoneer and joined the other women on the dock, not a few of them her patients. Girlfriends, mothers, wives—in Little Roanoke, they were indiscriminately known as "fishing widows," a detail Joe had duly noted and filed away in his extensive ethnographic notes. In sweats and curlers, a baby on one hip, another in a folding Kmart stroller, the village women—many still in their teens, yet already beefing up as though they got paid for marriage by the pound—idly smoked and chat-

ted, occasionally shrilling coarse chastisements at a tow-headed
boy amusing himself by chucking rocks at the fishhouse cat.

In understated urban black, Day, lean and thirty-one, a head
taller than anybody there, stood out in their midst like a letter
crisply printed on a blurred gray page. In a short-skirted bouclé suit
under her open overcoat, she wore leggings against the cold and a
pair of heavy, square black lace-ups purchased at some trendy
bootery off St. Mark's Place. Clunky, almost remedial-looking,
those shoes' subversive charms spoke to Joe at levels he could
hardly understand, like the man's Swiss Army watch she wore upside down on her left wrist, and her radical blond bob, which fell
above her earlobes, with shallow bangs across her brow. Whether
she'd paid a week's salary for that cut at some avant-garde salon or
had grabbed the Fiskars from the pen-and-pencil jar, poured a glass
of jug Chablis and gone on the offensive in the bathroom mirror
was a mystery that Joe, professional unraveler of mysteries, had
preferred to leave intact. In combination with her eyes, that haircut
gave Day a distinct resemblance to the little Dutch boy. Joe, however, could no longer see Day's eyes as the boat neared Gravesend
Head, where the Gut opened into the Pamlico channel, wending its
way through nine treacherous, shoaling miles to Oregon Inlet and
the most dangerous sandbar in the United States. He knew their
color, though: a pure Delft blue that lightened when she laughed,
turning the almost lavender of chicory growing wild in a ditch by
a New England roadside in July. Day, however, wasn't laughing
now. Joe didn't need to see her face to know that either.

She did, however, raise her hand, and he raised his, answering
back. Over black, open water, they faced off like Indian braves,
somber and unsmiling with the weight of everything that had gone
down. As the distance between them widened, Joe was struck
again, as he had been over Christmas, by how profoundly unlike
his own mother this woman was. Physically, morally, stylisti-
cally—the two women were virtual opposites in every way, as different from each other as Joe was from his father, Jimmy, which
was what made it so curious, and shattering, to try to understand
how today, at twenty-eight, on this bitter winter morning at the
start of 1983, Joe had arrived in exactly the same place his father
found himself at twenty-one, in 1954.

To the east, on Roanoke Island, a gust of wind moved through the cordgrass in the marsh, the depressed stalks darkening as though shadowed by a passing cloud. A raft of what at first resembled butterflies drifted slowly upward, like confetti in an updraft; then the white flash of sunlight caught their underwings, revealing what they were. Snowgeese. Rising helter-skelter, spooked by something, they gradually ranked themselves in order, forming a long fluid V, the arms rippling and fluctuating as they crossed the bow and circled back. Against the pale sky, their whiteness blackened as they climbed, till they suggested specks of dust or iron filings. Iron filings in a magnetic field—as he watched them waver and align, setting out on their remembered journey, following an invisible line of force, the image came to Joe together with a question: What was the field?

Whatever it was, a similar one now held him and Day. A scientist whose field was human motivation, Joe could no more answer how this had occurred than he could spread his arms and fly south with the snows.

PART I

One

I had a rotten feeling, watching them steam out that morning. Moving backward, away from me, Joe stood in the stern, six-four, with a grave expression on his clear, high-boned face; his shoulder-length black hair, straight and heavy as a Cherokee's, was pulled back in a ponytail from which a single tress had broken loose. That lock of hair disturbed me; why, I don't know. As though pledging allegiance to the flag, promising to tell the truth, the whole truth and nothing but the truth, he had his hand raised, and the look in his eyes—incompletely reconciled, gazing into the distance with a hint of misgiving whose true nature I don't believe Joe understood any more than I did—was one I'd come to know. I felt a little stab of premonition, which I wrote off at the time to the argument we'd had, if an argument was what it was, and the uncertain way we'd left it. Later, though, I had occasion to recall him standing in the stern like one of the newly dead in Charon's barge, gazing back as the infernal boatman ferried him over the black waters of the Styx.

The last I saw of him was his Day-Glo orange oilskins. They were Grundens—Norwegian, Swedish maybe, Scandinavian in any case. Joe, as it turned out, was exacting when it came to his equipment, a fact you might not have immediately put together with his professorial and somewhat unworldly air. He'd had them on the day he came into Beach Med with cellulitis, thinking he had dengue fever. Having a light afternoon on the women's side that afternoon, I took the call.

Joe was sitting on the table in Exam Room 4, with his coverall suspenders dangling, wearing the white rubber boots they call "Roanoke bedroom slippers" on the islands, perusing the book in his lap through a pair of scholarly, pink-framed glasses.

"Dr. Madden?"

As he looked up, a gleam of recognition darted, minnowlike, through intelligent green eyes before disappearing into deeper water. Our paths had crossed before, albeit briefly. Joe's face was a curious marriage of two types: John Kenneth Galbraith, say—that refined patrician chiseling—grafted onto something unrestrained and far less tame, reminiscent of someone like Neil Young. "Dr. Shaughnessey, isn't it?"

I smiled. "What seems to be the problem?"

Closing his finger in the book, he extended a right arm that four months of summer fluking had left as heavy and articulated as a piece of lathe-turned oak, with a plump blue vein running up his biceps, still visible at the shoulder, where it disappeared beneath the frayed edge of his sleeveless T. A surfer's arm, I remember thinking. Joe had that build—broad-shouldered, lean, flat-hipped. Though, as a rule, surfers are as dumb as posts, they have the best of all male bodies—this, of course, is just my personal opinion—carrying in their limbs some suggestion of the grace and love of what they do offshore.

"Just tell me it's not dengue fever," he said, nodding to an inflamed red streak running from his wrist to elbow.

I laughed, thinking he was joking. The look he gave me quickly corrected that impression.

"We're a little far from the equator for dengue," I explained, chastened and professional.

"I was in Bali last year. I'm not sure what the incubation period may be."

"Oh," I said. "Well, dengue, I believe, does cause inflammation, but what you have here looks to me to be a simple case of lymphangitis."

"Lymphangitis?"

"That's right."

"Can you define that?"

"A rash. Or, if you prefer, a diffuse, edematous, suppurative inflammation of the subcutaneous tissue."

He blinked. "Could you spell lymphangitis?"

With no great confidence, I gave him my best approximation, and Joe, to my amused surprise, took a small steno pad from his T-shirt pocket and wrote it down with a nib pen—a Mont Blanc, I noticed.

"I see this a lot in folks who handle fish. In Wanchese and Little Roanoke, they call it fish poison."

"I thought that was the sort of thing you get from eating bad sushi."

I smiled, though cautiously. "Different animal."

Frowning, he took note of this, then looked up with the keen gaze of a mental raptor. "What is it, bacterial?"

"Most likely." Dousing a cotton ball in alcohol, I began to swab his arm.

"Staph?"

"Could be. Or group A strep," I answered, liking his pursuit, but also noting how he'd quickly turned our consult to an interview, betraying the bent of an investigative journalist. "To know for sure, we'd have to run a culture, but that really isn't necessary. A course of tetracycline, and it should clear right up. If you handle fish a lot, you might try mixing a tablespoon of Clorox in a quart of water and rinsing down with that—it's a home remedy the locals use."

There was a brief delay as he jotted this down, too, in his compact script—block letters, like a child's, but neat and regular and tight, like glittering Roman phalanxes marching on a void white plain.

"I tried sea water," he said, putting away his implements. "That generally works pretty well as a disinfectant."

"Old wives' tale," I told him, stepping on the waste can pedal and tossing in the swab. "Sea water isn't sterile. Dozens of types of infectious bacteria live in it."

"Oh." The professor drew a pause on this. "Oh, well," he said. "There goes another childhood illusion."

And I would have laughed at that one, too, gladly, only from his expression you simply couldn't tell whether it was wit or accident.

"I must have got this lumping out last week."

"Lumping out?"

"Unpacking the boat," he translated.

"I don't think I've heard the term. Why do they call it that?"

"Lumping?" Joe considered. "Actually, I'm not sure. Based on somewhat limited personal experience, I'd say it has to do with taking lumps on a professional basis."

On that, I hooted, and just when you thought Buster Keaton was terminally incapable of a smile, there it came, a flush of half-surprised pleasure beaming through his reserve like sunlight through the stained glass window of a church; someone younger and warmer peeked out at me like a shy faun from behind the fluted column of a stone Greek temple.

"You know, actually," he said, emboldened by a success I was pretty sure he hadn't planned, at least not fully, "we've met. You probably don't remember."

"Actually," I said, "I do."

It had been at a town meeting, in the gym at Manteo High, convened to discuss the Oregon Inlet Stabilization Project, a hundred-million-dollar proposal by the Army Corps of Engineers to build a pair of mile-long jetties straight out into the Atlantic from the Inlet's mouth to stop the shoaling on the outer bar. Facing off across the center aisle that night, like resentful, socially ill-suited families at a shotgun wedding, you had, on the right side, the pro-jetty contingent, consisting primarily of bearded fishermen in flannel shirts and Redman hats; and on the left, opposed, the vacation interest, so-called, various upstate doctors, lawyers and Indian chiefs with their million-dollar ocean-front properties—and the locals who catered to their trade—all of them united in a not entirely altruistic crusade to keep the Banks pristine (protecting, along with the environment, the tourist dollar and their own property values).

Landless, none too gentrified, but deeply Green at heart, I'd gone that night with Gaither Holman, Beach Med's staff G.P., my boss, to rally round the environmental flag. As we sat down on the left, I saw, among the contra-jetty crowd, several men I'd dated—mostly blind and seldom twice. With their gold signet rings and graphite golf clubs rattling in the beamer's trunk, they tended to blur into a single image: Topsiders without socks, a starched madras shirt, a belt with yachting flags, a haircut like a twelve-

year-old's, that Tefloned, ultra-Southern, almost military-style politeness, so friendly on the surface, to a true and searching intimacy
so opposed. Over dinner, when I launched, with my second glass of
wine, into some choice war story culled, perhaps, from therapy and
punctuated by the first un-self-censored "fuck" for emphasis—stories that at a dinner in D.C. or New Haven or New York would
have got a laugh—I'd usually elicit stares in which the clink of blue
ice cubes was all but audible, leaving both me and young Robroy,
Gilliam, or Rhys the third, F.F.V., dying to escape before the coffee
came.

Romantically, the beach had been a small catastrophe for me.
The good news was, I'd developed one hell of a shell collection.
And jokes aside, apart from the professional opportunity Beach
Med provided—the chance to run a women's clinic according to
my lights, offering a level of service local women before had had to
drive a hundred miles to get—the ocean was the reason why I'd
come, the big sky with its shifting lights. After eight years in New
Haven, eight years of urban blight, eight years walking home from
the hospital down Howe Street in the middle of the night, my finger on the trigger of the canister of Mace in the side pocket of my
overcoat, I'd been ready for a break. The beach had given that to
me—the chance to walk the strand after northeasters, scouring for
shells, to fall asleep with my windows open. Listening to the
ocean's conversation with itself, systole followed by diastole, the
ancient yes and no, had helped me to hear the whisper of my inward voice again, a voice that had grown ever fainter during the
long forced march I'd soldiered through at Yale.

The bad news was, by that August night in Manteo, eight
months into my one-year contract, I felt in imminent danger of re-
gressing to the virgin state I'd sacrificed in my best friend Caitlin's
rumpus room in Chevy Chase the week I turned sixteen.

The moderator of the event was Grant Eustis, current head of
the North Carolina chapter of E.C.C.O., the East Coast Conservation Organization, whom I knew slightly through his wife, Cassie,
a patient. An agribusiness magnate who owned a 500,000-acre
spread in the northeast corner of the state, stretching from the
shore of Currituck Sound five counties deep, back through
Perquimans and Pasquotank all the way to Gates, Eustis bore an
unfortunate resemblance to my personal *bête noire* and nemesis of

nemeses, Jesse Helms, a resemblance that, I regret to say, wasn't solely physical.

He'd just given the floor to the evening's featured speaker, Professor Perrin Orkney, a geologist from East Carolina University, who spoke—persuasively, I thought—of the profound unwisdom of the jetty plan. Oregon Inlet, Orkney said, was one of the most dynamic watercourses in the world. In a single twenty-four-hour period, during the Ash Wednesday storm in 1962, it had opened from less than half a mile across to more than two. It was hubris and sheer folly to think human intervention could oppose the force of nature in a system so unstable, and an egregious waste of taxpayer money to try.

"In the seventeen years since the Bonner Bridge was built," Orkney said, "twenty-three lives have been lost at the Inlet. That works out to one-point-three a year. I don't want to make light of those deaths, but the truth is, thirty times that number drown here off the beaches every summer. Given the weekly traffic through the Inlet, crossing the bar is probably safer for the fishermen of Roanoke Island and Little Roanoke than it is for most of us to get in our cars to drive to work. Statistically, you have more chance of dying from a shark attack or lightning strike than . . ."

"Goddamn it to hell! We ain't talking about shorks or loightning stroikes!"

Unrecognized by the chair, Dolph Teach, the head of the Clam Teach Fish Company in Little Roanoke, stood up and, in a voice like Popeye the Sailor Man—only salted with the dipthongs of the distinctive local "hoi toide" dialect—shouted the professor down. Built like the butt log of a sequoia, with a tuft of coal black hair on top so thick it looked like fur, he glared at the geologist with angry eyes as black as creosote. Removing the unlit pipe from his mouth, he jabbed the air with the chewed stem. "There's people doying over here, you asshole—good men! Ain't a fam'ly own the oislands ain't lost a father or a brother or a son, and you, some Nancypants from E.C.U., got the goll to stand up there and tell us it's safe as droiving in your car to work . . .It's a goddamn loie and you're a goddamn loiar!"

"Dolph!" Grant Eustis rapped his gavel. "Dolph! Mr. Teach! Listen here, I won't have that kind of language. It doesn't do a bit of good to turn this thing into a shouting match."

"And you!" Teach roared. "I know who you are—don't think I don't! Up there own that farm of yours, you clear-cut half the Dismal Swamp and ditched it out and planted it in corn. There's foive hundred pounds of fortilizer to the acre toimes foive hundred thousand acres running roight straight down into the Albemorle, which, thanks to you, is polluted worst than Narragansett Bay. And that's proime breeding ground for all them fish you say you're so damn jealous to presorve. East Coast Conservation Organization my ass—the damn sport-fishing lobby is what you are! The only thing you're interested in consorvatin' is your privilege, so you and your buds from Roleigh and Richmond and Washington, D.C., can droive down here own the weekend in your shoiny four-by-fours and th'ow a loine in the worter and catch, for your pleasure, the fish my people count own to survoive and risk their loives to get every toime they cross the Inlet bar. Shouting match? I'm gonna shout! I'm gonna shout it from the rooftops, 'cause I'm mad as a wet setting hen! People own the oislands are flustrated to the seb'm toimes seb'mty-seventh power, roight up to the tops of their heads, and I intend to shout till someone storts to listen, and you don't loike it, you can kiss my round, red, hairy ass!"

"Order! Order, Mr. Teach!"

And just as things seemed about to degenerate into a barroom brawl, Grant Eustis, grateful for diversion, pointed his gavel, and I turned to see Joe Madden standing in the rear, steno pad at the ready, Mont Blanc raised for recognition. He was clad in jeans and a heavy denim shirt spruced up with a rumpled blue blazer with gold buttons that looked like a relic from a former tour of duty in some tony boarding school and made a curious contrast with his old work boots.

"Yes, sir!" Eustis hailed him.

"Joe Madden, Mr. Eustis," Joe called back in a strong, clear voice.

"I know who you are," said Eustis, his gaze going lidded and appraising. "What can we do for you, Professor?"

"I want to respond to Dr. Orkney's point."

"Go 'head," said Grant, and as the room quieted, you could hear the squeak and rustle of people turning in their chairs.

Joe raked his fingers through his hair. "As I was coming in a little while ago, I noticed a Mercedes in the lot beside a rusty pickup with crab pots in the bed. They both had the same bumper sticker: IF YOU WANT PEACE, FIGHT FOR JUSTICE." Speaking in a relaxed, natural style, he left a pause for rhetorical effect.

"What's your point?" said Eustis, frowning.

"My point," Joe replied, "is that both sides of this issue raise legitimate concerns. As eloquent as he was, Professor Orkney's 'one-point-three' doesn't convey the human cost of the Inlet to the island communities. I've been doing fieldwork in Little Roanoke for the last four months, and in that time I've made seven or eight trips aboard the *Father's Price* with Captain Jubal Ames. As you approach the outer bar, there's a rusty spar sticking up from the water. It's the mast of a dragger called the *Debra Jean*—some of you, I know, remember her. She went down three years ago in an October gale. Her captain, Billy Rabb, reached the Inlet six hours before slack water. It was blowing forty knots, gusting up to fifty-five, but they had fish going bad on deck, so Rabb decided to come in. Jubal and Cully Teach on the *Three Brothers* were out there jogging by the first buoy, waiting out the tide, so they watched this happen from a distance of less than a hundred yards.

"As the *Debra* came across the bar, a big sea caught her starboard quarter and shoved her up on the south side shoal. Rabb gunned her, trying to get off, but he had nine hundred boxes aboard—that's ninety thousand pounds of fish—and her rudder dug into the sand and snapped the steering cable. They said she swung around then till she was beam-to to those big combers rolling down from the northeast. Rabb was on the horn to the Coast Guard down in Buxton, but there wasn't even time to get the helicopter in the air. Randall Midgett, the ranger on Pea Island, came down in his truck and tried shooting a Lyle gun from shore, but the way those seas were running, the waves just washed the line away.

"This happened on a Sunday, around nine, nine-thirty in the morning. Rabb's crew had taken their showers, cleaning up to go to church. Jubal told me that through the glasses, he could see the comb strokes in their hair. They were all standing there on deck, clinging to the shrouds and stays, with long looks on their faces like they knew what they were in for. Then another sea washed in and raised her up, and when she dropped back down, it punched her bottom out. Within three minutes, she was matchwood. She was put together, too, the *Debra Jean,* only she was wood. The next wave swept her decks, Jubal said, and when the foam subsided, Billy and his crew were gone. They saved one man. Rabb's body was all the way to Salvo before it washed ashore."

The gym, as he concluded, was silent as a mausoleum. Joe's eyes, as he told his story, blazed.

"You asked me my point, Mr. Eustis. My point is simply to suggest that justice, as it appears to you and E.C.C.O. and Professor Orkney, and justice, as it appears to Dolph Teach and the fishermen of big and Little Roanoke, and especially to Linda Rabb, Billy Rabb's widow, who's forty-six years old and lives on Flower Street in Little Roanoke with four children under twelve years old and works on the fishhouse culling line for $3.65 an hour, justice in your universe and hers are two different things."

That was my first sighting of Joe Madden.

As the meeting started to break up, I tagged along with Gaither as he worked the room, and I overheard Dolph Teach and several other fishermen offer Joe shy and bumbling congratulations—"Way to go, bud"; "Reckon you told them"—which the professor received with a smile that failed to mask his deep unease at their assumption of straightforward partisan solidarity. Appearances to the contrary notwithstanding, Joe Madden could never be accused of anything so simple as partisan solidarity, or partisanship in general or straightforwardness of any kind. But I precede myself . . .

While I was chatting, I spied Cassie Eustis making her way through the crowd like a destroyer, parting the waters as she came. Wearing a take-no-prisoners Chinese red ensemble, she marched up to Joe like John Wilkes Booth approaching Lincoln at the Ford, and waited, none too patiently, for an opportunity to give him a piece of her mind, if not a naked bodkin in the heart. So, at least, it seemed to me, and Joe, showing signs of similar concern, broke off in midsentence and turned to her with a polite curiosity that did not preclude the possibility of self-defense.

"I'm Cassie Eustis," she said in her honeyed eastern Carolina drawl. "I think you know me."

Joe was clearly clueless.

"Cassie Lane, if that helps you any. From Chowan?" (Cho-*wan,* she said.)

"I'm sorry, Mrs. Eustis," Joe began, "I don't believe I . . ."

"You have no more idea than a hoot owl who I am, do you?" she interjected. "Well, never mind. I'm a friend of yo' mama's, sugar. Many's the time I've sat right there on the po'ch at yo' cottage and had cocktails with your mamindaddy. Jimmy used to make a diabolical martini." (Maw-tini, she said.) "We used to call him Maddog—did you know that?"

"I have heard that, Mrs. Eustis," he answered, smiling now.

"Cassie," she said. "Last time I saw Jimmy, he was climbing a trellis at the KA house in Chapel Hill in his skivvies, yodeling like Ta'zan, King of Apes. I don't even want to tell you how long ago that was. I want you to know, Joe, I loved yo' book."

"My book . . ." Joe said uncertainly. *"Ngirim?"*

"Simply loved it. When I heard May Tilley's little boy had grown up to become an aw-thuh, I went right out and bought twenty copies."

"Twenty copies!" Joe's manner warmed distinctly.

"Umm-hmm. Sent 'em to my Christmas list last year."

"Good heavens, Mrs. Eustis, you must have bought out the whole first printing."

"Cassie" she said, a hint of mischief sparking in experienced, unsurprisable dark eyes. "Cassie, please. If you make me tell you one mo' time, I may have to put you on my knee."

With highly developed social E.S.P., she caught my eye at just that moment while I eavesdropped shamelessly. Operating off pure instinct, like a birddog quartering a hill, she waved her bejeweled fingers, took my hand and reeled me in. "And look who's here. Day Shaughnessey, Joe Madden. Joe, Day's a doctor, down here on sabbatical and sharp as seven cards of tacks. Day, sugar, I just love that outfit. Where on earth did you ever find that shawl?"

She was referring to an off-white floral one I'd picked up at a vintage clothing store off Dupont Circle on a trip home to D.C.

"My Nana Lane had one just like that," said Cassie, fingering the silk. "The spitting image."

"Maybe it was hers," I said, giving Joe a friendly smile. "I got it at a thrift shop."

Cassie took the slightest pause. "You don't mean it. I swear, you girls today are so much more creative than we were. All we ever did fo' fun was drink and screw in the back seats of cars."

At that, I let out a delighted yelp. Cassie's manner owned no hint of the intention to amuse, yet she was obviously used to doing so and took our laughter as her due. For Joe laughed, too, and it was enlightening to see, once assassination had been ruled out as a possibility, the way she brought him out. With blush after blush, the somber young professor seemed, if only temporarily, like a happy bacterium suspended in a petri dish of nutrient-rich female attention, giving me a fairly definite idea of how he'd grown up, and where.

As though a thought had dawned in her small mind, Cassie cut her glance from me to Joe and back to me again.

"Joe's an author, Day," she said. "Did I mention that?"

"I'm afraid I haven't read your book," I told him.

"That puts you in a sizeable majority, I'm sad to say," he answered rather nicely.

"He's being modest," Cassie said. "I have no earthly idea what the title means, but it's a perfectly wonderful story, and, Joe, Day is wonderful, too. Did I tell you that she's down here on leave from Yale?" She touched his arm. "Let me ask you, sugar—are you seeing anyone right now?"

"Seeing anyone . . ."

"Romantically, I mean."

Joe's eye rolled like a nervous mustang's. "Well, actually, Mrs. Eustis . . ."

"Cassie . . ."

"Cassie. No. However . . ."

But Professor Double-Take was left masticating the disclaimer in his mouth. Cassie, with an arch-browed look, turned to me and poked her tongue into her cheek.

"You better strike while the i'on's hot, sugar," she said. "Else, I may have to go fo' 'im myself."

And just as Joe and I were both about to burst spontaneously into flame, Cassie's attention wavered; she spied her husband in the crowd and invited him to join the rolling, self-created "pa'ty" that she was.

"Now Joe and Grant," she said, with an expression like an orphan eating gruel, "I know you two have a diff'ence of opinion on the jetties, but I want you to shake hands and be friends, and I intend to hold my breath and pout until you do. If I expire, it'll be on both yo' heads. Grant, honey, Joe is May's son, May Tilley—did you realize that?"

Fifty-five, heavyset, Grant repaid her efforts with a smile that, putting in its appearance, extended less than it withheld. Despite careful grooming and ample evidence of wealth, there was something countrified and taciturn about Grant, as though even if he owned the entire northeastern corner of the state, he was, at heart, a dirt farmer with a shrewd, unforthcoming, hardscrabble view of things. I didn't know him well, but Grant Eustis struck me as a man in whom privilege and affluence produced not refinement but its opposite, a kind of coarseness that gave him license to regard his mental limits as the horizon of the world—the world that counts, that is.

"Umm-hmm," he said, in a drawl like Cassie's. "I knew yo' mama from way back, son, way on back. I 'member May down here dancing at the Beach Club prob'ly thutty yea's ago. She could cut the rug, May could. Knew yo' daddy, too."

"Jimmy and Grant were both KAs," Cassie said.

"Is that right?" A look of unconsidered, boyish pleasure lit Joe's face, that shy faun peeking from the peristyle. (That was my first glimpse of him.)

"Umm-hmm. He was always writing, too, as I recall"—Grant's gaze casually scanned the steno pad and the Mont Blanc—"scribbling on the backs of matchbooks, paper napkins, whatever he could find. We always figured he was writing the Great American Novel. Where is Maddog anyhow?"

"Key West."

"Right, right. Come to think of it, somebody told us that, didn't they, Cassie? Said they saw him selling ice cream cones off the public dock down there."

The unsuspecting smile on Joe's face flash-froze, then, thawing, melted quite away. "He has a shop actually," he answered in an even tone.

"Oh, then, well . . ." A look of bland exulting played like sun spangles over the dark water of Grant's lidded eyes. "A shop."

Until that moment, Joe Madden seemed intriguing, even vaguely possible. But right there—don't ask me why—right there, as he fielded the insult to his father, his green eyes clear and his shoulders held a trice more square, his cheeks burning bright as with the handprint of a slap—something about him in that moment pricked me like the needle of the magic spinning wheel in the old fairy tale.

"If you'll excuse me?" And with a question and the briefest glance at me, Joe beat a poised retreat. Our paths didn't cross again, not for another month, till that September morning in Exam Room 4 when he came in with a case of common cellulitis he thought was dengue fever.

As I wrote out his scrip and tore it off the pad, he got up from the table, unfolding and unfolding as he rose. The whole perspective tilted woozily—to tell the truth, at five-eleven and a half, I wasn't all that used to looking up to men, and feel free to take that any way you want. As I handed him the slip, I tilted my head to see what he was studying.

"*Tristes Tropiques,*" I read off the spine. "Lévi-Strauss . . . wasn't he the guy who invented blue jeans?"

The professor looked discouraged, if not morally gored by my remark.

"That was a joke," I said, clueing him.

"Oh." He didn't look convinced.

"I think it was on our syllabus in Anthro 101 at Georgetown," I said, making conversation. "As I recall, it's pretty good."

Joe nodded. "Someone—I think it was Clifford Geertz—once said it's the greatest book ever written by an anthropologist. Its status as ethnography is pretty dubious, though."

I widened my eyes. "Really, Clifford Geertz said that?"

"I think it was Geertz," he replied, as soberly as though challenged in his doctoral defense.

Belatedly, he caught my grin. "Oh," he said. "I'm being pedantic, yes?"

Apparently the charge was not entirely unfamiliar. The smile with which he took the news, however, was entirely sporting.

Call me crazy, call me irresponsible, but I thought he was adorable as hell. I liked the deliberate way he answered questions, taking them more seriously than casual conversation warranted, furrowing his brow to ponder first and then responding as though composing the thesis paragraph of an essay on which I'd presently be grading him. Something about him conjured up the notion of a bear—I don't mean an old bear, boorish and willful with self-rule—but a younger specimen, a leaner, better-natured bear who, rather than roaring and relying on his claws, had made ursine habits and behavior the subject of scholarly pursuit and learned to drink tea from a china cup with lifted dewclaw. The effect was not of lack of force but of force restrained or incompletely recognized.

Joe Madden was, at any rate, different from the men with madras shirts and belts with yachting flags. Those men had clear provenances and unclear faces, something Joe, with his clear face and unclear provenance, reversed. He was at least a member of a tribe I vaguely recognized—if not my own. But, no, that's not right either. It's probably closer to the truth to say that Surfer Joe, the Lumping Professor, Mr. Scientific Method, student of tribal customs, was not a member of a tribe at all. And that, too, had more than a little to do with his sojourn in Little Roanoke. If you ask me, that's what he was doing over there, searching for the time portal, the magic door back in. What neither of us had any way of knowing that morning at Beach Med was that the door, when it finally opened, would be through me.

Shouldering his suspenders, he took his book and started for the door, where he turned back. "By the way," he said, "do you like fish?"

"Fish?" I said. "Why, sure. Who doesn't?"

Perhaps a femme-none-too-fatale may be forgiven for thinking this was a romantic opening of sorts, albeit a rather odd one. The professor, however, as though satisfying a point of personal curiosity, merely pursed his lips and nodded, politely thanked me, and promptly disappeared.

Not two minutes later—I'd gone on to a patient in Exam Room 3—LuAnn Grissom, the obstetrical nurse who served as my right hand, knocked on the door.

"I think you'd better come. It's kind of an emergency," she said. An attractive brunette who'd grown up on a farm near Morgan's Corner, LuAnn exuded, even in her spotless whites, the blowsy sensuality of a country-western star, something big-hearted, warm, incautious, and a little roadworn at the edges, an effect compounded by her bad home perm, which had relaxed to the point where it was indistinguishable from simple piliform distress.

I followed her boom-boom walk toward the waiting room, which was absolutely crammed. There, in his sleeveless T and Grunden coveralls, holding what appeared to be a halibut or perhaps an enormous flounder—it was flat and green and roughly the

size of a Toyota—was the young professor, looking around un-
comfortably.

"Hi again," he said. "Sorry to interrupt, but I had two of these,
and I can't eat them both. I thought maybe . . ." Self-entangling, he
faltered.

At a loss, I stared at the leviathan.

"It's a gift," LuAnn said helpfully, taking on the thankless task
of jump-starting my dead love battery.

Joe gratefully tipped his head in her direction. "Not that it's a
big deal or anything, but I thought you might like to take it home."

"Oh," I said. "Oh, well, thank you. That's very . . ."

"Thoughtful," LuAnn supplied.

Behind her, the entire staff had assembled in preparation for a
Roman Holiday, including Gaither, who strolled up from his office
and stood rocking on his heels, hands stuffed in the pockets of his
Duckhead khakis, a grin on his shrewd, good-natured face.

"It's fresh," Joe said, as though my hesitation might be traced to
this.

"I'm sure it is. I'm just not sure what I'd do with it."

He hesitated, deciding where to go. "Well, what I generally do
is marinate it in a little olive oil and lemon juice. And black pepper," he added. "Then throw it on the grill."

I winced apologetically. "I don't have a grill."

"You have a hibachi, don't you?"

I cast a warning glance at Lu. "I don't think it could handle anything that size."

"What is it anyway?" Gaither interposed. "A flounder?"

"A fluke, actually. The eyes go the other way. See here?" Turning professorial, Joe pointed, his biceps moving like a languid
python under his brown skin as he hoisted the leviathan to instruct
the assembly on this arcane point of piscatorial anatomy.

"No kidding," Gaither said, making an effort to conceal his glee
which could not have been more insincere.

Beginning to go down in flames, Joe glanced at me as though I
might have a fire extinguisher handy.

"Thanks for thinking of me, but you should probably keep it. It
would be a shame to have it go to waste."

"Oh," he said. "Oh. Well, that's okay. It was just a thought."

"It was a nice thought," I said.

"I'll bet you have a grill, Joe, don't you?" LuAnn said.

The look I sent her way was positively black.

The professor blushed through his deep tan.

"Let me walk you out," I said, facilitating my escape along with his.

"Sorry," he said in the lot, as the big sky opened up around us. "I guess this wasn't such a good idea. Just a whim."

"It's okay," I said. "It was a nice whim."

"I do have a grill, though," he confessed, with redoubled earnestness, as though I were a bank officer and he was applying for a loan. "I don't know if you have plans tonight . . ."

And it's curious. Until that moment, I'd been hoping he would generate the nerve to ask me out. But as wish became reality, I wasn't sure it was such a good idea. After all, I didn't really know him. So on, etc., blah blah blah.

"That's awfully nice, Joe. Thank you," I said, taking a powder. "I probably shouldn't, though. I have a policy about dating patients."

"Oh," he quickly said. "Oh. I understand. Of course. That's probably smart. I wasn't really thinking of it as a date, though, just . . ."

I waited, curious to see what ingenuity would supply.

"Company," he said. "I'm sort of on my own down here."

"Company," I repeated speculatively, seeing how it played. As a concept, it was highly questionable, but it did have the advantage of supplying plausible deniability, something Joe seemed to appreciate as much as I did.

"And since you've already treated me," he said, catching the vibe, "don't you suppose it's reasonable to say I'm no longer your patient? Technically speaking."

"Technically, I suppose it is." I smiled at his joke, intrigued by another glimpse of the faun boy darting between columns, playing a shy come-hither on his pipes. And there was just something so preposterous and charming about him standing there with that fish and his earnest face. "I do like fish."

"Come," he said. "I'd really like you to."

"What could it hurt?"

Girlfriends, sisters, fellow suffragettes—beware! Famous last words!

"Seven-thirty," he said. "Here, I'll draw you a map."

And producing his Mont Blanc and steno pad, he proceeded to draft a document as detailed, baroque and compendious as a medieval cartographer's world map, including, in the lower right-hand corner, a compass rose indicating magnetic north, and designations of latitude and longitude. By the time he'd finished—five to seven minutes later—his chart showed the Outer Banks in their entirety as seen from outer space, including both the Albemarle and Pamlico drainage basins, and every state and secondary road extending back as far as U.S. Route 1, running along the fall line at the margin of the Piedmont and the coastal plain.

"So?" Lu asked when I walked back inside.

"So what?"

"So, are you going out with him?"

I frowned. "It's not a date."

Oh, how they laughed. Oh, how they rolled their eyes and poked their cheeks out with their tongues like happy little squirrels. The remainder of the afternoon was dedicated to a roast. Designated weenie: yours truly.

Two

As Jubal rounded the point, the southeast wind came up, running brisk at fifteen knots. There'd be swell outside, Joe reflected. Above the engine's numbing roar, which vibrated through the deck plate up into his groin, his shoulder blades, his skull, he made out the soulful-soulless tolling of the bell buoy off Gravesend, caught a ray of sunlight winking in the heavy optics of the lighthouse tower, where the light had been extinguished.

Day had vanished now. From this distance in the offing, Little Roanoke village, the whole poor, hard-bitten scene—the listing boats and canted pilings, the south wall of the fishhouse, with its blistered, peeling paint—fused together into the white vision of a waterfront, idyllic and serene, and then the waterfront became the town, the town the island, island, world. The farther off they drew, the more ordered and beautiful the scene became. Joe thought of Boston fourteen years before, the night his first world ended. Gazing out from the high floor of a hotel, he'd watched the blinking lights at Logan and the Mystic Tobin Bridge turn into whirling galaxies, and the thought of human intervention in the processes by which they turned seemed vain and of no use.

Gripping the transom rail, he watched the wedge of geese disappear to the south. The morning air was filled with correspondences, memory carrying a dark charge, like premonition. With cold hands, he reached inside his coat for his steno pad, only to find he'd filled it to the last line of the last page.

What is the field? Lacking other space, he wrote the question and underscored it twice on the back cover. Beyond the scope of his investigations, past the end, it stood like an epitaph to the months he'd spent down here, a last uncertainty, opening into something else. He'd hoped this notebook would see him through the trip, his last, but his estimate had proved overoptimistic, a rare mistake for Joe. As the *Father's Price* entered the Pamlico, proceeding east into the cast-iron dawn, he capped his pen and started below to fetch another pad.

When he entered the lazaret door in the aft wall of the deck-house, the engine noise assaulted him at a new, more violent level, rising from below with an oily blast of tropic heat. Slapping in and out in the light roll, oilclothes, hung to dry, brushed his shoulder, reaching out halfheartedly like restless orange and yellow ghosts, as he made his way down the steep companionway. Tacky with resid-ual oil, the engine room floor clung to the soles of his white Wellingtons, a faint adhesion like Post-it gum, as he passed the diesel, a Caterpillar 3412, squatting in the center, dull yellow, the size of a small tractor, curiously still and self-possessed amidst the shattering white roar.

Unwheeling the hatch door in the forward bulkhead, Joe entered the forepeak, the V formed by the converging bows. Here, four to a side, were eight stacked bunks, those to port crowded with tools, spare engine parts, various gear, including five type-one life pre-servers, one for each man in the crew. Joe's bunk was the bottom one to starboard. He shared quarters with Ray Bristow, the thirty-three-year-old, born-again ex-con who'd been one of his principal informants in the village. For reasons Joe hadn't fully understood or cared to question, Ray had taken him under his wing shortly after his arrival and introduced the young anthropologist to John Calvin Teach, the minister at the First Covenant Pentecostal Church, through whom Joe had met Jubal Ames and secured this berth.

As the boat rolled, a plastic milk jug, half-filled with sloshing yellow liquid, scraped across the floor.

"What is that, lemonade?"

His first trip out, Joe had innocently posed this question as his new shipmate, legs dangling from the top bunk, sat toeing off his boots. With his long brown hair parted in the middle and his soft, slight beard, Ray—who resembled a felonious Christ, Christ as He might be portrayed on a black velvet panel, with a bit of Charlie Manson mixed in, too—had grinned down with the intimate and risible suggestion that almost always lurked in his expression.

"Used to be," he said and winked at Joe with glittering violet eyes as soulless as a doll's. "Beats going topside in the middle of the night. Feel free to use it if you want."

With a queasy smile, Joe had thanked him, and Ray, nodding, went back to taking off his two-toned cowboy boots—black, with iridescent lizard uppers and gleaming metal toes. Gratitude notwithstanding, in the sequel, Joe had preferred to hold his water or to make the climb and go over the rail.

Ray's offer had held the same thread of vaguely alarming generosity that ran throughout Joe's relationship with him. For nine months, they'd shared this cramped, clammy iron cell at sea, a place that smelled at once like a locker room, a fishhouse and an oil refinery. Even with the hatch dogged down, the noise of the engine rang the bulkhead, jackhammer loud, vibrating the beds where, between hauls, they tried to catch an hour's desperate sleep, a scratchy Army surplus blanket pulled over their sweaty, filthy clothes whose cuffs were rimed with ice that slowly puddled the mattresses. Ray had opened doors in Little Roanoke that Joe could never have opened for himself, and Joe had gone through them, gratefully, but without feeling entirely comfortable in Ray's presence.

Like a *fiasco* of Beelzebub's own Chardonnay, the piss jug presently disappeared beneath the bottom portside bunk, whose edge was garlanded with Ray's sweat-stiffened tube socks, like a barbaric necklace of yellow teeth. Joe thought of something Rolly Hughes, his old mentor and adviser at Duke, had told him: *For an ethnographer, getting in's the easy part; the trick is getting out.*

When he opened his pack for the new pad, Joe found, resting on his spare wool shirt, a cassette he hadn't placed there. As he stared at it—black, unlabeled except for the brand name, Memorex— something in his chest began to tick like the radiator of the Wagoneer cooling when the engine is shut down. Day, he thought. She must have put it here this morning or last night. Steeling himself to deal with it, he bent on the headphones of his Walkman and punched the tape into the slot. But when he hit Play, he heard only hiss, and fast-forwarding produced the same result. There was no message. The tape was blank. That, apparently, was the message.

Topside, he proceeded up the starboard gangway, climbing the short external ladder to the wheelhouse.

"Morning, Cap."

Talking on the VHF, Jubal swiveled in his bolted chair and scanned Joe with unsmiling eyes the color of pig iron, with a hint of similar weight. In khakis and a hooded navy sweatshirt, he looked, at forty-two, as lean and athletic as a twenty-five-year-old, but long exposure to the weather had left a craze in his fair skin like hairline cracks in the glaze of an old china cup; it broke his features into jigsaw fragments when he squinted, as he did now, regarding Joe with a characteristic expression—stern, worried, principled, set for confrontation. With no more greeting, he spun back and went on mumbling into the handset.

15, 13, 12, 13, 12, 11 . . . As they made their way up the channel past islands of dredge spoil necklaced with black sandbags, Joe watched the depth reader blinking on the chromascope and did the math, adding six to compensate for the transponder's depth below the water line. The *Father's Price* drew eleven feet. Across the monitor's black screen, gray-green blips floated like bursts of flak in a night sky, entering at the left, departing at the right—schools of bait fish or some debris beneath them in the water. A second monitor, the plotter, showed their course, a solid yellow-green line inching erratically, Etch-a-Sketch fashion, over a black ground divided into purple grids of latitude and longitude.

These two video consoles—added recently, at considerable expense, by the Clam Teach Fish Company in an effort to update the fleet—seemed at odds with the dingy appointments of the cabin, its cheap veneer cabinetry and dated linoleum, speckled yellow-green, lending the place a resemblance to the capsule of a seedy spaceship. Scattered here and there was evidence of Jubal's occupation—a bottle of Extra Strength Excedrin, a tube of Ben-Gay and Joe's personal favorite, a blue tin of Four Seasons Danish Butter Cookies. On the countertop beneath the long aft-facing window, this rested on the hang log, a sort of bibliography of local wrecks and obstructions on the sea floor.

"YEP, JOINED THE LOIONS' CLUB LAST SPRING . . ."

The voice burst across the VHF, followed by a crackle of static. Jubal tuned the squelch.

"Couldn't make the meetins, though. Hord to plan on anything when you trawl boat. Come back."

A small commercial tuna boat, the *John Henry*, came toward them up the channel, her bow breaking a white furrow like a plow and pushing it ahead.

"How'd y'all do, Emmet?" Jubal broke in. "Come back."

"Not much good. Went a day early, I reckon."

Without comment, Jubal put the handset in his lap, his expression one that Joe, with practice, had learned to interpret as a smile.

"How's the weather look?" he asked the captain now.

"Southeast, ten to twenty. S'posed to hold up through the weekend. Then there's a clipper coming through."

"That sounds pretty decent."

"Not for fish, it don't. Nothing from the east no good."

"At least it won't be dirty." Employing the jargon for bad weather, Joe betrayed a residual pride in the fluency he'd acquired.

"Ruther dirt and fish," said Jubal, grounded in his more basic point of view.

To port, over the black cone of the radarscope, Joe could see the *Three Brothers* leaving the slip at Ice Plant Island, turning into the raised slick left by their boat's settling wake. A slanting shaft of sunlight caught her house and superstructure, enameling them a brilliant white against a northern sky that dawn had turned a bruised and sudden blue.

Steps rang in the companionway. As Ray Bristow appeared, Joe felt a reflexive inward clinching.

"Hey, Jubal, where you going? Ain't we taking ice?" Ray brought with him a buzz of bright, aggrieved intensity, like an electromagnetic field to which one half expected the compass to reorient, floating toward him in the gimbals.

Jaw squared, the captain focused ahead through the window panels. "There's a good twelve ton still in the hold from last toime."

"Hell, Cap," Ray said, "that shit's all melted and re-froze. It's hard as cured cement."

"So's loife," said Jubal, " 'cept the oice is paid for."

Against his better judgment, Joe released an involuntary laugh. Ray glared. "What's so funny?"

Joe shook his head. "Nothing."

"Then what you laughing for?"

"Come on, Ray, admit it. It was a good line."

"I guess you'll want to write it down then."

"Now that you mention it . . ." Attempting a defusing humor, Joe feinted toward his pocket as though to take out his pad.

Ray debated his next move. "Hey, Jubal, ever wonder what he's putting in that little book he's always writing in?" As Ray posed the question, his eyes never left Joe's face.

"Ain't my business, long's he does his job."

"You seen 'Star Trek' before, hadn' you?"

"What, that talent show with Ed McMahon?"

"Jesus, Jubal!" Ray, despite his grievance, couldn't resist a glance at Joe, sharing his delight in this. "Captain Kirk, the *Enterprise*? Hey, Scotty, beam me up?"

"Roight," said Jubal in a sheepish tone. "I seen that oncet own Mama's satelloite."

"Which one's Joe here remind you of?" Answering his own question, Ray held his fingers up like pointy ears. "Spock—that's him. Got a Vulcan brain the size of a computer, and he's half-human, too, but only half. What part you reckon they left out?"

Joe kept his smile, but the animation drained away.

"How did it go?" Ray continued. "To explore new worlds, but not to get involved? Something like that. I reckon that could be Joe's motto, too."

"You boys settle down," Jubal interjected. "It's a long trip ahead."

Having got his shot in, Ray let his mood ratchet down a notch. Joe, however, was stung by the remark, which, as Ray's remarks had a tendency to do, cut close to the bone.

As the Bonner Bridge loomed up in the distance, skeletal against the overcast, Joe recalled making the same journey with his father and his mother's father, Pa Tilley, bottom-fishing out here in a wooden boat when he was ten years old, in that other lifetime. That summer—1966—the Bonner had been only half-complete, ending in midair. Now it touched both shores, a grim steel rainbow. Looking through the finished arch, he recalled that unhappy trip. He'd almost drowned that afternoon.

The boat moved forward, and the autopilot ticked, making infinitesimal self-adjustments in the dash. Joe's glance drifted to the digital read-out on the water temperature gauge over Jubal's head beside the black box of the Loran.

"Forty-two," he read. "That's the coldest it's been."

"Here's a thought," said Ray. "Don't fall in."

Deflecting the thrust, Joe retreated into his typical mode of questioning. "How long could you survive in water this cold?"

Jubal's brusque, impatient exhalation was also typical. Challenged, though, he went on to speculate. "Live or swim?"

"Either," Joe said. "Both."

"You'd live a hour or two, I reckon. After fifteen, twenty minutes, though, I doubt you'd get much swimming done."

"Shit," said Ray. "I doubt you'd do no swimming after five. You kidding me? That water'd sting you like a cattle prod. Me, if I went in and didn't see the boat coming back in a big goddamn hurry, I'd suck brine and make like a anchor, straight for the bottom of the Nine-Mile Slough. Better that than stay up and turn into a floating goddamn ice cube." He cut a look at Joe. "Course you, it probably wouldn't bother you that much. What you think, Cap? Old Spock here could probably live out there a year, doing the backfloat and squirting water through his teeth."

Even Jubal, normally as sensitive to nuance as a post, looked around at this. Things, Joe saw, weren't off to a good start. Debating how to deal with Ray, he opened the starboard door, leaned against the coaming and watched the Pamlico narrow like an hourglass ahead, funneling through the Inlet's narrow waist. As the boat entered from the west, the outracing ebb tide made it feel as if she'd picked up headway. She slid between the massive concrete pilings of the bridge, whose shadow touched the bowstem, scanning the boat like a dark bar-code reader, and fell over Joe, a sensation he briefly recalled. High overhead an orange VW, toy-sized, labored toward the crest in second gear, where a gull no bigger than a snowflake hovered near the railing. The roadbed trembled.

Daylight touched his face again on the far side, and they entered the Inlet proper, going due east. Ahead, laced with white, the channel snaked between the two low landmasses, north and south, gauzed with haze; beyond, the lower bell of the hourglass, the iron-gray Atlantic. Above the engine, combers thundered in the distance, breaking on the outer bar.

"Close that fucking hatch," said Ray. "You want to freeze us out?"

Joe complied and came inside.

To port, sixty yards off, a pelican was perched atop a canted spar: the *Debra Jean*.

Frowning, neither Ray nor Jubal looked at her or spoke. Joe, in a subtle breach of protocol, spoke the thought that struck him now. "I thought she grounded on the south side."

"Three years ago that was the south soide." Jubal's iron-colored eyes briefly reposed their weight on him and then moved on.

Joe watched the ruined mast slip by to port, their north.

15, 13, 14, 12, 11, 12, 11 . . . The depth counter blinked and changed.

"Hemorrhoids of the world," Ray said. "That's what they call this place. And what you reckon that makes Little Roanoke, Jubal? The asshole of the universe, wouldn't it be?"

The captain's coarse guffaw surprised Joe; it subsided into a grin made doubly boyish by Jubal's failed efforts to suppress it.

On the mast, the pelican spread its wings and soared aloft, retracting its neck as it achieved a labored flight. It was somewhere along here that they had spied the fish that day, four red drum speeding underneath the boat like scaled-down, blunt torpedoes. Pointing with one hand, holding his Panama hat down with the other, Pa Tilley had called back directions to Jimmy, Joe's father, in the stern, who gunned the old one-lung Evinrude and sent them skipping like a stone toward shoal water, out there where the *Debra*'s iron bones lay rusting now. Casting from the boat, Joe—still Joey then—had hooked a forty-pounder and wrestled it for close to twenty minutes before the wake of a passing pleasure boat rippled beneath them like a three-foot concrete speed bump, sending everybody reeling. In the commotion, his brand-new rod and reel, a Christmas gift from Pa, had slipped away into the deep, along with the big fish.

That was the first time the men had taken him offshore with them. The last time, too, as it turned out. Two days after that trip, on Labor Day Monday of 1966, the thrombus in his pa's left calf, the bad one, dislodged in the night and broke up, sailing like a dark armada down the rivers of his blood, making its way into his heart and ultimately out into his pulmonary artery. Will Tilley, who'd passed his love for fishing to his grandson, who'd taught the boy to tie the fisherman's knot, which, once bent on, can never be undone but only cut, died in his sleep. Since that day seventeen years had passed, and Joey Madden had not been fishing once, not until the previous spring, when he came back to the Outer Banks, as Joe, to pursue his ethnographic task.

For almost a year, he'd studied Little Roanoke—its social and economic structure, its religion, politics; he'd interviewed dozens of informants, filled notebook after notebook in his compact hand, notes that had so little to do, finally, with him. Today, however, the question on his mind was a personal one. The scene through the windows of the *Father's Price* had the quality of a double-exposed photograph. If the surface image was his ethnographic mission, the ghostly underimage was that earlier trip; that's what held him now. Why was it there?

On the plotter, the solid line of their present course tracked a string of dashes like a highway's broken yellow line: an old trip called up from computer memory. Joe became aware of his reflection, ghostlike, floating on the screen, along with Ray's and Jubal's. Here he was again on a fishing boat bound for the Inlet between two older men. Was it his imagination, or was he repeating something with these men, and if so, what? What force had drawn him here, and to what end? If he was the iron filing, what was the field?

A burst of static broke into his reverie.

"Hey, Jubal, how you going out? Come back." The voice was Cully Teach's, captain of the *Three Brothers*.

"Loining number eight with the second pillar," Jubal said into the handset.

Rising from his chair, he fronted the wheel, looking aft toward the bridge through the slit window, forward, then aft again as he steered.

There was shoal water on either side, low dredge islands populous with rafts of chattering birds. Out of place, a green buoy slipped by to port. Outside the Inlet, the surface of the sea was fretted with whitecaps, like a moving picture shot in black and white. Risen now, the heatless winter sun threw a brilliant gleam on giant combers' backs, polishing them as black as anthracite as they made up, throwing off their crests in a white flash as they thundered on the beaches of Pea Island and the outer bar, leaving a low pall of hanging spray like smoke from detonated bombs.

9, 8, 9, 8, 8, 7 . . . Joe watched the depth tick down.

7, 8, 7, 7, 6, 6, 6 . . . Twelve feet of water beneath them. The handset lay abandoned in Jubal's chair, Cully Teach, on his end, silent, too.

6, 6, 6, 6, 5 . . .

The bow rose on a swell and dropped back, jarring faintly as the keel touched bottom—a whispered, grinding kiss.

No one spoke. Jubal's face was solemn, white.

Suddenly the number plunged to 15 . . . 16 . . . 18 now.

The number went to 3 as Jubal flipped a switch, converting feet to fathoms. Sitting down, he picked up his coffee mug. Joe, his heart still pounding, read the logo: FISH OR CUT BAIT.

In front of them, as sharply drawn as though with a Magic Marker, the tide line wavered on the surface like a blousing curtain—on one side, the turgid muddy brown of the Pamlico, on the other, the clean gray-green of the Atlantic.

The minute they were past the bar, the boat began to buck and plummet in the swells, each shock followed by a stagger in which a volley of spray flew aft, pattering the window panels and painting transitory rainbows in the air above the deckhouse roof. Spangling off the rippled crests, the light this morning had a wintry glare Joe hadn't seen before; no softness or shadow anywhere. Visibility was unlimited. The sea was like a former friend who, overnight in the rise to greatness, has forgotten you.

"It's wintertoime, boys," the captain said, thinking along related lines.

When he turned the wipers on, Ray turned to Joe. "Let's go."

Passing through the galley, they endured the unenthusiastic scrutiny of Curtis Bly, the cook, newly hired, who looked as if he'd just awakened after a lost weekend in hell. In his early fifties, with a ten- or twelve-day growth of beard, he looked to be around five-six and two hundred and forty pounds, with a heavy sack of gut spilling through an unbuttoned, food-stained shirt whose sleeves were ripped away, revealing flabby upper arms covered with a blue lacery of prison-style tattoos and tufted with a luxuriant crop of thick black hair. Beneath his pants, belted with a piece of rope like a medieval friar's tunic, Bly wore pink fuzzy bedroom slippers with pom-poms on the toes. He was nearly bald except for a combover consisting of a half-dozen plastered individual strands.

He was sitting at the tiny banquette table, surfaced with spongy black foam rubber to discourage slippage, listening to country-western on the tinny radio with its coat-hanger aerial and perusing a tabloid: SPACE ALIENS BUILD ON MARS, the headline on the rear declared. His unfiltered Camel, burning in the sandbag ashtray, added a charcoal overtone to the pervasive smell of scorched coffee grounds, bacon drippings, male funk, fish and industrial-strength floral disinfectant from the tiny head immediately adjacent.

"Having you a Maxwell House moment?" Ray said, pulling his slicker off a peg beside the door and shouldering into it. "There's twelve ton of ice needs to be broke up in the hold."

"Have fun," said Bly.

"Cook's job."

"Says who?"

"Says me."

They faced off, Bly visibly weighing the pros and cons of mutiny. "I'll get to it when I get to it," he said, retreating behind his paper.

"Don't strain yourself." Ray nodded to a NyQuil bottle and the half-full plastic dosage cup beside it on the table. "What's that? Having you a before-breakfast apéritif?"

"I'm sick."

"What, them polka-dotted dingbats and boa constrictors swarming you?"

Emerging from behind his paper, Curtis regarded them, his eyes as muddy and unconscious as a trout's, and held up his middle finger with a total absence of expression.

"Just don't let the captain catch you," Ray said. "He finds you drinking on this boat, you'll be swimming home to Seaford, or wherever the hell it is you come from."

"I told you. It's my med'cine," said Bly. "And I'm from Gloucester Point."

"Gloucester, Seaford—either way, it's still Virginia. Far as I'm concerned, it all sucks the same up there."

"I'm Joe," Joe said, "by the way." Bly, apparently holding him guilty by association, picked up the *World News* again without reply.

"He's a beauty, ain't he?" Ray said, as they exited the galley door into the port gangway. "Looks like a frog setting on a toadstool growing from a pile of shit."

When Joe laughed, Ray glommed him with an eager grin. "Don't he?"

"No comment," said Joe, though there was something apt in the tripartite image.

On the work deck, Ray pulled a rusty metal arm from the deckhouse wall, engaging the clutch of the hoisting winch. With a squeaky clank reminiscent of a tank on a World War II movie soundtrack, two corroded brass heads the size of milking pails with flanged, bell-bottom ends began to rotate slowly at knee height. These projected from and mirrored, in miniature, the hogshead-sized double drums of the big, squat winch, whose reels were crowded with turns of rusty one-inch cable.

Rousted from the engine room by the clank of the chain drive, Lukey Brame, the fifth and last man in the complement, appeared in the lazaret door, carrying a monster orange pipe wrench. He wore a watch cap, green skins and a black football jersey with large gold numerals, 23, the team colors of Manteo High. A former football star, part of the Redskins' storied, undefeated year, 1979, Lukey lived on Good Luck Street in Little California, the black section of Manteo, with his wife and their two-year-old son. Only twenty-two, he still had a wide receiver's build and a handsome face, with long, curling lashes that revealed themselves in profile over liquid dark eyes that fixed you for a moment with a calm attentiveness, then blinked and opened somewhere else. Though the youngest member of the crew, Lukey was, after Jubal, the most competent seaman aboard and as taciturn an individual as Joe had ever met.

"Hey, Lukey," he said, "how was your holiday?"

"Pretty good. Yours?"

Joe, whose holiday had proceeded like the third act of a play by Eugene O'Neill, nonetheless answered with a smile.

"Hey, Brame," Ray said, "you eat your pork and black-eyed peas for New Year's?"

"We did," Joe said, intervening. "Pork, black-eyed peas and collards. Got to have the greens for luck."

"Greens for money, peas for luck," said Lukey.

Interested, Joe asked, "Is that what it is?"

"What I always heard."

"How about the pork?" said Ray. "What you figure—government subsidy? Your people must pack away a lot of it up there in Little California, huh, Brame?"

By way of answer, Lukey turned away.

Ray's racist baiting, which still affected Joe like fingernails against a blackboard, had no visible effect on Lukey Brame. And it was curious to Joe, who'd studied crew dynamics for a year. Ray's off-island experiences in the Navy and elsewhere had made him, in many ways, the most worldly and sophisticated member of the crew, yet he was the one overt and unapologetic bigot. Perfectly aware of the political incorrectness of his views, he lost no opportunity to troll them before Lukey like a solemn trout trying to get a bite; and not only before Lukey, but also before Joe, who'd become, willy-nilly, part of the dynamic. Joe was Ray's disapproving audience, the audience Ray took it on himself to shock. In Joe's entire time aboard, he'd never once seen Lukey take the bait.

Just aft of the winches, a trestle was welded to the deck, a sort of hitching post with rebar belaying pins projecting up like the blunt tines of a pitchfork. Here, various hoisting lines converged from blocks aloft in the superstructure. Removing one of these, the starboard whipline, Lukey swung the heavy lifting hook to Joe, who'd climbed onto the deckhouse roof.

Navigating his way through a bristling undergrowth of antennas, Joe attached it to the starboard outrigger, which was still in its raised position, vertical beside the mast, then repeated the same process to port with Ray. As the radar's curved transponder dish rotated behind him, spelling out FURONO with each pass against the white egg of the plastic life raft shell, Joe watched Ray and Lukey wrap several turns around the rotating winch heads. They paid out line, and the derricklike towers of the outriggers—forty-foot-tall scaffoldings of plate and rebar welded around a central spine of six-inch pipe—creaked downward like skeletal wings in a slow motion downstroke, coming to rest over the rails a degree or two above the horizontal. Dangling from the tip of each—like a punk rock earring the size of an anvil, and not dissimilar in shape—were the stabilizers. Once released, they splashed away to either side, their retainer chains rattling through the sheaves, then thwanging taut when they reached planing depth beneath the surface. Creaking, slicing surgical white lines in the water, the chains slowly drifted back as the boat moved forward, her roll noticeably decreased.

"Here's another one for your notebook." Ray, standing in the lee of the deckhouse, hailed Joe as he dropped back to deck. "Know what they call outriggers up north?"

"What?"

"Sissy bars." Ray cupped his hands to light a cigarette and waved out the match as he inhaled.

"Why's that?"

The wind blew his exhalation to tatters, carrying it astern. He looked at Brame. "You know?"

"Can't use 'em 'cause of ice." Coiling the whipline, Lukey hung it on its pin.

Ray grinned. "Two points. Second question." He shoved the clutch arm back against the wall, abruptly stopping the hoisting heads. "What are those boys called?"

"Heads, winch heads," Lukey said indifferently.

"Err," said Ray and looked at Joe, who shrugged. "Come on, Brame, I know you know. Niggerheads? Don't tell me you never heard of that."

Profoundly unprovoked, Lukey picked up his pipe wrench.

"You ain't gonna frap me with that, are you?" Ray said, feigning terror. "That's the name, man. I didn't make it up. It's reality. You can't go getting hard-ons over that."

Lukey stepped inside the lazaret.

"Hey, Brame!" Ray called after him. "Brame! Come on, man, one more question. This one's serious."

From the landing, Lukey impassively stared back.

"This is important. I want you to take your time and think before you answer it. Who's the private dick who's a sex machine to all the chicks?"

A slow, liquid blink turned Lukey's pupils into empty blackboards, erased as though in expectation of a different, better lesson; then he went down the stairs.

Ray turned on Joe. "Shaft!" he sang, his expression charged with dark elation. "Shaft!" again, breaking into the high chorus.

Ray's aggression, Joe saw, was targeted at him.

"Listen, Ray, about Christmas . . ."

His violet eyes focused in like lasers. "What about it?"

"I'm sorry we never got a chance to hook up."

"Yeah," Ray said ironically, "I bet you're all tore up."

"Seriously," Joe said. "My family was down. When you called, we were in the middle of some stuff."

With an aggressive fillip, Ray flicked his cigarette over the rail, tracking it like a hunter shooting skeet. "Hey, man, enough said." Changing tacks, he turned back, holding up both hands as though surrendering at gunpoint. "I understand completely. Your folks were here, and who knew, I might show up with a ski mask and a .38, burgle the Rolexes off your mama and daddy's wrists, right? Hell, if it was me, I probably would've done the same. You can't be too careful. After all, it ain't like I didn't introduce you all over Little Roanoke and in church and get you on this boat. But that was *you* meeting my family, my people, and this was me meeting yours. It's completely different—believe me, man, I understand!"

"You're wrong, Ray. You're totally off base."

"Am I? Come on, Joe. You're the truth-and-knowledge guy, ain't you? That's what I always liked about you best. You're always lifting up the corner of the rug to see what kind of dirt's underneath. Don't disappoint me now. At least be honest with yourself."

Ray left a beat for Joe's response, but Joe, frowning, found his mind had suddenly gone blank.

"Yeah, well, I guess I'm gonna catch some *zzz*'s before we hit the grounds." And he walked off toward the lazaret, leaving Joe alone on deck, staring at vacated space.

The call had come on Christmas night at ten o'clock at the tail end of a raucous family dinner. Joe, who'd been drinking with his brothers since afternoon and was three-quarters advanced in his own long day's journey into night, had answered in the bedroom. It was Ray. "Hey, man, I got a bag of salty oysters over here. How about I bring some by?"

"This isn't a good time," Joe said. "My folks are here."

"Hey, that's cool. I hear you," Ray replied. "Just tell me where you are. I'll drop 'em by tomorrow."

That was the moment. Joe replayed it now, recalling his brothers' shouts and laughter coming through the closed plank door as they fired volleys of invective in the outer room like magnum duck loads knocking down each other, themselves and anything that moved. While he listened, the silence on the line between him and Ray had hissed like the white noise on Day's blank cassette.

"Ray, listen . . ." His brain fogged with wine, Joe led with this, unsure how to follow. In the sequel, though, no follow-up had been necessary, because Ray Bristow, who, under everything—the bad grammar and redneck, racist baiting, all the various miscues on the surface—was not only smart but sensitive, said, "Yeah, man, that's okay, I get it," and hung up.

That was where the frayed thread finally snapped. More than once since Christmas, Joe had rehearsed the reasons that had made him hang fire in that moment, hesitating to give Ray Bristow his address. The desire to maintain ethnographic distance, to keep an appropriately professional relationship with an informant; the fact that Ray was a convicted felon, a former heroin addict, who, prior to finding Jesus, had financed his habit by committing burglaries; Joe's intention to shield Day and his family from potential risk—these factors all had their due weight. In the end, though, they were excuses, so much intellectual fluff. The real risk Joe perceived wasn't to his family or to Day.

Ray was right. As one whose professional task consisted in unearthing the nonobvious and not infrequently unhappy truth in other people, situations, things, Joe had to face one in himself.

Gravesend Light shrank away in the distance over the port quarter, and the Bonner turned to a black bobby pin against a sky of burnished tin, bringing back once more the thought of that bad night in Boston half a life before. That night as he gazed down at the city lights after everything had come to grief, the sense of distancing and widened view had brought relief and peace to Joey's fevered thoughts, a sense almost of absolution. Today, half a life farther on, Joe watched the shore grow small and distance swallow up details, and he felt a twinge of panic, like an astronaut whose tether to the ship is cut. Tumbling and tumbling, this slow-motion freefall backward out of life seemed a journey he'd been on ever since.

Three

I was standing by my window
On a cold and cloudy day . . .

As the big v-8 of Joe's Wagoneer roared to life in the fishhouse lot, the voice—haunted, subtle, with the eroded terminal consonants of the Mississippi delta—came over the speakers together with the hiss and crackle of tape distortion.

When I saw the hearse come rolling
For to carry my mother away . . .

A flash of Mary Catherine, lying upstairs in the guest bedroom of our old house on Utah Street in her chaste nightie, without breasts or hair, too meek—and too invested in her own Catholic self-sacrifice— to inconvenience my father, even to die . . . When I was six, and briefly plump, and came home every afternoon from Blessed Sacrament with my Judy Jetson lunchbox empty, Mom, under guise of an embrace, ever so discreetly used to pat me down at the front door, as though I might be packing new, ill-gotten swag inside the waistband of my tartan skirt. And when she pulled away to look, there was something anxious, inquiring and ultimately discouraged in her face, an overcast that weighed down my whole childhood and that I later starved myself to break, but never could. Then she was gone.

As I pulled down Teach's Landing, I glanced at the cassette box on the dash: "Will The Circle Be Unbroken," The Staples Singers. Home-mixed, the writing was in Joe's brother's hand. As large and loose and unsteady as Joe's was small, compact and sure, Reed Madden's writing seemed scratched out hurriedly, as though he was distracted by more urgent business on the far side of some inward horizon, where no one could follow him or help.

I don't know what it was, but as I drove home that morning, the ghosts were gibbering. Maybe it was the music, scratchy, old, like something exhumed from a musty vault in the Smithsonian. Beautiful as it was, it got on my nerves like Little Roanoke did, and in exactly the same way. But how Joe loved it—the green where the old Bethsaida Methodist Church, with its bubbled window glass, faced off against the village schoolhouse on the south; on the west, opposite the water, Skaddle's Red & White, an old-fashioned mom-and-pop grocery, was flanked by Midgett's Marine Supply on one side and Midgett's Mortuary on the other. "One-stop shopping," Joe had said. "Purchase a survival suit while picking out your coffin." The professor, on occasion, could crack a joke. Today, it didn't seem that funny.

I thought about him as I drove past the trim saltbox houses with the salvaged World War II torpedoes in front yards, where sometimes you also saw an unexploded mine, a spiked giant like a medieval mace head, ominously crumbling to orange dust. These were what the Teaches and the Midgetts and the Flowers in Little Roanoke used as lawn ornaments, in lieu of pink flamingoes. The stacks of rusty crab and eel pots everywhere, the hedges draped with net, the old skiffs and wheelless, vintage pickup trucks on blocks in backyards accompanied, now and then, by an apiary standing against a dark line of loblolly pines where the forest began—Joe loved it all. To him, Little Roanoke was like a rare and precious human ecosystem in a state of fragile balance that had taken generations to create. When he looked, that was what he saw: simplicity and character, old folkways, seafaring traditions dating back to Devonshire in Walter Raleigh's time; Joe saw the villagers' originality and ferocious independence, their unwavering certainty as to who they were. When I looked, I saw patriarchialism, religious dogma, bigotry toward blacks and women. Our difference as lovers and as human beings somehow boiled down to our different views about this town, ending where it had begun: with Cleopatra Ames. As I drove through, I thought of Pate and was tempted to stop by.

On second thought, it didn't seem like such a hot idea. In the midst of planning a last-minute wedding, probably letting out her mother's antique dress to hide the pooch she showed, Pate might not be overjoyed to see me. Certainly her mom, Idail, was no great fan of mine. And even if they didn't mind, to tell the brutal truth, I wasn't all that keen on visiting myself. No, Pate had made her choice. Or maybe not. Maybe she'd let her mother and her church and her fiancé, James Burrus, choose for her. However it was, Pate too had become a ghost, and Little Roanoke, Joe's precious ecosystem, went humming on its merry way, having eaten her.

As I put the whole place in the rearview mirror, the song's refrain looped back.

Will the circle be unbroken?

Upset, I wondered what that meant. Will the circle be broken? Will it be completed? Those questions I could understand. Maybe my brain was fried—I'd stayed up half the night hashing and re-hashing things with Joe—but "unbroken"? That made no sense to me at all.

My bemusement blew by with the slipstream of the Wagoneer as I punched Eject. I didn't feel like listening to Joe's old shit today. What I was in the mood for was a little Pretenders—Chrissie Hynde now; Chrissie was my girl—or maybe some Talking Heads, say "Burning Down the House." There was nothing like that in the professor's tape box, though; take my word for it. In Joe's opinion, no good rock and roll had been composed since 1973.

Crossing the low concrete bridge from Little Roanoke to Roanoke Island proper, I drove north through the marshes, turned east on 64 and made my way out to the beach, where I fought the morning traffic on the bypass, listening to Rick and Dave crack bathroom jokes and blow the circus horn on the morning show on WDAR, making up in enthusiasm what they lacked in wit. In the shadow of Jockey's Ridge, I turned right, then right again on the beach road and into the drive of my little cottage.

Having lived, for all intents and purposes, with Joe for the last four months, I hadn't been to my place since before the holidays, and I arrived with trepidation, afraid that I might find the pipes had burst. Due to start my new gig in Boston in a week—a two-year fellowship in high-risk pregnancy at Brigham and Women's—I'd put off packing, as usual, to the eleventh hour. Now the eleventh hour had arrived.

But when I unlocked the door and looked around, I wondered, with a pang, what there was to take. My futon? My bookshelves—three raw pine one-by-twelves supported on glass bricks? Maybe it was time to pick up the phone and call Goodwill and have them cart away the lot. Maybe it was time to stop living like a student and grow up. After Joe's, this place looked unfit for human habitation—at least in winter.

I'd loved it, though, my sweet little falling-to-pieces dollhouse in Nags Head, with no curtains on the windows, just an old pink cotton sheet tacked up in the bedroom. (Mary Catherine's ghost said, "Iron it, Day," and I said, "Go away, you're dead. I don't have to listen anymore"). Here, in my rattle-windowed kingdom by the sea—well, not by it, but within walking distance of the public access—I'd eaten for eight months with a bent tin fork off beautiful earthenware plates, no two alike, and drunk iced tea from Mason jars and filled my ice trays only when it suited me and picked mint sprigs a former occupant had planted near the outdoor spigot and right up to October had late tomatoes, which I ate like fruit, licking the juice that dribbled down my wrists, or sliced in sandwiches with coarse black pepper, mayonnaise and dense white bread from the struggling hippie bakery.

The night of my "non-date" with Joe, I'd stopped here after work to change. Popping the reusable cork on a jug of Almaden Chablis, I poured a glass to keep me company in the shower, hefting my large green friend into the antique Frigidaire before heading to the breezy outdoor stall. By the time I finished, I'd achieved a mild gold blur that left me feeling semi-human, and I spent an inordinately long time contemplating whether to wear makeup. What message would it send? Effort? Availability? Just lipstick, I decided, as a compromise.

While I was taking the tube from the rusty medicine cabinet, I cast a baleful glance at my diaphragm case, growing peat moss on the bottom shelf; then I shut the mirrored door and saw someone familiar, prettier and not so old and roadworn as, most days, I took myself to be. Suspicious of her presence, I listened to two voices engaged in The Debate Within. The mature and realistic one advised me, a mature and realistic woman, to go prepared; the less mature, more idealistic countered that no preparation should be required on a first date. As I hashed the pros and cons, my pretty doppelganger, whose nose for once did not appear too large, benignly smiled, sympathizing with an ambivalence that had no claim on her.

As a compromise, I took the case but put it in the glovebox of my Karman-Ghia, not in my purse. The distinction was important: my action, you see, was without specific reference to Joe and our upcoming evening, but a general precaution for the future.

By the time I left my house, it was seven-thirty, a fine September night, with one bright star: Venus rising, I decided, maybe Mars, or Mercury with winged feet (love, war, or run like hell—why not cover all the possibilities?). Following Joe's cartographic masterpiece, I turned off the beach road a little north of Milepost 8, my tires crunching over loose sand in the old shell-flecked concrete driveway.

Holy Moly, I thought, taking a gander at the house in front of me, a shake-sided Nags Head classic, raised and rambling, weathered charcoal gray, with a steep-pitched dark green roof and prop-out shutters. Beneath a coolie-hat overhang, wide porches, painted a glassy, deep-sea green, circumnavigated the second floor above a double-bayed garage. A bit spavined and eccentric, but a head taller than the rows of spec houses crowding its back across the road, it gazed seaward like an old dowager with dated notions, nursing her memories and secrets.

Pulling past the garden wall, I found Joe peering into the orange cauldron of a Weber as his fire burned into coals, a junior soothsayer searching for the hidden truth behind the painted scrim of things. At my approach, he raised his meat fork: a caveman welcome. His comb-stroked hair was wet, and he'd shaved and put on a clean denim shirt. (In his closet, I would later learn, there were six or eight of same, a two-year supply, all top-quality, heavy, expensive goods, bought at the same place at the same time, on sale, to minimize the agony of shopping.) Barefoot, his sleeves rolled to the elbow, his tail untucked and a tear in the left knee of his faded Levi's, he looked placidly at home, firelit in last twilight, beside the dark hulk of a half-million-dollar house where not a single light was on. I could see behind him the heavy-headed sea oats stirring on the pale-dark dune. The sea beyond went *boom.*

"Nice place," I said out the car window. "Your parents'?"

"My mother's, actually. You look nice. Lipstick?"

Dig and counterdig. "Mmm," I answered, getting out.

"What about you?" Joe asked. "Where do you live?"

"I rent in Nags Head, south of the Casino."

"Who's your landlord?"

"The Winslets?"

"Not their guest house?"

I arched my brows. "You know it?"

Joe grinned. "I went to Amy Winslet's birthday party there when I was nine years old. She tried to talk my little brother Reed into eating sand and bloodworm pie."

I laughed. "And you went along with her nefarious design?"

"It was tempting," he conceded. "In the end I had to save him."

"Blood was thicker?"

A shadow darted through his eyes, then vanished. "Blood was thicker," he said, smiling, but with a slightly formal note that opened, for an instant, a vista into something long and sad.

"How about a drink?" he asked.

"I won't say no."

As he bounded up the stairs by twos, I peeked in the garage. The place looked like a camp—pairs of old, patched waders hanging upside down from the exposed joists, along with children's orange life preservers, sun-faded, threadbare relics that had done their duty in another generation. A collage of dented, rusty license plates on the east wall dated back to 1936, the year the house was built; the west was lined with antique fishing gear—old deep-sea rods of thick bamboo, lacquered to an amber tone, the frozen brass reels painted with a patina of green corrosion.

Overhead, something touched my hair and tinkled. I turned on the light and saw an old dog collar swinging from a rusty nail. I read the bone-shaped tag:

My name is
TAWNY
I belong to:
MAY & JIMMY MADDEN
RUIN CREEK RD. KILLDEER, NC
8-7596.
Please return me to my home.

"Here you go."

Silent as an Indian tracker, he startled me. And turning off the light as we went out, Joe handed me a green-gold something—Riesling, maybe—chilled and apple-tart in a condensation-frosted tulip glass.

"Shall we go up?" He nodded toward the gazebo on the dune and offered me a hand, which I took, but only long enough to toe off my black six-dollar Chinese slippers. I left them where the pavement ended, and we started our assault on the low summit of the hill.

"What about before?" Joe asked, continuing the interview. "Where did you grow up?"

"Chevy Chase."

He sipped his wine and nodded. "I almost could have guessed."

I was intrigued. "Is it that obvious?"

"I might not have gotten Maryland, but the D.C. metro area for sure."

"Your reasons, Professor Marvel?"

"You have the D.C. look. At boarding school, the kids from Washington always had more style than anybody else."

"Where did you go?" I asked, panting from the climb.

"Exeter?" He posed it as a question, as though I might not have heard of it, an affectation I noted but decided to forgive.

"I would have guessed the New York City kids," I said, picking up his thread.

"The city kids were more sophisticated," he conceded. "They could quote you Lenny Bruce routines and Marx Brothers movies; in writing, they were past *The Catcher in the Rye* and on to Paul Bowles, Malcolm Lowry, stuff like that. In the style department, though, they tended to be slobs. The D.C. kids, in comparison, all looked like junior rock stars."

"I see," I said. "And have you published on the subject?"

His hesitation queried me. "I'm being pedantic again . . ."

Obviously, he was alert to outbreaks in himself.

"A little professorial maybe."

"Professorial . . ." The repetition had a ring of doubt.

"It's cute," I said. "Somehow I think you know that, though."

The professor's expression, however, made clear that I'd overestimated him in this regard, and for that I liked him even more.

We sat on the benches and took in the gloaming. Brown and nodding, heavy-headed with their load of seed, the sea oats rustled in a light onshore breeze. To the east, down the dunes' far side, was a scoured strip of clean beach sand fringed with seafoam lace, beyond which lay the sea, dark-shining, breathing in end-of-day repose. As we sipped our wine, the floodlights at the Wright Brothers Memorial came on behind the house atop Kill Devil Hill, a half mile to the west. TO THE CONQUEST OF THE AIR; CONCEIVED BY GE-NIUS; ACHIEVED BY DAUNTLESS RESOLUTION AND UNCONQUERABLE FAITH. I recalled the words hard-chiseled in the granite base. Like a great illuminated fin, it floated above us, cruising in the dark.

"Nice night, huh?" I said.

Joe nodded. "When it gets a little darker, we'll have to look for falling stars. If I remember, the Perseid showers are right around this time, though it could be a little late. We may still catch a few."

"What do you do when you catch them?"

He smiled. "Put them in a little jar beside my bed. You?"

"I don't believe I've ever caught one. If I did, I'd probably let it go."

He took a musing beat. "So I like keeping things; you like to let them go."

His deduction pleased me. "Maybe we should just declare a draw, shake hands and go our separate ways."

Joe pressed his lips into a line. "Too soon, I think, by half."

My, my, I thought, *aren't we getting on.* "So, anthropology . . . how did you get into that? Looking at topless Masai girls in *National Geographic?*"

Joe spewed his wine.

"Sorry," I said, flushed with a success whose magnitude went well beyond my modest hopes. "Are you all right? I didn't mean to injure you."

"*National Geographic,*" he said, still laughing, pulling out the damp spot on his shirt. "Good one."

Using the cocktail napkin he'd provided—which was mono-grammed linen—I helped him blot the spill.

"I didn't personally experience the call that way," he said, "though it did have to do with nekit ladies. My grandparents—the ones who built this place—had a coffee table book of photos of Bali in their library in Killdeer. They'd been taken by a German, Gregor Krause, back in the twenties. When we were kids, my little brother and I used to take turns standing sentry while the other looked."

"Reed?"

Joe acknowledged my mnemonic effort. "Reed."

"Funny," I said, "you don't seem that Southern."

"What do I seem?" he risked.

Invited, I zoomed in. "If anything, more Western. Like a ranch hand." As he blushed, I took a deeper focus. "A prep school–edu-cated ranch hand," I amended, failing to repress a smile.

Joe blushed some more.

"So tell me about your book. What was it again?"

"*Ngirim.*"

"Which is . . ."

"It's a funeral ritual practiced by upper-caste Balinese."

"What sort of ritual?"

"Well," he said after a sip, "when the patriarch of an important clan dies, his family undertakes an elaborate burial ceremony that begins with the cremation of the body and ends with a pilgrimage to the sea. The ashes are put into a *wadah*—a sort of cross between a tree house, a pagoda and a giant Roman candle. Carrying it on their shoulders, the whole extended family walks to see the ashes scattered in the sea. I spent time chronicling it with a Triwangsa family in South Gianjar Province."

"From Bali to Little Roanoke," I said. "That's quite a leap."

"Well, yes and no. In the family I studied, the *raja's* eldest son, who'd been educated in the west, thought the ceremony was too old-fashioned and expensive; he wanted to dispense with it and put the money to better use. His younger brothers felt it would be disrespectful to their father's memory not to perform *ngirim,* even if it crippled them financially—which it nearly did. They won, by the by. The same collision between tradition and modernization is taking place in Little Roanoke. So, to answer your question in a circuitous way, no, it's not too big a leap for me."

"I see," I said, smiling at "circuitous." "That's why you're interested in the jetties."

"Partly."

"I have to say I disagree with you on that. I thought you made a strong case, though."

"I don't support the jetties."

"What!"

Joe calmly blinked. "What I was trying to get across in Manteo is that the fishermen's side was underrepresented at that meeting, and I wanted to redress the balance. Personally—to the extent that I'm involved in it at all—I have reservations about the jetties. A, would they work—they haven't been that successful up at Barnegat in New Jersey or down south at Masonboro. And B, even if they did, would the outcome be desirable? I'm inclined to think it wouldn't."

"And why's that?"

"Because," Joe said, "the condition of the Inlet is probably the only thing that's kept Little Roanoke from becoming the biggest commercial fishing port between Cape May and Florida. As it stands now, local skippers are the only ones who'll use it, except as a port of refuge. Solve that, and what you'll have is a superhighway from the ocean straight into the village. And what happens then?"

"I give up."

"Take a walk along the waterfront in Cape May or New Bedford sometime," he replied. "Up and down Teach's Landing, you'll have a string of sailors' bars, massage and tattoo parlors, X-rated movie houses and topless dancing joints. You'll have Portuguese sailors knife-fighting on the green and throwing up in Maude Teach's petunia beds. In other words, everything that makes the village culturally distinctive, everything that interests me as an anthropologist, will be swept away."

"Wait a minute; I'm confused," I said. "Now you're against them?"

"No, I don't think the jetties are our call one way or the other. I don't think we—and I mean people from upstate who come down to their cottages here for three weeks or a month each year—have the right to dictate the future of the land to people who've lived on it for two hundred and fifty years. Does it seem right to you?"

I couldn't help myself. I let my glance feint down the hill toward the seven-bedroom "cottage" where he was roughing it while doing his research.

The implication wasn't lost on Joe. "You notice I said 'we.' "

The irony of his situation by no means escaped him. When it came to irony, very little did. In a nutshell, if you wanted him, there he was, Joe Madden, Mr. Both-Sides-of-the-Question, Mr. On-the-Other-Hand, Mr. Yes-and-No. His chameleonlike ability to self-immolate and rematerialize, shape-shifted into one or more of any number of opposing points of view, was one of his best qualities—his capacity for empathy was large. Later, his double vision came to infuriate me—because the thing is, if there's always right on both sides of an issue, if everyone's entitled to his point of view, then you never have to choose. In fact, you can't. And that, too, was Joe: Mr. Uncommitted.

But not really. Really, Grant Eustis, who wasn't half as smart as Joe, pegged the professor better than the professor pegged himself. Joe—in his denim shirts and prep school blazer and his Gokey's workboots hand-sewn on a last custom-shaped to Joe's foot, oiled over the years to the burnished gleam of antique saddle leather—by class and background and education, belonged on the environmental side with Grant and me and Gaither and the sad, long string of Robroys and Gilliams I'd dated. By preference, though, at the bottom of the bottom, Joe's heart—all protests of neutrality notwithstanding—was with the fishermen. He loved them and everything about them—their rusty boats and winches with chain drives, their marlingspikes and otterboards and 3:1 reduction gears and God knows what all else. Something in Joe, deeper than his professorial reserve, got weak-kneed and breathy when it came to anything like that. And if you ask me, after his voyages as far as Bali, halfway around the earth, the reasons that drew him back to Little Roanoke, a stone's throw from the summer house where he'd grown up, weren't strictly professional.

What they were, I didn't know, but you might almost say that sitting opposite him on the gazebo bench that night, I started my own personal ethnography on Joe. My anthropologizing, though, was forged in warmth and, later, forged in love; Joe's was altogether colder. Joe searched his subjects for the hidden tic, the thing that you don't say about yourself, because you can't or won't, or because you just don't know. When it came to ferreting out that revealing clue, he was a veritable Sherlock Holmes; when the subject was himself, a Watson. But on the other hand—to use his signature expression—aren't we all? So I forgave that, too. I forgave a lot for Joe.

"So, tell me," I said that night, "in the end, who are we supposed to root for?"

"That's the question, isn't it?" he said, answering with a question. "Do you root for the villagers, hell-bent on destroying their unique way of life? Or do you root for Grant Eustis and Perrin Orkney and E.C.C.O., coming down here like a claque of Norman barons determined to mark the Outer Banks as their private hunting and fishing preserve, a sort of vacation Sherwood Forest? And if it means turning the fishermen into Saxon peasants poaching the king's deer, too bad. The issue, Day, is too complicated to take sides."

"So what do you do?"

"Me," Joe said, "what I do, or want to do, is get down as much of it as I can while it's still here. Because whether the jetties are built or not, whether it takes five years or twenty-five, Little Roanoke is on borrowed time. I want to preserve some part of it in amber before it's swept away."

That magic spinning wheel pricked my second finger. Don't ask me why, but I was touched by what he said, even if, in some way, it was sad.

Joe frowned. "But I'm lecturing . . ."

"Hey," I said, "as long as you don't charge."

He smiled. "So are you hungry yet?"

"Starved!" As we started down the dune, I felt a few languid stirrings, the ones you learn about in junior high that have to do with liking boys and boys liking you. I hadn't felt them in some time and made a mental note to slow down on the wine.

Tracking down the long, wide porch, Joe, remembering his manners like a good Southern boy, held open the front door for me, and I caught the scent of juniper, a hint of sap the fifty-year-old planks remembered from the time when they were green.

"It smells like a cedar chest in here," I said.

"After you've been here awhile, you don't smell it anymore. But you always catch it when you come back."

He turned on the overhead light, and I looked around the big, dim room, with its white wicker furniture—not rattan, but some sturdier stuff, with reeds as thick as drinking straws—its cushions covered in a regatta-striped chintz that must once have been festive and summery, before the white ground faded to bone. There was a ballast-stone fireplace in the long north wall and a bay window in the shorter east one, looking across the porch toward the dunes, beyond which curved the dark rim of the sea. There wasn't a plumb line or a right angle in the place, all the walls and corners canted off the square. The grayed oak floors, I noticed, had lay lines in them, ancient migration patterns scuffed by generations of wet, sandy feet; they tracked off in various directions toward plank doors with black wrought-iron hinges, behind which, I supposed, the bedrooms lay.

Beneath the bay window was a ponderous trestle table whose old heart-pine planks were distressed by the water rings of a thousand sweating glasses of iced tea in a thousand late-night summer feasts whose din and clatter seemed to linger in the air. A pair of slender ivory candles burned in bell-waisted chimneys. There were linen napkins—with napkin rings, no less—and a vase of wild-flowers. Jumbled at the head of the table was a heap of flatware, at the foot a black-and-gray Smith Corona portable that Joe, in his vigilance to make a good impression, had not felt it incumbent on himself to remove.

"It's all so sparkly!"

"Vinegar and water," Joe said. "An old family secret. Beats Windex any day."

In the kitchen, I sat on the island sipping wine while Joe transferred the marinating fluke from the refrigerator to a trenched pewter turkey platter. "May I ask you something?"

He looked up.

"How old are you?"

"Twenty-eight. How old are you?"

"How old do you think I am?"

"Thirty-one, thirty-two?"

"One," I corrected, a tad severe. "Just."

He smiled.

"Do you realize I could have baby-sat for you when I was in high school?"

He pursed his lips. "An obscure point, but true enough." And then, unfolding his improvisation with slow, deliberate attention, "I probably wouldn't have objected to you tucking me in . . . in high school."

"Umm-hmm. Well, not every childhood dream comes true."

"So I've noticed." He nodded to the fish. "This is set to go."

"What can I do?"

"In a few minutes you can turn on the water for the corn. It was fogging up the windows, so I cut it off. And pick some music." The screen door slammed, and Joe's lilting steps thumped toward the drive.

Topping off my glass, I went back to the big room and nosed around. In the crammed floor-to-ceiling bookcase there was a bit of everything in no particular order—canted stacks of humidity-bloated paperbacks, last summer's best sellers, alongside old Heritage editions of the classics with yellowed, water-spotted spines. Without consciousness of class distinction, *Moby-Dick* and *War and Peace* sat in the same row with *Valley of the Dolls,* where I also spied John Ashbery's *Self-Portrait in a Convex Mirror* and T. S. Eliot's *Collected Poems.*

On the mantelpiece, beside a swan decoy—its eyes concealed with a black domino—was a clamshell ashtray filled with ashes someone had forgotten to empty and a large sand dollar that had broken imperfectly in half, a bead of amber glue along the edge suggesting an unsuccessful effort at repair.

I finished setting the table and drifted toward a crowded wall of family photos, where one shot drew my eye. In it, a beautiful young woman around my age—she reminded me of Vivien Leigh without the vixen quality—stood barefoot in the gazebo on the dune, wearing bell-bottoms and a sixties' bandana-print shirt, her long black hair in a ponytail pulled forward over her right shoulder. Dark glasses failed to conceal the sadness in her face, the kind you hide till you can't hide it anymore. Against her left shoulder she held a swaddled baby in a tiny bonnet; her right hand rested protectively on the shoulder of a five- or six-year-old boy, laughing sweetly, but with incongruous dark smudges under his black eyes. To her left stood another child, ten or eleven, overweight, with an antique flat-top haircut and a stare that seemed both vulnerable and fierce. He was pulling away from her, yet not too far. Behind them, a bruised dark thunderhead, beautiful and menacing, was moving across the water—toward them or away, it was impossible to tell.

The screen door slammed, startling me.

"Find anything interesting?"

"I'm snooping," I confessed. "Is this your mom?"

Carrying the fish, Joe joined me at the wall, frowning slightly as he studied the photograph. "That was taken a long time ago."

"She doesn't look like a deb," I thought aloud. "Given Cassie, I thought she would."

"They're both a little past the deb stage."

"Do they get over it?"

Joe was caught off guard by the amount of top spin on my serve. "I take your point. May, however, was in recovery by then. This was well into her I-Hate-Nixon phase."

I laughed at his unexpected slyness. "She kicked the habit, did she?"

"Well," he conceded, "no, not entirely."

"I'm not, you know," I told him, "a deb, I mean."

"I noticed." The professor's unambivalent smile disarmed me, and I stood down from battle-preparation mode. Things were swimming right along. Where was anybody's guess.

"What about your dad?" I asked, scanning for a likely candidate as Joe put the fish platter on the table.

"Deleted from the archive."

I turned around. "For?"

"The usual crimes and misdemeanors," he answered lightly.

"And these are your brothers?" I nodded to the children in the photograph, letting him escape—though only temporarily.

"The baby's Gray. That's Reed." He pointed to the laughing six-year-old.

"So who's the fat kid?" I leaned closer.

When Joe didn't immediately answer, I glanced up and found him violently in flame, the blush spreading from his hairline down into his shirt.

Embarrassed, yet owning it, he looked me in the eye. "The proper term, I believe, is husky."

I laughed. "Nice haircut," I said, easing away.

"Thanks."

I found this whole reaction wildly interesting.

"Shall we sit down?"

As he pulled out my chair, I noticed him scratching his left arm with suspect gusto. "You really shouldn't do that."

"I know," he conceded, "but it itches."

"Here, let me look." I noticed that he'd opened his scabs. "You'd better get some alcohol."

When he returned, I put my foot up in the chair and laid his arm across my knee.

"What's the prognosis?"

"You'll live. Now that I think of it, you really shouldn't drink on tetracycline. I should have mentioned that."

"That wasn't the prognosis I meant."

He was waiting for me. "Oh," I said, aware that we were deeper into the game than I'd realized. The move, apparently, was mine.

In the armpit of his shirt was a thin, dark crescent like the rim of the eclipsing moon. Bold with wine and seized by other forms of madness, I reached out and touched it. "Do I make you nervous?"

His eyes lit like bonfires; the professor, it appeared, had not been stinting with his cups. Those fires warmed my cheeks. We leaned together and, for the first time, I caught his smell, released by sudden heat. There was ocean in it, salt, a hint of surfboard wax and body oils the sun had worked on, and, under everything, that peculiar boy smell, the one that turns bad in locker rooms. Ripe and bitter, it always reminds me of my first taste of beer—something you don't like that later becomes a necessary part of pleasure's structure in the world.

That was it. One minute I was on my feet, counterpunching like an old pro; the next, I was on the mat, watching little tweetie birds fly by my head. You never see the sucker punch.

"You know what I'm thinking?" he asked.

Here it comes, I thought, counting down inside: *ten, nine, eight* . . . "No, but if you're going to make a pass at me, you may want to stop and reconsider."

With every nuance of my come-hither keep-away, those bonfires in his eyes roared up, as though I'd doused the flames with gasoline. "I'm thinking that I'm attracted to you, and I'm wondering whether it has to do with my being wounded and your attending me . . ."

"That's flattering."

"Or whether your being a doctor has anything to do with it," he continued, undeterred. "If it's simple chance, or if there are powerful forces pushing us together, and if so, what they are, whether they're good or bad and whether they'll succeed. So what do you think?"

"I think you got on the express train by mistake. If I were you, I'd get off at the next stop and take the local home." And damning the torpedoes, I shot forth my most flirtatious smile.

He was game. "That's your advice as my physician?"

"As whatever," I said, thinking his advance had proceeded far enough and digging in while there was still ground left to give.

"I have an idea."

"Uh-huh, I'll bet you do," I said, watching the bulb light and then explode above his head.

"Let's go swimming."

Needless to say, this wasn't the idea I'd expected. "Swimming? Now?"

"Why not? It's beautiful out. The water's warm; the moon will be up soon. There won't be many more nights like this."

"I don't have a suit."

"It's dark out," the professor observed. "I promise I won't look."

Experiencing a brief arrhythmia, I acknowledged that the moment of decision was at hand. "This doesn't mean we're going to screw."

Joe put his finger to my lips. "I know. Come on." He took my hand. I didn't know where we were going then.

His instinct proved sound. Outside, the moist night air, the salt breeze stirring overhead, the faint hint of tingling autumn chill, all helped to wipe away the tarnish that fear had started to deposit on my spirit. Down the east side steps and, hand in hand, we ran up the dune. Toward the top I lagged, my breathing going heavy. Joe stripped his shirt off backward, hopped with awkward grace on one leg, then the next, and left his jeans where they fell, his white ass flashing in the dark as he went down the far side into the tide roar, calling, "See you there." Then the ocean said *ah-kooo, ka-sssss* and *boom,* lighting up a quarter mile both ways.

I took my time undressing, letting the soft breeze find the tender caves and hollows, the small of my back, my armpits, the damp crescents under my breasts. Then I pushed down my underwear, stepped out and ran—the damp sand cool and granular between my toes—straight into the bright splash of ocean cold.

When I came up, pushing back my hair, stars were running off my shoulders, down my stomach and my legs.

"Hey," said Joe, "look at this."

I couldn't see him, just two swirling galaxies where he stirred the water with his hands.

"I'm bioluminescing," he said, and a trail of stardust streaked toward me through the water as though fired from Glinda's wand.

"Greetings, fellow starchild." He surfaced near me. "Are we still in Kansas?"

"I don't know."

"Well, tell me this—are you a good witch or a bad witch?"

"Shut up and come find out." I pulled him toward me, his body wet and sculpturally cold, then warm, then soft, pressing my breasts flat. The kiss was simple, tender, crisp and short.

"Your mouth tastes good."

"Yours, too," I whispered. I didn't say the other thing: *I knew it would.*

The second time, we kissed down deep, to wetness; then Joe broke away.

"Ever seen this?" He let the phosphorescence drip from his fingers.

"No," I said, wanting back his mouth.

"It's called *noctiluca*. They're plankton, dinoflagellates."

"Thank you for that tidbit, Mr. Science." Turning away, I caught the dark wave rising toward me.

I came up alone out of the runny foam, and then his dark head bobbed up beside me, and he blew and shook his hair and his teeth gleamed in his dark face.

"Nice ride," he said. "I don't know too many girls who body surf like that, especially this time of night."

Girls? I almost called him on it, but stopped short. It didn't seem necessary. I felt watchful of myself, curious, less afraid. The concussion of the next wave trembled the whole surface of the ocean as if it were a bowl of satin gelatin, shooting through my feet and up my legs, deep into my body, where I wished to live, yet some-how spent so little time. But suddenly I was there again; the rest-less, dissatisfied something that had gnawed at me all summer relaxed, and I felt free and large, expanding till my arms and legs stretched northward all the way to Camelot Pier and south to Nags Head. Those winking green and pale blue lights along the shore were part of me, my twinkling cells, and then I snapped back like a rubber band and lost it all. *Sharks feed this time of night,* I thought, and I felt scared and cold. "It's dangerous to be out here," I said. "We should go in."

"We're safe," he said. "Don't back away." His hand closed on my shoulder, kneading it with a strong, gentle pressure. "I'm going to kiss you," he whispered.

"Be my guest," I whispered back.

And this time it was slight and soft, a wisp of ash borne upward from a bonfire where all the cartographic charts and boundary lines and diplomatic protocols were burning.

I didn't feel it end; the harmonic simply grew remote and thin and pure; and Joe was carrying me, like a naked bride, through the water, scooped up, lighting fires with every stride.

In the swash, he fell on his knees and keeled over, laughing, on top of me. A cold wave slid beneath us and receded, and he moved between my legs and I opened them.

"I don't have birth control," I whispered.

He kissed me, and I waited, tense, until I felt his willed pursuit relax. I reached down and found him hard and felt his cockpulse thump in my hand like a night moth trapped inside a taut skin drum. I grabbed his hair and pulled his mouth to mine, spreading my labia between my fingers as I pulled him in: a slight adherence, and then the long quicksilver shuddering glide.

"Come out now," I said. "My diaphragm's in the car. Let's go up."

"All right."

"No, wait. Don't move."

I felt his heartbeat thump inside, or maybe it was mine: *me you,* it said, *you me, youme . . . Ka-boom!* The bubble suddenly ex-ploded as the world came rushing back, a huge wave sheeting in around us, cold.

Joe rolled off me, laughing. "Shit!"

I got up and ran.

"Hey, wait!"

I didn't stop. Picking up only my blouse as I flew past, I kept going, rifling the Karman-Ghia's glovebox before dashing to the shower under the porch steps, where I turned on the hot water and ducked into the stream.

"Fee, fi, fo, fum. Who's that in my shower room?" The door swung in.

"Hello," I said. "Come over here."

We kissed like old hands then, all the way, and he lifted me off the floor, crushing me to him, overeager, showing me his strength.

"Whoa," I said. "You're freezing. Come in the water with me."

My arms around his back, his around mine, I laid my head against his chest, listening to the water drum the floor boards, running down my throat, between my breasts and his, bubbling and damming where we met as cool air swirled around our calves.

"This feels nice," I said, and he swept my hair off one side of my face, kissed my ear and turned my back to him. I felt his soaped hands slick over my breasts and belly; then his finger glided down into my bush, tentative, exploring, an archeologist moving through the jungle undergrowth, excavating with an artist's brush, and he found the wet warm trench below, the not-so-secret passage.

I faced him.

"Is it okay now?"

I kissed his lips and wrapped one leg behind, as he put both hands on my ass and hoisted me, dropped me back; reaching behind me, through my legs, I found his cock, struggling like a blind man, bumping down a corridor, and showed him to the door.

At the end, we were lying on the floor, spent, the water beating close beside my ear.

"Day," he said.

"What?" I raised myself to look at him.

He smiled and shook his head. "Nothing. Your name."

"You'd better not forget it."

He crossed his heart and held three fingers up, a Scout.

I lay back against his chest. "The water's turning cold."

"Shit, no towels." He started to get up. "Should I turn the water off?"

"Just a little more. I'm not quite melted yet."

I closed my eyes and heard his feet retreat, return, depart again. The screen door slammed upstairs. When the hot water heater finally rebelled, I climbed up on one knee and turned it off. The worn terry robe across the door turned green when I pulled the light string. None too clean, it had his smell in it, a history in several volumes. I buried my face and snuffed up the bouquet, surprised that there was something left in me still innocent enough to feel this eager—a whole new human being, another man.

Like a barbaric queen wrapping up in furs, I put it on and went upstairs.

Joe was at the table, naked, sitting sideways in a chair, his legs dangling from the sidearm. The candles had burned down to stubs, trailing frozen waterfalls of wax.

"Did you say grace?"

"Good bread, good meat, goddamn, let's eat." He grinned and pulled me into his lap. "Try this."

"Umm," I said, noting the professor's transformation into the friendly nudist. "Cold fish. No, thanks."

"It isn't all that cold."

I tried it. He was right. "Not bad."

Suddenly the overhead light flashed on with a faint zap.

"Pa!" Joe said. "Greetings!" And, to me, "He must have heard the blessing."

"What?"

"My grandfather Will Tilley. I called him Pa," he explained. "According to May, he inhabits that light bulb, like the genie in the bottle. He weighs in on things from time to time." Joe offered me another bite, but I declined, enchanted by watching him emerge, larking in the open air, playing a melody on his pipes, humorous, but with an edge, like old circus music on a steam calliope. "Of course, salt air and old wiring may have something to do with it."

The light dimmed, brightened, flickered out.

"He didn't like that comment," I observed in the spirit of the game.

"One of us must be lacking in faith."

"It's probably me," I said.

Joe laughed. "I was thinking it was me."

We held each other's eyes on that, and I turned to the wall of photos. "Which one was he?"

Joe pointed to a picture of a heavy, sweet-faced older man in wire-rimmed spectacles and a Panama hat. He stood before a rack of bluefish, his hand resting on the shoulder of the former Joe— Joey, the fat boy with the flattop and the troubled stare.

"He used to take you fishing?"

"Taught me everything I know."

I picked a flake of white meat from a bone. "And now you're fishing again?"

"I know," he said. "Curious, isn't it? So how about some tunes?"

I knelt and sorted through the fruit crate in which he kept his albums alphabetically arranged, with pop-up tags for all the major listings: Beatles, CSN, Dylan, Hendrix, Led Zeppelin, Rolling Stones, Stones (see Rolling), Zeppelin (see Led).

"Don't you have anything from this century?" I asked. "This looks like it was teleported here from someone's dormitory room in 1972."

"Basically," Joe said, "it was. You don't like my music?"

"Let me play you some of mine." I went out and fetched my tape box from the car. "Do you like Patti Smith?"

"I don't think I've heard of her."

"Jesus, Joe!"

"What?" he said.

I punched in *Horses*, and sat down.

Wrestling a pair of pronged yellow holders into the ends of a corn cob, Joe rolled the ear in butter, peppered it heavily and handed it to me.

"Oops," he said, licking his finger. "I think you lost an earring."

I touched my lobes. "Shit!" Given to me by a friend at Yale, those earrings showed newborn Diana turning back to catch her twin, Apollo, as he came from Leto's womb. "Damnit, these earrings are my faves!"

"We'll find it. It's probably in the shower."

"What if we don't?"

"It works as a single," he said, being sweet. Tearing off a hunk of bread, he went on chatting innocently. "I almost got an earring once."

"Why didn't you?"

He shrugged. "I guess it seemed too gay." His smile—trusting, ignorant—expected no rebuff.

"Oh, dear. You aren't a homophobe, are you?"

His expression dropped. "I don't think so. I hope not."

I don't know what it was—the earring; no, not just that—but I stared at the glum face of the picked fluke, the blind eyes staring upward, side by side, and the rising tipple cake of my sweet, tipsy mood whistled downward like a bombed soufflé. *You shouldn't have let him fuck you,* a voice inside me said.

"I had a brother who was gay," I said, granting him no quarter. The breeze through the open window brought up the muffled shorebreak. I stared out into that dark. "At least I think he was. He died before he ever had a chance to know."

"I'm sorry," Joe said. "How . . . ?"

"Vietnam."

Behind us, on the deck, "Gloria" was coming to its thunderous conclusion, G-L-O-AH-I-A conjuring up a younger and more radical epoch in my life when Patti and her bi lover, Robert Mapplethorpe, still playing open house downtown, seemed to me cultural heroes, prototypes, showing what love and sexuality might look like in a future finally freed from the age-old, outlived urge to reproduce. That theory dated to my East Village phase, when I tossed out my platform shoes and discotheque regalia in favor of an all-black Morticia Addams wardrobe purchased in a thrift on Great Jones Street and spiked my hair—a bad mistake—and wore tuxedo pants and skinny black suspenders like Patti, whom I briefly followed into the dark woods of sexual experiment, only to come smash against the disappointing wall of my intransigently hetero proclivities.

Joe got up and turned off the music.

"You don't like Patti?"

He made an apologetic *moue.* "Truthfully? Not that much."

"Too much attitude," I surmised.

"What I mainly hear," he said, sitting down, "is a yowl of pain, pain hammered down into defiance, my call on attitude."

The professor, intentionally or not, was elucidating something in me, I decided.

"I think she's great," I said.

"Is it okay if we disagree?"

"I don't know," I said. "Maybe we should lay down certain ground rules."

"To wit?"

"To wit: it's okay if I disagree with you, but not if you disagree with me."

Though I said it with a smile, Joe looked uncertain; not having caught the downswing, he also missed the upswing back. It struck me that the professor, unlike most of the men to whom I'd been attracted, wasn't quick. His mind, though deep, was essentially unfit for repartee; it worried the lightest, most casual remarks down to first principles, moving with the ponderous motion of a glacier across landscape, leaving crevasses in its wake. Peering into one, my heart began to pound with anxiety. It suddenly dawned on me that Joe was a man with whom, for me, anything and everything was possible. And whatever I'd come expecting, it wasn't that—not anything and everything.

"It's late," I said. "I probably ought to go."

"I was hoping you'd stay."

"Do you think that's a good idea?"

"If you leave, we'll never know."

I curled a lock of his black hair around his ear and lightly kissed his lips. "There'll be other nights."

"Not this night, though. We just get this night once."

There was in him, deep down, a spark of old-style romance.

And being a romantic sort myself, I hesitated.

"Come on. What could it hurt?" he said, throwing my line back at me.

More sure of the answer now, I allowed myself to be persuaded.

Following one of the old lay lines in the floor, we went to his bedroom, a corner on the ocean side, with windows facing south and east. Joe handed me a T-shirt and went into the bathroom, and I changed and turned back the quilt, a beauty, bearing the stitched signature of the women of the First Covenant Church in Little Roanoke. Pale green squares on white, each panel showed a local scene—a gnarled live-oak, the Wright Memorial, a fiddler crab, a wild pony, a church, a breaking wave, a lone man fishing in the surf. The bed was neatly made, the way boys do it, leaving out the pillows as too technically advanced.

On the bedside table was one of those lovingly abused Heritage editions: *Twenty Thousand Leagues Under the Sea*. I opened to the bookmark.

"Monsieur le Professeur," the Captain was quick to reply, "I am not what you would call a civilized man! I have broken completely with society for reasons only I have the right to appraise. I do not therefore obey any of its rules, and I suggest that you never invoke them in my presence."

The passage had been underlined. The bookplate in the front was inscribed, *Ex libris James T. Madden.*

"Your dad's?" I asked as Joe came in, toweling his face.

He nodded. "He used to read us that when we were kids. I found it on the shelf the other day."

"How is it?"

"Not as good as I remembered. It does have a useful sedative effect."

"Tell me about him."

"Who, Captain Nemo?"

I smiled. "Your dad."

"Oh, dear. And we were doing so well, too."

"What?"

Keeling over onto the bed, Joe looked at me with shining eyes. "I'm happy; let's don't spoil it. Tell me about yours."

"The old interviewer's trick?"

His smile conceded it a little grudgingly, like someone unused to being called out at his game.

"Okay," I said, "I'll go first. Don's retired. Thirty years at G.E. Drinks. That, in combo with a caustic Irish wit, kept him from rising past middle management, which is too bad really, because to Dad, G.E. isn't a corporation; it's a religion, and positive thinking is a form of prayer."

"He still lives in Chevy Chase?"

"Flagstaff, Arizona. He has a condo—doesn't have to mow the grass. He plays golf every day and microwaves his dinner, and if the microwave breaks down? God help the president of Samsung or Panasonic; he can count on getting a twelve-page letter, typed and single-spaced, sent certified, return-requested, threatening legal action and bewailing the collapse of standards and the American way of life. That's Donald . . . Now tell me about yours."

Joe stared up at the ceiling, where the knots in the old juniper stared back. "He was a tobacconist when I was growing up. He worked at the Bonanza, the warehouse my grandfather owned."

"Pa . . ."

"Pa. What he really wanted was to be a writer."

"So you grew up to become the writer?"

Joe swung his head. "No, what I do is different. Ethnography is factual, scientific. He wanted to be a novelist, to roll the universe into a ball and ask the overwhelming question."

"And he didn't . . ."

"He tried once. When I was eleven, he quit his job and moved out to a trailer at the lake, where he kept a trot line for gars and sank his beer in the lake to keep it cold and lived for a while like Huck Finn on the lam from Aunt Pol and the Widow Douglas. He was, oh, thirty-two or -three by then. I visited him once for what was probably the saddest two weeks of my life. Every night he'd sit in the kitchen with his spiral notebook open to a blank page and a row of number two Ticonderoga pencils lined up in front of him. I'd be in the living room, if you want to call it that, trying to watch the Yankees through the snow on the TV, which had a coat-hanger for an aerial. Every once in a while I'd hear him scratch out a line; there'd be a pause as he read it back, and then he'd say, 'Shit,' and I'd hear the paper crumple and the refrigerator door being opened and the snick of a pop-top. He'd sit down, and after a while, another scratch, another pause, another leaf torn off, another beer."

"He never wrote anything?"

"One morning I took one of the wadded sheets from the trash and looked at it. It said, 'Once upon a time . . .' That's all." The weight of it was in Joe's expression. "And he was probably the most intellectually vivacious man I've ever met, the most imaginative."

"What happened?"

"I've been asking myself that since I was twelve years old and I still don't have an answer."

"Do you get along?"

"I haven't seen him in two years. The truth is, I can hardly stand to be in the same room with him."

"Why?" I asked. "Because he failed?"

"No," Joe answered. "Because when he failed, he took everything down with him."

"How?"

Joe shook his head. "Let's save that story for another night." After a beat, he gave me a doubtful look. "So, are we having fun?" His eyes were gentle, sad.

"This is what it is," I whispered, suddenly sure; then, less so. "Isn't it?"

"I wish I knew."

I wondered whether another round of sex might solve the ambiguities, or at least distract us from them for a while; gentler and more intimate would have been my vote, though I wouldn't have said no to another panting, sobbing romp. Joe, however, slipped his hand under the T-shirt he'd supplied, resting it innocently on my bare breast, and fell asleep.

I lay there as the wind picked up, banging a shutter against the house. Somewhere I heard the bright tinkling of a windchime. Under everything, Joe's heartbeat, steady, warm and strong as his breathing deepened, slowed.

Lying there, I thought—not for the first time, but perhaps more clearly than before—there's something in us like a door: certain people have the key to open it and others don't. It isn't so much a matter of his general attractiveness or lack thereof. For me, it never was. It's not about respect, ideals, some vision you might share; not about the future, what you might stand to gain or lose from an involvement; not about what's good for you. Mainly it's something primitive and fundamental, like a pheromone. When the other person has it, you wake up in his presence, as though you'd been sedated and suddenly the sedative wears off and you come physically alive. What that something is, I don't know, nor how we recognize it in another. Perhaps my doppelganger in the mirror knew, who seemed clairvoyantly aware this would occur long before I gave consent.

Too disturbed to sleep, I slid from under Joe's arm and tiptoed to the big room and out to the east porch, where the moon he'd promised me had risen now, a waning, gibbous one, silhouetting the gazebo on the dune, painting a trembling white road across the open water. I could feel the strain in my leg muscles, twitching in a way that made me remember gym, when I was a gangly, knock-kneed girl, breastless and too tall, with braces, teacher's pet, a goody-goody, with pimples, desperately uncool. They called me Big

Bird then, behind my back, and Mary Catherine was dying in the guest room. My only relief was taking long rides in the car on weekend nights with Paul, my big brother, who was wounded and kind—so soft. Too soft. Standing on Joe's porch in the night air, I recalled the wind rushing in the open window of his dark blue Impala, and how one day I waved goodbye and Paul walked off across the tarmac and disappeared into the belly of the C-141 and went away and died.

With the new, the old comes rushing back. *What if he's the one?* I thought. *What if he's the one?* I felt so open, so opened up. I hadn't meant to be.

The truth was, I'd never had the discipline in love that came to me so easily in work. It's not that I was weak; I only wanted to find someone to drink Italian roast with me on Sunday mornings and squeeze fresh juice and read the *New York Times* for, oh, the next forty years or so, someone I could tell the dream I'd had the night before, and shower with, and have fond, unthreatened sex in the middle of the afternoon when there were bills to pay or gardening to do, someone who'd take half the responsibility for birth control, and for ending it when the time came, who'd willingly conspire with me to plan a loved and wanted child (which I was not), a man whose face would light with uncomplicated happiness when I told him I was pregnant, and not be shy of diapers and rising in the night and the vigils of fever, and would dance the dance with me, the ancient one, and stand the beautiful pain of living.

All I really asked was that he be as smart and strong as me, and that he have a job. That résumé hadn't seemed unreasonable to me at twenty-two when I left Georgetown, but by the end of my residency at Yale, having served eight years as a guerrilla operative in a world of smart and egotistical male troglodytes, what had once seemed reasonable now seemed . . . I won't say out of reach, but reachable only by a stroke of luck and grace. By thirty-one, after my year collecting shells and cataloging new varieties of bad blind dates, it had become a notable occurrence to find a man who could hold up under the first fifteen minutes of scrutiny, not as a human being, but as a potential lover. And yet, after and in spite of everything, I still felt lucky; I still felt I was going to find that man and that great love; I wasn't ready to settle. The difference being, I knew now that what I wanted wasn't reasonable, but a miracle, and you have to work at miracles, I think; you have to make your heart stay open, and maybe that's another kind of discipline.

Four months later, standing in the living room of my sweet little dollhouse cottage between the roads where winter had descended, I could see my clouding breath in the cold air, and I wondered whether I'd made the right decision that September night at Joe's. I still didn't know. But I knew I couldn't afford to be indecisive. I couldn't be like Joe, because on that answer, other, still more fateful decisions hung.

Wanting to put them off as long as possible, I took off my coat and filled a bucket at the kitchen sink. After pulling on yellow rubber gloves and taking the last pad of S.O.S., I lugged the sloshing bucket upstairs like an old Irish charwoman and, starting with my bedroom, scrubbed and scoured my little house as though intent on removing every trace that human life had ever taken place in it.

PART II

Four

When he left Bali, in August of 1980, Joe Madden returned to Duke to begin work on his dissertation, briefly re-establishing housekeeping with Beth Carneale, an assistant prof of physics, in the small brick ranch they'd shared before he left. Beth—whose wire-rims, trousers, cropped dark hair and chain-smoking habits were props in a lifelong campaign to minimize the florid natural beauty God, she felt, had afflicted her with in an effort to undermine her intellectual credentials—met Joe at the airport on his return. That night they stayed up to all hours drinking red wine they couldn't afford and making love, by the light of guttering candles, with the lusty abandon that had marked their sex from the beginning, surfacing there as though to compensate for its absence elsewhere in their intermittently shared lives. The following morning, over coffee and her first and second Marlboros, Beth told him she'd been offered a position at Stanford; ten days later she was gone. Having looked forward to their reunion during his whole time in Indonesia, Joe was disappointed, but he'd done the same to Beth the year before and had no fulcrum from which to leverage an objection. There were phone calls between Durham and Palo Alto, but as the school year kicked in, their frequency decreased, and in a way that was implicit, but mutual, drift turned to sundering. What troubled Joe in retrospect was how swiftly the break healed, leaving no scar. Having had his share of scarless loves by then, Joe, at twenty-five, began to wonder whether relationships—his, that is—weren't altogether too much like tires, good for a certain mileage, after which they had to be replaced.

With Beth's departure, he made up lost time on his dissertation, often working through the night, discovering that morning was imminent by the changed vibration of traffic rising off I–85 and the twittering of birds in the screen of pines behind the house. Once or twice a month, he met his adviser, Rolly Hughes, for breakfast at Minnie's, a black eatery on Guess Road not far from where Joe lived. Over the ruins of a soul food breakfast sufficient to overwhelm a small construction crew, Rolly, mopping perspiration from his luminous, orbicular bald brow with the pocket square from his seersucker suit and pressing his enormous horn-rims up his birdlike nose, vetted Joe's chapters in an accent that Harvard, Caius College and the London School of Economics had left pretty much unspoiled from a small town childhood in Dunn, North Carolina. ("Etta, I'll have another side of *bobby*-cue, if you'll be so kind. Now, Joe, I want you to go back and take another look at Durkheim"— "*Duck*-heim"—on this subjec' . . .") And as autumn turned to winter, deepening the sweet, cloying smell of bright tobacco over Durham and conjuring up bittersweet associations with Joe's childhood in Killdeer, forty miles away, his growing stack of pages took shape as *Ngirim,* published toward Christmastime in 1981.

Not long afterward, at Minnie's one morning, Joe noted an op-ed piece on the Oregon Inlet Stabilization Project in Rolly's *News and Observer*—the editors were outspokenly opposed to the plan— and, in characteristic fashion, wondered what the other side's points were, a speculation tinted with memories of bottom-fishing with Pa Tilley and his father in the Pamlico and eating chowder at a down-home restaurant in Little Roanoke called Teach's Lair. Before long, a North Carolina road map was push-pinned to the Sheetrock on Joe's kitchen wall. Having christened a new steno pad "Little Roanoke," Joe was penning notes, queries and epigraphs in its pages, among which appeared the following, from *Deadly Words,* Jeanne Favret-Saada's work on witchcraft in the Normandy Bocage:

> *The anthropologist's task is like learning an unknown symbolic code which must be taught him by the most competent speaker he can find.*

In his first, unsuccessful effort to root out such a speaker for himself, Joe, briskly pecking at the Smith Corona on the kitchen table of his Durham ranch, typed polite, straightforward letters to Dolph Teach, head of the Clam Teach Fish Company, and to his older brother, John Calvin, the pastor at the Lighthouse—as the First Covenant Pentecostal Church in Little Roanoke was familiarly known—explaining his intentions and requesting any assistance they would be generous enough to give. Along with these missives he included copies of *Ngirim,* fresh off the press—as well as copies of a complimentary notice the book had just received in *American Anthropologist*—as authentication of himself professionally and as an earnest of his serious intent. To these letters, Joe received no reply. He wasn't seriously discouraged. If Bali had taught him anything, it was that action at a distance is no more effectual in anthropology than in other walks of human life.

And so, prepared to press the flesh, kiss babies, put his shoulder to the wheel, oars or whatever else might be required to carry out his personal mission and advance the cause of knowledge generally, in April of 1982 Joe returned to the Outer Banks and his family's house in Kill Devil Hills for the first time in almost three years.

Having arrived during the night, he'd been spared the unhappy revelations daylight brought when he set out for the village the following morning at six-fifteen. In his absence, the ocean had all but disappeared behind a wall of chain motels, time-shares and multi-unit condos broken at great intervals by dwarfed and lonely cottages owned by old summer families like his own, still holding out against the tide.

Widening the bypass from two lanes to four, great yellow earth machines droned and beeped along the shoulder; jackhammers fired staccato blasts, rearranging the imperfect earth. The road was leveed roof-high with sand where they were ditching for the new municipal water and sewer lines. Where Kinakeet Wood once stretched from sound to ocean—a virgin tract of pine and live-oak forest with mysterious ponds some said had been formed by a rain of ancient meteorites—acres of fresh blacktop smoked and shimmered in the warming sun, providing parking for a new mile-long strip mall, anchored by a Kmart and a cineplex, whose marquee featured *Raiders of the Lost Ark.* Glancing at the store directory as he zoomed by, Joe reflected with astonishment that one could now have, in Nags Head, North Carolina, an Orange Julius and a slice while waiting for a pair of one-hour eyeglasses, the way he had done on West Fourth Street in New York City during his under-graduate days at Columbia.

Between his house and Whalebone Junction, he passed eleven new theme restaurants, with names like Bimini Twist and Margar-itaville. There were waterslides, bungee-jumping towers, go-cart tracks, amusement parks, video arcades and miniature golf courses—he counted six of these en route—one featuring a thirty-foot Tyrannosaurus Rex, pink with purple polka dots, disgorging a gout of solid orange flame. McDonald's, 7–Eleven, Wendy's, Motel 6, Ponderosa—the invasion was complete. It was a relief to leave the outer beaches finally, crossing the bridge to Roanoke Island. A left on Route 345 just before Manteo, and all the traffic and de-velopment dropped away. Alone on a narrow, two-lane blacktop, Joe headed south again through miles of open marsh, a castaway contentedly adrift in a newly greening sea of cordgrass and spartina.

A mile north of Wanchese, Joe turned west onto a still smaller county road, crossing the low concrete bridge from the big island to Little Roanoke. On entering the outskirts of the village, he had the sense of crossing through a time warp into another, previous America, a prehistoric world of small towns, tended lawns and family cookouts, a world whose demise had coincided with the death of his own family. It was a place of green quiet streets shaded by old-growth water oaks wearing Spanish moss like feather boas and crape myrtles with their smooth, curiously human-seeming limbs. Together with the mines and torpedoes, the front yards sported wooden ducks with whirring wings and painted plywood cut-outs of women leaning over to reveal their polka-dotted un-derpants. In one, a superannuated dory had been recommissioned as a planter filled with pink geraniums. Close beside it, a boy's red bike, a Schwinn, with plastic streamers in the handle grips, lay overturned, the rear wheel still spinning, a little out of true. Eyeing it in the rearview mirror as he passed, Joe felt like a hunter kneel-ing in the forest, turning a fresh spoor. *This is it,* he thought. *This is where it is.* What "it" was, however—on this, he was not yet clear.

At the center of the village, he pulled the Wagoneer to the curb along the green, which was dominated by an ancient live oak known as Teach's oak, one of those rare trees that in size and breadth and symmetry seem not just alive but sentient and aware, with a consciousness calibrated to a different time scale, one in which human years, perhaps, are single heartbeats. Beneath its branches, Edward Teach, a.k.a. Blackbeard, the supposed progenitor of Little Roanoke's dominant clan, was said to have buried his treasure before sailing south to Ocracoke on his last voyage, into Maynard's ambush.

Joe's initial plan was simple and twofold: first, to seek work on a fishing boat; second, to establish a beachhead at the Lighthouse—centers, respectively, of the village's economy and of its social and religious life. It had not occurred to Joe—who was young, healthy and athletically inclined—that prong A of his plan might be a problem.

Reality, however, quickly diverged from the agenda he'd so painstakingly drafted in his carrel at the library.

As he walked the docks, which were chock-a-block with boats of all descriptions, from crabbers' homely deadrise skiffs to hundred-foot steel trawlers, a shower of arcing blue and white sparks drew his attention to a teenage boy seated on an overturned milk crate on the deck of an otherwise deserted boat, cutting out a quarter-round of pipe. When Joe shouted good morning, the boy looked up through an unruly swath of white-blond hair, challenging the hail with suspicious eyes that made no effort to mask their hostility.

"How's it going?"

No answer. The boy held his stare.

"I'm looking for a job. I don't suppose . . ."

Shaking his head, the boy looked back at the smoking pipe and turned the oxygen feed until his cutting flame went sharp and blue. Stung by the rebuff, Joe could not help being impressed by the rude confidence with which it had been administered.

A few slips farther down, two burly men, with beards that might have been coiffeured by the application of high-voltage electroshock, traded amused looks when posed the same question. As Joe thanked them and walked on, one of them sang out the jolly taunt "Good luck."

With minor variations, this scene played out two or three more times, by which point Joe had worked his way down to the fishhouse, a hulking, barnlike structure, part on land, part on canted pilings projecting into the Gut. The sliding doors were open, revealing the bustle of the packing floor as an early trawler was offloaded. Joe could hear the grinding, squeaking clank of conveyor belts, shovels biting into beds of crushed white ice, splashing water, high-pitched shouts, and caught a heady whiff of fish, ocean-clean and rank.

As he stepped in, thirty pairs of eyes scanned him with the same radioactive stares he'd received outside. These belonged to the workers on the line, arranged, gauntlet-style, on either side of a conveyor that extended past the building's edge and over the open fish hold of the boat. Winched aloft at fearful speed, a metal bucket shot from the dark, where it hit a trip bar, spilling thirty pounds of fish onto the belt, and a sea hose washed away the bloody ice. In slimed transparent aprons and green rubber gloves, the workers sorted them by size and species, hands moving in a blur, as if they were poker players dealing cards. They were women mostly, middle-aged to old. Black and white were represented, but the races, Joe noticed, faced off down the line, standing on opposite sides. Two burly black men manned the scale, where the red needle jolted and trembled toward 50 as fish rained into a waxed cardboard box. There were no white men in evidence, none, at least, of normal working age, only one old captain with a face as leathered as an Apache chief's and one long-haired teenage boy, in a Zeppelin IV T-shirt, with a proud wisp of first mustache.

Stepping over an untended sea hose that was whipping like an angry blacksnake over the slab floor, Joe approached a group of women near the time-card clock, chatting and smoking as they changed from street shoes into boots in preparation for the shift.

"Excuse me?" he interposed. "Can you tell me where I might find Dolph Teach?"

Giving him the hairy eyeball as she pulled up her heel, one woman made a curt chin-toss to a glassed-in office perched on a mezzanine of sorts. As Joe climbed the trembling, fish-slimed metal stairs, he heard shouting inside and saw, through the half-glass door, two men. The first, with amber-lensed glasses and a stubble as colorless as nylon fishing line, sat in a folding lawn chair, hands in his pockets, legs outstretched, chin tucked between hunched shoulders as though he were riding out a squall.

The second, his back to the room, stood behind a desk cluttered with, among other items, a V-8 distributor cap and a half-eaten barbecue sandwich, and bellowed into a phone while jabbing the air with the chewed stem of an unlit pipe. Out across the docks, past the black-and-white spiral of Gravesend Light, winking pale in the morning brightness, a skeletal black trawler was steaming up the channel in a patch of sun dazzle, trailing a soiled bridal train of gulls.

Joe knocked, but neither man seemed to hear.

"Goddamnit, Kyle, I'm standing roight here looking at him now. Jubal's passing number fifty-foive with flukes poiled to the rails, been setting out own deck since yesterday at four o'clock—hell, I near 'bout smell 'im. What'm I s'posed to do with him? . . . Second crew? What second crew? Home in bed with hangovers, I reckon. How the hell do I know? They were here last noight till ten o'clock waiting own him, but Jubal calls me up and says he can't run the channel in the dark. I just got th'oo installing that new plotter and a foive-damn-thousand dollar Furono rador in the house. What the hell we spend the money for, if he's too chickenshit to use 'em? . . . What do I want you to do about it? What I want you to do about it, Kyle, is get in that piece-of-shit Ford of yours and droive to Terry Pilcher's trailer and drag his sorry ass out the bed. 'Cause if you ain't here in twenty minutes and he ain't with you—not thirty minutes, Kyle, not twenty-foive—neither one of you'll ever work for Clam Teach Fish again."

He hung up and jammed the pipe in his mouth. "I swear to God, Stump, if Jubal won't my goddamn brother-in-law . . ."

"Ain't no salter cap'm own the oisland than Jubal Ames," Stump said with a resigned but steady look. "You know it good as I do, Dolph, and if you don't, shame own you. Your daddy shorely did."

"Well, Daddy ain't here, Stump. Daddy's dead—he's the lucky one—and I'm still here doing the best I know to run this fucking business. Far as I know, I ain't paying you to disagree with every goddamn thing I say."

"That's true, son. I throw that in for free, from love."

Dolph's laugh rang out boldly, and in the lull Joe stuck his head around the door. "Excuse me? Good morning . . ."

"If it is, we ain't seen no evidence, have we, Stump?" said Dolph, now cheerful. "What can I do for you, son?"

"Mr. Teach?"

"That's moy name. Who the hell are you?"

"I'm Joe Madden, Mr. Teach," he said, advancing. "I wrote you a letter some time back."

Dolph did not so much as glance at Joe's extended hand.

"From Duke?" Joe said, withdrawing it. "The anthropologist?" With each uptick in specificity, Dolph's face descended one notch into a granitelike obduracy.

Joe tried another tack. "I'm looking for work, Mr. Teach. I was hop—"

"Great God from Goldsboro!" Teach said, bursting into animation. "You ready to go?"

"Now?"

"Roight now."

"Sure—I guess," Joe said. "We're talking about on a fishing boat, right?"

"Hell, yes, roight smack damn in the middle of one."

"I reckon he means crewing, Dolph," said Stump in a tone of mild reproof.

"Don't put words in the man's mouth—he said *own* a boat. Ain't that what you said?"

"Well, yes, but I meant crewing."

Dolph held up two stubby fingers that looked as if they'd been squared off by an axe. "Here she is, bud—was it Joe?"

He nodded. "Right. Joe Madden."

"All roight, Joe Madden. You can spend the day walking up and down them docks down there asking every man you see to take you fishing. Come foive o'clock this afternoon, you won't have another nickel in your pocket than you got roight now nor a job neither. Number two . . ." He folded back his index finger. "Run down them stairs as fast as them long legs'll carry you, punch the clock and start making three sixty-foive a hour. Work hard for me, some cap'm moight see you and say to hisself, 'Hey, now, there's a willing fella with a good strong back. Maybe I'll take him own at a quarter share and troy him out.' Next thing you know, you'll be carrying home your money in a burlap oyster sack. Now, you want the job or don't you, 'cause I'm busier'n a three-peckered billygoat in spring."

"What exactly would I be doing?" Joe asked warily.

"What you'd be doing," Dolph said, "exactly, is lumping fish own that boat roight there." He pointed to the window with his pipe.

"Lumping . . . that's like . . ."

"Jesus, Stump, he wants to go fishing and don't know what lumping is. You ever run acrost a shovel in your journeys, son?"

"Once or twice," he answered with a smile intended to be wry.

"Well, Joe, you take a shovel, stick it in a poile of fish—that's A. B, you throw them fish into a bucket and then go back to A and stort the whole thing over. That clear, or should I run it by again?"

"I think I got it."

The next thing he knew, Joe, feeling like a smutch-faced cartoon character after a juggling bout with lighted cannon balls, was descending the stairs he'd climbed, unemployed, only minutes earlier, following Stump, whose lopsided, wonderfully fleet and dangerous descent revealed the reason for his nickname: a prosthetic leg.

While Stump filled out Joe's time card, Joe suited up and walked forward, shoulders bound up in the cast-off skins Stump had given him—which fell a good six inches shy of his ankles and his wrists. His semi-comical appearance caused a gaggle of sallow-faced high school girls to break out in giggles, and a similar merriment, not entirely friendly, was mirrored on all the faces on the line. Enduring the scrutiny, a blushing Joe walked the gauntlet.

By then, the *Father's Price* had loomed up fifty yards off shore. A seventy-five-foot steel-hulled Western rig—wheelhouse forward, work deck aft—she was scab red from the rails down, with a house and superstructure painted white. In her stern beneath the gallows were her two net reels, like giant spools wound with green and orange nylon mesh, rusty chain and cable, and white and yellow polystyrene floats the size of basketballs. Hanging outboard on her quarters from enormous rusty G-hooks, were her great steel spreader doors. She was stolid, graceless, uglier than a pug dog, and some vestigial kid in Joe felt his breathing hitch with unreasonable and instant love.

A handsome young black man standing in the bow caught Joe's eye and tossed the hawser, which hit the dock with a dead, sodden splash. "Put it on that cleat." Pointing with his chin, he fixed Joe momentarily with curious, pacific eyes and turned away as Joe complied. Stretched taut, the line creaked and thrummed like a tuned bass string, shaking out bright drops. As Jubal killed the engine, her stern slowly swung around to dock with recoil motion in a strange yet booming silence; then the hull ground with a wrenching *skreek* into a fender row of dangling tires.

"Swing that boom own out, and let's see if we can't save a box or two of these damn flukes before they stink up this whole town, this oisland and this sorr'ful world." Dolph squared as the captain came out of the galley door, frowning and hitching up his pants. "Jubal."

"Dolph."

The air between them crackled.

"Didn't know as we were going to see you back insoide the month."

"Well, here I am. You mean to kiss me, come along, or else I'm going home."

At that moment a shrill wolf-whistle from the line drew everyone's attention to a cloud of yellow dust mushrooming above the parking lot. Out of it came barreling a horse, a palomino, its mane and tail aswish, successive starbursts winking from the slavered bit. Bent low against its neck, reins in one hand, the other wrapped up in a hank of champagne-colored mane, the rider, an attractive, freckled girl with an arresting shock of copper-colored hair, seemed intent on overleaping the work deck of the boat and swimming the Gut to Wanchese. At the last minute, though, she drew up, her horse's eyes showing white as it reared, dancing sideways, its hooves beating out a tattoo on the planking of the dock.

"Hey, Daddy!" she called, lifting her leg in a goosestep over the gelding's corded neck and sliding down the side. "How'd y'all do?"

"Best we could, sugar," Jubal said, his face breaking into a jigsaw of delight as she tiptoed up to kiss him at the rail.

"How about me, Pate?" Dolph asked, beaming stolidly behind his pipe. "Don't I get a kiss?"

"I don't know," she answered. "Does he deserve one, Daddy?"

Jubal laughed. "No, but let him have one anyway, or else he'll make it warm for me."

"Are you being mean to Daddy, Uncle Dolph?" she asked, giving him a peck.

"Got to, honey. Foighting foire with foire."

At that moment, a man in lizard cowboy boots materialized

against the flat black velvet panel of the cabin doorway, where he leaned for a moment, examining an apple core to see whether there was enough meat to justify another bite. Deciding no, he tossed it in the drink and, stuffing his hands in the back pockets of his jeans, rocked back on his two-inch heels and grinned at Pate.

"Miss Cleopatra."

"Ray," she said, her face transforming from a breathless schoolgirl's to that of an older woman giving shrewd inspection to some suspect bargain.

"The face that launched a thousand ships."

"That was Helen of Troy, Ray."

His smile was unabated. "Good-looking and educated, too."

Pate frowned. "Have you called to let your mama know you're in?"

"We just got here not thirty seconds ago."

"Well, do it now. You know she's worried. And take her a fish for supper, hear? Mama always appreciates it—doesn't she, Daddy—and so will Aunt Inez."

He saluted. "Yes, ma'am. Anything else?"

"Clean it," she said. "Don't leave it for her to do."

"How'd I ever arrange my life without you?"

"Not that well, from what I hear," Pate said. "And if you're going to be ironical, don't bother."

Ray laughed, taking obvious pleasure in her repartee, though it came at his expense.

Pate turned to Jubal. "Mama sent to know when you'll be home."

" 'Nother forty minutes or a hour, I expect."

"I'd better call her then. Uncle Dolph, may I use your phone?"

"Long as it's local."

"I was going to call the Ayatollah in Iran."

Dolph nodded. "Say hello from me and tell him Dolph Teach said that he could kiss my—"

"What?" Pate said. "Your foot?"

"That, too," said Dolph. Then he wheeled and jabbed his pipe toward Joe. "You there, Highwater, Long John. Don't be shoy. Jump own over here and grab a scuffle off that roof and lend a hand. Cap'm, here's a green one for you. Says he wants to be a fisherman."

For half a second, Jubal coolly appraised the stranger; then Joe, balancing one-footed on the rail, scouted for a clear footfall on deck and, finding none, plunged waist-deep into ten thousand pounds of summer flounder, a green-and-white mosaic that rearranged itself with a mucosy slosh around his legs as he waded forward.

He could only guess at what a scuffle was, but since the other items on the deckhouse roof—two deep-bellied shovels, a fire axe, a monster pipe wrench, a broom and a marlingspike—were known quantities, Joe deduced that X was the remaining implement, a wide-bladed aluminum hoe. He was shortly joined by the long-haired high school boy in the Led Zep T.

"Joe Madden," Joe said, extending his hand.

"Willie Flower," the boy replied, ignoring it as he picked up a shovel. "Let's get it own."

At that, the bucket whanged down from the block, bail clattering against the rim. Willie filled while Joe used the scuffle like a shuffleboard cue, sending the fish forward, platoon by platoon, man by slippery man. Within ten minutes, blood blisters the size of Egyptian scarabs had sprouted in the center of each palm. Within fifteen, they'd popped and run. Then the skin, not slowly, began to shred away in bloody strips, as though his hands were being flayed.

Feeling he was on trial and that any show of softness might defeat his cause, Joe leaned back against the deckhouse wall and, crossing a foot over his knee, shucked first one boot and then the other, stripped his socks and wrapped them around his palms. Thus padded, he worked on, and soon the pain subsided to a tingling numbness. Before long he was in a rhythm, sweating rivers in the clammy interior of the slicker top, which released a disturbing whiff of a former occupant's B.O. He stripped it off, along with his shirt, and from a little after seven till a little before noon, saw no more of Little Roanoke, took no further notes, but fell into a lost bodyworld he hadn't occupied for such a stretch of time since he was ten years old, shooting baskets in the driveway of his family's house on Ruin Creek in Killdeer, sending the ball toward the memory of the hoop as darkness fell, listening for the answering swish of net.

And the truth was, bloody hands aside, the work appealed to him. Lumping's repetitiveness, its simplicity and order—Joe liked this the way he liked to turn the pedals on his bike, liked the Coast Guard Station bar where the break was always left, liked to frame his queries in advance and write them in the steno pad with the Mont Blanc lest he forget and lose a thing of value.

When the whistle blew, he blinked like one emerging from a trance beneath a sky that suddenly seemed a richer and more saturated blue. On his way to lunch, he passed through the fishhouse, deserted now except for the old man with the Apache face—they'd called him Cap'm Ernal on the line—who was squatting in a corner on his hams, spooning potted meat out of a tin with a Barlow knife and eating off the rusty blade.

"Afternoon," Joe said, slowing down.

A pair of fierce blue eyes looked up.

Joe smiled. "Joe Madden."

"Jesus God Almoighty, boy! What in hell's blue thunder you done to your hands?"

Joe, who'd pretty much forgotten them, now saw the tube socks, red and sopping wet, like battle dressings. He unwound them; underneath, his palms from heel to just beneath his fingers were raw bloody pulp. "I guess I got a couple blisters."

"Blisters? You're tore up all to pieces. You rinse 'em off with corlocks?"

"Corlocks?" Joe said.

"Come own here." Putting down his tin, Teach stood up, brushing off his hands on his patched railroad coveralls, and pushed through a swinging door.

"Excuse me?" Joe said.

"Goddamnit, boy! Did you hear what I said? Quit yapping and move your ass!" Cap'm Ernal roared, like a man accustomed, at one point in his life, to giving orders without the slightest doubt that they would be obeyed.

Following him, Joe entered a small locker room with a mildewed shower stall whose plastic curtain featured sunken treasure chests and seahorses. In the out-of-order urinal floated a white cake of floral disinfectant, steeping in a yellow infusion dotted with floating bottleflies and sodden cigarette filters.

The old man took a gallon jug of Clorox from a shelf. "Stick 'em out."

Joe hesitated with alarm.

"You want fish poison?"

"Fish poison?" Joe said, mistaking it for something in the GI tract. "I don't think . . ."

Like an arsonist dousing his intended flashpoint with a canister of gasoline, Ernal clutched him with a bony talon and splashed a gout of full-strength chlorine bleach in Joe's raw, bloody palm. It was as if he'd set the boy on fire.

"Ow, ow, goddamn!" Joe hopped on one foot and danced in a circle. "Jesus Christ, goddamn!"

"Gimme the other," Cap'm Ernal said.

"No, sir," said Joe, who had no idea of the purpose of this anointment. "No, thank you. One will do."

Striking like a timber rattler, Ernal grabbed and poured again.

"Ow, ow!" Joe shouted. "Ow!" With violent motion, he waved both hands in unison from waist to shoulder, as though he was shaking down the mercury in twin thermometers.

"That ought to do 'er." Cap'm Ernal was satisfied.

"Whew," Joe said, sucking in his breath between his teeth. "Yowie."

"Go stick 'em in the Gut—that'll stop the smart a bit."

Joe speedily obeyed this time. Starting off at a brisk walk and accelerating to a trot, he headed for the dock and threw himself, full length, on the planks, plunging both hands gratefully into the black water.

As cool relief swept over him, he heard a wheezing laugh.

"Ow, ow!" the old man mimicked. "Sweet Jesus help me, ow!" He shook his head. "Ain't no sense for a man to ruin hisself over a pair of two-damn-dollar gloves. Here." Joe stood up, and Cap'm Ernal handed him an old, worn pair.

The gesture surprised Joe. "These are for me?"

"Who the hell you think they're for?"

"I can't take these."

"You cain't?" Ernal glared as though prepared to prosecute his point at fisticuffs. "Whoy in hell cain't you?"

"Well, let me buy them from you," Joe said.

Cap'm Ernal tilted his head, as though giving the offer due consideration. "They're pret' much wore out," he said. "Ain't worth but a quarter maybe. I reckon I can let 'em go."

"Thanks," Joe said, touched. "Thank you, Mr. . . . Cap'm Ernal."

The old man's fierce expression briefly simplified toward the stranger; then he nodded curtly, once. "You wash 'em again this afternoon before you leave, you hear? A man's hands are his loife. You cain't work, you don't eat. I'm sixty-three years old, and I ain't learned nothing else, I at least learned that."

Sixty-three, Joe thought, amazed. He would have guessed the man was eighty-five.

"There's no goddamn call to let yourself get all tore up loike that. It's a sin of goddamn foolish proide." And the old man stalked off to his corner and, squatting and turning his back on Joe, again applied himself with gusto to his repast of potted meat.

Carrying Cap'm Ernal's stern reproof, Joe made his way across the green to Skaddle's, where he chose bologna over olive loaf and topped it with a slice of orange hoop cheese from the glass bell sitting on the countertop beside a jar of Penrose sausages steeping in cloudy cider vinegar. Washing it down with the Sun-Drop Cola he found glowing like a frosty emerald in the old chest box—possibly the last on earth—Joe dangled his feet contentedly off the front porch and gazed up Teach's Landing, where he half expected the paperboy from *Our Town* to zip by on a Western Flyer or a candy-apple-colored Schwinn.

The spell of lost time was broken by the whiffs of marijuana Joe caught strolling back across the fishhouse parking lot. Lounging on their hoods and tailgates, Willie Flower and a crew of friends assessed him with looks that clustered near the colder, blue end of the spectrum. Joe gave them a friendly nod and took refuge on the boat.

They'd cleared the deck by then, and an ice-cooled updraft made him peer down into the fish hold, where a square of yellow light, stenciled through the opening on deck, undulated on the floor. Outside its sharp perimeter, everything was velvet black. Curious, Joe unhooked a worklight and vaulted down like a spelunker into an ice cave, trailing the extension cord as his belay. Landing with a splash in ankle-deep ice water, he raised the light and found himself in a narrow corridor running fore and aft between two dark walls of oozing boards divided vertically by metal stanchions. These were the fish bins, walled up board by board as they were filled from overhead. There were three on each side, one forward, one aft, all closed off except the last, where he made out the silhouette of an enormous halibut sharing ice space with a lobster that, despite having only one claw, must have weighed close to twenty pounds. Assuming that it was dead, Joe picked it up but promptly fumbled it into the bilges when it demonstrated vital signs.

A splash behind him made him jump. He wheeled and raised the light into a pair of glittering violet eyes.

"Find what you were looking for?" Ray asked.

"Excuse me?"

"You're a narc, ain't you?"

"A narc," Joe said. "Who, me? No way."

Ray appraised him through a grin.

"Seriously," Joe insisted.

"Seriously," Ray repeated in apparent mockery. " 'Cause you know what we do with narcs in Little Roanoke, don't you?"

The question was one Joe Madden did not feel professionally obligated to pursue. Ray, producing a crumpled pack of Kools from his shirt pocket, hung one off his lip and, frisking himself in search of matches, answered anyway. "Cut 'em up in little pieces, sell 'em to the charter boats for bait." Cupping his hands around the match flame, he leaned into it. "Fifteen cent a pound. Ain't real lucrative, but hard to beat for sport." He exhaled and flicked the match into the bilges, where it self-extinguished with a stinging little hiss. "Fella your size, you'd bring a good twenty-five, thirty bucks."

And the curious thing was that the amusement in Ray's expression undercut—without by any means eliminating—the overt threat the words contained. Overall, the effect was one of menacing conviviality.

"I guess it's a good thing I'm not a narc then," observed Joe.

"I guess it is. I told them other boys you won't. They thought you must be, but I said, no, you got the wrong face for a narc. Too clear. And even if you was, you ain't gonna find no contraband aboard of here. Jubal Ames is a straight arrow. So what you doing down here anyway? Stealing fish?"

"I'm not stealing anything," Joe said. "I was just curious."

"Curious," Ray said. "Uh-huh, I see. So, what's your name?"

"Joe Madden."

"Ray Bristow, Joe. Speaking for myself, I'm here to do a little piscatorial larceny. From the Latin *piscis.*"

Joe raised an eyebrow. "To steal fish?"

Ray grinned. "You have a agile mind. That ain't a common quality around these parts. Now if you'd shine that light this way . . ." And he started sorting through the open bin.

"Listen, Ray," Joe said. "I hate to mention it, but there's a lobster somewhere on the floor."

"Not that great big one-armed mother!"

"I dropped him," Joe confessed.

Wide-eyed with alarm, Ray wrenched away the light and aimed it down. A bit of segmented black-green shell breached and re-submerged between their boots.

"Holy fuck, it's Moby freaking Dick!" With an impressive darting snag, Ray slung the lobster skidding back into the ice.

"Nice shot!" Joe said.

"And stay there, too, you mother! Damn, boy, now I gotta change my underwear."

Joe laughed.

"Seriously," Ray said, wiping his hand, "what brings you to Little Roanoke? Taking a semester off from college?"

"I finished college several years ago," Joe said with dignity. "Actually, I'm an anthropologist."

"Bullshit! And I'm a brain surgeon."

"No, really. I published a book on Bali recently. I did fieldwork over there."

"What, studying cannibals and shit?"

"Well, not cannibals, but . . ."

"And now you're lumping fish?" Ray whistled and shook his head. "And I thought my life sucked. Well, hey, man, don't feel bad. You want to write a book on cannibals, stick around this place."

"Right now, I'd settle to get on a fishing boat."

"And you thought lumping was the way to go?"

"It's not?"

Ray laughed. "Who told you that? Dolph?"

"What would you suggest?"

"Talk to J.C. at the Lighthouse. Know who that is?"

Joe nodded. "I wrote him a letter not too long ago, in fact. He never wrote back."

"J.C. ain't too big on the old epistolary back-and-forth, but he knows every captain in this town and, better still, every captain's wife. There's a service Wednesday night. You feel like dropping by, I'll introduce you."

"Really?" Joe said. "I'd appreciate that, Ray. Thanks."

"No problem, man. We get a bounty anyway."

"A bounty?"

"Twenty bucks per Christian scalp . . ."

Joe was silent.

"Hey, man, I'm joking!" Ray punched Joe's arm. "Don't be so damn serious, and take some fish. I mean it, Joe. A man can't live on no damn three-fifty a hour."

"Three sixty-five."

"Whatever. You still got to eat. Wrap some in your coat with you when you go home tonight. Everybody does it."

"Thanks, maybe I will," Joe said, touched once more by the rough charity of one who seemed, in the big scale of things, less fortunate than he. In his offer of the fish, Ray Bristow was like Cap'm Ernal, but Cap'm Ernal after the apocalypse, returned from a term of years spent wandering the earth, where he'd picked up a veneer of bad knowledge through which his original island nature shone with a cloudy light. Jettisoning his prior plans and schemes, Joe recognized his "most competent speaker" right away, and this accounted—though not entirely—for the *frisson* Joe experienced that April afternoon, his bristling antennas reorienting to Ray Bristow like heliotropes toward a Plutonian sun.

Five

The Lighthouse was a mile south of Little Roanoke village at Gravesend Head, the smaller island's southernmost point, rising alone in a sere, beautiful landscape of high dunes dotted with wiry myrtles and sea oats. The church occupied what had formerly been the Little Roanoke Coast Guard Station connected to Gravesend Light, a nineteenth-century structure that had been retired when the larger lighthouse was built on Bodie Island. The tithing members of the church had purchased the abandoned complex from the government and restored both buildings, and as Joe drew near that Wednesday night, he could see the light beam sweeping the marshes before disappearing out to sea.

The station itself resembled a white, three-tiered wedding cake, the highest layer a glass-walled lookout post surmounted by an enormous cross on which an outsized plastic Jesus, head bowed, eyes upturned, hung from spiked, extended hands. Positioned behind the Man of Sorrows, giving Him an accidental halo, a satellite dish—an expensive hi-tech novelty for 1982—was aimed northward toward Virginia Beach to receive the signal of the Christian Broadcast Network.

Joe, reared as an Episcopalian, had scant personal experience with home-grown evangelical Christianity, no more than an occasional late-night channel-surfing encounter with the PTL or 700 Club. Despite his resolve to broaden his perspective, he approached this night's service in a forearmed and dubious frame of mind, and the amplified music that greeted him in the parking lot—thumping bass, the low squeal of reverb, Doppler-ing in the open air—did little to alleviate his doubt.

After shrugging into his blazer, he raked his fingers through his hair and breathed deeply to still his butterflies before he started up the ramp, which bore a not-entirely-reassuring resemblance to a gangplank, one he was walking in reverse, toward the body of the ship.

"Working up your nerve?" The voice came from behind him in the dark.

Joe turned around into Ray Bristow's neon Cheshire grin.

"You made it. I was wondering if you would. Come on, I'll introduce you to J.C."

Standing in the doorway to greet late arrivals, the minister faced in, clapping time to the music.

"Hey, Reverend," Ray called, "someone I want you to meet."

Expecting a family resemblance to Dolph, Joe was confounded when John Calvin turned around. A man of fifty in a cheap but sober suit, the reverend was his younger brother's opposite. Where Dolph was short and squat and powerful, John Calvin was wiry, lank and tall. In place of Dolph's dark fur, he had blond curly hair, thinned to the consistency of cornsilk, showing a gleam of freckled, sun-scalded pate beneath. His most prominent features were his eyebrows. Graying blond and thick, with little uptufts at the corners, they gave him an arch, even roguish look, ill-suited to the sternness of the expression beneath them. Something about J.C. conjured up a reformed pirate. This was partly attributable to his pale eyes, which had the confirmed sun squint of an old waterman, the left narrowed a bit more than the right.

"Who's this?"

"Joe Madden." Joe offered his hand, which the minister shook with a surprisingly soft grip.

"He's working at the fishhouse," Ray said, "looking for a berth."

"That so? You a fisherman, son?"

Joe shook his head. "Only recreationally, Reverend, and not really even that anymore."

"He's a anthropologist, J.C.," Ray said, working to advance Joe's cause.

The reverend's eyebrows pricked up like the ears of an attentive dog. "Not the one from Dook? Sent me that book . . . What was it again?"

"*Ngirim.* Yes, sir, that was me," Joe confirmed, gently attempting to disengage his hand. Like an angler with a wahoo on the line, the older man gradually tightened his grip.

"Well, son, I been remiss own that. I shorely have. Your book's been setting own my desk upstairs lo these many weeks, nagging at my conscience, but what with one thing and t'other . . ."

"I understand," Joe said, smiling as he risked a little tug to free himself and failed.

"So, a scholar, are you? Me, I never had much in the way of schooling," Teach said. "Just hoigh school and a year of Boible college in Topeka. But Boible study and the Word—that's always been a koind of hobby of moine, Joe. No, I shouldn't say a hobby; a love is what it is, a deep, abiding love. Are you a Christian, son?" Teach threw this in casually, like a karate knife-hand to the solar plexus, eyeing Joe as an angler might eye his fish, envisioning him deep-fried in yellow cornmeal in the local style.

Joe, who'd expected this question, though not quite so soon or quite so frontally, came to attention. "I grew up as an Episcopalian," he replied with truthful ambiguity.

The minister frowned as though he suspected the young anthropologist of levity. "A 'piscopalian . . ."

"Yes, sir."

"Well, in my Father's house are many mansions," Teach said, extending forgiveness in a sorrowful tone and dropping Joe's hand as though it had transformed into a red-hot coal.

The arrival of a group of parishioners spared Joe, for the time, from further vetting.

"You sweating there a little?" Ray asked as they moved on.

"It is a little warm in here, now that you mention it," Joe said, lightly acknowledging the implication.

With a laugh, Ray led him down the long, red-carpeted aisle toward a pulpit fashioned like a lifeboat, with a pair of authentic polystyrene life rings in the bow. Beneath one was written, "Cast thy bread upon the waters"; beneath the other, "I will make you fishers of men."

Having expected Shakerlike simplicity, Joe was surprised by the evidence of money, something gaudy and extravagant. The dais was dominated by a bank of Peavy amps that would have looked at home at Altamont. Leading the ensemble, a pretty, bird-faced high school girl, with waist-length brown hair and a long-sleeved floral dress that brushed the tops of her high heels, was ripping out impressive licks on a Fender Stratocaster with a pearltone pick, making liberal use of her vibrato arm and stepping on the *wah-wah* pedal on the floor. Accompanying her on a white baby grand was a meek-faced man with a high glossy pompadour, and a grim-faced fifty-year-old matron with a mesomorphic build and forearms like a pair of anacondas worked out on the drums.

Ray, slipping into a front pew, introduced Joe to his mother, Inez, the minister's sister, a pale, thin woman with a long-suffering mien that seemed imperfectly resigned to its own martyrdom. As she regarded Joe, two pinpoints of surmise as cold as January stars focused briefly in dark eyes. Then she turned to the front. Also in the pew were Pate Ames and her mother, Idail, the sister of Inez and J.C., a dowdy, gray-haired woman with thick-lensed glasses through which glared a pair of challenging gray eyes.

John Calvin's progress up the aisle—marked by smiles and kisses, winks, two-handed handshakes, spirited cross-court hails— was like that of a celebrity moving through a gauntlet of adoring fans. As he approached the front, the band kicked into a moderate-tempo instrumental number, to which the minister, beaming like a beneficent host, clapped time softly, nodding to late arrivals as they straggled in with long-day, after-dinner looks.

The congregants were mostly island types—old clean-shaven fishermen and bearded younger ones, all in faded, sweat-stained baseball caps. The wives of the older men tended to have mild faces and bodies as puffy, soft and white as Wonder Bread, while the younger women wore defiantly slight clothes in bright, harsh colors and looked as thin and dangerous as knives. There was a smattering of professional people, too, perhaps from Manteo or the beach, including a pair of neatly dressed young men in suits who could have been junior loan officers at a local bank.

At a nod from the minister, the band kicked into an up-tempo hymn, "Jehovah Jirai," the words flashing down the wall from a projector in the rear, complete with bouncing ball. The song proceeded in the manner of a bluegrass breakdown, the singing growing more and more spirited as the tempo ratcheted upward, faster with each verse. As Joe shyly glanced around, he was struck by the way the hassled, worn-out faces grew flushed with happy transport as the congregants belted out the words and clapped their hands like thunder. Ray offered to share his hymnal, but Joe thanked him and declined.

When the music subsided, John Calvin raised his hands and dropped his head back, eyes closed, smiling beatifically, and, in a voice that thundered off the ceiling, echoing backward through the church, shouted, "THANK YA JEESUS THANK YA! Puh-RAISE THE LORD!"

And the congregation shouted, "PRAISE THE LORD!"

And he shouted, "THANK YA THANK YA JEEESUS! O MY SAVIOR! O MY DEAR REDEEMER! THANK YA THANK YA THANK YA!" Teach looked up, his cheeks streaked with unembarrassed tears, and Joe, his ears ringing, blinked his wide Episcopalian eyes.

"Praise God, brothers and sisters," the minister began, "we made it through another week, and that's a vic'try, ain't it? Now I want to welcome y'all to Wednesday prayer. We got something roight special to share tonoight in Jesus' name, but 'fore we git there, we got a visitor I want to introduce."

He held out an open hand toward Joe, and on that signal the whole congregation turned in unison, irradiating the stranger with such gravely concentrated stares, the hair follicles tingled individually on Joe's dark head.

"This young fella here is Joe Madden. He's a scholar down from Dook, here thinking to maybe wroite a book own oisland loife. He's looking to go trawl boating, so come own up here, son, don't be shoy. Let the good folks get a look at you."

The moment he realized where the reverend's initiative was headed, BB–sized beads of sweat popped out on Joe's brow and upper lip. He'd come prepared, he thought, to witness almost anything. But to be witnessed himself, wrenched so swiftly from observer to observed—this Joe had not foreseen in his strategizing sessions in the carrel at the library. Since Teach left him little choice, Joe wiped his sleeve across his brow, stood up and proceeded down the aisle with red face, furrowed brow and a thin, fixed smile.

Removing the mike from its stand, John Calvin wrapped the

cord around one wrist and came down the steps like a TV talk-show host entering the audience. "Why don't you say a word or two own who you are and what brings you to Little Roanoke."

Joe reluctantly accepted the microphone, feeling like a bloody steak presented to the delectation of a den of hungry Christian lions. "The truth is, Reverend," he said in a subdued voice, "I don't have anything prepared."

"We ain't fancy here," Teach said. "Just speak from your heart; we'll troy to overlook your grammar."

Joe smiled at the sly pleasantry. "Well," he said, "after reading about the Oregon Inlet situation in the Durham and Raleigh papers for the last few months, I thought I'd come down here and see how it looks to the folks on the scene who have a good bit more riding on the outcome than the newspaper editors."

The minister narrowed his eyes, giving the visitor a look in which gratitude for Joe's sympathetic interest played little part.

"At least that's the answer I gave the oversight committee at Duke when I applied for my grant," Joe continued. "What I didn't tell them was that I was looking for a plausible excuse to eat lunch every afternoon at Teach's Lair and write it off on my taxes."

J.C.'s smile acknowledged the bonhomie with which this was offered, but the eyes beneath the tufted brows maintained a frosty watchfulness, as though their owner was still deciding whether to be charmed or not. "My mama runs that restaurant."

"Maude Teach. Yes, sir, I know," Joe answered, working harder and perspiring more. "I knew her when I was a little boy. My grandfather used to bring me over here to buy fish off the boats, and we'd always go upstairs and have a bowl of chowder. Every year around Labor Day, he'd buy a half-dozen quarts and freeze them for the drive home to Killdeer, where he'd dole them out over the winter like so many lumps of gold."

"That so. And what's your position own the Lord, Joe?" he asked on redirect, returning to the central point. "I still ain't clear own that, and I 'spect the good folks here would also loike to know."

Joe squared to face it, astrally projecting himself to a point in space somewhere in the vicinity of the earth-orbiting satellite that beamed down CBN's signal to its paid affiliates. "I'm interested in faith as a student, Reverend," he said, "particularly in what it means to you and to the people here."

"But you ain't in the market for yourself . . ." Teach swiftly drew an inference Joe made no move to deny. Like arm wrestlers in deadlock, they faced off, and even as Joe returned the reverend's smile, he felt the tensile force of Teach's will in opposition to his own. "Studying's foine, so far as it goes," Teach said, "but studying faith, seems to me, 's a bit loike taking you a picture of the borthday cake."

"I'm not sure what you mean."

"I mean you can hang that picture own the wall and count the candles. You can measure it and send it to the lab at Dook and git it analoyzed, but study it from now till Kingdom come, and you still ain't never gonna know the way it tastes."

Looking at Teach's face, Joe encountered something knowing, calm and old that channel-surfing past the PTL and 700 Clubs had not prepared him for, and briefly he felt like a swimmer in a riptide.

Before he found a response, John Calvin stepped forward. Grappling Joe's shoulder the way his pirate ancestor boarded a disabled ship, he administered a rolfing that made Joe wince and stiffen and then, to his vast surprise, gentle like a colt.

Teach bowed his head and closed his eyes. "Brothers and sisters, we cain't look in this boy's heart and know what brung him here any more than he can look in ours. All we can know is that he's followed some call to be with us tonoight of all the noights of his loife. Joe here may think he knows the nature of that call, but Saul thought he knew where he was going, too, own the Damascus road, before the good Lord struck him with the loightnin' bolt and he rose up as Paul. All we can know is Joe's washed up far from home and empty-handed, asking us for help. Now all you cap'ms out there—Jubal, Cully, Erb, and all the rest of y'all—Joe here may be a little green, but I ask you, which one of us'd be where we're at today if someone didn't fly bloind oncet and take a chance own us? If there's a one of y'all who can help this boy or point him where to go, I call on you to do it in the spirit of the Word that you all know, which bids us do the same as we'd be done to.

"But I didn't mean to preach a sormin and leave old Joe here twisting own the hook, so I'm'own cut the loine and th'ow him back and ask him to set down again."

Returning to his seat, Joe felt lightheaded and disoriented, as though his inner compass had been temporarily degaussed by the charged neutrino blast the minister had beamed toward him from his Christian ray gun. It was a profound relief to have the spotlight pass away, yet for a moment, as the preacher spoke, Joe had felt a hitch in his breathing, a stinging in his eyes, and as he sat down, he felt adrenaline's suffusing afterrush.

The truth was, at St. Paul's in Killdeer, Joe had never experienced anything as charged and raw as this, not in all the years he'd attended, repeating, Sunday after Sunday, the sonorous, majestic cadences of the Episcopal liturgy worn smooth as river stones with centuries of rote affirming. The service moved on, leaving him like a bit of flotsam bobbing in its wake. He slowly recovered and relaxed, and as he did, the question the minister had posed played insistently through his mind: *What brings you to Little Roanoke?*

The truth was, he didn't know. All Joe could think by way of an answer was that something was missing from his present world—the beach with its new strip malls and theme restaurants with specious Caribbean décor—that hadn't been missing in the world where he'd grown up. What that was, that *it*, he didn't know. But sitting at his kitchen table on Guess Road, he'd had a dim intuition that if *it* still existed, the place to look was here.

Six

"Now one more word from me," John Calvin said, "and I'm'own step asoide and clear the deck myself. All of y'all know Inez Bristow, my sister, who's one of the foundation stones of this here church, and most of you know Ray, her boy, or knowed him oncet upon a toime before he left and went out in the world. Now, brothers and sisters, Ray's had quoite a loife, and loike the rest of us he's took a wrong turn here and there and stove his boat and sunk roight down and woinded up a place or two that it was better not to go. But at the bottom of the bottom, Ray found Jesus, Praise the Lord, though I reckon it's the other way around, Ray, ain't it? Jesus foinds us when the toime is roight and lifts us up. Now I been after Ray, me and his mama both, since he come back own the oisland, to testify and share with us his pow'rful story, and here tonight he's going to take the plunge, so come own up here, Ray, and y'all give him a hand."

Wearing black leather pants and a matching vest, with a heavy silver key-chain, Ray, looking as if he'd acquired his fashion sense from a tour with the Hell's Angels, came forward, squeaking slightly.

"Brother, if you will, share with us what transpoired to bring about this joy we see here own your face tonoight."

Looking less joyous than ill at ease, Ray took the mike, tapped the head and blew. "Testing, one, two, three. Everybody hear me in the back?"

"Loud and clear, Ray!" someone shouted.

"Well, let's see . . . I guess I ought to start off saying I grew up in a Christian home—y'all all know Mama. But my dad run off when I was four months old. I knew he was a petty officer in the Navy, but I never met him till I got my license. He was in this crappy apartment out near Oceania, and I knocked on the door and this fat old unshaved dude with red eyes and dirty yellow underwear opens it and looks out across the chain. 'You from the collection agency?' he asks. There's liquor on his breath—it's maybe ten A.M.—and I say, 'I'm Ray, Ray Bristow . . . your son?' and he just blinks like maybe I was a pink elephant he got from some bad liquor, closes the door in my face.

"So when I was seventeen I joined the Navy myself to keep from getting drafted. I went out to the Tonkin Gulf on the U.S.S. *Enterprise*—I was a gunner's mate—and that was where I started getting into dope. We use to call it *Starship Enterprise,* and every night it was, like, hey, Scotty, beam me up. My first night back from Nam, I met this sailor in a bar in Newport News, and we got high and did a burglary, bought a bag of smack—that's heroin—went back to his place and shot up. Within a month I was a addict.

"So I showed up at Mom's on Christmas Day—hadn't even bothered telling her I was home—and she looked in my eyes—I never will forget it—and said, 'You aren't even the same person, Ray. You don't cry, you don't laugh, you don't care about nobody.' And I didn't, man. By then I'd become a person with no feelings. I was running around with a .44 Magnum on me at all times, waiting to be killed or kill somebody else. I was at the tail end of living, I would say.

"Now one day I'm shooting up in the apartment, watching this evangelist on TV. Me and my roommate used to get our ya-yas running around slapping each other's forehead, going, like, 'Praise *Gawd!* Be *haled!*'—how they do. Well, something happened. The sound went off, and suddenly the whole afternoon got dark outside. I thought, oh, man, Bristow, you done O.D.'d, fool. And then I hear this sound. Outside, over the roof. Wings.

"I picked up the phone—I couldn't hardly dial the number—and called home. 'Mom, I'm a drug addict,' I said, first words out of my mouth, and she said, 'I don't care; just come home.' So my buddy locks me in the bedroom for eight days while I go cold turkey. When I get home, Mama opens the door, and there was all of y'all—Jubal, Aunt Idail, John Calvin. There was this big turkey and a chocolate cake. It was like the Prodigal Son or something, man. I mean, I couldn't handle it.

"I tried for a week, then I fell off the wagon. Got drunk, stole Mama's car and drove back to Norfolk, where I been locked out of the apartment. So I break the door down, but the neighbors already dialed 911. Squad car pulls up. I yell, 'Get the you-know-what away,' fire a shot out the window—won't even aiming. Next thing I know there's a SWAT team deploying in the parking lot. Phone rings, it's this detective. I tell him, 'I want a plane to South America.' Guy laughs. 'What you think this is, Bristow, the movie of the week? Cut the crap. You fired at the police—right now it's gonna be a miracle if you walk out of there alive.' Ended up a seven-hour standoff. Eventually I just passed out and they come in and got me.

"So I woke up in the county jail and had my bail hearing before Judge Stone. Judge John Stone—they called him Maximum John. My attorney asks for a ten-thousand-dollar bond, prosecutor wants a hundred thou. Stone glares and raps the gavel, gives the DA what he asked. I was going to get a hundred and twenty-eight years in prison—that's what they said.

"So one night in jail there's this evangelist service, and I just busted out crying in the middle of the sermon—I knew it was the end of my life—and the preacher looks out in the audience and says, 'What's the matter, son?' and I told him. He said, 'Ray, it's not too late. If you'll turn your life to the Lord right now and ask Jesus for help, He'll help you.' And I said, 'I ain't worthy,' and he said, 'Ray, none of us are. Just do it.' Well, I didn't believe him, but I got down on my knees and I begged God for forgiveness, and the weight just lifted off me. I can't explain it, but for the first time in my life I was at peace, and if I spent the rest of my life in jail it didn't even matter.

"Well, by time it come for court, they'd miraculously reduced my hundred and twenty-eight years to six. Because of my honorable discharge, they gave me a suspended sentence and sent me to rehab in Chesapeake for thirty days. When I got out, I went back to my apartment, and my roommate, who's a atheist, said he won't living with no Jesus freak and slammed the door in my face. So I sat down on the steps and slit my wrists. Ambulance come and took me to the nut house. I woke up in the insane asylum pumped full of Thorazine. They kept me there for ninety days, then shipped me down here to face this DWI I'd been running from for years.

"The prosecuting attorney comes to me and the man says, 'Ray, if you'll just plead guilty, we'll give you two years, and in North Carolina the average time served on two years is twenty-one days. You'll be in and you'll be out.'

"So I pled guilty. Shipped me to the Triangle Correctional Center. When I got there, they promptly lost my paperwork. They contacted Virginia, and Virginia issued a detainer on me for violatin' probation. I became a fugitive from justice. I mean, I was in jail, but I was a fugitive from justice—figure that. They locked me up in solitary with all the murderers and child molesters and the mentally ill. North Carolina warehouses the mentally ill in prison—a lot of people don't know that, but it's true. I got into a cell nine cinderblocks long by three and a half wide with no windows. But I just kept saying, 'It's gonna be all right. God's gonna help me.'

"Three months later they lost my paperwork *again* and shipped me to the Warren Correctional Center, a maximum security lockup in Warrenton, N.C. Folks at Warrenton didn't even know who I *was*. Locked me back in solitary. So one morning I stand up in my cell and holler, *'Praise the Lord, I'm in prison!'* And all these guys started laughing and screaming and rattling the bars. They said, 'Bristow, you've lost your dadgum mind. What you doing down there?' I said, *'Thank God I'm locked up in solitary confinement!'* Well, before long, every day there'd be twenty guys waking up, going, *'Praise the Lord, I'm in prison!'* The guards thought we'd lost our mind.

"And there was a guy in there for murder in the cell next to me, and he liked to argue about the Bible. He kept saying, 'Well, you're so happy, there must be something to it,' but he wouldn't turn his way to the Lord. So I asked God to give me the words to say, and I open my mouth—don't even remember what I said—and next thing I know, this dude is on his knees crying and begging for forgiveness. It was the most exciting thing that ever happened in my life, and I've seeked every thrill there is.

"And the next day, on my *birthday,* I was paroled from the state of North Carolina. On my birthday, swear to God. I got shipped back to Virginia, and they told me, 'Ray, you'll have to go before Judge Stone again and you'll get your original six years. He won't want to hear nothing.' My attorney tells me if I'll wait six weeks to go before Judge Bennett, he can work a deal. I said, 'Nope, whatever happens'll be the Lord's will.' Lawyer says, 'Don't do it, Ray. The man'll give you three years minimum even if I cry and beg and take my britches off and stand on my head.'

"Well, Mom and everyone said listen to your lawyer, but I wouldn't. So the day come for court, and in the waiting room outside, I flipped my Bible open—this habit I picked up in prison—and read where it hit: *'He that findeth his life shall lose it; and he that loseth his life for my sake shall find it.'* Matthew, 10:39: I was, like, *'Whooooah.'* You know? And there's this other drunk listening, and he goes, 'Have you lost your mind? This is John Stone, man. The guy's gonna burn you.'

"Well, Stone comes out, sits down on the bench and stares at me a long time, don't say nothing. People start coughing, fidgeting in their seats. There was something different about him—I didn't know what to think.

"My attorney tells him all about what happened. Stone says, real quiet like, 'Did you have a window, Mr. Bristow?' I blinked my eyes, like, huh? 'In your cell,' my lawyer whispers. 'Oh. No, sir, I didn't.' So Stone says, 'I understand you had a really rough time,' and I say, 'Well, they drug me around a little bit down there in North Car'lina.'

"Stone nods, looks out the window. 'There isn't anything I can do to you, Mr. Bristow, is there, worse than where you've been?'

" 'No, sir, I guess there's not.'

" 'You realize that by the time the day's over you'll probably be across the bridge in the state penitentiary?'

" 'Yes, sir,' I said.

" 'And you're willing to accept my sentence?'

" 'Yes, sir, happily.'

"Stone just nods. 'The fine I deem uncollectable,' he says, 'the original sentence I waive. I now give you six years in prison . . . suspending all but the time you've served. And now I terminate the sentence.'

"I was, like, *what?* Didn't even know what it meant. I stuck my hands out to the cop, and he goes, 'What you doing, Bristow?' and I said, 'You gotta cuff me, man. You trying to get in trouble?' He said, 'Man, he just let you go. I been in this courtroom twenty-six years, and you're the first man I ever saw that he *ever* let go.' And that was it—no probation, no parole, cut out all the money I owed, nothing.

"And I don't know what else to say except it was just the biggest miracle of my life, and I thank all of y'all for the opportunity to share it, and I hope everybody in this room stays in these rooms the rest of their life."

And handing back the microphone to John Calvin, Ray casually returned, squeaking, to the pew and took his place beside his mom.

"*Hallelujah, Jesus!*" John Calvin shouted. "Let us sing that song, 'Amazing Grace, how sweet the sound that saved a wretch like me . . .' "

By the conclusion of the hymn, when Pate Ames turned to pass the peace, embracing Joe with steamy Christian love in her tear-reddened eyes, he was asking himself, *What world have I fallen into now?* Whatever it was, it was every bit as strange as Bali—stranger perhaps, because this was Dare County, North Carolina, the place where he'd more or less grown up and still considered home.

Whether Ray Bristow was Professor Moriarty reincarnated or a budding prophet—or some combo of the two—Joe didn't know, but he was mesmerized. Here was a group of people who claimed not merely to believe in God as a matter of unverifiable personal faith, the polite and unprovocative Episcopalian position; they claimed direct knowledge of supernatural power, special connection to that power and the ability to conjure it to intervene in their lives in such a way as to suspend or reverse the course of nature. And they adduced evidence for their claims.

Reeling with the ethnographic possibilities, Joe watched a fellowshipping mob gang Ray Bristow as if he were a newly anointed Pentecostal rock star. Flushed from his spiritual exertions, John Calvin approached, herding a reluctant congregant.

"Here's a feller you moight want to talk to, Joe," the pastor said, dabbing a few residual tears with a paisley hanky.

"We met the other day," Joe said, offering his hand, which Jubal Ames appeared not to notice. Regarding Joe with a doubtful frown, the captain began, in a tone both regretful and mildly argumentative, "Now, son, I'd be loying if I said I wouldn't ruther have a 'sperienced man. But fish are thick, and everybody that can work is working. I been short-handed for a month, and if I got to break in a green hand, I'd ruther give it to a boy as goes to church."

"You're offering me a job?" Joe asked.

"That's the long and short of it," said Jubal. "Now, I cain't offer no more'n half a share to stort, but ain't a fisherman in Little Roanoke got more his first toime out, and many's took a quorter and been glad to git it, too. You want to check that statement, you won't hurt my feelings none. Things work out, we'll bring you up to scale soon's you can do the work. We don't git along, we'll all shake hands and drop you at the docks."

"But, Captain, you don't have to pay me."

Jubal frowned. "Don't have to pay you . . ."

"No, sir," Joe said. "I guess I should have made that clear, but my research is funded."

The captain mulled over this pronouncement with a look of grave misgiving. "I don't know what you think trawl boatin' is, son, but we don't set around in deckchairs, lollygaggin' and drinkin' tea. It ain't the Love Boat. You mean to work for me, I'll 'spect you to hump it like the other men till your oyeballs pop. Otherwoise, you ain't no good to me. So you best tell me roight up front which one it's going to be."

"I'll give you everything I've got," Joe said.

Jubal Ames did not seem noticeably reassured.

"Be at the dock tomorrow morning at six o'clock. And six o'clock means six o'clock—it don't mean foive past six or six-fifteen."

"Yes, sir. I'll be there on the . . ."

But before he could finish, his new employer, still looking doubtful, nodded to the pastor and walked unceremoniously away.

Once more the beneficiary, or victim, of hospitality, Little Roanoke style, Joe gave the minister a slightly flabbergasted look.

J.C. winked. "Ask and ye shall receive, roight?"

"I don't know how to thank you, Reverend."

"Don't thank me. Thank the Good Lord, whose foot soldier and willing pawn I am. Now 'scuse me, son. I got to run off here and say good noight to folks. Hope to see you back real soon."

As he left, Ray strolled up. "So, man, I hear you're going fishing." He grinned. "Didn't I tell you you should come?"

"You were right," Joe said enthusiastically. "You were absolutely right. I owe you."

Ray shrugged. "No problem. I don't know 'bout you, but I got a right powerful thirst on. You got a car?"

"A car?"

"Yeah, you know, has wheels and runs on gas?"

"Right," Joe said. "Sure, it's right outside." He hung fire for an eyeblink before taking the inevitable next step. "Why, you need a lift?"

"Yeah, thanks," Ray said. "Mama's going with Idail and them. Come on, let's bail."

As they stepped together off the gangplank, Joe felt a wave of unaccustomed nervousness and attempted to face it down with typical directness. "That was quite a story, Ray."

"You thought?"

"Absolutely."

"True, too," Ray said. "Mostly."

Sorting his keys beneath the single streetlight, Joe glanced up and found Ray waiting for it, grinning.

"I may have left out a part or two," he said. "Stuff you wouldn't necessarily want to get into in front of a bunch of old ladies, including your own mom. Know what I mean?"

Joe did not press for elucidation.

Ray swung into the shotgun seat. "Hold on."

Key in the ignition, Joe paused as Ray cut a look down the lot, where the brake lights of the last departing car flashed, then dimmed as it turned out.

"Ta-da," he sang, producing a joint from his shirt pocket and wetting it between his lips. "You're sure you ain't a narc, now."

"I'm sure," Joe said in a tone that failed to mask his dubiety at being cast, unconsulted, in an accomplice role. "Pot's not exactly standard issue in the church, is it?" he asked as they pulled out.

"True enough." Ray pulled the pristine ashtray from the dash and fired up. "J.C. don't go for it in a big way. But like the Rasta boys say, God made ganja, right? You got to write your own instruction manual on certain things. Toke?"

Joe hesitated. "I should probably pass. It's been a while since I smoked dope."

"How long's a while?"

"Six or seven years, I expect."

"Jesus Christ!" Ray said. "No damn wonder!"

"No wonder what?"

"Hey, man, don't take this wrong, okay? You seem like a nice guy and all, but just a wee bit on the stiff and squeaky side. Know what I mean?"

This observation had been made to Joe before, if in less gleeful notes.

"Wuff of this'll put you right down in your body." Ray made a downward finger-walking motion. "You're kind of a head man, Joe. Am I right?"

Honor challenged, Joe frowned and took the joint.

"You sure now?" Ray said, brows arched, amused. " 'Cause I wouldn't want to blow the lid off nothing or nothing."

Joe shrugged. "What the heck."

"What the heck." Ray broke into a nasal, equine laugh. "You kill me, man. Who are you, the Beaver? Here, pull in the restaurant a sec."

Joe swerved into the fishhouse lot, where Ray, crimping his joint in the ashtray, got out.

"A headman." The ethnographic pun occurred to Joe in delayed reaction. He snorted.

"Good shit, huh?" Ray said.

"So it would appear."

Ray laughed. "So it would. Come on."

Ray led him up the rickety external stairs to Teach's Lair, the down-home restaurant above the packing floor, where Miss Maude Teach, Little Roanoke's aged grande dame, held sway. As they walked through the door, Joe caught a briny whiff of her famous chowder, which was neither New England nor Manhattan, but Roanoke style, a clear, though distinctly greenish broth with a surface sheen exuded by earlobe-sized chunks of fatty bacon. The smell briefly transported him to his grandparents' house in Killdeer, where, standing shoulder to shoulder with his mother at the kitchen sink in 1975, the year the house was sold, he watched his Pa's handwriting appear through the dissolving frost of one of those old quarts they'd hacked out of the stand-up freezer's shaggy ice like a chunk of prehistoric mastodon from a glacial wall. MAUDE T'S CHOWD: SUMMER '66 it said in Will's fine old cursive; then the paper lid began to disintegrate, bleeding ink into the warm stream, where it disappeared like magic handwriting down the drain.

Flickering through his brain like a strip of silent film from an old archive, it brought home to Joe the fact that he was stoned, officially, and the accompanying wave of sadness also helped to remind him why he'd stopped.

It was after closing, and the restaurant was empty except for a trio of waitresses in pink polyester uniforms with white bib aprons. They were sitting on stools at the bar, shoes off, smoking and laughing as they filled cocktail and tartar sauce containers under the blue arc of an enormous marlin, whose odd grin, Joe decided, was also probably attributable to cannabis. Another waitress, middle-aged, heavyset and gray, with a curious paper crown in her hair—the sort waitresses wore in the fifties, when drugstores still had soda jerks in clean white caps and coats—was setting a window table with her back to them.

With a wink at Joe, Ray crept up on her with exaggerated stalking steps, then grabbed her from behind, planting both hands firmly on her bosom and giving a vigorous jiggle.

"Lor'!" she screamed, scattering the silverware. "Ray Bristow, you little shit ass!" She clapped her hand over her mouth. "Listen what you made me say."

"Hey, Toxey." He pecked her cheek.

"Don't you be kissing me, boy. I ought to slap your face and backsoide, too. Look-a-there, you made me drop a knoife, and that's bad luck."

"Means a man's coming to see you, Toxey," called a gravelly voiced woman from the bar. The oldest there, she took a searing drag on an unfiltered Camel.

"Well, then, Ray, come own," said Toxey, "grab away. I'll see if I cain't drop a couple more . . . I thought that was a fork, Pol."

"Nohuh-uh. Fork's a woman," Pol replied. "Which way's it point?"

Toxey checked. "To the door."

"Then that's the door he's coming through." Pol stabbed out her cigarette.

"What if it was pointing to the window, Pol?" asked Ray.

"Have to be part bird, I guess, or angel one."

"Ain't no angel men," said Toxey. "I know, because I spent my sad loife looking."

"Amen, sweetie," said another.

"What about me?" Ray asked.

"Especially you, Ray Bristow. You're the devil if you're anything."

"Come on, Toxey, that ain't nice," said Ray. "I know you don't mean it."

"Mean it till I have to clean it. Who's your friend?"

"That's Joe," Ray answered, and all the women turned in unison and scanned the visitor with X-ray stares.

"What about a spoon, Pol?" the youngest waitress asked.

"A spoon?" She shook her head. "Ask Miss Maude. She'd know."

"Where is Gram, anyway?" Ray said. "We want to get some beer."

At that moment the kitchen door swung open and out came Miss Maude Teach, whom Joe hadn't seen since his last visit here with Pa, in 1966. Eighty if she was a day, she was recognizably the same woman, only vastly aged. Whereas she'd once been a redhead with a spiffy, if somewhat bluff-bowed figure—she'd had a waist, at least—she was now ponderously heavy and used a cane, moving across the floor with a lumbering bearlike stride, her stockings rolled down to the tops of her black orthopedic shoes. Her hair, pinned up loosely on her head, was silver, her face one shade paler than her hair, and her black eyes had that same frosty pinpoint focus Joe had noted in her grown children, Inez Bristow and J.C.

"Hey, Gram." Ray went to meet her as she shuffled toward the bar.

"He must want money," she said, balking his attempt to take her arm. "Who's this man?" Abruptly stopping, she looked up in Joe's face with a challenge so fearless and profound that it somehow canceled the impertinence.

"This is Joe Madden, Gram, a friend of mine. He's going fishing with us."

"That so? Well, you should cut that hair, good-looking boy like you. Are you married?"

"No, ma'am."

"Git Dolly out here! I got just the one for you."

"Gram!" said the young waitress.

"Don't Gram me." Shuffling on, she hooked her cane over the bar and hoisted herself onto a stool. "You do loike girls, don't you? I mean, you ain't the other koind."

"No, ma'am," Joe said. "I'm rather partial to them."

"Well, I don't mean nothing by it, only nowadays it's hord to tell sometoimes."

"Ray's the one that worries me," said the young waitress, smirking.

"That's funny, Betty," Ray replied.

"Aw, honey, I'm just joshing. You know I'd never think a thing loike that."

"Well, she may not," Toxey said, "but someone will, you don't get married soon."

"Hey, Toxey, I'd marry you in a heartbeat, if you were available," said Ray.

"Who says I ain't? Just let me leave the old man a note—I owe him that, I reckon. Though come to think of it, I don't see whoy."

"You're in trouble now, Ray," said Pol.

"So where's he from?" Miss Maude asked, still interested in Joe.

"I grew up in Killdeer," he said. "Recently, I moved down here to the beach."

"Joe's a anthropologist, Gram," Ray explained. "Went to Duke and then was over there in Bali Hai, studying the cannibals and all. Now he's here to write a book on Little Roanoke. She's the one to talk to, Joe."

"What's he want to know?" the old lady asked.

Ray arched a brow at Joe, giving him the floor.

"Well," Joe said, a little stoned and off his game, "I'm interested in local customs." He nodded to Toxey. "Like the knife?"

"He means superstitions," the youngest waitress said.

"Lor', there's a blue scadrillion of 'em," Toxey owned.

"What is it when you drop a spoon, Miss Maude?" asked Pol.

"Spoon's a choild," she said. "Knoife's a man, fork's a woman, spoon's a choild."

"Tell him some others, Gram."

"Here, lemme see your hand." Miss Maude reached out peremptorily to Joe and turned the surrendered article palm up. "Now t'other one."

"What is it, Gram?" the young waitress asked.

"He'll git married, but he won't stay married."

"How can you tell that?" Joe asked.

"See here? You got a M in one palm, but not t'other. If you got a M in both, you'll git married and stay married, only I don't know as that one's true or not, 'cause look at me." She turned over her old gnarled, liver-spotted specimens and held up the left one. "I just got one M loike you, only my man doied, so maybe that's the reason. But look-a-here"—she touched his fingernail—"see that itty whoite spot there? Oncet that grows up to the top, you'll be receiving a surprise. And this scar here? It's roight acrost your loifeloine. That's something you'll be living through real soon. No, wait. How old are you?"

"Twenty-eight."

She frowned and shook her head. "May be in the past," she said. "I'm koind of rusty; cain't quoite tell."

"What about Ray, Gram?"

"Here, lemme see." She took his hands. "Well, Ray, you ain't got no M's a'tall, so I reckon you won't never marry. But, see here, this wart? You go back in the kitchen, git Nadine to pick a corncob out the trash and wash it good. Then you take a pin and prick this wart, see, put blood own the cob, take it in the morsh somewhere and bury it. Once you forgit where it's at, that wart'll disappear."

"Easier to just go to the doctor, ain't it, Gram?" Ray winked at Joe.

"I reckon, but we didn't always have 'em, and doctor does it, sometoimes it comes back. Corncob, though, one toime and that's the end."

"I thought of one," said the young waitress. "If your palm itches, you'll get money."

"That's right," said Pol. "And if your foot itches, you'll walk on strange land."

"Yeah, and if your whole body itches," Toxey said, "it's toime to take a bath."

Everybody laughed, and Ray said, "Well, Gram, reckon we could get a six-pack?"

"A six-pack? What you want with all that beer."

"I guess we'll open it, walk down to the Gut and pour it in, git the fishes drunk. Make 'em easier to catch, don't you reckon?"

"Well, long as you don't mean to drink it yourself," she said. "Betty, git him what he wants."

Ray reached for his wallet. "How much do we owe you?"

"Put that thing away," Maude said. "Just send me a borthday card next year, if I make it."

"Don't I always?"

"Lord," she said, "don't stroike 'im, he ain't hardly worth the loightning bolt. Y'oll going out tomorrow?"

"Plan to." Ray bent to peck her cheek.

"Well, don't say goodboye or else you'll doie at sea. That's what Clam used to say, and t'other one he loiked was 'Good luck and shitty fishing.' Some Frenchie told him that one in the wor, so out with you, so I can close this place and go own home to bed."

Seven

Before they made their exit from the restaurant, Joe excused himself to the men's room, where he closed the stall door and sat down on the lidded toilet, writing out, in urgent shorthand, key words and phrases he might later use to reconstruct the women's conversation. On the trail now, in a state of keen, if circumspect excitement, he was startled by the creaking of the outer door and left off abruptly, overwhelmed by a rush of unaccountable panic.

"What, you on the crapper?" Ray called out.

"I'll be right out."

"Hey, don't rush on my account. Take your time. Enjoy."

Through the crack in the stall door, Joe watched him stroll to the mirror. Producing a black comb from his back pocket, Ray raked the large teeth backward through his hair, smoothing after it with his free hand, a gesture that briefly teleported Joe back to junior high, to the bathroom of A. M. Spaulding Elementary, where, ambushed, his pants around his ankles, Joey quickly lifted his white hi-top Converse sneakers and ceased to breathe as a gang of older boys from Dyer Road, the meanest of the mean streets in North Killdeer, cruised in to check the luster on their pompadours and scan their private hunting ground for morning prey.

"Catch you outside," Ray called.

Like an intruder moving in the basement of a house, Joe's heart continued thumping heavily after Ray's departure.

When they were both outside on the landing, Ray broke a Bud out of the plastic rings and, dangling a cigarette from his lip, handed it to Joe. " 'Good luck and shitty fishing.' She's a card, ain't she?"

"No doubt about it," Joe confirmed, his smile a little stiff.

"You still with me?"

Joe considered it. "I think I've got another hour left in me. If I'm wrong, just leave me where I drop."

Ray grinned. "Come on, let's walk down to the point and check out the moon."

Almost before Joe realized it, they'd left the hard-packed lot and struck a trail through waist-high grass that whispered in the breeze above the steady crunch of footsteps in soft sand. Still spooked by his reaction in the bathroom, worrying it down in characteristic fashion, Joe found himself pondering the wisdom of accompanying his new friend into remote and lightless areas. Through his anxiety, however, vibrated a buzz of fear-tinged curiosity.

He shadowed Ray as they proceeded south, then east, and struck out for the point. Across the dark, low landscape, the sharp-edged beam of Gravesend Light swung slowly, accelerating as it came toward them, passing like a whipcrack overhead and slowing as it disappeared at sea.

At the water's edge, Ray stopped.

"What the hell is that?" Joe said, shelving his hand above his eyes.

Twenty yards off shore, opaque against the glassine limpidness of the horizon, loomed two great hulking shapes.

"Never been down here?" Ray asked. "They're a couple of old pogy boats. Clam had 'em towed down here from Norfolk and scuttled off the point to hold it from erosion. Been here twenty-five, thirty years, I guess, rusting away."

Above the soft repeated slap of waves, a deep stressed-metal groan rang out as the sprung keel of the closer vessel shifted like a sleeper in a tortured dream.

Ray toed off his boots and started rolling up his cuffs.

"You aren't going out there?"

"It ain't deep."

Reluctantly, Joe followed.

The water was warm and, on the low tide, hardly rose above

their ankles. The nearer boat lay canted over on her beam, her lower rail at chest height. Grabbing hold, Ray vaulted onto the slanted deck, then offered Joe his hand. Like mountain hikers, they made their way up, taking handholds where they could—a fallen spar, the coaming of the uncovered hold, which lay like a gaping pit in center deck. When they reached the upper rail, Ray went up, twisting on his seat the way a swimmer comes out of a pool. Joe followed him out onto the hull, which was flat enough to sit down on before it angled sharply toward the chine and then the water.

As another eerie creak echoed through the ruined hold, the whole boat shifted infinitesimally. "Shit, Ray, you sure this is safe?"

"Been out here a million times." Joe heard his pop-top snick and the foam-fizz splatting on the hull. Ray licked his fingers and passed the can. "Got it?"

"Yeah, thanks. This is why I stopped smoking pot," Joe mused aloud.

"Why's that?"

"Makes me paranoid."

"Maybe it ain't paranoia," Ray said with a contented belch. "Ever think of that?"

"What would you call it?"

"Reality?"

The suggestion, all too plausible, did little to alleviate Joe's doubts about the expedition, or the company.

Ray, however, jolly over his bon mot, clapped him companionably on the shoulder. "Hey, look." On the east horizon, where before there'd been a formless glow, the rim of the moon now peeked up, orange as a carrot. "Damn," he said admiringly. "Evil-looking bitch, ain't it?"

"I don't know; it looks sort of beautiful to me."

"That, too." Like a sword swallower, Ray extracted a second joint from between his lips and submitted it to critical inspection.

"So," Joe said, forcing himself to focus on the task at hand, "which part wasn't true?"

Ray gazed innocently up from his cupped match. "Which part of what?"

"Your testimony . . ."

Laughing, Ray coughed out his smoke. "Damn, boy, I better watch what I say around you, hadn't I?"

Joe smiled narrowly. "Just curious."

"Uh-huh. Well, you heard right much for one night." Ray waved out the match as he inhaled. "I wouldn't want to blow your circuit breakers or nothing."

"My circuit breakers are fairly durable, I think."

"That right? Well, I don't go all the way on the first date."

"Why not?" Joe retorted, in the spirit of the game.

Ray's laugh approved his new companion's cheek. "You might not respect me in the morning."

Joe smiled at this as well, though a tad uncertainly.

"What about you?" Ray asked. "You ain't said a whole lot about yourself so far."

"Not a lot to say. Until Bali, I'd spent most of my life in school."

"You grew up down here, though."

Joe nodded. "Summers. But I haven't spent much time on the beach since I went away to boarding school."

"When was that?"

"Sixty-nine."

"Where'd you go?"

"This place in New Hampshire," Joe replied, "about an hour north of Boston."

"Sixty-nine," Ray mused. "I was on the *Enterprise* in sixty-nine. We went to Boston once on liberty. There was this red brick road running all around the town."

"The Freedom Trail."

"You been there?"

Joe nodded.

"What's that church? You know the one I mean—one if by land, two if by sea?"

"The Old North Church."

"Right," Ray said. "Right. Took us all afternoon to find it, and once we did, it won't that much to look at."

Joe accepted the joint on the second pass. As a cat's paw crossed the water, roughing it like suede, he recalled his first exposure to the town, a walking tour he and Reed had taken with their parents the afternoon before they dropped Joey off at school—the sharp tang in the September air, the fresh-rank breeze blowing in off the harbor, the cry of gulls, a cobbled street.

The New England sky, on first encounter, had seemed two or

three times wider than it ever had down south. They were somewhere in north Boston, an Italian neighborhood, tired and slightly
lost. To the west, a sulfur-yellow sunset was dissolving over Water-
town or Newton. They'd tried a shortcut that hadn't worked, Jimmy,
a devotee of shortcuts, always searching for the easy way that always
ended being hard. He had the map, but he'd stopped looking long
before. Still in her dark glasses despite the failing light, May had
fallen half a block behind. "Hey, Mom, hurry up!" Reed shouted
from the corners as Jimmy glared, the band of muscle twitching in
his jaw. Joey's parents were barely speaking by that point, and he remembered how the somber, brilliant northern light had a quality of
impersonal sternness that showed things as they truly were, as opposed to what he'd hoped and made himself believe.

". . . the Boston Tea Party." Pulling out of his stoned reverie, Joe
caught the tail end of something Ray was saying.

"Sorry, what was that?"

Ray scanned him. "You okay?"

"Fine. Why?"

"You look a little green around the gills, is all."

"It's this grass. It isn't like the nickel bags we used to smoke at
Exeter."

Ray's laugh was easy. "Yeah, baby, the world changed while you
was sleeping, huh?"

The subtext of this remark seemed so obscure and rich that Joe
risked a glance at his companion's face to read what it might tell
him. Not retreating, Ray grinned back. Unsure of his ground, Joe
averted his gaze first.

In the distance, off Gravesend, the doleful clangor of a bell
drifted faintly from offshore.

"Know what that is?" Ray asked.

"A buoy, isn't it?"

Ray nodded. "Number one. That's where the channel opens. My
whole life, ever since I was a little kid, I been listening to that. Sum-
mertime with the windows open, you'd fall asleep to it, and it'd be
there in the morning first thing when you woke up. In high school,
before I went away, I used to come out here a lot to think." He
raised his chin, surrendering his smoke. "All that water out
there . . . What you figure? Hundreds of square miles, thousands,
prob'ly."

"At least."

"And out of all that, this one little channel a hundred foot wide, some places barely fifty. Everybody in this town, everybody own these islands"—and in that "own" Joe heard for the first time Ray's accent, jettisoned somewhere along the way, like his—"all their life they go back and forth and in and out the same way. They grow old and die, and all they ever know is that fifty or a hundred foot of water. The rest of it's just something to be scared of, something they never know . . ."

"Maybe they figure fifty feet's enough," Joe said, intrigued by the metaphor and by the wistful note that had crept into Ray's tone.

Ray clicked his tongue dismissively. "Me, I hate that sound. That's what I left Little Roanoke to get away from, part of it."

"It wasn't enough for you," Joe said, slipping comfortably into his subject's point of view.

"What I think," Ray said, inhaling, "I think there's this other group, five or ten percent—maybe only two or three—but something pushes 'em. It ain't necessarily a choice. They just have to go outside. Now you . . ." In an unanticipated move, Ray turned the magnifying lens of his attention on the anthropologist, his features concentrated and intense. "I don't really know you, right? Like you don't know me neither, but the other day, docking, I see you standing there, sticking out like a sore thumb with that clear face and that long hair; we get to talking, I tell myself, here's this guy, educated, smart, not too bad-looking, what's he doing here? What's he looking for? I mean, how come you ain't, I don't know, what—at the country club, I reckon, in silk suspenders, having a martini and smoking you a fat cigar?"

Joe laughed at Ray's succinct description of him in an alternative universe he might have occupied, and at the same time ran a finger around the collar of his denim shirt, which suddenly felt tight.

"What I tell myself, what I figure," Ray went on, in hot pursuit of his own inference, "is something somewhere once upon a time pushed you outside the channel just like it done me, so to that extent we maybe got some common ground. So, tell me, am I way off base?"

"I can't refute your theory out of hand," Joe said with a wry note.

"But you ain't admitting nothing neither," said Ray with a still wryer one.

Joe acknowledged the perspicacity he hadn't expected. "I see you have me pegged," he observed with only partial irony.

"Now correct me if I'm wrong"—Ray sucked the joint with an enthusiasm born of intellectual success—"but I'm getting the impression you maybe ain't the most deep-down faithful kind of guy. Am I right?"

Joe's amusement level dropped a notch. "I have faith," he countered with studied casualness. "If I fall off this boat right now, for instance, I'm fairly confident I'll sink and drown unless I move my arms and legs to swim."

"I hear you, man," said Ray appreciatively, showing an innate grasp of good ethnographic field technique. "Me, I used to feel that way myself. Now, though, since I got with Jesus, I know I'm going to float. Know what I'm saying?"

"Mmmm," Joe responded noncommittally. "Me, I think I'll stick with a standard life preserver for the present."

"Good one," Ray conceded. "Stranger things have happened, though."

"I'm sure they have, though I can't think of any right off hand."

"So, man, what is it?"

"What is what?" Joe asked.

"What is it you're looking for out here?"

The query was entirely natural and obvious, yet Joe, pondering it, had no immediate or easy answer. So he said nothing.

Ray filled the pause. "Mind if I ask you something personal?" After politely requesting permission, he didn't wait to receive it. "You seeing anyone right now?"

"Not recently, no."

"Me neither," Ray offered, as though Joe had inquired. "Since I been home, I been kind of on a solo gig."

All of a sudden, there was something in the wind.

"You know, in my day, this was sort of like your local lovers' lane, what passed for it." The match flared as Ray relit the joint, which had gone out. "Still is." He held it to Joe's lips, reversed.

"No, thanks."

"Sure?"

Joe nodded, and Ray, as he withdrew his hand, reached out and curled a lock of hair around Joe's ear.

At the gesture, Joe felt the cold glissade of a zipper in his spine. Something in his bowels dilated like the shutter of a lens, and he experienced a freefall into an abyss.

"Listen, Ray," he said, with a mildness his inner state belied, "if I've put out some sort of misleading signal, I apologize, but I should tell you, I'm not gay."

"Gay . . ." Ray repeated, confident of his ground. "That what you think this is about?"

Joe blinked, attempting to fathom the nature of the negotiation they were in. "If I'm misreading something . . ."

Ray cut him off. "Forget it, man," he said in a suddenly deflated tone, tinged with irritation.

In the awkward silence, embarrassment and threat vied in Joe with the concern he felt for Ray. "You know, Ray," he eventually began, "I appreciate you letting me tag along tonight. Some of the things you've shown me might have taken me months to discover on my own."

"Hey, we're just hanging, right?"

"Right," Joe said disingenuously.

Ray's soured, knowing look made Joe feel transparent.

"Maybe I should go," he said, sensing that other options were foreclosed.

"Don't you want to know what it was?"

"What what was?"

"What pushed me outside the channel?" Patting his pocket for his cigarettes, Ray glanced up, looking almost wizened. Something in the offer struck Joe as unsavory, manipulative. Prudence whispered it was time to leave, but curiosity, partly professional in nature, partly not, once more prevailed.

"Everybody's heard them stories, I suppose." Lighting his Kool, Ray picked a tobacco flake off his tongue and casually inspected it. "You go inside the joint, you're just so much fresh meat, somebody's little kewpie doll. Me, it was this dude named Elton Lewis"—and now he pinned Joe with a look—"they called him Baby, I don't know why, his size I reckon. He was six-five, around two-sixty, solid muscle, didn't do nothing but work out all the time. He was the strongest man in Warrenton, and he was a sick, insane fuck. Talking to Baby was like trying to have a conversation with a dog. He had this gold front tooth—he was proud of that—and these eyes . . . The whites looked like bloody egg yolk. Looking in them eyes was like staring into fucking outer space, nothing there. Baby, he was like a shark, just moved and fed, nothing else. Why he picked me, I don't know, but he made me his sow, his wife—that's what they called it—we was married, only this was the kind of wedding you don't get no say in. My third or fourth night there, he comes up behind me, grabs my hair and slams my face into a wall, knocked out my front tooth, and he says, 'Hey, crackuh, you can go easy or you can go hard, but you goin', baby, one way or the other.' I tried to fight him. It was like hitting a brick wall, nothing; he just stood there taking it, patient, like a cow. And then he grabs my wrist and twists it up behind me, puts me on the floor. When he's done, he gets up, tucking it back inside his pants. 'See you tomorrow, sugah,' he says, zipping up, and he grins at me, this little whatyoucallit, sparkle, winking off that tooth."

Ray took a long drag and exhaled slowly. "That was what it was for me up there. All day every day I just wondered where it was going to come from. 'Cause, see, I don't know about you, but all my life, I was terrified of that, getting fucked up the ass. Don't ask me why, but it was like I wouldn't be a man no more, my soul would be destroyed, and all of a sudden, see, it's happening. That's why I busted out crying at that evangelist service.

"Then one night something happened. I was laying there sobbing with Baby behind me, cuffing me upside the head with that big paw, going, 'Shut up, shut up,' almost gentle, like I was distracting him. It was like I drifted toward the ceiling and just floated up there, looking down. And I didn't feel exactly calm, but calmer, because the thing I feared, that I wasn't gonna be myself no more—that hadn't happened, see, and I realized it wasn't going to.

"Floating up there, I could see it was a act, just a physical act, it won't like the universe was going to end or anything, so all this fear I had of it, these ideas and shit you pick up from the time you start to walk—that was just unreal. Then you start to look around and ask yourself how much of what they teach you is the truth. Know what I mean? How much of what we take to be reality, the absolute last word on things, really is? Know what I think, Joe?" And Ray once more impaled him with a look. "Not that much. I think what we take to be reality is like that channel out there, fifty to a hundred foot wide, and there's hundreds of thousands of square miles outside it we don't know about. Most people, they don't want to know, but others, see, like you and me, we got no choice except to go. Baby Lewis made that choice for me; he pushed me past some edge I thought was the end, but it was only the beginning. And what I found out, see, I found out there's something in us it's like water. If the channel's there, it runs inside, but once it gets out, getting it back in ain't all that easy. Water's got a law, but it ain't human law. The law of water's to take the path of least resistance and flow down, and anything gets between it and where it's going just gets washed away.

"Now Baby Lewis, I'll tell the truth . . . If hell exists, I hope there's some bigger, blacker, meaner nigger there, or better yet some redneck cracker from the Aryan Brotherhood, to service him through all eternity the way he serviced me. But in another way, I owe him. See, Baby taught me the meaning of surrender, and it may seem like blasphemy, but, to me, the love of Christ is of this sort. Whoever you are—man, woman, straight, gay—when it comes to God, you have to play the female part and receive a love that shatters you.

"This is what I didn't necessarily want to get into with J.C. and them other people at the Lighthouse. But you, see, this educated guy, out here off the beaten track, way to hell and gone in Little Roanoke, asking questions, looking for truth, I figure maybe you can handle it."

With this pronouncement, Ray flicked his cigarette over the side, a falling star shedding sparks in its descent. "So how about it, Joe? Them circuit breakers holding up?"

"A little frayed," the anthropologist replied in a subdued voice, "but still intact, I think."

"Yeah?" Ray said with a note of clear delight. "That's great, man. That's really good." And slapping both his leathered knees, he got up with a squeak.

The truth on Joe's end, however, was profoundly otherwise. Unlike several semi-disingenuous statements he'd made to Ray, this one was unequivocally dishonest. The truth was, Joe Madden, student of cultural differences, felt out of his depth—terrified.

"I don't know about you," Ray said, with a hint of his previous, more innocent volubility, "but all this yapping, I worked up a pretty decent case of the munchitoes. Mama made cookies this afternoon—tollhouse. You feel like stopping by, we could palm a couple?"

"I'd better pass," Joe said, his tolerance for adventure exhausted for the night.

In the parking lot as they took leave, Joe watched their shadows on the ground touch in the illuminated circle of the lamp and merge into a single silhouette. He offered Ray his hand and then made his exit, politely, circumspectly running for his life.

Driving home, Joe realized that what disturbed him most was the fact that he was disturbed at all. Homosexuality and bisexuality, for someone from his background, could hardly be construed as shocking facts. At Duke and elsewhere, Joe had had numerous homosexual acquaintances and been on friendly terms with them. He'd even been asked out on one or two occasions. In academia, however, these advances had been rebuffed in a mutually painless and mannerly Episcopalian sort of way. Perhaps it was that Joe, until this night, had never been touched, personally and specifically touched, by another man with unmasked sexual intent. Sitting in the driveway of his cottage, lost in a brown study as the converter of the Wagoneer ticked under him, he unenthusiastically mulled the possibility that Ray's advance, however uninvited, was less objectionable and frightening than expected, less frightening than it should have been—less frightening than Joe might have wished.

Seeking refuge in unconsciousness, Joe went to bed but was too keyed up to stay there. Defying better judgment, he retrieved the roach Ray had deposited in his ashtray and fired up in the gazebo. Risen now, the moon had lost its ocher tinge and turned a pure, untainted white. As he smoked, Joe thought of J. C. Teach's birthday cake—*Study it from now to Kingdom Come, and you still ain't never gonna know the way it tastes.* In his stoned condition, it seemed to Joe the minister's remark contained a proposition not unlike Ray's, and, further, that his resistance to the one wasn't entirely unrelated to his resistance to the other. At the bottom of the bottom, Joe trusted God Almighty no more than he did Ray Bristow. And why?

This question wasn't one he'd come to Little Roanoke to pursue, wasn't one he even wanted the answer to. As he took a final searing toke, burning his fingers on the roach, the tinkle of the wind-chime on the porch brought back the doleful clangor of the bell buoy off Gravesend Head and Ray's talk of the channel. And from somewhere in those thousands of square miles of dark, uncharted water, the image of that Boston trip flashed back, his father's brooding, still-young face, darkening ominously as Reed on the corner cried, "Hurry up, Mom!" and May, in dark glasses, made her sullen and deliberate approach.

Obscure links on a rusty chain that vanished into opaque black water.

PART III

Eight

Within a month, my toothbrush had found its way into the holder in Joe's bathroom beside the medicine cabinet, where my diaphragm had also found a home away from home. On a brass hook behind the door, my bikini hung by a shoulder strap, together with my Wayfarers on their hot pink safety cord.

When Joe wasn't fishing, I spent almost every night with him. At first—a nod to my developed views on relational parity—we alternated houses, but, in the end, my little dollhouse, for all its threadbare student charm, couldn't compete with the graciousness of his and its access to the oceanfront. So we landed there, and Joe cleared me a bank of drawers so that I wouldn't have to rush home every morning before work, and I did my laundry in his garage instead of trekking to the Laundromat, and garment by garment, piece by piece—garlic press, espresso maker, boom box and selected tapes—my life moved toward his. I'd like to say the shift occurred so gradually that it was almost unperceived, but that would not be very true. No, I knew where we were going from the start, or thought I did; the major question on my end was speed.

When Joe was out at sea, though, I always went back home—preserving the knack for independence has always struck me as the prudent move, keeping the solo muscles toned and fit. That was okay for a while; Indian summer held on and on, deep into October. And then, overnight, it changed. A gray overcast descended and the wind swung around to the northeast, driving a cold mist off the ocean. For nine straight days it blew, and sand drifted across the road; even though the temperature held in the fifties, it felt miserable and raw. Every night in my little cottage, I listened to the wind howl in the eaves, rattling the windows till the ancient putty fell in grayish, sun-chapped strips. Sand found its way into my sheets and down the chimney and into the closed kitchen cabinets, and when it rained I lay in my damp bed listening to the *plink, plink, plink* of a half-dozen roof leaks, dripping into old tin pots.

When Joe came in after that trip, he bought a log load and began bucking up his winter firewood. One afternoon when I returned from work I found him, shirtless and sweating, on my front porch, adding to the head-high stack he'd already built for me.

"What's all this?"

"I don't want you to freeze," he said, wiping his arm across his brow.

"That would put a damper on your love life, wouldn't it?" I kissed his salty lips, noting how his jeans slumped around his lean hips, revealing a sweat-darkened band of boxers—plaid.

"I'm serious, Day." He followed me inside. "How are you going to heat this place?"

I pointed to a rusty baseboard strip.

"Electric? Jesus, that'll cost a fortune." Frowning, he placed his ear against the wall and palpated the Sheetrock. "These walls aren't even insulated. You'll never keep it warm in here."

"Really?" I batted my lashes, damsel-like, as though this info came as news.

"Look, we're going out again tomorrow. Why don't you stay at my place?"

"While you're out, you mean . . ."

Sacrificing points, he hesitated; the hesitation, though, was brief, which gained him back a few. "While I'm out, while I'm in. Why don't you just stay?"

"You mean move in?"

"Why not?" His expression went as grave as though he'd announced a terminal prognosis.

"I don't know, Joe. It's sort of a big step."

"Why?" he asked. "For all intents and purposes, we're already living together. Why keep paying rent? Think how much cheaper it'll be. We can split utilities."

"So you're a romantic after all."

He made a semi-stricken wince. "I'm trying not to make too big a deal of it."

Oh, I was fond of him. I swept away a strand of wet black hair from his cheek. "Are you sure you want me to?"

He blinked with eyes as honest as a piece of slate. "Do I need to answer that?"

"Yes," I said, "you do."

"Okay, I want you to."

"I'm going to Boston after Christmas. You know that, don't you? What do we do then? Shake hands, salute and go our separate ways?"

"Why don't we cross that bridge when we get to it?" he said.

"What if there's no bridge when we arrive?"

He hesitated. "What's our option?"

"Stopping now."

"Could you?" he asked.

"Could you?"

Both of us were bad that way, to answer questions with a question. Having had a few sawed out from under me, I was shy of going out on limbs, and Joe wasn't exactly Mr. Act-on-Impulse, either. He was right, though. At that point, stopping, however feasible in theory, wasn't a practical possibility. I won't say I had no qualms, but I stayed at his house while he was out on his next trip, and from then on, pretty much. Despite the potential economic benefits, though, I never did give up my place and once or twice a week I headed back to check the messages on my answering machine.

Things were going well, better than they'd gone in quite some time. But the course of true love never did run smooth, or so they tell me—however suspect generally, the old bromide certainly held true for me. Pretty much on schedule, the first cloud sailed over the horizon; a distant boom of thunder shook the sea.

That cloud, by name, was Cleopatra Ames.

I'd first met Pate three weeks after my arrival from New Haven, when I was invited to speak at Manteo High by Edna Driscoll, the school nurse, a blue-haired Roanoke Island institution, who'd vaccinated several generations of children while inculcating the girls in her home ec class with the principles of household husbandry. When sex ed became part of the required curriculum, Nurse D. dealt with it as an unsavory fact to be squarely faced with common sense and proper hygiene. Hence, my summons—and a summons it was, delivered over the phone in a decrepit, but magisterial monotone. For me, everything about Nurse D. conjured terms from an antique and obsolescent feminist vocabulary—words like bluestocking and virago—feminism as it had been practiced, say, in 1910 by vanished suffragettes.

When I arrived at the office on the appointed day, I found Pate waiting to conduct me to my destination. She was a tall, smiling, green-eyed girl with the most astonishing red mane, bright and raveling like flame.

"Hi, Dr. Shaughnessey," she said stepping up and putting out her hand. She was a little overweight, dressed in jeans and a demure white blouse, with a small gold cross around her neck; and her fair skin was heavily freckled, yet, with that amazing hair, she was quite beautiful, like a Scottish lass in some old ballad. From my own long-vanished high school days, I instantly recognized her type—the reigning star, the Good Witch Glinda sort that every teacher holds up as an example and every mother wants her child to be.

In the cafeteria over lunch, Pate, with sweet ebullience, gave me the salient facts about herself. She came from Little Roanoke, had a horse named Prince and, after graduation, planned to go to UNC and become a vet. As the conversation ranged, we somehow touched on Patti Smith and her first album, which Pate hadn't heard.

"If it has to do with horses, though," she said, "I'd probably like it. *Black Beauty* was my all-time favorite book."

That line made my day.

I also met her boyfriend: James Burrus, a broad-shouldered football-player type with a flattop haircut straight out of 1955, where he also seemed to have picked up most of the opinions he wielded like a set of leaded Christian nunchucks. My fame, it seemed, had preceded me, along with the topic of my talk to Nurse D.'s class: birth control. Neither, I think it's safe to say, had made James's limited approval list, which he made evident by glowering at me from the moment he walked in, bringing conversation to a crashing halt. So confident and talkative till then, bright, vivacious Pate, to my dismay, dropped her eyes and from that moment forward, blushing, let him answer for her.

In the way an older woman assesses a younger, I'd recognized a breadth in her. Pate was in a larval stage, on the way to something, and I couldn't help rooting for the metamorphosis, wondering who the butterfly would be.

After that, I saw her picture in the *Coastland Times* as a National Merit Semifinalist, with her hair all curled and set and an everything-is-just-so-wonderful-someone-help-me smile frozen on her pretty face.

Then one day at the beginning of November, LuAnn caught me coming out of Exam Room 3.

"I'm going to lunch," I told her, pointing to my watch in a preemptive act of self-defense. "It's twelve-fifteen."

"One more."

"I'm hypoglycemic, Lu," I whined.

"I know. Me, too." She handed me the chart with a smile both tolerant and devoid of mercy. "It won't take long; it's just a bee sting . . . Pate Ames, remember her?"

"Pate? Sure, of course I do."

"She's on her lunch break, so she's in a rush."

"Gaither's busy?"

"She asked for you specifically."

"What's the problem? She having a reaction?"

"Not that I could tell. She says she's not allergic. Her BP's normal."

"Sweating? Hives?"

LuAnn shook her head. "She isn't anaphylactic, but she told me she feels nauseated."

"Nauseated," I said. "Where is it?"

"What?"

"The bee sting."

"She wouldn't say."

I looked up from the chart, and LuAnn shrugged.

"Knock, knock," I said, breezing in. "Hey, Pate, I saw your picture in the . . ."

The look she gave me stopped me in my tracks. "Pate?"

Sitting on the table, hands clasped in her lap, she gazed at me, her green eyes forthright and ashamed. "It's not a bee-sting, Dr. Shaughnessey." Then she burst into tears.

Pate already knew beyond a shadow of a doubt that she was pregnant. She'd known it for two unhappy months and hadn't talked to anyone and had, apparently, a desperate need to. Apart from all the other items on her résumé, she was head of Little Roanoke Christian Youth, local Pentecostalism's poster girl and darling own. Who was Pate Ames going to talk to?

"It was like this little flashbulb," she said, her face turned to the window. "Of a camera? Like that. I felt it go off somewhere deep inside, and I knew right then, that very second. You remember James?"

I nodded.

"But you don't want to hear all this." Gathering herself, Pate brushed her fingertips across the hollow under her right eye. On her finger was a birthstone ring, a garnet no bigger than a BB, on her wrist, a charm bracelet with a four-leaf clover, a scissors, a spool of thread, a tiny horse.

"Anything you want to tell me, Pate," I said, "I want to hear."

"We broke up," she said. "I wanted to ever since last spring, but it was hard. We've been going steady since ninth grade, and James's parents . . . two years ago, when he graduated, they gave James half their lot to build on, that back part by the creek? The idea was that he'd build the house in stages, so by the time I graduated, we'd have a place to live. James and his daddy poured the slab and built the sill and stud walls and put on the roof and shingled it. By the beginning of last summer, James had paid the first installment on the windows. Whenever I tried to talk to him about college, he'd say he supported me. But I can tell you for a fact he never gave five seconds' thought to what it would be like with me halfway across the state in Chapel Hill for four long years while he stayed home and fished and lived alone in that new house he said was all for me—except he never once asked my opinion on what went in it or where it went, not one single time.

"Knowing James, I can tell you once I said I do, he'd walk through that door the next night and want his supper on the table. That's how he'd have ended up 'supporting me,' and Mama would have been right there behind him, cheering him along, because to her—and I don't mean any disrespect, Dr. Shaughnessey, because I love Mama; I truly do—but, to her, it's from God and proved in Scripture that Eve was made from Adam's rib and therefore meant to be his helpmeet and subordinate herself to him as to her lord and master. That's how Mama's lived her life, and I try to be a Christian, too, but I have mixed feelings over that, and so do lots of girls my age."

"I understand," I said, trying to maintain a look of appropriate professional sobriety and not stand up and cheer.

"But this house," she said, "it just got to be this huge, enormous thing. Everyone in Little Roanoke knew. And we were engaged, which was a promise, and I wasn't raised to break my promises. But I shouldn't make it sound like something good, either, because it wasn't. What it was was weakness, plain and simple—not James's weakness; mine. It got to where I couldn't stand to look at my reflection in the mirror, I was so sick with self-disgust, but I couldn't bring myself to do it; I don't know why. I made a promise to myself, though, I swore I wouldn't start senior year still going out with him, and the last night of revival—this was at the end of August? After the service, James was all pumped up and wanted to go, you know, parking? I was quiet on the way to Gravesend, working up my nerve, and when we got there, I took off his ring and tried to give it back, and he said, 'What's this?' and wouldn't take it. He got mad, and when he saw I was serious, he started crying, and I felt so terrible, Dr. Shaughnessey, I felt so bad for him. I was going to get out and walk home—I should have—but when I opened the door, he grabbed my arm, he got all pitiful and begging, and I don't know why, I don't know why, but I let him do it, Dr. Shaughnessey. I let him do it one more time. I thought it would be worth it just to, you know, get it over with? That's when it happened. That's when I felt the little bulb go off.

"When he finally dropped me off, he was so immature he wouldn't even hold his hand out for the ring, so I had to drop it on the seat and climb out of the car. Mama was so furious we broke up, she wouldn't speak to me for two whole days. And now I'm pregnant."

"Pate," I said, "based on the dates we're looking at, you're only ten weeks along. Termination's legal through week twenty-one."

Her whole demeanor suddenly went grave and small. "Termination . . . You mean abortion?"

"If that's an option you're considering," I belatedly put in.

"I don't know," she said. "I don't know if I could do that, Dr. Shaughnessey. I know you disagree, but in our church . . . I mean, it's just how I was raised."

"I understand," I told her. "As a Catholic, I was raised that way myself."

I saw her mull the implication. "But I can't have a baby either. I don't want to marry James."

"What about adoption?"

"But my parents would find out, wouldn't they? If I had it, they'd have to know."

"Yes," I conceded, "they probably would."

"I can't do anything." She cut her glance back toward the window. "I don't know what to do."

Run, I wanted to tell her. *Get on your horse, head west and don't look back until you get to UNC.*

Let's face it, if I didn't think having babies was a pretty swell idea, I'd have gone into another line of work. But when it's right, it's right, when it's not . . . At Yale–New Haven, I'd seen scores, maybe hundreds of young women in that moment, receive that news. Rich, poor, black, white, Ph.D.'s and high school dropouts, when it was unwelcome, it was the same each time. Whatever was diverse and rich about their backgrounds, their personalities, their losses and achievements, all leveled out and disappeared. They all looked like Pate, frightened cattle moving up the chute toward the dark door.

I didn't tell her, though. You can't. As she left, I simply pressed a pamphlet in her hand—*Choices,* the standard handout from the D.O.H.

"You've got some time, Pate," I told her. "Not tons, but some. Think about it. If you want to talk to me, call any time." In the margin on the back page, I jotted down my office and home numbers.

A week passed, two, three. I never heard from her.

Then the week before Thanksgiving, a late-season hurricane targeted the Banks while Joe was out at sea. After listening to the weather report one morning, I stood in the gazebo looking north as the combers roared in, sending plumes of spray aloft like solar flares, and, against my normal practice, I called Clam Teach Fish to find out when his ship—excuse me, boat—was coming in.

I spoke to an old man named Stump.

"What boat's he own?" he asked.

"He doesn't own a boat; he just works on one."

"What's this feller's name?"

"Joe," I said.

"Not Joe Tillet, is it? 'Cause I know his woife, and you ain't Bess."

"Joe Madden."

"Oh, Joe Madden. He's own the *Father's Proice*. Jubal's coming up the channel now. Be here in another fifty minutes or a hour."

And so, forgoing my morning jog, there I was at seven A.M. as the boats paraded in dramatically against the bruised sky of the approaching storm. In Joe's honor, I'd put on red Vampira lipstick and the shortest miniskirt I owned—black leather, from the old days in New York. Like a lamia shoehorned into a discarded skin, I was experiencing symptoms of mild respiratory distress, thanks to too many morning doughnuts at the clinic and too much jug Chablis.

The true dimensions of my sartorial blunder didn't dawn on me until I reached the dock, where the other women had congregated to await their men. To be honest, I hadn't imagined that anyone else would be up at that godforsaken hour, but there they were, at the landward end. Cigarettes in one hand, babies in the other, they broke off their chatter, eyeing me with hangdog looks, as though I'd defected from the cause, some cause, leaving them to shoulder my share of the burden. Suspended over water, alone at the far end, I felt a tad unpopular, like the whore of Babylon, in fact, sent to walk the plank, an option that was beginning to look seriously attractive.

It was worth it, though, to see Joe's face when he spied me there; it modulated through surprise to happiness and ended up in pride. Something in me bloomed toward him, confirming what I must have known already. It was that moment starting out, when everything is new and it seems possible to choose the bricks in the history you're going to build, this time selecting only what is good and laying all your courses true.

With his tan and dirty hair and three-day growth, Joe stood in the bow, his expression as clear as the ocean when an onshore breeze has blown all night. Six days at sea, in the sun and salt air, had removed a tarnish, and the slow way he raised his hand to wave brought home in a flash that what seemed complex in his nature wasn't native there. At bottom, there was a simplicity in him that something in his former life had hurt.

"Welcome home!" I called.

Joe grinned, cupped his ear, shook his head.

With the boat still moving, he leaped to the dock, landing squarely and then teeter-tottering as he straightened up.

"Whoa!" Extending his arms for balance, he tightrope-walked toward me, woozy as a toddler. "Hey, Ray, check it out!"

Leaning over the side, a man on deck scanned me in a manner not precisely rude, but brazen. "He's still got his sea legs on," he said to me. "It'll wear off in a couple hours. Engine noise'll take a little longer. I'm Ray Bristow."

"Day Shaughnessey."

"I know who you are."

I smiled with minimal politeness and turned to Joe, who introduced me to Jubal Ames; it was the first time I'd met Pate's father. As he shook my hand, his confident, paternal manner with his men evaporated in a mumbling shyness. He struck me as a man still young, straight-limbed and strong, imprisoned in the weathered flesh of an aging one, the sort who would remain intact and hale far into his advancing years, then overnight turn old.

As we walked hand in hand toward the parking lot, Joe drew me up short.

"Hey, sailor," I said, vamping.

He started to kiss me, and I caught my first undiluted whiff. "Oh, my God."

"What?"

"Eeee-uuu." I pinched my nostrils.

"What, I smell?"

"Smell? Sweetheart, honeybunch, like the end of life on earth."

He sniffed his armpit. "Come on, it's not that bad. Give us a kiss."

"No chance, bud-weiser. Not until you burn those clothes."

"Just one?" He batted his lashes.

Shamelessly manipulated, I caved, and it was there, *ka-boom,* the tingling where our bare shoulders touched.

"All right," I said, as his lips brushed my throat. "Enough. Shove off there, matey."

"Oh, crap, we have to take two cars?" he said, as it dawned on him. "I don't know if I can stand to be away from you for twenty minutes."

"You made it for twenty-eight years. You'll manage."

"Not that well," he said, his whole face open, revealing something new.

"See you later, 'gator." I pecked his lips, and at the clopping sound of hooves, we swiveled and saw Pate entering the lot at a slow canter.

"Hi, Pate," Joe said.

"Hey, Joe. How'd y'all do?" She focused exclusively on him.

"Seven hundred boxes."

"Not bad." Then, as Prince danced sideways, she turned a grave look to me, one that conjured the outlaw in an old Western, tracked down in her hideaway by someone who knows the secret of her past. "Hi, Dr. Shaughnessey."

"Hi, Pate. I take it you two know each other."

"Yes, ma'am."

"I came to pick Joe up," I said, clueing her.

Her gaze discreetly flicked from Joe to me, checking out my clothes, then off above our heads. "There's Daddy. I should probably go." Clucking her tongue, she rode ahead.

"How do you know Pate?" Joe asked, fishing out his keys beside the Wagoneer.

"She's been in a couple of times."

"To Beach Med?"

I blinked in a way meant to terminate the line of inquiry. For an instant, the easy sunlight left Joe's face, replaced by something speculative, complex, his Sherlock look.

I waited to see whether the jeep would start. When it did, he kissed me through the window.

"See you at home," he said and roared out of the lot.

Holding back, I cast a fretful glance toward the dock, where I saw Pate's shock of copper hair burning amidst the nondescript assemblage. One hand holding the bridle, the other on her father's shoulder, she tiptoed up to kiss his cheek. Idling, I saw how at home she was with the other women, of their world yet different, too, that hair like a spark which they had let burn out. She'd said she wanted to go to college and become a vet. I wondered whether she'd make it, or if a year from now, she'd be out here in her sweats, a baby on her hip, waiting for James, the trophies she'd won in 4-H and debating club accumulating dust in a box at home.

I pulled out feeling angry, at what, I didn't know—the women, Pate, my mother, motherhood itself. And then there was that little voice—not theirs, but mine—that occasionally sounded off, accusing me of my childlessness as though it were a crime, the mindless imperative that said, *It's time, it's time,* dismissing my logical objections as excuses to disguise my failure to be real. Occasionally, it seemed that everything, even biology, conspired to extinguish that spark, not just in Pate, but in women everywhere, and towns like Little Roanoke were the embodiment of the forces that had held us down and back. What was it that made Joe blossom here?

What Pate was going to do—make the break or let James answer for her the way she had that day in Manteo—I didn't know. If I felt invested in the outcome, more than was probably appropriate or wise, maybe the reason was because Pate reminded me of someone I once knew, in that previous lifetime at Blessed Sacrament in Chevy Chase, a cheery, positive-thinking Catholic go-getter who dotted her *i*'s with hearts and put smiley faces at the bottom of her notes. That morning as I put the village with its rusty mines and unexploded bombs in the rearview mirror, I thought again of the heroines in those old Scottish lays and ballads. Things never turned out well for them; things never turned out well at all.

Nine

The hurricane veered off at the last minute, making landfall at Cape Fear. We got some storm surge, heavy rain, nothing to write home about. That Saturday, Joe took a rare day off, and the two of us, starved for culture, made the drive to Norfolk and took in a matinee. There was a Hitchcock festival at a little art revival house in Ghent. We saw *Rear Window*, which Joe claimed was on his all-time top-ten list.

"Number eight," he specified unnecessarily.

At the theater, after a preemptive pee, I spotted him at the refreshment counter, standing to one side, picking absently at a large popcorn bucket. A toddler, unbeknownst to her mother, had formed a wide-eyed, blue, mesmeric fix on Joe, who didn't notice it, then did. For a moment, the two of them faced off in somber appraisal. The little girl looked at Joe, looked at the bucket, back at Joe and took a heaping, tiny fistful. Unsmiling, Joe put a finger to his lips, sealing the conspiracy, and at that moment mommy turned around.

"Elsbeth! Oh, I'm so sorry."

"No, no, I gave it to her," Joe said, copping.

"Say thank you to the nice man," she said, hurrying as the sound of music swelled up from within and the usher moved to close the doors. As her mother led her off, little Elsbeth reached back in Joe's direction, dropping puffs of popcorn on the dark rug.

Watching the scene play out, I discovered that I was keenly interested—don't ask me why. I took Joe's arm, and we proceeded down the aisle, following Elsbeth's edible white trail into the dark.

Hitchcock, with his dry, macabre wit, and Earnest Joe—not a pairing that exactly leaped to mind. But after seeing the movie, I had a better sense of it. The film's about watching, about interpreting what you see, and the wide gulf that potentially exists between appearance and reality. It's about how watching isn't an innocent or neutral act, but one fraught with consequences that can get you into twenty kinds of dire and unexpected trouble.

Over lunch, Joe, animated, slathering butter on my bread and his, talked about Heisenberg's uncertainty principle, and how particle physics had changed the classical notion of reality as something out there, fixed and other, going its independent way without us, and had made our observation an intrinsic part of the reality we see.

It was interesting to me, the way his mind ranged, and I was pleased to see him so pumped up, though the subject wasn't one I'd pondered much since college, if then.

Afterward, each nursing double scoops of pistachio—a sugar cone for Joe, a cup for me—we strolled the rain-shiny streets, smiling, green-lipped, at the yuppie pioneers we passed, couples not so different from us. On the gentrifying tide they'd brought with them, a number of good shops had come in, and we stared at the windows, went into a few. In an antique print shop, sorting through the bins, I lost sight of Joe and found him in the rear, perusing a framed etching. In the manner of Doré—as meticulous, but starker, more affecting—it showed a long-haired man with a sea-weathered face standing at the masthead of a square-sailed ship, his wrists lashed to the crosstrees, his eyes wide with rapt, hallucinatory bliss. A single tear rolled down his cheek.

"The Ancient Mariner?" I said over Joe's shoulder.

"Odysseus." Joe pointed to three women in the distance, standing in a circle on a bare outcrop of rock. Their chins were lifted, as though singing. "The Sirens," he said.

"You may be right."

As we studied it together, leaning close, Homer's story drifted back to me, how, passing the headland where the sisters lived, the wily Greek devised this means to hear their music without being tempted off-course and smashing his ship to pieces on the rocks.

"Nice, isn't it?"

"Mmm," I said. "Reminds me of someone . . ."

He glanced around. "Me?"

"I was thinking me." I smiled, and he smiled back.

Back home that night at dinner, topping off my wine, he gazed at me across the table with matched candle flames reflected in his eyes. "You know, it looks as though I'll be wrapping up my field-work by New Year's."

"Really?"

"After that," he continued, filling his glass, too, "I won't need to be here."

"You won't?"

He sipped and shook his head. "Basically, once I sit down to write, I could pretty much be anywhere."

"You don't say." I airmailed this with a smile meant to fill his circumspect and timid heart with courage. But subtlety, as usual, was lost on Joe. "And you mention this because . . ." I prompted him.

"Oh, no particular reason. I just wanted to keep you up to speed."

"Oh," I said. "Well, thank you for apprising me."

"Don't mention it." And just when you despaired of him, there he was again, the faun, winking from the candle flame in his left eye. With a restrained, sweet demi-smile, Joe looked down and sipped his wine.

Later, when I came up from the outdoor shower before bed, I found him giving his hairline a minute examination in the bathroom mirror. Our eyes met in the reflection, and I gave two sideward nods toward the bedroom.

"What's this?" Joe said, mirroring back the gesture.

"It translates, do-ya-wan-na-screw."

"You are a bold dame, aren't you."

"I do have a certain *je ne sais quoi*, don't I?"

He faced me and smiled. "If you do say so yourself." Slipping his fingers, just the tips of them, inside the lapel of my silk robe—another vintage find—he let his hand drop till the weight broke loose the sash.

"You brute," I said, reaching to close it.

Joe stopped my hand. "I like to look." And his eyes traveled down me, palpable as touch.

"So I noticed. Is looking all you do?"

"You're asking for it now."

"Hey," I said, "see me shaking in my boots?"

Our sex was changing. I noticed it for the first time then, the athleticism, mutually exhorted, passing off in favor of episodes more languid and prolonged, a kind of slo-mo swimming that seemed to take place in an altered medium as viscous as a jar of honey. Afterward, amid the reassuring smells of soiled sheets, soft with thrashing, I fell asleep, my body as relaxed as water.

When I woke up the next morning, I was disappointed to find myself alone in bed. I had to work—Beach Med was open on Sundays from nine to one—but it was only a little after seven. I thought Joe might be surfing—he'd said the break was shaping up. But then I heard him splitting wood in the driveway, and I lay for several minutes, listening, following the process in my mind—first the clean thwack of the axe with its splintery undernote; then the two splits hitting concrete with a sound like toppled bowling pins; the dull clunk-clunk as Joe tossed them on the pile. The succession of the sounds was reassuring to me. They possessed a sense of order, the idea of a loop that changed as it progressed but always recurred to its first term; slowly it advanced, and underneath it something mounted, something built.

Wanting to surprise him, I started a Chinese omelet in the kitchen—the first time I'd made Joe the dish that I was semi-famous for. Tapping hardened Five Spice in the eggs, I stared at the tiny bright red characters on the yellow tin, recalling what they were: long life and happiness. The sound of frying filled the kitchen; coffee dripped into the carafe, releasing its black steam. I felt a little larking flight of happiness, realizing that I'd landed—quite to my surprise—in the middle of my dream, the one of Italian roast and Sunday mornings. Having used up twelve or fifteen—fifteen at the most—we had another forty years' worth still to spend. At that thought, something in my cautious, semi-jaded heart filled like a little red balloon and, in the bright square of the kitchen window, floated into a cloudless sky and out to sea. Oh, yes, indeedy, my thoughts by then were ranging far and free.

When Joe came up, innocent and unsuspecting, I put his plate in front of him and stood, arms crossed, like a prairie farm wife serving her man breakfast when he comes in from the chores.

"What?" he said, noticing, his fork halfway to his mouth.

"Nothing."

The Professor looked doubtful and took a taste. "Hey," he said. "Hey, wow."

"You like?"

"Superlative." He took a second, more enthusiastic bite. "What's this spice?"

"It's an ancient Irish secret, passed down from mother to daughter in an uninterrupted line from days of yore."

"Irish?"

I laughed and started to turn around.

"Hey, wait," he said. "I was thinking. Any chance you'd go with me to church today?"

"Church?"

"I'm going to videotape the service at the Lighthouse. I've been after John Calvin ever since I got here, and he finally gave permission."

I shook my head. "To be honest, a recreational root canal sounds more appealing, but thanks for asking. Besides, I have to work. I'll be home early, though."

When I left, he was in the bathroom, checking his hairline again and tweaking the dimple in his four-in-hand as carefully as though he were going to St. Peter's to see the Pope serve Mass.

I got to the clinic twenty minutes early, hoping to catch up on some paperwork before we opened. God, however, had other plans for me.

LuAnn met me at the door, and hell immediately broke loose.

"Thank God you're here," she said. "Pate Ames has called twice in the last ten minutes."

"What's the matter?"

"She wouldn't say. She said she tried your home phone last night, but kept getting the machine."

"She must have called my house."

"That's what I figured. I just tried you at Joe's, but no one answered."

"Did she leave a number?"

LuAnn shook her head. "She said she'd try back in five. I think she was at a pay phone."

At that second, the phone rang at the desk and LuAnn rushed to pick it up. "Hold on. She just walked in." She nodded at me.

I double-timed it to my office and picked up there. "Pate?"

"Dr. Shaughnessey?"

"What's wrong?"

"Mama found it," she said. "In my purse? I borrowed the station wagon and forgot to give her back her keys, and last night she went in my room to look for them and found it there."

"What, Pate? What did she find?" She sounded frantic.

"That little book, that pamphlet thing—the one you gave me at your office?"

Choices, I thought.

"*Choices?*" she said. "Last night when I came in from the game, they were waiting for me, her and Uncle Johnny, sitting on the couch. The minute I walked in the door, they looked up, and right that second I knew, something balled up inside me like a fist, and then I saw it laying open on the coffee table next to Uncle Johnny's Bible, *Choices.*"

"Oh, Pate," I said.

" 'Where did you get this?' Mama asked me, pointing like she wouldn't even touch it with her finger, and I said, 'Mama, did you go in my purse?'

" 'Answer me right now, young lady!' she said. I could tell she was beside herself, but Uncle Johnny made her hear me out. He was trying to be nice, but it was awful, Dr. Shaughnessey, just awful.

"I told them I got stung at school, the same thing I told you, and in the waiting room, see, there was a whole stack sitting on the table, and I picked one up, just for something to read, and didn't even realize what it was until I opened it. When the nurse called me in, I guess I must have stuffed it in my purse, I said.

"For a second, I thought it was going to be okay, but Mama asked why I didn't tell her I'd gone to the doctor. Five seconds later I thought of twenty things I could have told her, Dr. Shaughnessey, twenty reasons why, but right then my mind just went completely blank. Mama looked right straight down deep inside me, and Uncle Johnny took my hand and said straight out, not mean, but kind, 'If you're in trouble, darling, we want to help you, your mama and me both, that's why we're here, only we can't do a thing unless you tell the truth.'

"I didn't, though. I couldn't, Dr. Shaughnessey. I said a bee-sting, that was all it was. I don't think they believed me."

"What can I do, Pate?"

"I want to do it, Dr. Shaughnessey, the thing we talked about before."

"Termination?" I said.

"Yes, ma'am."

"Are you sure, Pate?"

"I'm sure," she answered. "Positive."

I took a beat. "Then let's set up an appointment for next week."

"Not next week," she said. "Next week may be too late. I have to do it now."

"I'm here today till one. If you want to come in, we can sit down and discuss it."

"Church lets out at eleven-thirty. I'll come right after that. Oh, hey, Mr. Midgett!" Her bright voice away from the receiver. "Yes, sir, yes, it is. It's gorgeous out today!"

And I was listening to a dial tone.

When she hadn't arrived by noon, I began a debate against the dark presentiment lengthening like a shadow across my mood. At twelve-fifteen, I marked her late officially.

"Don't worry, Day, she'll be here," Lu kept saying.

By one o'clock, I was resigned.

"Maybe she's changed her mind," Lu said.

"She'd have called."

I waited till two o'clock, long after Lu and everybody else had left. When I got back to Joe's, I found him in his rocking chair in front of the TV.

"Did anybody call?" I asked.

Hitting Pause on the remote, he said, "I think you'd better take a look at this."

On the screen, I found a frozen image juddering and bristling as though too charged to brook restraint. In the pulpit at the Lighthouse, J. C. Teach, in a hellfire pose, was leaning out over the congregation, his mouth open, his right arm raised high overhead. In it was a pamphlet.

Ten

An exterior shot: the enormous plastic effigy of Jesus hanging with upturned eyes, against a backdrop of blue November sky . . .

"Little Roanoke. Sunday, November 21, 1982. First Covenant Pentecostal Church."

Handheld, slightly unsteady, the camera pans across the scene. The road is lined with rusty pickup trucks and cars for fifty yards, spillover from the filled church lot. Along the shoulder, rough men, most of them tieless, looking confined and chastened in wash-and-wear suits with double-wide lapels, out of fashion since the sixties, help their wives, in polyester florals, off the running boards. Holding down a flowered hat in the strong wind, a woman with a rough, good-natured face peers into the lens.

"What you doing there, Joe?"

"Recording you for posterity, Toxey." His tone is marked by circumspect bonhomie.

In a sudden gust, her hat flies off.

"Jesus, there it goes!"

Several men reach for it along the road, but it eludes them, skipping with a prankish *joie de vivre,* until it falls into the runoff ditch and disappears into the dark maw of the culvert.

"Hold on; I'll get it for you," Joe says.

"Never moind. It's ruint now. I been looking for a excuse to buy a new one, anyhow." Her glance suggests a certain doubt about the camera but does not obscure her obvious goodwill.

The scene abruptly fades to black, then opens on the packed interior. Elbows on the pew backs, people chat with neighbors in a mood of restrained festivity. Alone in front, his head supported in his hand, J. C. Teach kneels at the prayer rail in silent communion. After several moments, the members of the band trade looks, uncertain whether to proceed. Finally the pianist, moving to the synthesizer keyboard, launches into a tremulous old hymn, and the minister stirs, looking stiff, almost hobbled as he mounts the stage. For a long moment, he peers into the open cabinet of the baby grand, as though mesmerized by something in its works; then, shaking his head, he walks into the pulpit and takes the microphone.

"I had my sormin all worked out to preach to y'all today, brothers and sisters," he begins in a subdued voice. "Last week my boy Matt and me took a droive up to the beach to see that picture show ever'one's been talking about, *Raiders of the Lost Ork*. It's about this feller foinds the Ork of the Covenant with the tablets of the Ten Commandments locked insoide, broke from God's displeasure with the Isru'loites and turned to dust with toime but still brim full of magic pow'r. That got me to thinking about Moses and the covenant he made own Sinai, and all the other covenants between the Hebrews and the Lord before the last and greatest, also called the New, by which He sacrifoiced His ownly begotten Son to redeem your sins and moine. That's what I was going to talk own— covenants. Had it all worked out. But I ain't going to preach it now."

Teach lifts a sheet from a yellow legal pad and tears it in two. The pieces, in a drifting, asynchronous ballet, fall to the floor.

"I'm tore up, people. I'm tore roight half in two. Last noight I went over to the house of a dear friend, went there for nothing more'n a cup of her good coffee, thinking we moight turn the Boible open and spend half a hour in prayerful meditation own the Lord. What I found instead was a woman troubled in her moind, brother and sisters, troubled sore.

"She has a choild, this woman does, a daughter, and not two hours 'fore I got there, she walked in that girl's room looking for a set of borrowed keys and what she found instead was this roight here . . ." Reaching into his inside jacket pocket, he takes out the pamphlet, raising it in his right hand as he fumbles open his reading glasses with his left. *"Choices* . . . that's the name of it. Let me read you how it starts. 'If you're pregnant, you have the right to choose . . .' "

Letting this hang, Teach stares over the rims of his glasses. "Goes own. 'Reproductive freedom is guaranteed to every woman in the United States by the decision of the Supreme Court in *Roe v. Wade* in 1973.' " He removes his glasses and dangles them over the lectern's edge. "Now every mother in this room today, every father, too, already knows what was going through that woman's heart when she read that. The truth come to her in a terrible loightning flash, same as it done me, and she knew the trouble her little girl had got herself into. And what did she do? Did she hunker down and hoide? No, she done what a Christian should; she took her trouble straight to Jesus and asked her pastor for his help.

"And what did her pastor tell her? I got to tell the story own myself now, people. I told her, hush it up. I acted as a friend, a neighbor, but all the whoile another voice was whispering in my ear. You boys out there, I want to ask you. You're setting in the den after supper with a good game own the set, your woife calls out from the kitchen asking you to take the garbage out or maybe run to Skaddle's for a quart of milk. Any of y'all ever maybe turned the volume up a notch own the remote and acted loike you didn't hear?"

There is a scatter of laughter in the congregation, but it's subdued and quickly stifled.

"I don't reckon any of you fellers here this morning ever been guilty of a indiscretion of that koind, but I have. Mildred, I confess it!"

The laughter now is genuine and loud. The camera closes on a beaming Mildred Teach.

"Well, brothers and sisters, that was what I done last noight, ownly the voice won't Mildred's; the voice was Jesus Chroist, and what He was telling me was just one thing over and over: *Loight heals and darkness festers.* Last noight Jesus Christ put out His call to me, and I set there in the easy chair pretending not to hear. I failed Him, people. I failed the Lord my God who never yet failed me, and He let me know it, too. I didn't sleep a wink. But I had a chance to get roight in my moind, and here I am, back own my feet again, ready to take the trash out for the Lord. And what I want to tell Him, what I want to tell you all is THANK YA JESUS! THANK YA FOR THE WAKE-UP CALL!"

A volley of corroborating cheers sounds throughout the church.

"Amen, brother!"

"Praise Him!"

"Hallelujah!"

" 'If you're pregnant, you have a choice,' " J.C. repeats, shaking the pamphlet over his head. "That's what it says here, people. This booklet was printed up by the Department of Health and Human Services with our tax dollars, and I don't think I have to tell you what they mean by choice. 'Terminating the pregnancy'—that's the words they use to hoide the awful meaning. According to this booklet, this is the law of the land, determined by the highest tribunal in the nation; what it don't tell us about is that other court where Jesus Chroist our Lord and Savior sets as judge. I ask you, people, does Jesus Chroist deny this troubled girl a choice? Is He a hard, cruel toyrant who tells her my way or the hoighway? No, sir. What Jesus tells this girl is the same thing He tells all of us who follow Him: you have a choice, but once you make it, darlin, that's the end. At the gambling table, when you ante up and place your bet, do them other fellas setting acrost from you let you change your moind and get a refund when the cards don't fall your way? No, sir. If you bet wrong, you lose your money, end of the discussion. That's what choosing is, a thing you do one time, up front, and then you live with what you done. And when it comes to men and women, when they make a choice own Saturday noight, say, after a go-round own the dance floor and a couple beers, that choice ain't to be undone in here own Sunday. It ain't to be undone own Monday neither, out there at the clinic own the beach—you know the place I mean. That's having it both ways, and both ways ain't a choice. *One way, one toime*—that's what grownups mean by choosing, and that's all Chroist asks of us. That's the law we must obey as Christians, and it's higher than the Supreme Court, higher than the U.S. Constitution. Render unto Caesar what is Caesar's, and unto God's what is His.

"Now what about the choild this girl is carrying insoide her body—whose is that? You mothers and fathers out there, let me ask you: Do you own your choild the way you own your house or car?

Is it a dog that you can beat it? We've had a few of that opinion down the years, and I don't need to tell you what happened. The social worker come down here from Raleigh and put them children into foster care, and their daddy went to jail. Y'all all know who I mean, but that same choild, if he ain't been delivered yet, though he has eyes and fingers and a human heart and dreams with brain waves they can read the same as they'd read yours or moine . . . if that child's mama decides to 'terminate her pregnancy,' the gov-'mint just shrugs and tells her go ahead. Is that sense? Is that logic? Is it justice? Let me tell you what the good Lord told me, people, as I was kneeling with Him in communion here: a human soul's a gift God gives, and who He gives it to ain't us, the parents—we are only stewards and protectors—not to the federal gov'mint. God gives it to the choild and that choild owns *himself!* His loife is sanc-tifoied, and only God who gives it has the roight to take it back!" And on the full flood tide of passion now, Teach's voice rings through the church like a martial fanfare.

"How do I know this? We've heard what this here booklet has to say about the laws of the Unoited States, but what about this other book"—he holds the Bible up in his right hand—"the one that comforts us in our affliction, which we all dearly love? Broth-ers and sisters, Jeremoiah, Chapter One, verse four and foive: 'Then the word of the Lord came unto me, saying, Before I formed thee in the womb, I knew thee; and before thou camest forth out of the womb, I sanctified thee.'

"Now, you'll notice here, the Lord don't say to Jeremoiah, I knew you at eight weeks or twelve or twenty-one. He don't even say I knew you at *conception.* No, brothers and sisters, what the Lord tells Jeremoiah is '*Before* I formed thee in the womb, I knew thee and sanctifoied thee.' And the promise God made to Jere-moiah is made to each and every one of us, and, brothers and sis-ters, it is made to the unborn child that troubled girl is carrying in her womb today. When her mama turned to seek my help last noight, I asked the cup to pass, but if it couldn't pass from Jesus' lips own Calvary, it cannot pass from moine. Nor yours either, dar-lin. I wish with all my heart it could, but it cannot, not for you and not for any.

"When you laid down with that boy in carnal lust, you took own a responsibility. You made a promise, darlin, even if the promise was imploied. And maybe I worked around to covenants after all, because, brother and sisters, that's all a covenant is, a promise made involving God. The covenant we as parents make our children is the golden chain that boinds the human generations, link by link, a chain of shoining love. To break it through abortion is a sin there's no forgiveness for. I warn you, darlin, in tender care of your immortal soul, amend your error, or from this pulpit now, armed with the sword of God's almoighty word in my roight hand, I will sunder you from us, requoiring every member of this church—even your mother and father—to turn their back and cast thee out forever into darkness and hellfoire, which burneth but consumeth not!"

Teach's face, as he utters the imprecation, is intransigent. In the utter stillness that attends his threat, a gust of wind outside makes the roofing timbers creak. And now the preacher bows his head.

"All of y'all out there, I ask for your supportin prayers and love to help this troubled girl git back straight with God. You know who you are, darlin. Come own up here now, do it of your own free will, don't make me say your name and put you under conviction here before this congregation. That's the bitter cup I have not wished to drink from, but Jesus Chroist has tapped me own the shoulder here today, He's asked me to step up, I'm under His command, and, darlin, if you won't, I will. You'll force me to it. Come own, take my hand, confess your sin and shame the devil, and let us through the love of Christ in us, love you and lead you from the darkness into loight."

With this, John Calvin concludes. In the silence, the soundtrack registers a woman's muffled weeping. The camera tracks her down, a dowdy, gray-haired woman with thick, outsized glasses sitting in the second row. Idail Ames. Her face streaked with tears, she holds her daughter's hand, their fingers interlaced. Pate isn't crying. Her pale face is attentive, like that of a woman on a dark street, pausing beneath the streetlamp at the sound of footsteps. And she turns to face whatever is pursuing her. Only now does her uncle allow his gaze to single out his niece. With tear-filled eyes, John Calvin, holding out his hand, nods, and Pate gets up.

"Praise God!"

"Thank you, Jesus!"

"Hallelujah!"

Relieved cries sound throughout the church.

There's radiance on John Calvin's face as he draws his niece into his arms and holds her, while the digital readers in the lower right-hand corner of the screen count twenty seconds, twenty-five.

"And the father," he says finally, wiping his eyes, "if he's here, let him be a man and stand up and get roight with this girl and with the Lord. The mark of a man ain't that he never strayed or troied to run, but that, come Monday morning, when the car was gassed and the engine idling and he was set to go, instead he turned around and went back where he was own Saturday night and looked her in the face he wronged. Come forward in the loight of day and own in public what you done in private in the dark of noight."

Wheeling, too swiftly, the camera finds a tall, dark-haired boy with a flattop haircut and a thick weightlifter's neck. James Burrus. His expression is curiously belligerent, though his eyes, wet and red, belie it.

"It was me," he says in a choked voice, trembling with uncensored sentiment, and his tears overflow. "I'm the daddy, I want to make it roight."

There is open weeping in the church as he moves up the aisle. On either side, women dab their eyes with handkerchiefs. Their men are also moved. The uninitiated might interpret their looks as belligerence, but Joe Madden doesn't make this mistake. He knows exactly what he's seeing. And as the camera registers these large and shattering events, on the soundtrack, barely noticeable, there's the sound of sniffling, rhythmic and repeated, while the ethnographer, capturing it in celluloid, getting it on tape, pulls the trigger on his Betamax and weeps along with all the rest.

Eleven

"Jesus," I said for perhaps the fiftieth time since Joe punched in the tape. "Jesus fucking Christ!"

"Are you okay?"

As he turned off the set, the driving gray electronic snow settled on a white horizon, contracting to a single pixel of white light before it disappeared, like Pate Ames's life.

"Me?" I said.

"I was afraid you'd be upset." He regarded me with concern. "But I thought you ought to see it."

I kept saying it. "Jesus! Jesus fucking Christ!"

"You're angry . . ."

"Ah, gee, you think?" I leaped up and began to pace. "I'm furious!"

"At me?"

Till that moment, it was nonspecific, but I ran with the suggestion. "How could you just sit there, all of you, and let him trash her?"

"Trash her? I don't know if I'd say he—"

"Jesus, Joe! Jesus Christ! Don't you see what he did? That ignorant, self-righteous prick, that fascist redneck bastard, that goddamn Jesus Nazi—he's ruined her whole life!"

Like an astronaut re-entering the atmosphere, pulling six or seven G's, he buckled in, weathering the ride. "You don't think you may be overstating it a bit?"

His calm, with its hint of reproach-by-contrast, infuriated me further.

"Hell, no, I'm *under*stating it. Jesus—think what that poor girl must be going through right now. Goddamnit. God*damn*it! It makes me fucking ill." And then the next thought—what to do. "I should go over there."

"And do what? I don't know, Day. Maybe it's better to let them sort this out themselves."

"Oh, yes, they're doing such a hell of a fine job! Joe, this is abuse. That bastard violated her. As far as I'm concerned, it's rape—morally, it's rape."

Joe held up both hands, palms out. "Okay, hold on. Hold it right there."

"What?" I challenged.

"Look," he said, "you're upset—I can understand that—"

"You worked that out yourself?"

"Some of what you're feeling went through my mind, too," he said, ignoring my sarcasm, which was reckless, I concede, but I was in ballistic mode. "Initially, it did. But violation? Rape? Come on, Day. Maybe the tape misrepresents it, but it didn't have that tone at all."

"You're defending this?" I asked. "Please tell me you aren't defending this."

"I'm not defending anything, but I think we should be clear on what actually happened."

"How would you describe it then?"

"Well"—he paused—"if I had to pick a term, catharsis is probably pretty close. When they went down front together, Pate and James, that's the feeling that swept through the church."

"Catharsis . . ."

"And forgiveness," he emended, specifying further. "It was remarkable. They were like—I don't know—two athletes who've won the race and brought the victory home for the whole town. I mean, let's face it, these aren't the most emotionally forthcoming folks you're likely to run across, but by the end of the service I'd say the congregation's mood was one of adoration, or bordering close to it."

"What about Pate, Joe?" I said. "What do you suppose her mood was bordering on?"

In his deliberate way, he pondered this one, too. "Well, I'm sure she must have been shocked when she understood where J.C. was going. By the end, though, I'll bet she felt relieved."

"Relieved? Are you insane? This is her uncle, Joe, her uncle and her fucking mother! The people she loves and trusts and counts on just sold her out in public. They invaded her privacy, they trampled her feelings, her dignity—not to mention her legal rights. They pounded the crap out of the girl and when she'd been reduced to a compliant pile of bleeding mush, they bullied her into submitting to their backward, intolerant hick values. Do me a favor, okay? For one second, one fraction of a second, put yourself in Pate's shoes and tell me that 'relief' is what she felt. Would you?"

Joe's jaw set a squarer line. "I don't know. In terms of what I might have felt, maybe you're right. As for putting myself in Pate Ames's shoes, though, that's exactly what I'm trying *not* to do."

"Hell, no—why would you want to?"

"You're missing the point," he went on. "What I'm saying is that we can't try to understand Pate's feelings based on what mine may have been—or yours. That's a failure of imagination and sympathy."

"A failure of sympathy . . ."

"Yes, I think so. Because there's another way to look at this— which I suspect is closer to the way Pate looks at it—and that's that her uncle performed an act of spiritual leadership, a deeply compassionate one. Do I think she felt relieved? Yes, absolutely."

"Do you hear what you're saying?" I asked. "What kind of fairy tale is this?"

"I'm completely serious," he said. "And it's because the event is susceptible to such different interpretations—because we disagree so strongly over what it means—that it's so important."

I gaped at him, unable to grasp his detachment from Pate's emotional reality, how she felt, what had been done to her. "What are you saying, Joe?"

"I'm saying that you and I and most educated people like us have no ready explanation for how Pate Ames could have experienced spiritual benefit from an action that would have been an injury to us. Day, we look at Pate and say she was victimized. But that's not what the congregation saw. They saw a hero, someone engaged in a morally transcendent act. I think that's what John Calvin means by 'covenant'—an act of surrender to God, or whatever you want to call the force outside and higher than the self that you and I and people like us, who worship personal freedom as the highest aim of life, don't take seriously anymore."

I cupped my hands around my mouth and called toward the stratosphere. "Joe! Listen to me. Pate doesn't want to marry James. She doesn't love him."

His space shuttle lost a wing but kept on flying. "And you know this how?"

I hesitated.

"You gave her the pamphlet, didn't you?"

I didn't answer.

"You don't have to tell me if it's a violation of her confidence."

"What confidence does she have left?" I said, exhaling a hot sigh. "Okay, yes, I gave it to her. Yes, she's my patient. She was scheduled for a D and C at noon today."

"A D and C?"

"An abortion."

"Ah," he said, circumspect and grave. "I see."

"Pate doesn't want this baby. She wants to go to UNC and become a vet, okay? You want to talk about covenants? God put a spark in this girl, the same one he put in you and me. Isn't it Pate's right to fan it to the brightest flame she can? And, beyond her right, isn't it her responsibility? Isn't that a covenant, too? Doesn't Pate Ames have a covenant with herself?"

"I think J.C. would call that selfishness."

"Is that what you believe?"

Joe shook his head. "No, I agree with you."

"What?" I said. "Goddamn you, don't start agreeing now. Don't you dare agree with me!"

"But I do." His expression was earnest, sweet, unrepentant. "There are two, Day, two covenants—self-realization and self-sacrifice—and they're completely incompatible, and both are right."

He stood there, the little sorcerer, wooing me into his universe of levitating relativities, ever onward into the revolving pinwheels of his eyes. I gave him nothing, though. Fuming, I stared back my defiance and refused to budge.

"Do you see? Everything I came to Little Roanoke to study comes to ground right here, in Pate Ames's case."

"Her 'case'?" I said. "You aren't going to write about this!"

His whole expression crashed. "What do you mean? You can't be serious? How could I not?"

I despaired.

"Look, Day, I didn't learn about this from you. It has nothing to do with your ethics."

"For God's sake, Joe, this isn't about me. You can't expose this girl to any more humiliation."

"But she's been exposed," he countered, "exactly as you say. Everyone whose opinion Pate gives a damn about already knows, so if five hundred or a thousand academics read the story two years from now in a professional journal, with the names and details changed, where's the harm? In my opinion, what I'd be 'exposing' reflects far more to Pate's credit than the opposite, so, again, what harm? And even if that weren't the case, I came down here to do a job. Whether your ethics are involved or not, mine are. If I soft-pedal what's probably—no, certainly—the most important thing I've witnessed since I've been here, what does that make me?"

"A nice guy?"

"A nice guy?" He was sincerely incredulous. "This isn't about being a nice guy, Day."

"What's it about?"

"How about the truth?"

"Fuck the truth!" I said. "The truth is overrated."

That, I think, may have been the only time I ever saw Joe shocked by an idea. "Even if you're right," he said, milling it swiftly down to grist, "what else is there?"

"Lots," I told him. "Compassion, tolerance, respect, forbearance . . . love—for starters. How about those?"

That shut him up. Only for a moment, of course.

"This is what I do."

"So maybe just this once, do something else."

"I don't think I can give you that," he said. "But I can change the name of the village, disguise its location on the map. That's as far as I can go."

"And you think Pate won't find out," I said ironically. "She will, Joe, no matter what you change, and she'll be hurt—her whole family will, including Jubal. Don't you owe him something? If nothing else, I'll know. I can't believe this doesn't register on you—it's like a public vivisection."

"Excuse me?" The sudden bloodrush made his face go dark. "Vivisection? If there's any vivisection going on, it seems to me you're the one performing it."

With that, we crossed over into terra incognita, and the terrain was dark and strange and new.

My eyes stung, and my voice dropped. "What did you say?"

"I shouldn't have said that," he acknowledged swiftly. "I apologize. Look, Day, I didn't want this to turn into a fight." He reached for my hand, but I jerked it back. "I don't see why it should, but you seem hell-bent on beating me up."

"That wasn't my intention," I said, "but this girl's suffered major injury, and you see it as a professional opportunity. You want to track her like a wounded animal you mean to skin and eat. For Christ's sake, be a human being: the girl needs help."

"What are you going to do, Day, drive over there and kidnap her from Idail and Jubal's house? What, you're going to teach her to eat tofu and drink twig tea and listen to Patti Smith and explain that shaving her underarms is capitulating to the patriarchy? Then what? Off she goes to UNC and completes her indoctrination; she becomes ashamed of her accent and her parents and her church and the three-hundred-year heritage they stand for, she loses her faith and registers Democratic and becomes a feminist and dons the obligatory wire-rims and chukka boots and goes around with her demerit pad, citing retrograde offenders for infractions . . ."

"Such as you."

"What the hell, okay, such as me. And my question is, at the end of all that 'helping,' what have you accomplished?"

"I guess you'd better tell me, hadn't you?" I said as my anger sank into a deeper and more quiet place.

"Basically you've cloned an image of yourself," he said, "you've created an homunculus, a miniature Day Shaughnessey."

"I guess that's a pretty terrible thing to be."

"Yes, for Pate Ames, it very well may be. Look, Day, I know you aren't a fan of Little Roanoke, but there's no other place like it. There's a fragile balance here that's taken generations to achieve—"

"Oh, shit, not the ecosystem speech," I interrupted.

"I'm serious," he said. "For ten or eleven generations, they got along with no help from us, and I don't think we have any business—or right—to interfere now. Let the battle be joined by the players over there. If Pate doesn't like the way things stand, let her stake another claim and defend it; let the others have their say. At the end of the day, there'll be a resolution everyone can live with."

"Sure there will, Joe," I said. "I can see it now. Pate marries this troglodyte, James, and has his baby, and he drinks a six-pack every night and beats her recreationally, and one morning, ten years from now, when she's fat and has five kids, she wakes up and sees that by keeping her self-sacrificial covenant with God, she's ended up in redneck hell, and she walks out. She ends up a divorcée without skills living in a rundown trailer park on welfare, and the precious ecosystem hums along its merry way. That's how homeostasis will be restored to Little Roanoke. Screw it, Joe. I'd rather see the whole damn island sink into the sea than have that happen. It's just so damn pompous of you to take this line. Pate isn't some aborigine dropped in Times Square with a loincloth and a spear. She's no different from the way you and I were twelve or fifteen years ago. We got out and survived, didn't we? Were you ready? I sure as hell wasn't. Why can't she? Why should she be condemned to live in some nightmare version of 1955?"

Joe walked to the window. "I guess my question is, is what we have so much better?"

"Are you kidding?" I said. "Would you want to go back to your parents' lives? Your dad's? You wouldn't last five minutes."

He stood looking out for a moment more and then walked back. "Did it occur to you that your argument is exactly the one we used in Vietnam? *We* know better, the superior white colonialists, with our electric toasters and fragmentation bombs and outstanding personal hygiene. We'll show you the light, and, by God, if you won't see it, we'll bomb your slope asses back into the Stone Age. Now have a Whopper and get over it. I hate to say it, Day, but you're showing your activist Catholic ass."

"For your information, I haven't been inside a Catholic church since I was seventeen—Pate's age."

"Well, to adapt your phrase on debs: Do they get over it?"

That was it. "Joe, I'm not going to argue with you anymore.

You're a smart man, but I'm going to tell you something, not as your opponent in debate, but as the woman who, for the moment, lives with you. However sound your logic and your arguments may be, your heart's in the wrong place on this."

"Why, Day?"

"Because whatever faith is, in my heart I know it isn't about coercion and manipulation. It's about compassion and tolerance and love, and if that's what you think you saw in church today, then answer me one question: What if Pate hadn't stood? What if she'd been too embarrassed or afraid or just plain fucking didn't feel like it, and J.C.'d gone on and named her anyway, the way he threatened to? Would all your weepy Christian friends have rushed forward to pat her back and cheer her on? Would it have been the happy lovefest you describe? I don't think so. Pate would be in outer fucking darkness now, they would have excommunicated her, or whatever the Holy Roller version is, and the one and only reason why they didn't is because she caved. That's not faith; that's bullshit." And I walked out.

He followed me onto the porch. "Where are you going?" he called as I headed down the steps.

"I have no idea."

"Come on, Day. So we have a difference of opinion; that's no reason to be mad. You're the one who said I wasn't human. If anyone should be mad, it's me."

"I'm sorry I'm not logically consistent," I said, opening the car door.

"Don't go," he said.

"I need some breathing room, Joe, okay?"

"Breathing room?" he said. "There's a whole house right here, sixty miles of beach, the whole Atlantic Ocean. How much breathing room do you need?"

The question, shouted above the Karman-Ghia's puny roar, rang in my ears as I scratched out of the driveway. Quite a bit was the apparent answer. Because I was all the way to Whalebone Junction before I came out of my angry fugue and pulled over on the shoulder. As Joe's remarks repeated on me like a bad dinner, I found myself wondering who the hell *was* he, this man I was sleeping with? What next? A gunrack in the Wagoneer and a constitutional amendment supporting prayer in schools?

Seeing red again, I had to do a round of yogic *ujai* breathing to calm down. When I did, it struck me that Joe was right. Here I was, idling on the shoulder at the intersection of Route 158 and the Manteo Causeway—halfway to Little Roanoke, in other words. Rescue Pate? Abso-fucking-lutely right! If the Ghia had been an M-1 Abrams tank, I would have stormed the village and taken her away with me. And on our triumphal exit out of Hooterville, as a parting shot, I would have swung around my turret and blown the Lighthouse of the First Covenant Pentecostal Church to smithereens.

If I was showing my activist Catholic ass, so be it. Maybe we don't get over it, but you still have to *do* something, don't you?

Casting professional propriety to the winds, I drove straight to the village and asked the first person I saw where the Ameses lived.

In the driveway, I steeled myself. Then I climbed to the porch and knocked. The inner door swung in, and there, in the flesh, was J.C. Teach. We faced off through the screen.

"I'd like to speak to Pate," I said politely.

Idail's face loomed over his left shoulder, her gray eyes, through her glasses, unblinking, avian and fierce. "Pate's indisposed," she said with clipped finality. J.C. stepped aside.

"Mrs. Ames, I don't know whether you know who I am, but—"

"I know *exactly* who you are."

"I heard what happened," I said, resolved to give rapprochement a try. "I just stopped by to see if Pate's okay."

"Pate's fine," she answered, "and I'm sure we all appreciate your concern, but she has a family to see to how she is."

"I understand that, Mrs. Ames," I said. "I don't want to interfere, but as Pate's physician, I have a responsibility to—"

She cut me off. "You aren't Pate's physician."

"As of this morning, I believe I was."

"Well, as of now, you're not. Her doctor's Teddy Pendergast in Harbinger."

"If Pate wants to change doctors, Mrs. Ames, that's certainly her prerogative, but she'll need to tell me so herself."

"Pate's seventeen," Idail replied. "She doesn't need to tell you anything. I'm her mother, and I'm telling you."

"You aren't going to let me speak to her?" I addressed the query to her humanity.

"No," she said, "I'm not. Now I want you to leave my property, and don't come back here again." And with that, she slammed the door so violently, I came down with tinnitus in both ears.

I ground my teeth and wept with fury all the way home—my place, not Joe's. I hadn't been there in two weeks. And waiting on the front porch, guess who. I have to admit that I was glad.

As I pulled in, Joe came to meet me.

"Hey," he said with a questioning look.

"Hey." I wiped my wrist across my eyes.

"I said some things I didn't mean—the vivisection thing?" He winced.

"Is that really how you feel?"

"Do we have to do that now?"

I shrugged. "Why not? We may as well."

He sat down on the steps and hung his head, staring at his clasped hands. "Put it this way, Day." He looked up. "If I were a woman and someone wanted to control my body, I'd fight like hell. To that extent, I can honestly say that I'm pro-choice. On the other hand . . ."

I rolled my eyes; the moment veered toward comedy, albeit black. "You just can't stop while you're ahead, can you?"

"Do you want the truth or not?"

"Not."

He frowned and persevered. "On the other hand, when you switch the frame of reference to the child, J.C.'s arguments have a lot of weight for me."

"So where do you come down?"

"I don't," he said. "For me, it's a both-and, not an either-or."

"But it can't be, Joe," I said, asserting my bottom line.

"Why not?" he asked, asserting his. "Can't we disagree? I can honor your position. Can't you honor mine?"

"I don't think I can give you this one, Joe."

"That upsets me, Day. A lot. Because I think I'm in love with you. No, let me rephrase—I am in love with you." He looked grave and vulnerable and young.

"You know what?"

"What?"

"Your timing really sucks."

"What can I tell you?" The professor shrugged.

He didn't mean it as a joke, of course, but I had to laugh. I laughed loud and I laughed long. As he studied me, a shy, sheepish, rather faunlike grin broke through, as though, on the one hand, he really was quite fond of me and, on the other, he suspected I might be dangerously insane—sentiments with which, at that particular moment, I thoroughly agreed (both A *and* B).

PART IV

Twelve

On deck, the winch's giant drums were rolling, winding in the tow wire. Dripping and juddering with strain, two strands of rusty cable rose from the water astern to blocks atop the net reel, shot forward to another pair halfway out the outriggers, then right-angled back toward deck and spooled onto the drums, making pops as loud as whipcracks as crowding turns of cable split apart the pairs below to find a place.

Five hundred yards off the port beam, Joe could see Cully Teach dragging parallel and just behind—beyond the *Three Brothers,* in the offing sixty miles away, Cape Henry and the mouth of the Chesapeake Bay.

Suddenly a dirty bit of raveled marker twine burst from the water, racing forward with the cable through the blocks—the seventy-five fathom mark; seconds later, the fifty. At twenty-five, Lukey Brame began tamping down the footbrake, harder and harder, till he mounted it with his full weight. Still, the cable crawled in, squealing and groaning like a braking locomotive, till the net doors breached astern, a wet-dark metal gleam as of two great creatures' backs, shedding whitewater with a noise like air rush into a pierced vacuum.

"You wanna help out over here?"

Joe joined Ray at the starboard net reel, and they began to wrestle confused strands of chain and cable into order as Lukey spooled them in hydraulically. Shading his eyes, Joe squinted into the dazzle off the stern, searching for some sign of the nets. Far back in the wake, several hundred feet away, a faint smudge hovered at the surface, moiling like a swarm of bees. As it drew nearer, he could see what it was—birds, hundreds of them, a staggering commotion, whirling, screaming, diving down and flapping up out of the corkline's green and yellow floats. Long before the net reached the boat, the noise had become deafening, a thunderous chittering that drowned the diesel, conversation, any hope of independent thought.

As mesmerized this time as he'd been the first, Joe watched them circle and attack the swollen tailbag. Wings spread, coptering in place, the gulls dropped toward the surface cautiously, picking choice bits with their feet, their movement jittery and awkward like puppets on strings.

The gannets were something else again: head divers. Starting fifteen or twenty feet above the surface, they suddenly inverted, tightly folding back their black-tipped wings, stretching their long necks until they resembled not birds as much as sleek white diving animals, ermines, spearing splashlessly down into the water. Tunneling deep below the surface, they left white tubes of oxygenated water like the veins in *verde antique* marble. At every instant there were scores, hundreds, in all the various stages of the dive, too fast for the eye to follow, blurring into trails.

Jubal popped a butter cookie in his mouth and planted his elbows on the rail as he silently appraised the bloated cod end, extending fifty feet back in the stern wash, wide and buoyant enough for a bride and groom to walk abreast on. As the swell rolled under and through the bag, it gently bumped the boat, sending the fish tumbling back and forth like doubloons in a net purse. From compacted weight, hundreds of tiny heads had popped through the mesh and gilled themselves; they looked like prairie dogs peeking from their burrows. Around the net the sea appeared to boil as accumulating weight and pressure burst tens of thousands of swim bladders.

"Two-fifty, maybe three?" Lukey said.

Jubal nodded.

Joe did the math: twenty-five to thirty thousand pounds.

"Look small," said Ray.

"Too many heads?"

Ray gave the ethnographer a dour look but nodded.

"Always look small in the bag." Jubal straightened up. "Cain't tell much till they're own deck."

Using the two whiplines in combination, Ray and Lukey cinched off a portion of the catch in the cod end to be brought aboard, letting the rest roll back into the net extension, remaining in the water. Connecting the hooks as Jubal shouted orders, Joe watched the creaking whiplines, lifting in unison, slowly raise the cod end from the water, straining inch by inch up the indented slideway between *Father's* and *Price*. Bit by bit, it loomed over the transom, a giant sunball shot with pinks and green-golds, pricked with heads and dripping in the brilliant January light. When the tailbag cleared the bulwark, it hurtled forward between the net reels like a giant bowling ball aimed up center lane toward the deckhouse; then it reversed, swinging aft again, scouring bright a paintless scuff on deck where rust had formed since the last trip.

At the winch heads, Ray and Lukey quickly slacked their lines. The bag slammed to deck with a thunderous squashing noise, and a wash of blood squirted out in all directions, covering the deck and running up against the bulwarks in a small wavelet that broke back over itself before draining through the scuppers.

Down on one knee, Jubal groped for the tripper line and snubbed it around the net reel's leg. At his signal, Ray and Lukey began to hoist again, and when the bag reached knee height, the captain gave a violent yank, and the net escape yawned open, sending a wall of fish, five thousand pounds, rolling forward with a wet, crepitating sound, flipping and sloshing, covering the deck ankle-deep up to the fish hatch.

While the net fluttered overhead like an empty sleeve, Jubal solemnly toed through piles of fish with his white boots, his expression inscrutable. To Joe, the uniformity of the catch was astonishing. With the exception of a few gray-winged skates and a peppering of sharklike dogfish the length and thickness of an arm, there was virtually nothing there but croakers, wall to wall.

Cinching the escape, Jubal whanged shut the brass tripper with a marlingspike and dropped the cod end over. Winding several feet of gained net onto the reel, the crew washed a new load of fish into the tailbag, which they split off and raised to deck again, exactly as before.

By the fourth split, the deck was covered from the fish hatch to the transom, leaving no way for anyone to move except by wading through the waist-deep swamp. At every step, Joe's long legs plunged and vanished; he could feel the croakers' seachill through his oilskins, the living carpet rustling and shifting as he crossed, communicating something through his boot soles, a twitch of alien nerves.

Jubal rinsed his boots and coveralls and started up the gangway. As Ray vaulted down into the hold, Joe and Lukey removed the cover plate in deck above the starboard forward fishbin and constructed a sluiceway to the hole with two converging boards.

"Hey, what the fuck is this?"

Halfway up the gangway, Jubal turned back, frowning. Ray's head appeared, like Kilroy's, over the coaming of the hold. "This ice ain't busted," Ray said. "Bly ain't broke one single fucking cube."

"He's been down there half the morning," said Jubal. "What the hell's he been doing?"

"I'll tell you what." Ray vanished, and an empty NyQuil bottle flew up from below, like a Ping-Pong ball bobbing on a jet of air, and landed with a wet smack in a pile of fish. A second bottle followed. A third. Then Ray reappeared, lugging two stacked cardboard flats. The cook's stash consisted of twenty-four bottles, six already M.I.A. The *Father's Price* had been at sea for not quite forty-eight hours.

"Go git him," Jubal said in a dangerously low voice.

Joe found Curtis Bly frying chicken at the range in a relaxed and semi-stuporous condition.

"I think you'd better come."

Wiping his hands on his apron—which featured ruffles on the straps—the cook emerged in his pom-pommed slippers, blinking his muddy eyes with innocence, prepared, once more, to be misunderstood. "What's up, Cap?"

"What in hell is this?" roared Jubal, pointing to the flats. "I told you I wouldn't have no drinking own this boat. Didn't I tell you that? You swore to me up one soide and down t'other you was droy."

"You said liquor, boss. That ain't liquor; it's my med'cine."

"Med'cine, my ass! You stole these boys' grocery money and

bought this mess at Skaddle's and been down there in the fish hold drinking it for breakfast, lunch and supper for the last two days."

Imploring mercy, the cook now freely whined. "Come on, Jubal, I ain't drunk. Do I look drunk to you? I cain't cook if my hands are shaking, can I?"

"There you go," said Ray, lighting a Kool. "He done it for us, Cap. It was a selfless act of Christian love."

"Shut your fucking yap, Bristow," Bly said.

Ray laughed. "I thought them scrambled eggs you served this morning had a greenish tinge to 'em, Curt. Last night I had a ticklish feeling in my throat, but after the first plate it cleared right up."

"Come on, Jubal," Curtis said. "Gimme one more chance."

Jubal shook his head regretfully. "Cain't do it, Curtis. You loied to me, you stole and now these other men got to cloimb down in that hold and do your job own top of theirs. That's all the chance you git with me." He nodded toward Lukey. "Don't bother setting out."

"Where we going, Cap?" Ray asked, but Jubal stalked past without so much as a look.

With that, the stack kicked back an angry belch of smoke, the bow lifted and they set out east-southeast, into the heavy swells rolling toward them from the distant coastline of Virginia.

At a loss, the men consulted in shy glances that rapidly recoiled away across the rail.

"This is awkward, ain't it," Ray said gleefully.

"I got a moind to kick your ass," Bly said in a shallow pant, looking wall-eyed.

"That sure leaves me faint with terror, Curt. See me trembling?" Ray held up a fluttering hand.

"Fuck you, Bristow."

Ray formed his lips into a silent O. "Y'all getting this? I beg the man for mercy, and here he's singed me with another lightning bolt of smoking repar-tay. You're a hard case, Curt."

"You're lucky I don't sloice you up and th'ow you to the shorks," Bly said. "Only they got too much self-respect to eat you."

"Pull a knife within a hundred yards of me, I'll slit your gizzard with it and shit right down your throat," Ray said, turning on a dime, "you fat, pencil-dicked, bald-headed piece of shit."

For an instant, the cook weighed his chances, then decided in the negative. He started for the house, reversed and, with a look both skulking and defiant, swiped up a fresh container of his preferred cold remedy—on second thought, took two.

"Think that'll do you?" Ray asked, relishing the moment. "It's a long way to Hampton Roads."

Bly, however, vanquished and demoralized, retreated without reply.

"We're going all the way to Hampton?" Joe asked.

Ray asked Lukey, "What you figure, Brame? That'd be my guess."

Lukey nodded. "Closer than home."

"But it must be six or seven hours."

"More like eight or nine," the mate corrected.

"Principle's a bitch, ain't it?" Ray said. "Here." He lagged Joe the twenty-pound maul from the lazaret. "You're always asking me what prison's like; here's your big chance to find out."

Grabbing the fire axe for himself, Ray handed Brame the pick, and they applied themselves to the Matterhorn of cloudy ice rising in the forward bin, attacking it sequentially with ringing, rhythmic blows, bit by bit reducing it to its prior state of virgin snow.

Climbing topside an hour and a half later, Lukey bulldozed the first slithering fish pile forward to Joe, who received it on the run, slamming his scuffle into it like an option tailback taking a lateral and driving through the line—bent forward, legs churning for traction on the pitching, slimy deck. Complicated by the roll out here, he moved as if careening up and downhill on a slippery skateboard. Through the dinnerplate-sized hole on deck, he occasionally glimpsed Ray below, chucking shovelfuls of white ice into the slapping waterfall of fish Joe sent raining down, walling them off, board by board, alive in the dark bin.

Though the temperature had risen close to freezing, the wind had picked up, too, blowing out of the southwest now at twenty-five knots, Force 6 on the Beaufort scale; everywhere they looked, the big seas were bucking off their whited crests like the tossing manes of spirited and restive stallions. Spray was constant, a driving horizontal rain that stung their cheeks and eyes, beading in their lashes, coating everything—each line and vang and spar—in a chrysalis of gleaming wet that dripped uninterruptedly.

As the boat shot up the face of an oncoming swell, the men, leaning for balance on a deck as steep as an 8:12 roof, stared aft into a dark abyss of water, a perspective that woozily reversed, turning to an unmoored panel of nacreous sky as they surfed down the back of the same wave.

Once or twice an hour, taking refuge from the bitter wind, the men ducked into the lazaret, huddling on the narrow landing like street people on a New York City subway grate, stamping their numb feet. Shucking his gritty gloves, Joe blew into his blanched, swollen hands, which had contracted into claws around the scuffle's helve, extending them into the heated updraft from the engine for a relief more imaginary than real.

"Think we'll stay out long in this?" he asked hopefully.

"Shit," Ray said. "This? This ain't nothing. We seen a whole lot worse than this, ain't we, Brame?"

"Seen better, too, I guess," the mate replied with a gallantry so understated it was possible to miss.

Back on deck, Joe gazed at the blur of fish around his feet, a mosaic that resolved into its individual bits of glass as his pulse descended out of the aerobic range. Within the prevailing gold and pink-tinged greens, sea-wet and gleaming, he made out the occasional blue-silver flash of a fingerling trout, the dark, intense green of a sea mullet or menhaden.

For the last hour before dinner—as lunch was known aboard—he and Ray worked the deck alone while Lukey went inside to deal with Bly's defection from the galley. With fifteen thousand pounds packed down and fifteen thousand more to go, they went in to eat, only to find Bly holed up in his stateroom, refusing to come out, like a diva in her dressing room after a bad review, sipping Bristol Cream in her peignoir while threatening suicide.

Ray rapped on the door. "Hey, Curtis, ain't you coming out to eat? Brame here's already done your job for you."

"Let me be!" roared Bly in a voice besotted with self-pity and doxylamine.

Ray winked at Joe. "Reckon he must want to contemplate his sorrows in a solo state."

"Go fuck yourself!" Bly cried behind the door.

Ray laid a hand over his heart. "You done blew me into smithereens with that one, Curt. Look at me; I'm tore to shreds."

"Holy Moly, Lukey!" Joe said, eyeing the spread. Heaped on a paper platter on the table, fare for three, were eighteen or twenty chicken pieces, fried to mahogany perfection; there was potato salad topped with slices of hard-boiled egg and paprika, cornbread, link sausages, an array of pickles—including watermelon rind, first-rate and eye-watering sweet—and, last but not least, a bowl of greens—Hanover salad—steaming in pot liquor, sequins of liquid fat winking near a half-pound slab of sidemeat, like ambergris jeweling the wake of the white whale. This was all to be washed down with brimming glasses of ice cold whole milk, supplied at the liberal allowance of a gallon per man per day.

"Jesus Christ!"

"What's the matter?" asked the mate, alarmed by Joe's apostrophe.

"The matter? It's beautiful!" he said, a bloom of misty love in his eyes as he recalled the comforts of his vanished childhood.

Brame looked shy and pleased.

"Ain't suppose to compliment the cook," said Ray, piling his plate with a six-inch tumulus of potato salad as he slid into the banquette. "Might go to his head." Co-opting the serving spoon, he gripped it like an oar and took a bite, continuing to talk with his mouth full. "Fella cooks as good as you, maybe ought to do it permanent."

"Huh-uh," said Lukey. "I took my turn. Tomorrow's one of y'all."

"The hell you say," said Ray, his tongue yellow as a daffodil from the mustard in the potato salad.

"Whoy not?" said Jubal, coming down the companionway to top off his twelfth or fifteenth cup of coffee of the still young day. "You loike eating good enough. Whoy cain't you cook?"

" 'Cause I ain't a cook. You didn't hire me as no cook and I ain't cooking."

"I'll cook tomorrow," Joe volunteered.

The others turned and briefly appraised the volunteer in a manner that did not suggest overwhelming confidence.

"Shit, that's all we need," said Ray. "He'd probably whip up ratatouille or pigeon shit on points of toast or God knows what. We don't eat that froggy shit out here."

"Least he's willing," Jubal said. "What can you make, son?"

"Maybe I should check what's in the pantry and go from there."

"Long's it ain't fondue," said the captain. "Idail made that oncet." He shook his head in dire remembrance. "I cain't aboide with no fondue."

"No, sir, Cap," Joe said with a straight face. "We'll scratch fondue off the list right now."

"Well, boys"—Jubal put the fourth heaping spoon of sugar in his mug—"Curtis says he wants to be let off to home, at Gloucester Point."

"Gloucester? The hell with him," said Ray. "Put him off at Hampton, the fat fuck. He can walk from there. Exercise'll do him good."

"Bristow, you dorty dog!" shouted Bly, following proceedings closely with an ear against the door. "You can kiss my ass!"

"Learn to wipe it, then we'll talk."

"It ain't that much fu'ther," Jubal said, rendering his equitable decision. "Now, t'other thing. This low up north is shaping up roight mean. By Froiday evening, I reckon she'll be peeling the green out here."

"We going in?" Ray asked.

"We'll shoot to git another day of fishing in and head home before she hits." Jubal shook his head. "I'll tell you, boys, we ain't never gonna pay for Chris'mus making trips loike this." The rare confession added ten years to his undefended face.

"Short trip," said Lukey as the captain climbed the stairs.

"Suits me," Joe said.

"Why wouldn't it?" Ray said. "You got you a fucking grant. The rest of us got rent to pay."

"You pay rent at your mom's, do you?"

Ray fired a dark look at Joe, then grinned with malice and approval. "Well, well, he barks, but does he bite? Touché, Professor."

Joe faced him squarely. "You going to let me off the hook or not, Ray?"

Lukey discreetly occupied himself with KP duties at the sink.

"I guess I'll let you know when I decide."

"I'd appreciate that, Ray."

They briefly held each other's stare and turned away.

Dusk was already well advanced by three P.M. as they were rinsing down the deck. On the masthead and the gallows, the 1000-watt halogens had come on, bathing the deck in a surreal illumination that picked out a pinkish neon shine in the eyes of a few dead croakers washing toward the scuppers on a stream of pressured brine.

After cleaning up, Joe joined Jubal in the house, where he'd been at the wheel for over fifty hours.

"How's it going, Cap? You must be getting tired."

"Not to speak of. First thirty hours are the worst. After that it koind of smoothes out some."

As they approached the roadstead, Joe could see the big navy ships silhouetted in the distance, like massive cutouts in gray tin, or mountain ranges glimpsed from the windows of a train. Reposing in a companionable silence, he thought once more of Pa, and a need to sleep, both aching and delicious, stole over him. He went below.

"Hey," he said, dogging down the door behind him.

Reading on his bunk in the beam of a small tensor, Ray made no reply.

With a capgun pop of metal snaps, Joe pulled off his slicker, unshouldered his suspenders and pushed down his coveralls over his jeans, leaving the wadded bottoms where they lay, boots sticking out of them like smokestacks, ready to go again.

"What're you reading?"

The query, too, went unacknowledged. As Joe approached his bunk, he saw that his roommate was absorbed in the steno pad he'd stowed there the first morning of the trip—securely stowed, along with Day's blank Memorex, under his spare wool shirt near the bottom of his pack.

"Ray, that's personal. I'd like that." There was no response. On a stiffer note: "Now, if you don't mind."

Ray glanced up, a studied languor in his eyes, and casually went on reading.

Joe reached out, and Ray blocked his wrist, darting him a look of overt threat.

"I'm serious, Ray. That material's private. You have no right to look at that."

Ray sat up, swung his legs over his bunk and stared into space for a moment before he pounced to deck and faced Joe in the narrow space. "Pardon me." He shoved the pad into its owner's chest, not hard. "I didn't mean to pry." Pushing past, he spun the wheel and shut the door behind him with an iron clang.

Unnerved, Joe looked at the open page and read:

qq: Ray Bristow:
A) is he gay; and, B) does he know?
i) is he in denial only with his family and the church, or also in the closet with himself?
ii) and if he knows, what is it to dedicate oneself to Christ in a church where what you are is reviled as a perversion of the human body and an offense against God's will?
iii) having left Little Roanoke to escape local prejudice, why did he come home?

Written during a summarizing session before Christmas, this was the penultimate entry in Joe's journal. Beyond lay only his concluding question: *What is the field?*

A small grunt escaped Joe's lips, the sound a boxer makes as he takes a gut punch on the ropes. When he raised his eyes, his reflection in the shaving mirror gave him a start, as though someone had stolen on him unawares and caught him, like a thief, red-handed in the act. Vibrating with the bulkhead, the outlines of his face were tremulous and indistinct, and it was as if Joe Madden were dematerializing, turning to a ghost.

Behind him, the piss jug scraped across the floor and roused him from his reverie. Throwing the notebook on his bunk, he hurried topside, after Ray.

Thirteen

In the head, the toilet flushed, a terrific whoosh accompanied by a death rattle.

"We need to talk," Joe said as Ray came out.

"You may need to talk, not me."

"Listen, Ray—"

"No, you listen." He pressed a finger into Joe's chest. "You and me been talking now for going on a year. Fuck it. I'm through talking. Fuck it, and fuck you."

He vanished up the companionway. Standing in the empty space, Joe felt confused and guilty. Yet hadn't Ray come on to him? What was he supposed to do, pretend it never happened? And what he'd written wasn't meant in judgment anyway, but in sympathy, the fruit of Joe's attempt to pose himself the question: "What does it feel like to be you?" and to answer it in the deepest way he knew. His arguments seemed sound, yet he couldn't overcome the sense of having trespassed.

This is what I do, he reminded himself, repeating the case he'd made to Day. And wasn't what he'd witnessed and recorded in his notebook true? It was to this that he kept coming back. The answer was clear: it was. And if the truth was a betrayal, wasn't it a greater one to turn away?

Outside, night had fallen, and the boat, rolling gently in the Bay's light swell, entered the mouth of the York River, approaching

Gloucester Point on the north shore, a fishing town that in the dark had little to distinguish it from Little Roanoke.

At the fishhouse, a big scalloper, the *Carolina Girl,* was lumping out while her contented captain watched from dock, sipping coffee as the crew hoisted the white linen bags from the hold, each fat with forty pounds of eye meat, sweating drops like breast milk. As Jubal eased in the *Father's Price,* a few workers acknowledged Joe with nods of terse and noncommittal friendliness.

Behind him, the galley door clanged against the wall, and Curtis Bly emerged, carrying a stained nylon duffel.

"Far's what's in the hold roight now," said Jubal, following him out, "we'll share out foive ways. You call Dolph and tell 'im where you want the check. Aport from that, I cain't do nothing for you, Curtis. Man your age ought to long since knowed that alcohol and fishing boats don't mix."

Registering the hit, Curtis fished a pair of wraparound dark glasses from his pocket and shoved them on. "You redheaded, cold-hearted, freckle-faced, cocksucking, no count, peckerwood motherfucker," he said, releasing the torrent of invective in a surprisingly halfhearted voice, "I'll laugh the day the barracudas gnaw your pecker, if you got one, which I doubt." He spit perfunctorily and tossed his bag to dock, leaping after it with unexpected nimbleness. Beyond their reach, he gave the crew a last salute, shooting the finger out of doubled, pumping fists before shouldering his kit and heading off across the parking lot, pursued by Ray's wolf whistle and a jeer or two from the crowd.

Within two minutes they were steaming at full throttle south across the Bay. In the green glow of the wheelhouse instruments, Jubal resembled a grim Norman king behind the stone walls of his keep.

As Ray left the house and started down the gangway, Joe tried again. "Ray?"

He didn't stop.

Joe pursued him to the lazaret. "Look, I'm sorry you saw that, Ray. It wasn't my intention to upset you, but you had no right to read it, and you damn well knew it before you went rooting through my pack."

"That's it?" Ray said, stone-faced.

Joe waited, expecting more.

"Blah blah blah." Ray walked away, but Joe grabbed his arm. "Ray, I know you're angry . . ."

"Angry? You think I'm angry? Angry ain't it, Joe."

"Then what?"

"You want to know? I'll tell you what. That first night you come to church, I remember setting there on the boat as we passed that stick, and you know what I thought? I thought, hey, here's someone I can talk to. Me and this dude here might end up being friends. That's a good one, ain't it?"

"We did, Ray," Joe said. "We are."

Ray sneered.

"I had a job to do here, Ray, and I've done it, but we've hung out and shared a lot. We are friends, Ray. I consider you mine."

"Naw, man. Naw, baby, I don't give you that. Don't kid yourself. I tried to be your friend, but you . . . you come out here like bwana in your safari outfit with your notebook and your little brownie camera set to take some Polaroids of the nekit jungle bunnies gittin' down and swingin' off the vines. It was a real hoedown, won't it, Joe, listening to us speak in tongues and testifying in the blood and God knows what. Mad? I ain't mad. Five years ago if I'd met you out here slumming for kicks, I would've tore you a new asshole. But I ain't mad. I feel sorry for you."

"Sorry for me?"

"Yeah, ain't that a kick? Me, ol' Gay Ray sorry for you, and you know why? Because you spent all this time out here looking for answers, searching for the truth, and what did you find? Far as I can see, you're still the same scared little chickenshit who walked in the Lighthouse that first night, and after all the notes you took on me and Pate and God knows who, did you ever once look in the mirror and ask the truth about yourself? I don't think so, and if you ask me, you never will, 'cause you're just too fucking terrified of what you'll see."

"I don't know, Ray," Joe said slowly. "Maybe I deserve that, maybe I don't, but for me the bottom line is you came on to me and I'm not gay. Ever since, you've been making me your official whipping boy, and what did I really do to you apart from turn you down? Maybe I could have handled that episode better. If I hurt your feelings, I apologize; I didn't mean to. You've helped me in ways that meant a lot, and however you may feel about me, I consider you a friend. But the other, the sexual thing—that I can't return, and I'm sick and tired of being punished for it."

"That's what you think this is about?" Ray asked, clearly incredulous. "That old shit? Me being gay?"

"You aren't?"

"I don't know what the fuck it even means." Ray patted his pocket for his Kools. "Straight, gay—I used to think I knew, but now?" He lit up and flicked the match over the rail. "You have no idea what I'm even saying, do you?"

Joe considered it. "I know what it is to be confused. But not on that."

"Yeah, but, see, to me, it don't feel like confusion. To me, what you think and feel is what's confused. I know, because I used to feel that way myself. Growing up in Little Roanoke, that was the worst thing you could call another man—faggot, homo, queer—the worst thing you could be. I said them words and laughed at 'em a thousand times, but it came back to haunt me after Nam.

"But why should it be dirty, Joe? If your own body don't disgust you, why should another man's? If your body's beautiful and holy like a woman's is, why not mine? And how can two beautiful and holy things add up to something wrong and ugly? The answer is, they can't. Two human beings in the act of love can never be disgusting. Never. That's what I figured out in prison, Joe; I didn't read it in no book. The book was me. You think I'm confused, well maybe so, but to me the way two people fuck, which end they use, that's like do you cook it in a skillet or a pot. What difference so long as the food is good? The way you fuck is just the means; the end is love, and what love is to me is just two human beings beholding each other fully, not in judgment, but with the eyes of faith.

"You, though . . . you don't believe in nothing. You think doubting and questioning everything makes you strong. But it don't; it makes you weak. You think it makes you big, but it makes you small. Mr. Wait-and-See—I used to be like you. Hell, I tried to tell you this the first night you arrived, so did J.C., but you didn't get it then, and you ain't gonna get it now. What's the point of talking?"

"Don't walk away," Joe said. "Tell me what I did, Ray. If I misunderstood, what did I misunderstand? If sex wasn't it, tell me what you wanted from me."

Ray narrowed his eyes. "You don't even know, do you?"

Joe just held his stare and blinked.

"You know what I wanted? I wanted you to look at me and see the truth of who I was and accept it. That was the whole deal, Joe. I didn't want to be your spy or science project. I didn't want to be the little white rat running through the maze. I wanted you to see me as a human being, the way you see yourself, and treat me like a friend, the way I treated you. But when I looked in your eyes all I ever saw reflected back was the mad, ignorant, redneck motherfucker I used to be before I went to Warrenton and fought like hell to overcome. And that's what I see right now. You ain't no friend to me—don't kid yourself. You never was and never will be. What the hell happened to you, Joe? What are you so scared of?"

Ray left an interval, but Joe, in pain, searched deep within himself and found no answer that might balance in the scales with the rebuff.

Ray shook his head. "Yeah, well, I guess I had something to say after all. I'll leave you some private time so you can write this down while it's still fresh."

He vanished down the steps and left Joe with the question ringing in his ears above the engine's roar: *What happened to you, Joe? What are you so scared of?*

PART V

Fourteen

Then it was Christmas, and his family came.

The day they were slated to arrive from Richmond—December 23—I made my groggy way to the kitchen at eight o'clock to find the floor long-since mopped and Joe cleaning the refrigerator crevices with a Q-tip doused in 409.

"What's up?"

"Just neatening a bit," he replied defensively, acting like a nervous junior officer before a dress parade.

"Can I help?"

"Actually," he said, looking relieved, "you can. I need to run out to the store. While I'm gone, maybe you could make the beds and, you know, straighten up a bit?"

"Your mother isn't going to put on a white glove and run her finger down the mantelpiece, is she?"

"May's not like that." May's son took a beat. "Though now that you mention it, you may want to give it a quick wipe."

The second beat was mine.

He grinned. "Got you."

"Ha-ha. You know I don't do well with this whole Junior League DAR thing, Joe."

"Just be yourself. I love you, so will they. And it's Colonial Dames, not DAR."

"There's a diff?"

"Try DAR on May, and you'll find out."

An hour and a half later he breezed in with two hundred dollars' worth of groceries, a prodigality that made my eyes bug, considering Joe's Raskolnikovian propensities. Given his druthers, I think he'd have lived in a garret on shoe-leather soup and pumpernickel crusts. Among the bourgie haul that morning were such items as a ten-dollar bottle of vermouth-soaked olives for his stepfather's martinis, an eight-pound beef tenderloin and two bottles of Château Margaux. As Joe placed them on the island with tender hands, I could tell from his wistful expression that the purchases had cost him, in addition to the cash outlay, a degree of moral pain located in the region of his sphincter. Good soldier that he was, though, he had done his duty. It was Christmas, after all, and when you get right down to it, nothing, I suppose, is too good for your mom—so they tell me. His family's visit had become educational long before they actually arrived.

Showered and dressed—he'd eschewed his typical denim on denim for a blue oxford shirt and khakis—Joe put the roast in at seven, expecting them at any minute, but at eight, when it came out, they had yet to show. By nine-fifteen, we'd finished the first bottle of the good stuff and gone ignobly back to my jug Almaden, a change I rather welcomed, like returning from a papal audience to relaxed dish with some good, down-and-dirty friend. Checking the kitchen clock continually, Joe had become a trifle grim.

Trying to lighten his mood, I twitted him about his getup. "I take it back; I do begin to see it now."

He challenged me with a distracted frown. "See what?"

"Your Southernness." I nodded at his feet, in Topsiders without socks.

"The giveaway," he said with a resigned, but sporting note, under the lens himself for once. It was as if the princeling in the fairy tale, surprised in his boudoir, revealed an animal's clawed foot when stripping off his boots.

And speaking of animals' clawed feet, at that moment the telltale sound of tires crunching loose sand in the drive was followed by footsteps on the stairs—padded, non-human ones.

"Bad dog! Stay! Lie down! Not there! Don't move! Come here! That's right! Good girl!" Dispensing contradictory commands like

God Almighty hurling crooked thunderbolts, the deep baritone broke like a sonic boom outside the house.

I looked at Joe, who said, with fearful wonder, "Jimmy?" He was barely out the door when an amber retriever with hazel eyes full of transparent schemes of self-aggrandizement pinned him to the wall with clublike paws, lapping his face with shameless love.

"Down!" he cried. "Down, damnit! You mutt!" And there was thunder in his voice, too.

"Meet Tawny." The voice came from the darkness at the bottom of the stairs, where one of Joe's younger brothers presently appeared, wearing baggy trousers and a puce designer T with outrageous braces—orange and pink chameleons skittering up one shoulder and down the next. Clearing his hair with a fifteen-year-old's chin toss, he took us in with a friendly grin. "Professor," he said, his gaze, approving and unshy, on me as he shook his brother's hand.

"Tawny?" Joe said.

"Reed's new dog."

"He named her *Tawny?*"

"What's wrong with Tawny?"

The owner of the plangent baritone now showed himself. At six-seven and two-fifty, Reed Madden made his brothers look like pygmies in the shadow of a giant banyan tree. With Clark Gable's looks and dashing black mustache, he wore a canary yellow sweater and a signet ring the size of a large English walnut and looked as if he might be on his way to a kegger on frat row in Chapel Hill.

"Jesus, you poor mutt," Joe answered obliquely as he scratched the retriever's ears.

"We used to have a dog named Tawny," the youngest musketeer reported for my benefit. "Hi, I'm Gray, the good one."

I smiled. "Day."

"I know." His precocious confidence and warmth were an immediate contrast to Joe, whose social manner was marked by hesitations, footnotes and punctilios. Gray's smile, though, had some emergent sameness in the bones.

"I guess that makes me the bad one. Hi, I'm Reed." With the easy, self-effacing manners of a well-bred Southern boy, he offered me his hand, then turned. "Hey, Joey."

"Joe," Gray corrected.

"That's right. We're under orders to remember that." Reed's smile included me.

"Jesus, Reed!" said Joe. "I thought you were Dad! So help me God, you sound just like him. I thought Jimmy was right outside the house."

"I'm surprised you didn't exit out the back," said Reed.

The brothers' laughter had a guilty tinge, but in Reed's "huh-huh," there was a ragged note that tugged at something in my chest. A second glance showed me sleep-rings smudged under his black eyes, as odd in his high-colored, twenty-three-year-old face as the silver threads sprinkled like early frost through his black hair.

"Knock, knock?"

In the spotlight at the bottom of the stairs, May, in a black-and-green plaid suit, loomed up, smiling with happy expectation as she took a final, searing puff on a pencil-thin, brown More, crushed it beneath the toe of her black flat with a twisting dance step and spread her arms toward her eldest son.

"Joey Madden, come here this instant and kiss your mama!"

"Joe," Gray corrected as the bumbling professor went to take his medicine. When May pulled back after the kiss, a bloom of sentiment misted her eyes, and she could not refrain from wiping lipstick from her eldest's cheek. Though she'd shorn her long hair in favor of a shorter, more current do, May was recognizably the woman in the photo on the wall. Middle age had made some inroads in her face, but she was still impressive, her beauty rooted not in flesh but bone, the sort that's like a fine antique that subtly enhances everything in the room around it.

"Day?" she said, peeking around Joe's shoulder. "You come kiss me, too, right this minute. Lord, I thought we'd never get here! Where's Sumner? Did we lose him? Sumner, are you lost?"

"Right behind you," her husband's voice called from the driveway, followed by the slam of a car door.

"Let's go in," May said. "It's cold as bejesus out here."

The moment we were in the house she lit another More, reaching for the clamshell ashtray on the newly dusted mantel and sliding it two inches to the right—its previous position—as she deposited her fag. "What, no tree?"

"No ornaments," said Joe.

"Sugar, there are, too! A whole trunkful of Mama's downstairs."

"Oh."

"Never mind; we'll bring them up tomorrow."

"Can we get you something to drink?" I asked.

"What are y'all having? Is that white wine, Day?"

"You probably don't want this," I said. "It's Almaden."

"That's my house brand! I drink it by the gallon!"

"I have a nice red," Joe offered.

"Oh, sugar, don't waste it on me. Reed, fix us one, would you? And Day could use a refill, too—yes?"

"Absolutely."

"Okay," Reed said, taking my glass but directing his remark to his mother. "But I'm not putting any ice cubes in it."

"Why not? I like ice cubes. Don't you, Day?"

"Ice cubes are good," I agreed.

"I'm only trying to save you from yourselves."

"That's what they all think, don't they, Day? Only we aren't the least bit interested in being saved." She took my arm in a gesture of female solidarity, and, like a wood chip in the hurricane, I bowed to *force majeure*.

At that moment, Sumner, bags in both hands, hooked the screen door with his pinkie, jerked it open, blocked it with his toe, then raced it toward the threshold, giving one last bravura backkick as it closed, superfluous except as it supplied a flourish. "Friends and Romans," he said, grinning like a man capable of taking satisfaction from an exploit as simple as successfully entering a door with both arms filled. In a camel's hair blazer and a crisp, open-collared shirt the deep-dyed aquamarine of a Caribbean atoll, he exuded a faint cloud of expensive aftershave and breath mints, a man of medium height who looked, beside the Madden boys, a bit like Gulliver in Brobdingnag. My initial hunch was that Sumner was one of those men, like my colleague Gaither Holman, who, a little portly, surprises you on the dance floor, where he turns to Fred Astaire.

"Dr. Shaughnessey, isn't it?" Depositing his cargo, Sumner smiled in a way that seemed to promise he would laugh at the next joke I made and thank me for the effort.

"Day."

"Sumner's a cardiologist, Day," May said. "I'm sure Joey told you."

"Yes, he did," I lied. Not only had "Joey" failed to mention his stepfather's medical specialty, he'd never mentioned him at all, except under provocation.

"So," he said, "think this will get us through the weekend?" A dark green Tanqueray bottle appeared over the edge of one bag, followed by others—Absolut, Maker's Mark, Cutty, all half-gallons. "Ladies?"

"We're all set, honey. Help yourself."

"Where have you *been*?" Joe asked.

"Got sidetracked in Virginia," Sumner said.

"Sidetracked?" Gray said. "If you call spending two hours chasing Tawny's sorry Chesapeake retriever ass through the Great Dismal Swamp sidetracked. Look at my shoes! These are Cole-Hahns, Reed. You're buying me new ones."

"The check's in the mail," Reed said with a shy, wicked little smirk as he handed out our wine.

"I'm serious!" Gray reiterated in a teenage whine.

"It was your fault she ran off. You should have used the leash."

"She ran away before I had a chance to put it on."

"She heard something in the woods and went after it. She's a hunting dog; that's what she's bred to do."

"Yeah, but isn't she supposed to come back when you call? I mean, didn't she just get back from obedience school?"

"Hunting school," Reed said. "She's a water dog, Gray, not a house pet."

"If that dog retrieves a duck tomorrow, I'll eat it raw, feathers and all."

"Yeah, well you'd better stock up on dental floss," Reed said, showing signs of offense on his canine protégée's behalf, "because she will."

"Boys, now," May said, intervening, and I noticed her for the first time in covert study of her middle son.

"You're going hunting tomorrow?" I asked diversionarily, thinking she could use a hand.

Reed nodded, examining his beer.

"You have a guide?" Joe asked.

"I don't need a guide," he said.

Joe gave May a questioning look, which went unacknowledged. "Should we eat?"

The idea seemed to have occurred to the nonhuman constituency as well. At that moment, from the kitchen came the resounding crash and clatter of the roasting pan, followed by a sodden *whump* as the tenderloin, left on the countertop to rest, hit the floor. And there was Tawny, shoving backward off the island with both front paws, following the meat in its descent.

"Tawny!" Reed bellowed, his heavy footsteps making china tinkle in the cupboard as he rushed to the rescue. "Bad, girl! Bad! Lie down!"

Thrusting legs out fore and aft as though prepared to fly, the dog hit the deck directly in the Worchestershire spill.

"Great!" said Gray. "Now what are we going to eat?"

"It's all right," May said, "we'll rinse it off. I don't think she touched it."

"Ah, Reed, like, ah, why don't you try *feeding* her?"

"Excuse me, Day." Ignoring Gray, Reed took a small pistol from beneath his sweater.

"You're going to shoot her?" I asked, with a nervous laugh.

"It's just a cap gun."

"Yeah, well, I still think it's cruel," said Gray.

"Listen, penile implant, that's how Daddy trained Tawny."

"Sweetie," May intervened, "our old Tawny never hunted."

"Mom, she did, too," Reed said, with a whine like Gray's. "Her mother was the field champion of Maryland."

"Maybe so," May said, "but one of her eyes was crossed and she had hip problems. I doubt Tawny would have recognized a duck if one quacked at her."

Gray hooted.

"Shut up, Gray. You don't even remember her."

"I do, too! Whenever we went in the ocean, she'd swim in a big circle and not let any of the children go outside, and if you grabbed her tail, she'd pull you back to shore."

"You've just heard us tell that story."

"No, I remember," Gray insisted. "And she'd dig for sand fiddlers. She'd stick her nose in the hole and get sand on it and paddle it back between her legs, and we'd make castles."

Reed dismissed this with an older brother's condescension and turned to the source of true authority. "And anyway, Mom, it isn't true. When Daddy took me to Mattamuskeet that time? Tawny fetched lots of ducks. The guide said she was as good a water dog as he'd ever seen."

As she looked at him, May's face settled back into that imponderable place. "All right, sweetie. If you say so."

"I was there, Mom. You weren't," he said, and something in his level of investment hurt my heart for him.

I caught Joe, who hadn't spoken through this interchange, standing on the threshold, a frown of concentration on his usually clear face. It was his watcher pose, the mental raptor look I knew so well, yet there was something pained and fretful in his study that was new to me. I can't explain it, but the image of him standing there, half in and half outside the room, seared me like a brand.

In the momentary silence, the kibble clattered loudly in Tawny's plastic bowl. Like a jailer leading the condemned to execution, Reed conducted the dog onto the porch as we tried not to watch.

"Sit, girl. Stay." As he raised the cap gun over his head, Tawny began to tremble and salivate in anticipation. "Good, girl." When the shot exploded, she flinched violently. *"Stay!"* A dime-sized drop of saliva hit the floor, followed by another and another, pattering like rain. "Stay . . . stay . . ."

"Reed!" Gray protested.

"Shut up, Gray. All right, girl." Released, the dog attacked the bowl with desperation.

"See?" Reed said. "You just have to let her know her job and be consistent."

Brushing past Joe in the doorway, he turned on the radio in the living room, sat down on the sofa and lit a Lucky Strike. As Sumner engaged him in conversation, I watched Reed reach his match toward the clamshell. His movements had a slo-mo quality, dreamlike and submarine, and there was a tremor in the big hand that wore the ring. In the midst of family, something about him in that moment radiated isolation, brittle dignity and something else impossible to specify, but sad.

The consciousness of it was there in Joe's face, too, and May's. She met Joe's look head on now in a way that brought out their resemblance.

"I have to ask you something, Joey. Reed has his heart set on this hunting trip tomorrow. It's the first thing he's been interested in in weeks. I'd like you to go with him."

"I doubt I could even load a shotgun anymore, much less hit anything with one."

May made no response.

"It's started again, hasn't it?" said Joe.

In his mother's eyes, the mist appeared like a skim of ice over black water. "I'm sorry, son. I don't want him alone out there all day with those guns."

Like a breakwater, Joe took the whelming sea and simply nodded once.

May tiptoed up and kissed his cheek. "Excuse me, Day."

When she left the room, Joe walked to the window and stared out for some time.

"What's going on, Joe?"

"Reed's manic, Day." He made the announcement to the dark sea out beyond the dunes.

"Manic-depressive?"

He turned to me, his expression flayed and the trace of lipstick on his cheek. "That's the current diagnosis, anyway."

"Is he on lithium?"

Joe nodded.

"You never mentioned it."

"He's been stable for a while. I guess I hoped it was over. I don't think it's ever going to be over, though. Is it okay if we not get into this right now?"

I held up my hands.

"Sorry," he said, picking up the meat. At the door, he turned back with the platter. "Welcome to the family."

Fifteen

The clock said 4:25. It was pitch dark outside, and Joe could smell strong coffee and bacon frying in the kitchen and hear the drone of a radio turned low. Conjured up by the good smells, Pa Tilley's ghost hovered in the vicinity as Joe lay in a suspended state.

Already dressed and shaved, Reed was making sandwiches at the kitchen island with the previous night's steak, spreading mayo on a row of bread—six slices—with a butcher knife and A.1. on the row of six below, exactly as their grandfather used to do before fishing trips. There, too, were the obligatory cans of Campbell's beanie weenies, one per man, and the old plaid thermos, into which Reed poured the coffee he'd made in the blueware percolator Pa had used.

"Ready to go give them ducks what-fo'?" Joe said in the old lingo, studying his brother's face.

"You betcha." Reed's grin was semi-doubtful.

"They'll take one look at that outfit and fly down to ask who your tailor is."

He had on a porkpie hat with a leather band, heavy tweed trousers and a white turtleneck under a navy blue boiled wool sweater with suede elbow patches and a shoulder pad for shooting; over this was a waxed canvas utility vest, its double row of shell loops swagged with brass-capped Magnum loads. The vest had roughly twenty pockets, ranging from a large zippered one in back for game to a cunning small one for Reed's bamboo duck call. Dan-

gling from D-rings, a silver dog whistle and a compass clanked sac-
erdotally as Reed concluded preparations.

"Does that inflate into a life raft, too?" Joe asked.

"Listen, Joey, you don't have to come. I know Mom's making
you."

"She's not making me."

Reed made a wry face, knowing better. "Well, if you're going to
eat, you'd better hurry up. I want to be in the blind before sunrise."

They stepped outside into cold that was startling and solid. The
porch thermometer read 23 degrees.

"All right, you," Joe said to Tawny, ensconced in the shotgun
seat of Reed's Blazer. "Out, damned Spot."

Her tail pummeled the leather bucket seat.

"Don't make me come in there after you!"

Tossing his gear in back, Reed laughed. "Tawny, come! Come,
girl, now!" Getting no response, Reed scooped her up and dumped
her over the seat into the back.

"She comes by her name honestly," Joe said.

Reed grinned, remembering, too.

Every June when they left Killdeer for the beach, they'd come
out on the fateful morning to find the original Tawny encamped in
the back seat of the Country Squire. Terrified of being left behind
and engaged in nonviolent civil disobedience, she'd jumped
through the window in the middle of the night. After dutifully
wrestling with her for several minutes, pulling her ears until she
yelped, Joey would trudge into the house and tattle to the boss.

"Goddamnit, what next?" Jimmy would slap his morning *Sentinel* on the breakfast table, put down his coffee and go out, with
May and Reed bringing up the rear, unwilling to miss the show.

"Tawny?" His most coaxing, come-hither tone.

Whomp! Down she'd go, undeceived and playing dead, her only
trick.

"It's a sit-in, Jimmy," May would say, trying not to laugh.

"Damnit, May, what does she think, that we're going to leave
her? Have we ever left you? Once?"

Tawny did not seem reassured by this citation of historical
precedent.

"We aren't going to leave you, Tawny," Reed always promised,
dislodging his thumb from his mouth to speak. Holding his stuffed

tyrannosaurus by one soiled paw, he watched the eviction with concerned black eyes.

And then the final warning: "Goddamnit, Tawny! Don't make me come in there after you!" And Jimmy would shake his head and mutter, the crack of his ass dawning over the khaki horizon of his still unbelted pants as he leaned in and nabbed her. "You're heading for a world of sorrow, dog."

Now, waiting for the heater to come up to speed, Joe warmed his hands around his coffee mug and remembered, as he and Reed rolled up to the stoplight on the strip, a neon ghost town at that hour.

"My battery died on me in Little Roanoke," he said. "Think you could give me a jump on the way back this afternoon?"

"No problem," Reed said. The light changed, and they drove on in silence, heading south.

The blind that Reed had arranged to use was on state land, assigned by lottery, the last one north of Oregon Inlet. Once they crossed the Whalebone Junction intersection onto Route 12, the houses quickly thinned and vanished; marshes opened on the right. Though there was no moon or stars, sunrise still far off, the enveloping overcast shed some diffuse light that made the meadows of black needlerush and cordgrass distinguishable from reaches of open water, lit by a ghostly sheen against which hundreds of bristling waterfowl stood out like coarse black pepper in a milky soup.

They pulled over near a wooden observation platform beside a narrow estuary. Released, Tawny exploded into the marsh, her excited bark mingling with the sere clattering of disturbed grasses, the sumping whomp of paws through mud. Where she vanished, a fairy trail of eider catkins from burst cattails drifted slowly downward in the headlight beams.

Reed opened the tailgate, took out a pair of sleek new hip waders and handed a patched pair to Joe. "I don't know how watertight these are; they were hanging up in the garage. I think maybe they were Daddy's."

"Jesus, I'll sink like a stone."

"Huh, huh, huh," said Reed, slipping his bare feet into battery-powered warming socks. Tossing two mesh duffels filled with decoys on the ground, he unzipped a leather sleeve and took out a new Browning .12-gauge pump.

"Nice gun," Joe observed, wondering how much it had cost and who had paid for it, though of course he knew. If he had any doubts about his mother's motivation, they were answered by his brother's happy grin.

"Thanks," Reed said. "Check this one out."

Unzipping a second fleece-lined case, Reed lifted out an antique double-barreled bird gun and, with reverent hands, passed it to his older brother, who read the elaborate engraving on the sterling panels in the stock, in letters time and human touch had almost worn away: A. A. FOX & CO., PHILADELPHIA.

"Where did you get this, Reed?"

"Daddy gave it to me for my birthday," his brother answered proudly.

Joe blinked at him, then gazed back at the gun, remembering Christmas Eve at his grandparents' house in Killdeer when he was eleven. Called from the party by his Pa, Joey had followed out to the garage, where his grandfather opened the secret compartment in the wall in which he kept the antique guns and swords and bayonets that were his special treasures. That night Will Tilley told his oldest grandson to pick which would be his, and Joey chose the A. A. Fox, and in all the intervening years since Will had died, Joe had never known what became of it.

Discovering it now, he studied Reed's pleased face, and something wallowed in his gut. "Pa gave me this gun, Reed."

"What?" Reed's expression curdled instantly.

"All these years I've wondered where it was."

"Daddy said Pa gave the Fox to him."

"You think I'm lying?" Joe asked.

"You're saying Daddy is?"

Both queries went unanswered.

"You realize Pa's daddy blew his brains out with this thing?" Joe said. "I'm surprised you even want it."

"Why do you?" Reed retorted.

The question stopped him. Tempted to stake his claim, Joe assessed his brother's focused, unambivalent expression and felt once more something that had dogged him all his life—the sense that the contest is unclean, and victory leaves an aftertaste as bad as defeat. And so, making his characteristic move, he withdrew. "I don't," he said. "Personally, I'd like to sink the thing in the deepest part of the Puerto Rico Trench, but if you want it, take it."

"To hell with it, Joey. If Pa gave it to you, it's yours. Tawny, come!" Shouldering a bag of decoys, Reed disappeared into the high grass, and Joe, shouldering the second bag, humped after him, bemused at how quickly things were spoiled and at his role in spoiling them.

A beaten footpath led into the marsh, the ground thinly crusted with ice their boots punched through to slippery mud. In places, the way was flooded midthigh deep, the water black as ink and so cold it made Joe's heart race till he came up dripping on the other side. With each in-breath he felt his nostril hair crisp with frost the exhalation melted. The walk in was half a mile and took them close to forty minutes. At one point they passed within a hundred yards of a pond where a large flock of snow geese lay sheltering, their throaty chortling communicating a state of brooding, alerted rest. From behind them there was suddenly a loud splashing, then Tawny's high-pitched bark, and the geese erupted, a pale fountain jetting a hundred feet straight up into the dark, the thunderous *whoosh* of hundreds of wings making a dampened concussion in the air like a helicopter prop. The dog's eyes gleamed in the Maglight beam and she exploded on them, her dangling tongue six inches longer than before and redder than the uncooked tenderloin.

"Tawny, heel!" Reed said. "Heel!"

Braking, she gave herself a violent shake, spattering them with foul black mud, and then plunged into the marsh on the far side of the footpath and ran on.

"That dog is hopeless, Reed," Joe told him sympathetically.

"Once she settles down, she'll be okay."

When they came to a hummock with several pine trees weathered into bonsai shapes, Reed unshouldered his duffel and unzipped his pants, modestly turning his back and leaning straight-armed against the nearest tree. Waiting, Joe remembered camping out in the garage with his grandfather and cousins, sleeping in Army surplus bags on Army surplus cots with Army surplus periscope-type flashlights, which they beamed into the rafters periodically, on the alert for vampire bats.

Inevitably, after everyone had settled in, one of the boys would pipe up, "Pa, I have to pee," and he'd call, "Who else needs to go?" Unwilling to be left behind, they'd formed a line and marched to the edge of the driveway, where they stood in military silence, waiting for the first trickling stream to release their communal powers.

Joe listened for that sound now, but thirty seconds passed, then a minute, and nothing came. "Come on, baby, you can do it. Unh," he grunted, "unh . . . unh . . . Try imagining a waterfall, the roaring torrents of Niagara, the headwaters of the Nile."

"Shut up. Don't make me laugh," Reed said, laughing.

"Why, does it make your sphincter tighten up?"

"Go on, I'll catch up with you," he said.

"No way. There might be bears out there."

"There aren't any bears."

"Yeah, well, just in case, I'm letting you go first."

Giving up, Reed zipped his fly.

Another five minutes' walk brought them to a second pond, eighty yards across and almost perfectly circular, its shore rimmed with a gray, slushy ice like a soiled ermine cuff. Boxy and half-heartedly disguised with brush, the blind stood fifteen yards from shore on the far side. They crossed a sluggish tidal creek spanned by a punky bridge missing several planks and waded out, tossing their gear on the raised deck of the blind. Joe helped Reed set out the decoys, dropping the lead sinkers in knee-deep water.

"Is there some principle to this?" Joe asked.

"Just make it look like an attractive family gathering."

Joe laughed.

"Shhh." Reed put his finger to his lips. "We have to keep it down now."

Joe hoisted himself aboard and Reed passed him a sandwich, dropping a slice of meat to Tawny, who caught it in midair and inhaled without bothering to chew. Reed's hand trembled slightly as he poured the coffee and spiked it from his silver hip flask.

"Is that Seagrams Seven?"

Reed smiled and shook his head. "How did Pa drink that stuff?"

"By the gallon."

"Did his father really kill himself with the Fox?"

"Blew his brains out in the library."

"How old was Pa?"

"Nineteen? Twenty? I know he was still at Chapel Hill."

"That's who they named me for, isn't it," Reed said.

Joe studied him. "There were others, too, Reed. It's an old family name."

Reed sipped his coffee without comment. "I wonder if that's why Pa drank."

"I don't know," Joe said. "That probably had something to do with it."

Having reached this somber terminus, the conversation died, and they ate in silence as a gray, sourceless light came up, without actual evidence of sunrise, revealing their position as castaways adrift in a dun world of grass, uninterrupted to the horizon on all sides, except for an occasional myrtle bush or hummock like the one they'd passed, where the sea-weathered pines formed indecipherable calligraphs. To the west, they could see Gravesend Light and, southward, the monumental hump of the Bonner Bridge arching up from a low mist. As the light increased, it revealed a late-December sky blanketed with low striated clouds, dark layers of bruised blue-silver shading almost indistinguishably into paler layers of silver-blue. Motionless as a painted skrim, it bathed the world in a beautiful, somber light.

"Did I tell you I saw Daddy?" Reed said.

"When?"

"My birthday. He was supposed to take me out for dinner, but he didn't show. About ten o'clock, I got a call at Mom's. He was somewhere in the boondocks in Prince George County with a flat."

"Is he still driving that old Ford?"

Reed nodded and gave Joe a shy, wicked smirk. "The Batmobile. He's got a mobile phone in it now."

Joe hooted. "Did he ever make it?"

Reed shook his head. "I went down there."

"So you ended up changing his tire for him on your birthday?"

Reed mugged, and they both laughed with happy malice, savoring all the levels of the joke, the subtle blend of disappointment and appreciation, the mischief sweetened with affection, the punch-drunk, bitter, ever hopeful love of sons for the large, doubtful character their father was, rendered larger and more doubtful by his absence than presence could have ever made him.

Dying out, the laughter left a gamy aftertaste. Finishing his sandwich, Joe was startled when Reed suddenly reached past him for the Browning, retracting the pump and shouldering it in a single motion as he stood. From behind and to their left, the direction of the hummock, he heard a cry, *hoo-week, hoo-week,* and turned in time to see three dark shapes streaking from the trees, their bodies straight between the blur of wings. *Wham! Wham!* The shots rang out by his right ear, striking almost with the force of blows. *Wham!* Joe barely registered what was happening before two birds, the middle and last, went still in midair and began to drop, wing over wing, with a looping casualness that seemed odd after their furious, streaking flight. Veering upward from its track, the first bird seemed on the point of turning back, then, with a plaintive *hoo-week,* continued on its way across the marsh alone.

"You son of a bitch," Joe said. "Where did you learn to do that? That was beautiful."

Reed pursed his lips. "I missed that first one, though," he said, aiming for understatement but smiling despite himself.

"What were they anyway, pigeons?"

"Fuck you, Joey. They were wood ducks."

"You sure? They looked awfully small, like a couple of whizzing bad-assed bumblebees."

"They're fast," Reed said, unclipping his whistle. "The fastest ducks." He blew a shrill, loud blast, and Tawny, trained to sit facing him on this command, instead lay cowering under the rough bench on the blind's back wall. *Whrrrt!* Reed blew again. "Tawny, come! Come, girl! *Now!*"

When she refused to move, he grabbed her collar and dragged her, skidding on her paws, toward the opening. He blew the whistle a third time and gave a hand signal, pointing toward the fallen ducks, but the moment he released her collar, she collapsed and hunkered down again.

"*Fetch!*" he shouted, the muscle popping in his lower jaw. "*Fetch, goddamnit! Go!*"

The dog looked up with seductive submissiveness and beat a tattoo with her tail, trembling violently. Gobbets of saliva pelted the weathered floorboards, spreading to dark dimes.

"I think she wants her kibble."

Reed turned a murderous look on Joe.

"GET YOUR ASS OUT THERE AND FETCH THAT DUCK!" he boomed. His shy sweetness gone, he once more sounded ominously like Jimmy.

"Take it easy, Reed. I don't think she understands."

"I spent two hundred and fifty dollars sending her to training school," he bellowed. "She'd better understand. *Get out there! Go on! Go!*"

Beside himself, he scooped up the dog and threw her, squirming, out into the water, where she went under and bobbed up, paddling furiously, a look of solemn panic in her hazel eyes. Paying no attention to the ducks, she swam back toward the blind, then veered away, afraid to come in. Blowing repeated whistle blasts, Reed stood frantically signaling, like an oversized Boy Scout signing some demented semaphore.

After a while she waded ashore and slunk off, her drenched tail tucked between her legs. In disgust, Reed cocked his arm and threw the whistle into the pond, which swallowed it without a splash.

"Shouldn't we go get her?"

"Fuck her, let her go," Reed said. "If she gets lost, it serves her right. I hope she does. I'm going to get the ducks." And he slid off the platform.

"Be careful. It's deep," Joe called, but his brother trudged grimly on, agitating the black surface of the mirror.

Taking the leash, Joe tracked the dog back down the trail they'd followed in, calling her in a soothing voice. Each time she heard her name, she wagged her tail doubtfully, but when he approached, she crept away again. They were halfway to the car before she let him apprehend her, lying down fatalistically as he clipped her collar ring. "All right, Mighty Mouse," Joe said, and the moment she realized he wasn't going to punish her, she perked up and began to frisk, ready for new adventure.

Walking back, he caught sight of Reed from a distance. On the hummock, he stood exactly as before, his left arm propped straight out against the tree, head bowed. In the time it took Joe to cover the intervening ground, perhaps five minutes, Reed never moved.

"Need some assistance there?" Joe called.

"No, thanks." His voice sounded small, deflated.

"Get the ducks?"

He shook his head, not looking back.

"I ran into a friend of yours."

Reed nodded. "Hey, girl."

At his voice, Tawny wagged her tail, the rest forgotten.

Joe stood there for another awkward beat. "You okay?"

Reed made a face. "I'm having trouble peeing."

"So I noticed."

"Did you ever feel like you couldn't go till you got grounded?"

"Grounded?" Joe felt the laugh reflex trigger and defuse. "What do you mean, electrically?"

"Yeah." He regarded Joe with a strained expression, a crease between his brows. "It doesn't have to be metal, though—just something that conducts."

Joe stared at his arm, still touching the tree. "Not really."

"Do you think it's possible?" Reed asked. "Scientifically?"

"I don't know."

Taking Joe's answer as reproof, Reed nodded and looked down. "I know it's kind of weird. I just find it easier to let go if I'm holding on to something." He zipped up and turned around.

"Maybe you could hot-wire your pecker to that D-cell in your socks."

"Huh, huh, huh," Reed laughed raggedly. "Huh, huh, huh."

He knelt and snapped his fingers for the dog, wincing and turning his face aside as Tawny eagerly lapped his face. "What's wrong with you, girl? I did everything they said."

"You can't really blame her. I wouldn't want to go in that cold water either, would you?"

"That's what she's bred for, Joey," Reed said with a look that hurt his brother's heart.

"She may have a better future as a house pet, bruh. That's a noble occupation, too."

Reed's face went sad. "I wanted her to hunt."

Joe knelt, facing him. "Have you been taking your medication, Reed?"

"Yeah."

"Is it helping?"

"I don't know. Some. It just makes it hard to pee, is all, and . . . you know, other things."

"Sexually?"

The muscle in Reed's jaw corded once again. "Yeah." He looked away. "You remember Leora?"

"The girl you're dating?"

"She found out I was manic."

"And?"

"We broke up." Reed stood up and brushed off his knees. "I guess you can't really blame her."

"Why not?" Joe said. "I blame her. I blame the hell out of her."

"Wouldn't you do the same, if it was you?" Reed stared at him. There was no intentional reproach, but something in his expression made Joe wonder whether he would have; whether, in fact, he had.

"I would," Reed said mildly. "Only it's kind of hard to break up with yourself." He started to laugh but broke into a croupy smoker's cough. Watching Reed wade toward the blind, Joe remembered coming home from Columbia that first time and driving with May to the private clinic outside Richmond, nestled inconspicuously amidst woods and hills. There he found his brother, disastrously thin, in pants from which the belt had been removed and laceless shoes, sitting on his narrow bedstead, gazing blankly out the window toward the James River and the rich fields beyond, where the plow still regularly turned up old musket balls and the bones of the Confederate and Union dead. The moment he saw Joe, Reed covered his face with his big hands and wept in a way his older brother, already a student of behavior, had never seen a human being do before. And he said, "I'm sorry, Joey, I'm sorry," repeating it again and again in shame, apologizing for what his older brother didn't know.

As Joe held him, whispering, "It's okay, Reed," he looked to May for some clue to what Reed's illness meant and what would be required of him, but his mother, answerless herself, simply stared at him with streaming, imponderable black eyes. And Joe had run.

Returning to Columbia, he'd discovered his keen interest in the Balinese. He'd been running ever since. Even now, watching Reed wade toward the blind, Joe had to fight down the flight reflex, as visceral and strong as the need to breathe.

Yet it occurred to him, today, that there was no place left to run. In the somber daylight, the vastness of the marsh, the overarching sky above their heads, all nature seemed to press in like the four walls of a doorless room that there was no escape from—no beyond, no outdoors to escape to: the outdoors was the room.

As Joe joined Reed in the blind, it began to snow, a few large flakes at first, falling straight in the still air like tiny parachutes, a white army airdropped in, hitting the black pool and dissolving with a hiss, transformed into the thing they came to fight.

Reed passed out another sandwich and poured the last half-cup of coffee, tepid now. "They say as long as you think you may be crazy, you probably aren't."

"So I've heard," Joe affirmed without enthusiasm.

"Only I don't think I'm crazy, so maybe I am." The grin that flashed back now, Joe realized, was Reed's response to being terrified. As he tried to light a cigarette, his hands trembled so violently that Joe had to bite his tongue to keep from offering help.

"Mom's scared I'm going to kill myself, isn't she?"

"No. What makes you think that?" Joe answered with a trace of heat.

"Isn't that why she asked you to come with me?"

"She never said anything like that, Reed. Why? Is it something you've thought about?"

He shrugged. "I guess I've thought about it. I'd never do it, though. I'm too much of a wimp."

"Not killing yourself isn't being a wimp," Joe said. "It's the opposite."

"Not for me. I'm scared it might hurt too much." He broke into his wheezing, croupy laugh, and Joe felt as though someone had split him open with a knife and gutted him.

The snow fell harder, and Reed toweled off Tawny and spread her blanket in the corner, tender now after the tirade. The dog sat facing him, attentive and obedient, and Reed opened his sandwich and fed her the meat, piece by piece, and stroked her ears, giving her so much more finally, in her failure, than she would have earned through a success. Joe thought of their mother, the way she treated all of them, but Reed especially, and would have treated him, too, if some instinct for self-preservation hadn't made him run. He wondered once again, as he had many times, long ago when they were children, if Reed possessed that instinct, or enough of it. Maybe that was why May indulged him, because she had the same question, and what to Joe seemed excess was offered as a form of consolation for what she wasn't able to repair.

"This snow looks pretty serious," he said. "Maybe we should go before the path gets covered up."

"There's not much chance of getting lost out here," Reed said. "You just face east and go."

"You want to stay?"

He shrugged. "Nah. The visibility's closing down, and I don't really feel like hunting anymore."

In the fishhouse lot, the Wagoneer was slowly piling up with snow. Reed popped the Blazer's hood, and Joe fetched the cables and connected the two batteries.

Exhausted by the morning's ordeal, Tawny had been prostrate on the drive, but the minute Reed got out, she began to whine and pace in the back seat. "It's okay, girl," he said, "I'm not going anywhere."

Giving the dead battery a minute to warm up, the brothers stood silent, stamping their feet, Reed hatless, shoulders hunched, hands shoved deep in his pockets. From the marsh across the road, they could hear the restless chortling of a flock of tundra swans.

"Remember leaving her at Nanny's?"

"Who?" Joe asked.

"Tawny?"

Joe shook his head. "When was this?"

"After the divorce," Reed said. "When we moved to Winston, to the Sans Souci? They didn't allow pets in the apartments, so we had to drop her off at Nanny's house. You don't remember that?"

"Was I there?"

"Maybe you were still at school," he said. "After the movers left, we went to say goodbye. Nanny was standing on the front steps in those cat shades she wore, the ones with glitter on the frames and little bat wings on the temples?"

Joe smiled, remembering.

"I'll bet she didn't weigh a hundred pounds by then," Reed said. "She looked so old. And Mama was crying, and Gray started, too. I don't think he was more than two. Tawny wouldn't get out of the back seat. She just lay there, whining, and I had to drag her up the steps to Nanny. But the minute we started pulling down the drive, Tawny broke away and came after us as fast as she could go. I looked back through the window and yelled, 'She's coming! Hit it, Mom!' And Gray screamed, 'Hit it, Mom!' copying me. Mom was bawling, and she floored it. It was like a getaway. And here comes

Tawny up the street, kind of hobbling and galloping at once. We're all blubbering, and I'm yelling, 'Go, goddamnit, go!' Mom went straight through the stop sign and fishtailed onto Raleigh Road, and when Tawny came around the corner, she skidded on her claws and rolled into the ditch, and when she got up, she started running back and forth across the road. She couldn't catch us; we had too big a lead. And then we couldn't see her anymore, and Mom kept driving and no one said a word."

"What made you remember that?"

"I was thinking, I guess we left her after all."

Joe felt his eyes turn suddenly hot. "No one's leaving anyone." He put a hand on his brother's massive shoulder.

"I know," Reed said. For a moment, though, his eyes engaged Joe's with a rare directness, and he smiled an unresentful and completely disbelieving smile as snowflakes filled his lashes and mustache and turned his black hair prematurely white.

"I'm okay, Joey," he said.

"Are you?" Reed let the echo of the question die away.

"I'll catch you at home."

As he drove away, he touched the horn and spooked the flock of swans, which rose like snow within the snow, the one flying upward in defiance of the force that made the other fall, or subject to another force, more tenuous than gravity, obscure and difficult to name. Gaining altitude, they formed an angled wedge, rippling as they circled and started south, on their way now, following something in the blood, deeper than remembrance. Joe wondered what force was leading them. Their hoarse braying honk supplied no answer, merely growing fainter as they grew faint and disappeared into the snow.

Sixteen

By the time Joe arrived, the party was already well advanced.

In an old sun hat of May's bedecked with large petunias, Gray stood beside the TV, one arm akimbo, mimicking Vi as she twitted George Bailey in downtown Bedford Falls. Everyone was howling, even Reed, who'd barely beat his brother home. In a state of helpless dissolution, he chuffed and wheezed, wiping tears as they rolled down his cheeks.

"The Iceman cometh!" Gray shouted as Joe walked into the hoedown.

"Behold, Grim Creeper!" Reed.

"Y'all, y'all, stop! Stop it now! Stop!" May, in fits, stirred her Bloody Mary and tasted off her fingertip.

"Ahoy, there, matey! Arrr!" Converted to their jolly, doubtful cause, Day squinted as she flexed her long, attractive arm.

"Hi, guys." Joe's smile for them was game but uninspired. His observant eye went to the almost empty pitcher on the table, the stalks of leafy celery like bromeliads, obscenely prospering in a medium of blood.

"What's the matter, sweetie? Don't you have the Christmas spirit?" May asked, attuned more closely than he wished.

"Sure," he said. "Sure, I do. I'm just a little beat."

"Fix a drink and come relax and watch," Day suggested.

"I think I'm going to take a bath and read a bit."

"Yo, Ebenezer!" Gray said. "You can't defect! We're almost at the good part. Clarence is about to come."

"Come on, sit down with us," Day coaxed, patting the arm of her chair.

Joe hesitated, then settled his hand lightly on her shoulder and, still standing, looked at the TV.

It was the moment everything goes wrong for George. Uncle Billy has lost the money. George has yelled at everyone; he's overturned his old drafting table, the one on which he'd intended to sketch skyscrapers and bridges for the cities of the future he was going to build. Finally, Mary yells at George, and Jimmy Stewart, mumbling an apology his family can't accept, stumbles out into the snow without his coat as Donna Reed picks up the phone.

Joe watched the antique images flicker and, after only a few moments, turned away.

"You can't leave now," Gray said. "We're almost at the bridge."

"To be honest, I was never a big fan of this film."

"What! You don't like *It's a Wonderful Life*?" Gray made a cross as if to ward away the Antichrist.

Joe smiled. "You guys go ahead and watch."

"We're going to see if we can find a tree a little later," May said. "Should we wait for you?"

"I'll see you when you get back."

"Hey, Joey?"

At the hail, Joe turned back at the bedroom door.

Gray, one arm akimbo, doing Vi. " 'Don't you ever get tired of just *readin'* about things?' "

"Good one," Joe said, exiting stage right, pursued by Reed's gleeful catcall: "REOW!"

Steeping in the bath, feeling the thaw work slowly into his cold limbs, he heard the merry wassailers depart amidst a volley of bluff cheers.

And the house, returning to familiar stillness, once more was his.

Restored and warmed, grateful for a solitary interlude, he poured a drink of his stepfather's liquor and sat down in his rocker with his father's Verne. Wincing at the bourbon's sting, he felt the small explosion deep within and then the liquor's ease dilating like a gentle shock wave slowly from ground zero. As Joe opened to his place, he stopped and looked around the room.

Something in the house seemed strange this afternoon. Sounds were muted, and the light had taken on a curious amber tone like museum light. After a moment, he realized that Gray had put up the storm panels while he and Reed were in the marsh. On the east side, they were already salting up, obscuring the view, lending a gauzy vagueness to the tufts of spindrift clinging to the thumping screens.

> *One day, perhaps, some volcanic eruption would bring these sunken ruins back to the surface! Numerous underwater volcanoes have indeed been reported in this part of the ocean and many ships have felt inexplicable tremors as they sailed over these tormented depths. Who knows but what, at some time in the distant future, through the accumulation of volcanic eruptions and of successive layers of lava, these glowing mountaintops may not appear on the surface of the Atlantic!*

What had possessed his father to underscore this passage, along with so many others? Joe imagined him, twenty-five or thirty years before, sitting perhaps in this very chair, reading the words and, stirred by some thought or feeling, reaching for his pen. Now across the years the message washed up in the bottle. Joe could only partly decipher it, yet it evoked a troubled bittersweetness. The passage was about Atlantis, a great civilization that sank into the sea.

He closed the book and threw a log on the fire, setting out in search of simpler occupation. A hand or two of Idiot's Delight seemed just his speed. Once upon a time, on an inclement day like this, his grandmother, Nanny Tilley, had taught him how to play the game. Looking for cards in the coffee table drawer, Joe found a broken set of crayons and a coloring book from the 1970s, featuring Penelope Pitstop, the perpetual damsel in distress, kidnapped every Saturday morning and rescued by her faithful canine friend. The bold color scheme and careful work revealed the *auteur* as his baby brother, Gray. He'd had a powerful fascination with these characters when he was two or three, around the time Joe went away to boarding school, the same time May and Jimmy got divorced. Rifling the bookcase cabinets, Joe found a Ouija board and a stack of ancient board games, War and Clue. No cards, though.

Finally, he went into his parents' bedroom—though May and Sumner's now, Joe still thought of it that way. This scuffed lay line, the oldest and deepest, was one down which Joe rarely ventured anymore. Avoiding his reflection in his mother's dressing table mirror, he sat down on the bench and stared at her vials of ointments and cosmetics, as obscure as an alchemist's retorts. There was a small frosted bottle of perfume with a blown-glass stopper in the shape of wings. He took it out and sniffed. It was a scent she no longer wore. Joe recognized it, though. He put the stopper back. There were just a few drops left.

One by one, he tried the banked drawers on the side without result. Yet as the bottom one creaked open, with a musty whiff of rust and woolens, he found his grandmother's old jigsaw puzzle of a Paris street scene, the Champs-Élyseés under snow, coal smoke in the air and horse-drawn wagons. Joe hadn't seen this in twelve or thirteen years and had assumed it was long gone. Yet he should have known; his mother was a packrat from a long, illustrious line. She threw nothing away, unlike her son, who'd jettisoned it all. Joe recognized the artist as Utrillo now.

As he lifted it out, his eye fell on a yellowed folder underneath. With a deckle edge and a double border of gold piping, it had a photographer's tag line embossed in the lower right-hand corner: "CANDID" BY BYRON WELLS, STATE LINE, SOUTH CAROLINA. Flipping it open, Joe discovered a black-and-white eight-by-ten of a well-dressed couple, college-aged, standing at the curb before the open door of a white Chevrolet, a 'fifty-five Bel Air. He recognized the car before he recognized the couple.

Younger than he'd ever known her, ten years younger than he was now, in a dark dress and a wide-brimmed hat that looked as if it might have sheltered generations in its shade, May clutched a pair of elbow-length gloves in one hand, the other fiddling with a spray of stephanotis in Jimmy's buttonhole.

Like an alcoholic gazing at the deep-sea twinkle of an ice cube bobbing in a glass of gin, Joe blinked and blinked again, realizing what this was: a wedding photograph. And he could hear his mother:

You know that old dirt turnoff back of Pa and Nanny's house? Y'all might not remember it, but that was where your

Daddy parked the car to wait for me. He had one suit and fifty dollars for the license, and every time a car went by, he ducked so the headlights wouldn't hit his face.

In his mind's eye, Joe saw her, May, the way he best remembered her, twenty-eight or -nine, dressed to go out for the evening, sitting on the foot of Reed's bed in the room they'd shared. As she began the story, she always lit a cigarette from the pack of Pall Malls in her lap, the same color as her lipstick, the same color as her summer dress.

"Me," she went on, smiling through the inhalation, "I lay awake in bed till everybody was asleep, and then, at quarter past eleven, I tiptoed in my stocking feet down the back stairs and ran across the yard . . ."

"The grass was wet," Reed would remind her with a trace of sternness, vigilant to see that their mother made no errors, omitted no details in the tale he frequently petitioned.

"Yes, it was," May confirmed.

"And you tore your stockings, didn't you?"

Smiling, she made her eyes go wide. "You know, I think I did."

"What did you do with them?"

"I can't remember, sweetie. I guess I took them off."

"Mama!"

"Y'all go to sleep now."

"But why did y'all run off instead of getting married in a church?" Reed asked with a note of urgency as May began to stir, though he knew this answer, too, but saved it, the best for last.

"Because we were so much in love we couldn't stand to wait," their mother whispered. "Sweet dreams now, children. Go to sleep." And crushing her Pall Mall in the clamshell ashtray balanced in her lap, she leaned down and applied a crimson imprint to Reed's brow.

The story always lasted precisely through the smoking of one cigarette and ended the same place.

In his bed across from Reed's, Joey listened to this story, keenly interested, and for a long time, the whole unbroken skein of days that formed their childhood, on which those summer nights were strung like pearls, there had been a bright conviction in his mother's tone that he believed. Listening to her interchange with

Reed, Joey's love of things predictable was cultivated and advanced.

As she tiptoed out, May always checked on him as well, but Joey, too old for such maternal ministerings, closed his eyes and pretended to be asleep.

Numberless times throughout his childhood, he'd heard this story, as familiar as the arcane credos of the Nicene Creed. Yet until that moment, Christmas Eve of 1982, when he was twenty-eight, Joe had never seen the photographs commemorating these events. Here they were. Here was the church, here the steeple, here State Line, the seedy South Carolina border town whose only claim to civic fame was that it provided rushed weddings, cheap, with no blood test and few questions asked.

Behind the brand-new car, behind the bride and groom, on the chapel steps, the elderly minister and his wife gaze into the camera, the gender of their pale, slightly bloated faces distinguishable only through his baldness and her hair. Around them, ranked on either side, stand the Tilleys and the Maddens, May's and Jimmy's parents. An Old Gold dangling off her lip and a string of pearls as big as grapes around her neck, Zelle Tilley—Joe's Nanny— holds a box that says Mahatma Rice in one hand, the other cocked to throw. Holding his fedora at his waist, Joe's Pa looks sweetly frazzled, his tie askew and the "two-mile strand" of side- hair he raked across his bald spot sticking up, a small prank at his expense. Jimmy's father, Thurston Madden, principal of Killdeer High, a stern man with steel-rimmed glasses and a ramrod spine, grasps a small boutonniere with large, uncertain fingers, a shy, almost sheepish grin on his normally uncompromising face. Only Jimmy's mother, Lilith, manages to look composed, flashing a so- cial smile as glib and depthless as a mirror.

As he studied the picture, Joe's forehead slowly creased. Around him, his mother's bedroom darkened, like a Southern spinster's parlor in July, as though a cloud had passed across the sun.

For no reason Joe could identify, a premonition stole over him. He homed in on Jimmy's face and found the trouble there. Where May wears the coquettish smile of a young debutante, the result of years of covert social training, the sort of smile that can mean any- thing you want it to, his father's expression is another story and an open book. Six-six and a hundred and eighty pounds, if that,

Jimmy faces the camera squarely, settled in himself in a way that makes the picture seem clairvoyant, like an X ray. Not smiling, clasping his hands in front of him in a pose of forbearance, he looks more like a pallbearer than a groom. His eyes, however, shine with an almost fevered cast. Twenty-one years old, he looks like George Bailey on the siding in Bedford Falls, listening to the lonesome whistle of the freight train slowly moving toward a future he's imagined and will never see, laden with the cargo of his dreams.

Joe realized that of all the many faces his father wore throughout his boyhood, this was the face he remembered best. It seared him now as it once had in the trailer beside the lake, listening to Jimmy scratch a line out in his notebook at the kitchen table then crumple up the page, scratch another and crumple that, while Joey watched the Boys of Summer through the snowstorm on the TV set, going down the batting order, waiting for Maris's at-bat.

Mesmerized, Joe continued staring. From the big room, he could hear the green wood in the fireplace hissing as the sap came to a boil, bleeding out of the cut ends. There was a loud pop and a whistle, followed by a strange low noise, like birdsong in a summer wood.

Hearing that sound, for one brief instant Joe felt himself poised on a swaying rope bridge over an abyss. Far below, a distance not in space but in time, his father's young face was the rushing torrent tempting him to leap.

Jerking back from it like someone starting from a dream, he stood up and quickly left the room.

Seventeen

The tree lot at the mall—manned by a blue-lipped surfer boy in a Peruvian wool hat, who kept blowing in his gloveless hands—had been pretty well picked over by the time we got there.

"A Scotch pine?" May replied to his suggestion, huddled in her swath of mink. "No, thank you. If I wanted a Scotch pine, I'd give these boys a hatchet and send them out to Nags Head Woods. To me, there's nothing worse than a Scotch pine. Don't you agree, Day?"

"Yes, ma'am," I said, though we'd always had Scotch pines and liked them well enough. At that particular moment, though, a little looped, I was preoccupied with a comic vision: Reed and Gray, with shouldered axes, entering the wilderness astride a large blue ox named Babe.

"Especially all tackied up with tinsel," she went on. "And those big colored bulbs they use?" She wrinkled her attractive nose. "Hate them. Myself, I only like the teeny white ones. Now don't you have a fir?"

"No, ma'am," said Surfer Boy, failing to appreciate the esthetic lesson he was getting free of charge. "I do have a couple spruces left, though."

May made a small *moue*. "Well, I'd prefer a fir, but if spruce is all you have, spruce, I suppose, will have to do. Give us the biggest one you've got."

With the Bunyan brothers' assistance, the attendant trussed the tree—a mildly misshapen giant with a bald spot in back destined to go against the wall—and lassoed it to the top of the Mercedes.

Back home, we found Sumner—whose golfing afternoon had been rerouted by the weather to the nineteenth hole and a Hollywood or two of high-stakes gin—mixing eggnog in May's sterling punch bowl. "There y'all are. I was starting to worry."

"We got the tree," May said. "Did you have fun?"

"Lost everything except my shirt." His smile was unperturbed. "I managed to spread around consid'able Christmas cheer, though. Those other boys thought Santa Claus had come to town. Come try my eggnog."

May tasted from the dipper. "Mmm."

"Need anything?"

"Maybe just a pinch of cloves?"

Sumner smiled at me. "Dr. Shaughnessey, a cup for you?"

My glance slipped involuntarily toward the kitchen clock. It was a little after three.

"No," May said preemptively. "Don't look. It's Christmas Eve. The rule of five o'clock does not apply."

"Maybe a glass of wine."

The doctor nodded his approval. "Good girl."

"Me, too!" cried May, and, following her to the kitchen, I poured two healthy gouts of Almaden and plunked the ice cubes in.

"So were you surprised when he went into anthropology?" I asked, continuing our intermittent conversation on a topic that interested us both, namely, her eldest, an investment in which I had acquired a few small shares.

"Surprised?" Turning from the fridge with two quarts of oysters in her arms, another prized beneath her chin, she laughed. "I couldn't even spell it, sugar . . . Now, tell me, you do like scalloped oysters, don't you?"

"Scalloped oysters? I'm not sure I've ever had them," I confessed.

"Day! You can't be serious!" She gave me a heartfelt look, as though I'd informed her of my tragic childhood, an orphan stealing loaves of bread. "Never?"

"No, ma'am."

"Well, come right here and let me show you. This was Mama's

recipe. Of course, Mama never really cooked. Our maid did. But the recipe came from Mama's *side,* you see. Now there's really nothing to it, just oysters with the juice and saltine crackers." And she proceeded to demonstrate, pouring the quarts into a Pyrex baking dish, adding milk and pulverizing the sleeved crackers— *thwack, thwack!*—on the island countertop. Last of all, she cut two sticks of butter into pats and sprinkled them on top. "And, voilá, ready for the oven!" She nodded down at our mysteriously diminished glasses. "And don't look at the clock."

I shrugged with happy fatalism. "Damn the torpedoes."

"Damn 'em!" May cried. "Now let's go find those ornaments! Aren't we having fun?"

Though I think her question was rhetorical, I answered anyway. "I am."

"Are you? I'm so glad." She lifted a heavy key ring from the hook by the front door, and we started down the stairs. "Because you never know, sugar, do you? It's always a little—what's the word?—well, touch and go is all I mean. Now I remember Mama—when I started dating the boys' father? First, it was Jimmy's hair; he had a duckbill. Then it was his clothes. The first time he came to meet her, he had on purple corduroys with stovepipe legs and two-tone shoes and one of those black-and-white checked sweater vests, and he weighed about a hundred soaking wet. He looked like Jughead from the comic book, so help me God he did. Mama took one look and flared her nostrils. 'Who is this, the flimflam man?' she said. 'Mama, Jimmy's a poet,' I told her. 'He's flam*boy*ant.' And she said, 'Hmph.' Poets and flamboyancy weren't way high up on Mama's list. And Jimmy's mother, Lilith, was the same to me. The more I did to please her, the more she found to criticize. I hated that woman, Day, simply *hated* her." Lowering her voice confidentially, May made the confession with a gusto I couldn't help admiring.

"But why on earth am I telling you all this?" she asked as we entered the garage. "Oh, I know what it was—I was wondering why it is mothers have such problems when their children bring somebody home. I swore I'd never do that to my own, and I don't think I have. I've liked all Joey's friends. But I probably shouldn't say that, should I?"

"As long as I'm your favorite."

My boldness apparently took her by surprise, if only briefly. "Well, you certainly are!" she said, breaking out in a delighted smile. "You *certainly* are!" She squeezed my arm. "Me, though, Day, my principle was always, whatever Mama and Daddy did, do the opposite, and I followed it from marrying Jimmy right on down the line. And then, of course, you wake up one day as old as they were, older than you thought you'd ever be, and you realize they knew a lot more than you thought they did and wish you'd listened. But you can't go back, can you? What about you, sugar? Are your parents . . ."

"My dad's retired," I said. "My mom died when I was twelve."

"Oh, Day, I'm so sorry." That mist bloomed in her eyes again. There was a rich and ready empathy in May, not lacking in her son, but so dispassionate in Joe. His mother, by contrast, was a fierce and unapologetic sectary, in that way more like me. Listening to emotion play, in her, its natural music made it easier for me to recognize the damaged note in Joe; made me wonder, too, given his luck in mothering, exactly where and how the damage had occurred.

"Saints preserve us," May said as the door to the back room of the garage creaked inward. "I simply have to get down here and organize. I've been meaning to for years."

The dingy overhead revealed a large shuttered room, refrigerator cold and littered with an unpredictable assortment, like a dynastic tag sale offering several generations' rejected treasure. Along one wall, stacks of boxes mounted almost to the ceiling, where the bare joists were covered with milky cobwebs. A silting of dust had found its way, wind-driven, through the heavy shutters, which kept out all but an occasional knife edge of daylight. There were jumbles of chairs with broken rockers, rush seats that had given way. On an old sleigh bed, too small for any modern grown-up, I saw a porcelain Bopeep, her shepherd's staff snapped off and laid aside, a dark question mark against the ivory counterpane beside an ailing sheep.

There were piles of fine old linens and two sets of lead-crystal glasses—the first monogrammed with T, the other, M, one line extinguished, the other superseded, wedding presents that reproached the vow whose making they had been engraved to celebrate, yet too expensive to discard.

"Look at this." May held up a yellowed *Washington Post*, announcing Nixon's resignation in bold type. Protected, the four copies beneath looked fresh. These sat on a rusted filing cabinet with a collection of picture books—*The Brothers Grimm for Children, Mother Goose*. Delving beneath them, May unearthed a Bible with a scuffed leather binding and an antique brass clasp.

"My Lord. I haven't seen this since Daddy's funeral. I thought my sister June had stolen it."

As she opened it, a pressed flower, no longer recognizable by type, fell from the pages of the Old Testament. Written in an old-fashioned penmanship with elaborate flourishes and arabesques, the first entry was the record of a wedding that had taken place in Bel Air, Maryland, in 1701, the year the Act of Settlement was made by which no Roman Catholic could be crowned king of England—the date came back to me from Blessed Sacrament, where I remembered red-faced Sister Frederica, still irate at the injustice after two hundred and seventy-odd years, calling June the twelfth a day of infamy. The name Tilley first appeared toward the bottom of the page, in 1746, the year Bonnie Prince Charlie and the Jacobites went down on Culloden's stony field.

As May shared the book with me, I watched as, page by page, entered in other hands and different colored inks, the family gradually migrated southward through Virginia, and finally into North Carolina. Most of the entries had been made at a place called Rose Hill in Killdeer County—births, baptisms, confirmations. The last two entries were a wedding and a funeral. MAY TILLEY AND JAMES MADDEN, M. THIS DAY, SEPTEMBER 21, 1954. WILLIAM G. TILLEY, D. SEPTEMBER 2, 1966.

"Your father?"

She nodded. "Labor Day Monday. I remember leaving here that night, following the ambulance back home. I thought everything was over, my marriage to Jimmy, too. I was pregnant, though. I didn't know it then."

"With Gray?"

She nodded. "I didn't find out till the week after the funeral. I would have left Jimmy otherwise. I probably should have anyway. I told myself I was staying for the children's sake, but I'm not sure it did them any good . . . Poor Gray; I need to put him in here. He always seems to get left out." She sighed and closed the book. "Look, there it is."

She pointed to an old steamer trunk partially concealed beneath a child's deflated life raft.

"Now let me ask you something, sugar," she said as she opened it and lifted out a blown-glass ball. "May I?"

"Sure."

"Did Joey seem all right to you when he came in?" The fretful little furrow I knew from her son's face appeared between her brows.

"A little down, maybe."

"That's what I thought, too. Maybe it was just the movie, though. I have to say, I agree with him on that. I always found it terribly depressing."

"*It's a Wonderful Life*? But it's so uplifting!"

She frowned, considering. "Well, I suppose the ending is, but he has to go through so much tunnel to get to that one little bit of light. Or maybe it's because it was Jimmy's favorite movie. Jimmy always reminded me of—what's his name, the one Jimmy Stewart plays?"

"George Bailey."

"George Bailey. When we started out, he had those same big dreams, to see the world and do important things. That may be why Joey doesn't like it. But you were asking me something . . ."

"How you felt when he went into anthropology."

"Oh, right! Right! I completely lost my train! What on earth possessed him, Day, I couldn't comprehend, not for the life of me. But you know what I think now? Bali and Little Roanoke, these threatened places where he goes? When he was small, I think Joey wanted more than anything to keep his father and me together, to save our marriage and the family, and of course he couldn't. No child can. In his heart, though, I think that's what he's still doing— trying to do for someone else what he never could for us."

She dropped this casual jewel in my lap, a lump of glistening uranium, and held my stare, her black eyes as grave and studious as Joe's.

And speaking of the devil, at that moment we both turned and found him there, silent as a Cherokee, standing on the threshold in deep meditation over us.

"Sweetie!" May cried, putting her hand on her bosom. "You scared me half to death! How long have you been there?"

"Not long."

"Look what we found!" She handed him the Bible, and he dutifully examined it with careful hands, his manner that of someone feigning respectful interest while preoccupied with something else. He put it on the trunk and laid a yellowed folder down on top. "I found something, too."

"What's this?" The brightness in May's voice underwent a dampening.

"Open it," he said, and there was a quietness in his tone as well.

She opened it, and I saw a photo of a young deb with gloves draped, just so, in the crook of her elbow and a hat the likes of which you don't see anymore except on Paris runways. The young May was a dead knockout and knew it, too, gazing at the camera as though seeking its approval and not about to be denied, charming the pants off everything in sight.

What interested me as much or more was Jimmy Madden. Lucifer incarnate turned out to be a tall, skinny boy with Bozo-sized shoes and a pimple on his chin. Maybe it was having watched the movie, but he did resemble a young Jimmy Stewart, a baggy suit draped on coat-hanger limbs, only darker and with that same soulful, incompletely reconciled expression that Joe wore in certain moods and slants of light—that he was wearing now, in fact, as I saw when I looked up.

"Where on earth . . . ?" May said, amazed.

"It was in your dressing table drawer. I was looking for a deck of cards." His expression as he answered her was questioning, marked by delicacy, yet the observation light was on.

For several seconds, they held each other's stare. What the moment was about, I couldn't tell, except that something was afoot.

And then in came Reed and Gray, like Dogberry and Bottom wandering into the wrong play, interrupting an intimate domestic scene between Prince Hamlet and the queen.

"We got the tree up, Mom. Come look," said Gray, eating a Hostess cupcake and swilling Jolt out of a thirty-two-ounce go-cup.

"What's this?" Like a guided missile, Reed instantly homed in on the picture, leaning down to look.

"Mom, is that *you?*" Gray picked up the folder. "That hat! That hat is *too* outstanding! You look like Audrey Hepburn in *Breakfast at Tiffany's.*"

"More like Audrey Hepburn being beamed aboard a UFO," Reed said, grabbing it out of his hand.

"Give that back, you butt!" Gray said, leaping as Reed held it out of reach above his head.

"Don't you dare make fun of my hat," May said, laughing with relief. "It came from Fanney's in Rocky Mount. It was very *comme il faut.*"

"*Comme il faux pas.*" Defeated by his own bad pun, yet chuffing anyway, Reed relaxed his guard, and Gray snagged the folder.

"What *is* this, Mom?"

"It's the elopement, dimwit," Reed replied.

Gray's eyes widened and his jaw went slack. "What elopement? You *eloped*?"

"Come on, you've heard that story," Reed said in that tone of elder-sibling Weltschmerz.

"I have not!" Gray answered with offended innocence. "In case you haven't noticed, no one ever tells me anything around this place!"

"Don't whine, Gilligan. Tell him, May," Reed said.

"Sweetheart, that was all so long ago." She cast a complex glance at Joe, who stood in the center of the room, unhappily upstaged. "I doubt I even remember it."

"Sure you do," said Reed. "Daddy parked at that old turnoff in the woods, the one that leads to Collie Pond . . ."

May's smile acknowledged an ebullience she failed to share.

"Daddy had one suit and fifty dollars for the minister," Reed went on, prompting. "Every time a car went by he ducked. . . ."

"What are Pa and Nanny doing there?"

Reed broke off, and everybody turned to Joe.

"What do you mean, sweetie?" May asked, aspiring toward innocence.

"Pa and Nanny," Joe repeated in that voice one note too soft. "And Dad's parents. If you eloped, what are they doing there?"

The question seemed to stymie her, but only for a moment. "Oh," she said, "well, you know what I think happened? I think we went back later and had the pictures taken."

"You went back later," Joe said. "To State Line?"

"I think that's what we must have done," she said. "To have something to show?"

"But that's past Charlotte, Mom," Reed said, catching on. "That's three hours at least. Three and a half. Each way."

In the pin-drop silence, Gray, with a troubled expression, looked from his brothers to his mother and then back.

"Well, I don't know!" May said with a note of petulance, reaching for her cigarettes. "I don't see how you can expect me to remember every little detail that far back."

"That's right!" Gray said, stepping up to her defense. "What's the big deal? Stop giving her the third degree!"

As Joe listened, the gravity in his expression deepened together with the tenderness, and the furrow he and his mother shared appeared between his brows.

May, inhaling, raised her face toward the cobwebbed ceiling and closed her eyes, and when she opened them again, she rested their full weight on Joe like a weary animal at the end of a long hunt, asking for the mercy stroke.

They weighed each other—son and mother. Joe clearly had no relish in the task he'd taken on, yet neither did he waver or retreat. And then, without fanfare, he turned and walked away, the only time I ever saw him, in pursuit, relent and let his quarry go.

Eighteen

"Joey?"

Standing in the square of worldlight at the end of the dark tunnel of the garage, Joe, like Orpheus, turned back. "Sweetheart . . ." When she overtook him, May clutched his arm and searched his face.

"There was no elopement, was there?" He posed the query softly.

"I thought you knew," May said.

Surprised, he blinked and pondered this and blinked once more. "How would I have known?"

"I'm sorry, Joey, I . . ."

"No," he said with a fierce note, then "no," again, more gently. "Don't apologize," he said. "Not to me, not for this."

"Joey . . ."

"I understand," he said. "You didn't have a choice." And he kissed her upturned brow and walked out into the light at the tunnel's end, into the rushing wind.

His intention was to keep walking, but when he reached the gazebo, his resolve deserted him and he sat down. The temperature had risen into the forties, erasing the last trace of snow, but the wind had picked up, and below him now the black sea was boiling out long streaks of storm-tossed confection.

Because we were so much in love we couldn't stand to wait. In his mind's eye, May once more in her red dress, sitting on Reed's bed with her Pall Malls and the clamshell washed up from the deep on a storm tide like this, balanced on her knees and filled with ash. . . .

Something else came back to Joe, another question Reed had asked back then: "And you still are, right, Mama? You still love Daddy, don't you?" This had crept into the catechism only toward the end, unasked till then as unrequired.

And up until the end, May had always made the same reply. "Of course I do. I'll always love your daddy." But then one summer night in 1966, she finished it, adding a new and terrible last line: "even if we don't live together anymore." And leaning down, she pressed the crimson stigma to Reed's brow. He stopped asking for the story after that.

"Joe?"

He looked up. Day, her shoulders hunched against the wind, her hair blown wild around her face, handed him his coat. "I thought you might need this."

"Thanks." He put it on the bench as she sat facing him, her clasped hands thrust between her thighs for warmth. "I don't understand," she said.

"She was pregnant."

"Your mom?"

He nodded. "With me."

"You didn't know?"

Joe shook his head.

"Are you okay?"

"I'm okay," he said, "but it's a little bit unsettling, you know? To believe one thing for almost thirty years—that your parents were this young couple who defied everything for the sake of a great love—and then find out your father had a shotgun pointed at his head."

"Is that how you think it was?"

"Did you see that picture, Day? His face? No, it's probably invisible to everyone but me and Reed and maybe Gray. But that's a look I know. That's George Bailey listening to the whistle of the train and knowing he's not going to go. That look was our whole childhood. He didn't want to be there. Yes, I absolutely think that's how it was."

"It happened to a lot of people, Joe."

"You're right," he said. "It's a common story, isn't it? Like Pate and James . . ." His eyes briefly tracked something off across her shoulder, where it vanished in the distance. "Twenty-eight years—seems like an awfully long time for such a little secret, doesn't it to you?"

"Maybe she was ashamed," Day said.

"Of what? At eighteen, she made a sacrifice that I, at twenty-eight, have never made for anyone. My father made it, too, Day, only Jimmy didn't want to be there. It's written in his face. The truth was common, but the lie they made of it was great."

Joe gazed down toward the house, where the white lights on May's tree twinkled through the window as afternoon declined. "You know, when I was a kid, looking at this place from up here always made me think of a great ship, like the *Titanic* in Southampton with her four great stacks. Reed and I were the little kids in plus fours and sailor suits; we climbed the gangway holding our parents' hands, and the bosun piped us on, and the captain saluted with a little wink. And you know the story. The greatest ship that ever sailed the seas wasn't even a very good ship, as ships go. She went down like a stone on her maiden run, and I made it to the lifeboats, Day, I survived, but I heard the cries behind me in the water—I still hear them now—and one of them was Reed's. You make a career of helping people, Day. My brother needs me—he needs something—and all I ever learned to do was swim."

"What does he need?" she asked as Joe, more moved than she'd ever seen, wiped his eyes, the despair having broken through his cool demeanor.

"I don't know; I wish I did," he said. "But I look at him out there in that blind today and what I see is a little boy who wanted and needed his father to teach him how to be a man, who wants and needs him still. So help me, Day, with his thousand-dollar shotguns and that dog—that hopeless, fucking dog that he names Tawny, *Tawny*, after all this time—Reed was like some tyro acolyte trying to self-administer the Eucharist of manhood in the absence of the priest. The priest was Jimmy, and Jimmy's gone. All that's left is the hole in the wall he punched on his way out. You want to know what's wrong with Reed? The doctors can call it manic-depressive syndrome or what they will; they can throw the whole damn pharmacopoeia at it; but those wedding pictures are the reason. The reason's the expression on Jimmy's face. Reed's problem is the problem at the core of our whole family, and it boils down to one thing. One."

"What?"

"The difference between who we thought we were, who we were told we were, and who we were in fact. That's the iceberg we collided with, Day. That's what made the *Titanic* sink."

"How did it sink, Joe?"

"Jesus, Day, do you really want to hear that story?"

"Yes," she answered, direct and clear, "I really do."

"I'm not sure I even know how to tell it. This happened fourteen years ago, and I never have—not to anyone."

"Maybe it's time to try."

"I'm scared," Joe said.

"Of what?"

"I don't know. Maybe that if I tell you this, I'm going to lose you. That you'll want to run away and I wouldn't even blame you if you did. That's why I've never told it, Day."

"You aren't going to lose me, Joe. I'm not going any place."

He scanned her face as though seeking confirmation, and Day could see that he did not believe but wanted to, and it struck her that for Joe Madden much, perhaps everything, hung on that desire.

"It was in Boston," he said, looking off. "It happened when I first went away to Exeter, the fall of sixty-nine. We drove up, Mom, Jimmy, Reed, me. Gray was too little. He stayed with my grandmother. Some of the circumstances are hard to remember now, but I'm pretty sure May didn't want to go. Things between her and Jimmy were already bleak by then. They'd been bad for years. The main image I have of that drive is her in dark glasses leaning against the passenger-side door, arms crossed over her stomach, staring out the window mile after mile—Virginia, Maryland, Delaware—saying nothing, not a word.

"Jimmy, though . . . I think he saw the trip as a chance for them to wipe the slate clean and start over, united over something, namely, me. You see, it was this good thing they'd accomplished; they'd raised a son and seen him to the point where he was going off to a good school. Jimmy'd ordered all these maps and planned our itinerary. We were going to take the walking tour and see the

Freedom Trail and the *Constitution* and the Old North Church. But May just sat there staring out the window, mile after mile.

"When we hit town, we checked into the hotel and set out. By dusk we were in North Boston somewhere, lost, and May was following half a block behind in her dark glasses, and Reed—who was nine, no, I was fourteen, so ten . . . Reed would stop at every corner and call back, telling her to hurry up. He didn't get it, Day, but I watched Jimmy's face getting darker and darker, and that little muscle in his jaw—I don't know what it's called—"

"The masseter," she said as her own flexed in sympathy.

"Right, the masseter, just going right to town, never a good sign in my dad. When we finally got back to the hotel, she crawled in the bath and locked the door and wouldn't answer when Jimmy knocked. He just began to blow, Day. He ordered a fifth of Scotch from room service and sent me out for ice, and he tossed the first one off and poured the second and knocked again, banging now. 'Goddamnit, May, I spent all this money, I took this time from work, I wanted it to be nice for Joey. Come on! Our dinner reservation's in fifteen minutes—why can't you cooperate?' And she still didn't answer. Jimmy looked at us. He was sixty pounds heavier than in that photograph, but the expression—that was the same. 'Talk to her, boys. Maybe she'll listen to you.'

"I didn't want to, Day. 'Maybe we should just go, Dad,' I said, but Reed wasn't having it. 'Come on, Mom, we're starving!' he yelled through the door. 'You boys go on with your father,' she said, and he said, 'No! You have to eat, Mama—come *on!*' And May said, 'Do you really want me to?' and he said, '*Yes!*' and there was this long pause, and then we heard the water stir, and she got out and came.

"By the time we reached the restaurant, Jimmy was talking way too loudly, slurring words. We were at Anthony's Pier Four, the tourist joint—he picked it from his guide—and I remember people at the other tables staring. I wanted to slip under the table. After dinner, we saw a film, and back at the hotel, May and Jimmy put us on the elevator and headed to the bar for a nightcap. We were all in the same room, Reed and I on rollaways—Dad was cheaping it—and I remember helping Reed spit-shine his shoes, showing him the technique Jimmy had taught me. The next thing I knew, glass was breaking somewhere and I woke up."

He faltered briefly, his eyes fixed on the middle distance, as though some old silent film were being screened there just for him. Then he continued, radiating a grim power Day had never seen in him before, as though some part of him, long withheld, had been released. He was impressive. It was terrible.

"When I opened my eyes, there was a seam of light beneath the bathroom door. I heard Mom say, 'Stop it, Jimmy. No,' and everything just stopped.

"I lay there, I don't know how long, maybe only a few seconds, but I remember being drenched with sweat. Then I heard another sound, a kind of thrashing, glass sliding over a tile floor like claws, and May was sobbing, begging him to stop. Reed was sitting up on the other cot, his eyes wide, showing white all the way around. 'Joey?' he said, and I put my finger to my lips and told him, 'Shhh. Stay here,' and I got up and knocked on the door. 'Mom?' I called, and Jimmy—Jimmy had this deep voice, Day, like Reed's—Jimmy answered, 'GO BACK TO BED!' This voice like thunder. 'GO BACK TO BED!' This voice like fucking God.

"I didn't, though. I knocked again, harder. 'Mom, are you okay?' 'I'm all right, Joey,' she said, in tears, and somewhere in the room behind me Reed said, 'Mama?' in this pathetic, frightened whine. And Jimmy shouted, 'GET BACK IN THE FUCKING BED!' and I said, 'Please, Daddy, let her out,' and for a moment everything went still. Then I heard stirring on the other side and I stood there without the spit to swallow. The door swung open, and there he was, Day, six-six and two-fifty . . . Reed's size. When they weighed us in at Exeter, I was six-one, one-fifteen. Jimmy's eyes were bloodshot, one lid, the left, drooping this way that made it look as if he was about to fall asleep on that one side. The right one, though, was wide awake. He had this look it's hard to describe, almost ennui, but with malice in it, too, something absolutely deadly. The towel around his waist partially concealed his erection, but only partially. 'Get back in bed or I'm going to kill you.' His voice was calm, entirely reasonable. I backed into the closet and fell into the hanging bags.

" 'Jimmy? Jimmy! *Jimmy!*' May called him from inside, but he hesitated before turning. Day, in some way, that's the clearest moment. Because it was as if my dad was almost sorry to break it off, what was happening there between the two of us. And, you see, that was the first moment in my life it dawned on me that some-place deep inside, my father hated me."

Day's eyes glowed with tears, but Joe's face was cold as stone.

"Behind the parted door, I heard them whispering, and finally May said, 'Sweetie, it's okay, go back to bed. We're coming out.' And they did.

"They climbed in the big bed, and I lay down on the rollaway with my back to them. I don't know where Reed was then. I don't remember seeing him again till it was over. What I remember is that my sheets were sopping wet, and I could feel my heartbeat jar the springs. I thought that's what the creaking was—my heart. It wasn't. It was coming from the other bed, and May said, 'No! No, Jimmy, stop!' By the time I rolled over, she was halfway across the room, and he was rising to go after her. At the window, Mom ran out of room and turned to face him. There was a bed lamp on the table and I remember thinking I was going to have to pick it up and act. For a long time afterward, in my own instant replay, I did it, Day. I picked up that lamp and bashed my father's skull with it, but in the moment I did nothing—or I did what I guess I do best: I sat there, petrified, and watched as Jimmy reached for her, both arms out like the creature, Frankenstein's, the moment in the nightmare when he comes for you. Then it was over." Joe snapped his fingers. "Just like that. He tripped on the coffee table, crashed down, face first, on the floor, groaned once, rolled over on his side and went to sleep."

Joe took a beat and stared northward toward the Croatoan Hotel, where the big combers sliced themselves to pieces as they roared in through the bones of the old wreck.

"We were on a high floor, twenty stories up, maybe twenty-five. I could see May's silhouette against the backdrop of the city lights. She didn't speak, just stared past me and began to shake her hands, both of them, as though they were asleep and she was trying to get the circulation back. When I turned on the lamp, I saw what she was staring at. Reed lay face down on the floor beside his cot, banging his head over and over into the carpet. She knelt beside him, her blouse ripped and mascara running down her cheeks, and called his name and stroked and soothed him, but he wouldn't an-swer her or stop. Finally, maybe twenty minutes later, he sat up like a zombie, and Mom wept and kissed his cheeks, and he sat there with these dead, vacant eyes that had a spark of anger in them somewhere like a drowned match. Mom said to me, 'We have to go. I have to get him home,' and I took the wallet from Jimmy's pants and gave her everything we had, and she dressed Reed while I tied his shoes, and I rode the elevator down with them and helped her get Reed in the cab to Logan.

"I went back upstairs, and for the rest of the night I sat in a chair, waiting for him to wake up. I remember I could see the runway lights at Logan streaking the harbor, and off the other way the Mystic Tobin Bridge, and I composed the speech I was going to deliver when he did." Joe touched his fingers to his lips and blew, fluttering them like petals scattered on the wind.

"Around eleven in the morning, he sat up, looking rested, and rubbed his eyes. 'Where's your mom?' he asked, covering himself modestly. He didn't remember anything. I had to tell him, and I did—I told him the story exactly as I'm telling you now, only I wasn't calm then; I was hiccuping down great sobs of rage. 'You raped her,' I said, and he said, 'No, Joey, you misunderstood,' and I said, 'No, I didn't, I did not.' And that was the first time, Day, the first time I recall having this feeling that the truth was all I had, my one defense, and if I let him talk me out of it, then I was lost."

"Joe." Day leaned toward him, starting to slip her arm around his shoulder, but he stopped her gently and pulled away. "No, I'm sorry. Let me finish, please. There's not much more.

"That afternoon he dropped me off in downtown Exeter. He still had on the rumpled suit from the night before. It reeked of smoke and alcohol, a whiff of Mom's perfume. We were on Water Street, the lower end, below my dorm, and the Country Squire was idling at the curb. Jimmy was hung over and unshaved; his eyes were red. He was suffering by then, but he bucked up and squared himself and clenched his jaw. He looked me in the eye and held his hand out, Day, and I refu—" Joe's face contorted, then relaxed. "I refused him, the man who taught me what a handshake meant and was. He took the hit and climbed into the station wagon with that look, the same one from the photograph, and pulled away uphill. In some way, that was my last glimpse of my father, on the lower end of Water Street in Exeter, New Hampshire, in 1969, above the boathouse, with a cold wind blowing off the river at my back.

"That night May called the dorm. I took it in the housemaster's study, and the minute I heard her voice, I just dissolved. The poor man and his wife gave me these solemn looks and left, closing the door. I begged her to let me come home, and you know what she said? She said, 'No, sweetie, I'm sorry; there's no home to come back to anymore,' and there never was again."

Joe stopped. And now Day, slipping close beside him on the bench, slipped her arm around him and held him fast with all her strength and he did not resist, but he was lax and uninvolved. She looked at him in profile as approaching dusk cast shadows in his eyes and made a marble sculpture of his face, and she understood now what had made the faun go into hiding, bunkered there in the Acropolis of knowledge behind a solemn stone facade.

"I'm so sorry, Joe," she said again.

West of them, the house lights had come on. In the kitchen window's yellow square, May was at the stove, stirring something in a pot. She looked up, as though someone had called her from the other room, and then, though it was hard to see her from that distance in the dusk, she seemed to search the dark for them. Inside Day, from some old place, the thought of Stella Maris drifted up, Stella Maris holding out her light.

"I know that on the big scale of human suffering, what happened in that hotel room was small," Joe said. "I know that, Day. Other people suffer worse and make it, and I made it, too—don't get me wrong—but I'm not the same person. Joey Madden, the boy in the photos on the wailing wall in there—that kid's gone, and so what. I mean, after all, so what. Things happen, you deal with them the best you can, you fight the battle and carry out the wounded and the dead you bury. You put them in the ground and say goodbye and you go on. But that's the problem, Day. For me, it won't stay down, and it isn't even me; it's us. It's Reed. Reed's the one.

"My sad story's nothing compared with what my brother's in the middle of, and I don't know how to help him. I don't even really know what's wrong. I only know the answer's in that photograph, it's in our father's face. What happened in that hotel room and in this family isn't something in the past. The stone drops in the ocean and the stone is gone, but the rings still spread, and through the years instead of dying down they turn to tidal waves. Now the undertow has Reed.

"I don't care what my mother says; I don't care about the shrinks. Who we believed our father was and who he showed himself to be that night in Boston—that's what Reed never got over. I don't believe he ever will. I know, because what made him what he is made me what I am, too."

"And what is that, Joe?" Day asked.

"Exactly what you said." He fired the answer back. "Exactly what you said I was the day we argued about Pate."

"I was angry, Joe."

"Maybe so, but you were right. I keep thinking about it. This is who I am, Day. The kid in plus fours grew up to become a forensic engineer. I visit human crash sites. That's what ethnography is for me." There was no more make-believe. Joe was coming to the end. "I heard what May told you downstairs, that I'm this kindly man who wishes to do good and save these people who can't save themselves, but that's not true. She sees me through the tinted lens of mother's love. That's just another great story, like the elopement, but the truth is, I'm a man who visits sinking ships on their way down. I'm drawn to them. I look for unsuspected stressors, hidden cause—impurities in the steel, the discrepancy between passenger manifest and lifeboat capacity. That's what I did in Bali; that's what I'm doing now in Little Roanoke. They're in their final hour over there; the band is all geared up, playing 'Nearer My God to Thee.' The whole island's sinking down into the Albemarle, like Atlantis, and I'll chronicle the end and maybe shed some dim light on the cause, but it won't prevent it from occurring, it won't save anyone. When the final moment comes and they go down, I won't be with them. When the last rat swims, I'll be right beside him in the water, paddling for all I'm worth. Their world's ending, and I'll go away and write it up, and it'll be a chapter in my book.

"This is what I didn't want to tell you, Day. We've come this far, and I love you as much as I know how to love—and I thought we could go on this way and I'd slip this over on you and you wouldn't have to know. But you must, and I have to tell you. All my life I've made a cause of truth in everybody else, and if there's any hope for me, I have to look you in the face and tell the truth about myself. You and everybody else I know watch *It's a Wonderful Life* and your hearts swell; me, I can't get past the fact that Potter gets to

keep the money. It ruins the whole film for me. Did Capra just forget? To me, it would be truer if the whole thing ended at the bridge.
George jumps; no angel comes. You see, that's really what it is. My
father was the George who never made his peace with Bedford
Falls. That's why I hate that film. Because when he was at the
bridge, no Clarence came; the good townsfolk didn't form a line
and dump their savings on his table when he was in trouble; no one
serenaded him with 'Auld Lang Syne.' In my heart, I wanted him
to be George Bailey and forgive us for the sacrifice he had to make;
I wanted him to love us and to love his life, but he didn't want to
be there, Day. His expression in that picture is the one I know the
best, not George putting Zuzu's petals back, but listening to the
whistle of the train, the Wabash Cannonball, and wanting to be on
it, regretting everything about his life, including me and Reed and
Gray and May, who used to be his wife.

"May said she thought I knew the whole elopement business
was a sham, and maybe in a way I did. Somewhere deep inside I
knew that story wasn't what we'd lived. It was the movie version,
but in our real Bedford Falls, Donna Reed got pregnant and Jimmy
Stewart never got to leave, and he stayed mad as hell, and at the
bridge he jumped. The bridge was Boston, and before he leaped, he
set fire to the house with us inside. There wasn't any happy ending.
Sure, it's a common story, but even now the rings still spread, and
my brother's in the water and I don't know how to save him; all I
know how to do is take notes and ask the questions. Remember the
one you asked me that first night? You asked what happened to my
father, what made Jimmy fail? That photo is the answer, Day. The
reason why was me."

His conclusion hit her like a gut punch, and she clutched his
hands. "Oh, no, Joe. Honey, no, you can't take that on. You aren't
responsible for that."

"I know, you're right; I can't," he said. "You're absolutely right.
It's unreasonable, it's grandiose, it's incorrect politically and psy-
chologically and every other way. But this is what they did, Day—
May and Jimmy took it on for me. Knowing so much less, they did
so much more. And isn't it strange? I come back from Bali and I
think, what next? Basically I throw a dart toward the map and it
hits Little Roanoke; I come down here, stumble on this church and
walk inside—and there at the altar are Pate and James. That be-

comes my case, and today I'm looking for a deck of cards and I find this picture. It's some goddamn coincidence. And you know what else? There's one last thing I want to tell you, and the truth is I don't think I've even told myself until this moment, but when Pate and James stood up that day, I wanted to go with them. I wanted to put down my camera and go to the altar and fall down on my knees and give my life to Jesus Christ—or not even Him, but something, Day, anything, Design or Cosmic PBJ, just something outside and larger than myself. That's what it really was, not skinning Pate and eating her alive. I was so moved by her courage and her sacrifice, and I want to make one, too. I'd like to make a sacrifice for Reed and you, for you, Day."

Tears were streaming down his cheeks, glistening in the house lights. He wiped them and controlled himself. "But I don't know how. That's my dilemma. I want to be George Bailey, too. I want to find my Mary and my Bedford Falls. I want my Mary to be you. I want to give this thing between us everything I've got. I want that more than anything. But I'm impeded. The impediment is me—I know, but knowing doesn't help. This is what I didn't want to tell you, Day. You see?"

"You aren't your father, Joe," she said.

"I know, I know. But what if, under everything, I really am? I want to love you completely, Day. I want to love my brothers and my mother and my life and God, whoever He or She or It may be, but way down in my deepest soul, I'm afraid that when and if I ever find Him, under the distinguished silver hair and beard and His white robes, He's going to turn out to be a deranged bull queer, and the minute I surrender, the minute I let down my guard, He's going to bend me face down across a Dumpster and fuck me up the ass." Joe frowned and pointed down the hill. "There's the boardwalk, run."

Day let go of his hands. "That's it?"

"You want more?"

"I want it all, Joe," she said. "Give me everything you've got. I'm strong. You think I'm not?"

And only now the fierceness in his face began to melt. "Jesus Christ," he said and shook his head. "Jesus Christ, have you been listening? Did you hear what I said?"

"Every word, and now I'm going to do the talking. I'll be honest with you, sweetheart; I didn't know you had that story in you. You put your heart on the line for me tonight, and I accept it with gratitude and pride. Before, I thought I loved you. Now, I know I do.

"And that's why I have to tell you this. In everything you say about yourself, there's truth. I'm not going to let you off the hook, but it's not the truth I see. Your truth leaves out too much."

He challenged her. "What does it leave out?"

"It leaves out your fundamental decency; it leaves out how much you care. However cold you say you are, the man I know is the one I fell for the first time I laid eyes on him, standing up at that meeting asking justice for people who couldn't ask it for themselves. The first night I came over—remember? We sat right here, and when you said you weren't really on their side, the fishermen, remember how I laughed? That's what you left out, Joe. And you say you stand by and take notes while Reed's drowning. But yesterday, when your mother asked you to go someplace I know you didn't want to go and make sure he came back, you went without a second's hesitation. Don't you see this?

"I look at you and I see someone on a quest for truth. Maybe there are other quests, Joe, bigger, better ones—love, compassion, tolerance; I've told you what mine are—but this is yours. Don't sell it short. I see you thirsting after it and fearless at your work. The truth can be a goddamned drag to live with—when we argued about Pate, I didn't like it when you held the mirror up and made me look. You say some of what I told you that day was true; well, so was some of what you told me. The truth is no small quest, and I respect you for it, but the thing I respect most, the thing I didn't know till now, is that you have the heart to hold the mirror up and see yourself. Good for you. I'm proud, and however paralyzed you feel, however fearful, Joe, I see what you had to overcome to tell me this, and what an act of intimacy it is . . . Run? Sweetheart, honeybunch, this girl's not going anywhere. I mean to stay right where I am, and if you don't know the reason, if you can't see how good you are, look in my eyes, Joe, you'll see."

Had this been a movie or a fairy tale, the wounded prince, redeemed by love, would have wept for joy and fallen in the princess's arms, and wedding bells would toll. But in the book of life this outcome is forever suspect. What Day told Joe that night moved him with wonder, hopefulness and thanks. But however much he wanted to believe Day's portrait, Joe, through long acquaintance, was more invested in his own. No external power can erase this in a human heart, not even love, which they fully entered there that night, and only then, on Christmas Eve in 1982. Joe wanted to believe, but—being Joe, in truth to his own nature—when the dust had settled, he was optimistically inclined, but unconvinced.

Nineteen

The little drummer boy was rum-pa-pumming on the Dumont Bal-
ladier when we finally made it back.

"There y'all are!" May said, and her eyes engaged Joe's in a moment's private inquiry and seemed reassured by what they read.
"Aren't y'all frozen stiff? Have some eggnog and come stand by the
fire. Look who I found."

She was putting the finishing touches on her tree and held up an
old ornament, a mouse in wire-rimmed spectacles wearing a green
vest and holding out a tiny cup. On one brown velvet foot were
small black nails; the other foot was gone, a piece of lead wire
sticking through.

"Remember Mouse?"

Joe admitted nothing, but a warmth rose to his eyes, and his
half-smile betrayed him.

"What is it?" Gray asked.

"This belonged to your great-grandfather," May said, "Pa's
daddy."

Gray examined it suspiciously. "What is he, a beggar?"

"Nosuh, that's his wassail cup," Reed barked. "Diddy git his
Chris'mus drink?" He posed this in their antique nekit-lady dialect,
and they all laughed—at what, I didn't know—some old joke
they'd shared before things went wrong. Yet I laughed with them
anyway, and it seemed to me, whatever Joe might say, there was a

rightness in the laughter and remembrance that balanced in the scales, weight for weight, against the hurt.

May's tree, of course, was stunning. Decorated according to ancient ritual passed down from mother to daughter in a long, unbroken line from the first deb in Eden's good West End, it was, in its own way, a masterpiece, as beautiful and transitory as Tibetan butter sculpture. Decked with her mother's ornaments, it set a retro, fifties' sort of tone that seemed appropriate somehow, a nod to what departs and also what remains. And I have to say, I began to see her point about Scotch pines.

The feast, by candlelight, was sumptuous and impressive, enough for twenty-five. It started with the enormous turkey at the head of the table and proceeded, dish by dish—oysters, wild rice, pearl onions in a cream sauce, candied yams and more—toward the foot, where it ended with the country ham, a blushing pink outlined in filigree of fatty white and pricked with cloves, an exclamation point at the end of a well meant and happily received death sentence administered by means of humane overdose of LDL cholesterol.

The musketeers vied to hold their mother's chair. May, frowning at her napkin as she pulled it from its ring, waited till the rest of us were seated, then looked up. "Joey, I've been thinking all afternoon of what you said, and I have to tell you you're wrong on something, honey. Sumner won't mind if I tell you this—it was all so long ago—but I want all you boys to know your father and I did love each other, for many years we did, and we did have a choice, Joe. When I found out I was pregnant, I could have gone to Philadelphia—we had a doctor's name up there. I considered it." She paused. "But when we came home from my appointment—Daddy took me—I walked down to the pond. I was so upset; I felt humiliated and ashamed. I lay down on the bank and cried myself to sleep and dreamed there were three little boys on the far bank, undressing to go in, and the oldest said, 'Watch out for the alligator,' and the littlest stopped dead, and I called out, 'There aren't any alligators here,' and they all turned and looked at me exactly like you're doing now."

"Who were they, Mom?" said Gray.

"Sweetheart, they were you."

The Brothers K. sat mesmerized.

"That was why?" Joe asked quietly. "Because you had a dream?"

"That was why."

As he heard her out, Joe's expression was serious and tender, yet there remained a trace of unsurrendered doubt. He weighed it for a beat, then let it go.

"I have a *dream*!" said Reed, reprising Dr. Martin Luther King, and we all laughed and wiped our eyes, especially May. Thinking of that young girl in the photo and looking at the woman at the table, the woman she'd become after three sons and almost thirty years of mothering, not to mention a divorce and a new love and marriage, I accepted what I had suspected all along—that my programmatic dislike of debs as a species was unjust. And I'd be lying if I said the thought of her in my life in a new and more substantial role didn't cross my mind. I figured I could handle that just fine.

"Now, who's going to carve?" she said, harking back to the proprieties.

"That beef worked my tendonitis pretty hard last night," said Sumner. "I'll leave the ham to someone else."

"What is it, Smithfield?" Reed asked.

"No, sir. This is salt-cured ham, the real McCoy, Tarheel born and bred. Why don't you do the honors, Joe?" Sumner suggested.

Joe hesitated. "I'd probably ruin it."

"Oh, do, sweetie," May encouraged. "You aren't going to hurt it."

"Yeah," said Gray, "it's dead already. What else can you do?"

"Good one!" said Reed. "Reow!"

May got up and took a rosewood case from the drawer in the bar. In it, an antler-handled carving set lay embedded in worn velvet. "This was Pa's." She pushed the case toward Joe. "Go ahead, sugar."

But Joe nodded to Reed. "You do it, bud." And we looked on in silence—May with the mist across her eyes, Joe with a tender frown—as Reed shaved the meat, his mouth set in a determined line, his hands trembling in the steady light of tapers, safe in their glass bells.

"How's that?"

"Outstanding!" Sumner said.

"Exactly right," said Joe.

"Your Pa would be so proud, sugar," May said. "And Nanny, too. I wish they could be here with us tonight, but I expect they are, one way or another. Let's all join hands. Something else I was thinking of this afternoon was how Mama always used to say, 'Remember who you are.' I took that as criticism then, but now I think she meant we should be thankful for the blessings we've received. I feel so many, looking around this table. I want to give thanks that we're all here and healthy, able to share this meal and this time; and for a new friend in Day; and for my husband, whom I dearly love, and for our marriage, and for my children, all of them precious, each in his own way, smart and good and brave."

"And kind to animals," Reed slyly interposed.

"We got it, Mom," Gray said, embarrassed, too.

May sniffed and glared at them, defiant in her sentiment. "I'm not talking to you. I'm talking to God."

"No name dropping, Mom," Joe said.

"Good one, Professor." Reed.

And the Brothers Three slapped five and, yucking it, attacked the groaning board.

After dinner, Reed brought his guitar out, unasked, and played for us.

"Play that one I like," May said. "You know—about the circle?"

"You mean this?" he said, and as he played, I was surprised by the authority and character that sounded from the strings. Closing his eyes and lifting his chin toward the ceiling, Reed sang in an eerie, high falsetto that shivered through me like a shot of cold against the filling of a tooth.

> *I was standing by my window*
> *On a cold and cloudy day,*
> *When I saw the hearse come rolling*
> *For to carry my mother away.*

When he stopped after the first verse, everyone protested.

"That's all I know," he said.

"You've been practicing," Joe said, stroking him.

"What does that mean?" I asked, speaking my thought aloud. " 'Will the circle be unbroken?' "

"It's obvious, isn't it?" said Joe.

"Well, no," I answered. "Not to me. I mean, why unbroken? Is it broken now? And what exactly is the circle anyhow?"

No one answered me. The professor frowned.

"Play something else," said May.

"Remember this?" Reed's hand, on its precarious journey, trembled as he reached his cigarette toward the clamshell.

This time he played in a broader style, big, jangling chords, using a pick he'd slipped from between the strings up near the tuning pegs.

> *From the calm Pacific waters*
> *To the rough Atlantic shore,*
> *Ever climbing hills and mountains*
> *Like no other did before.*
> *She's mighty tall and handsome,*
> *And she's known quite well by all,*
> *She's the Southern combination*
> *Called the Wabash Cannonball.*

This time, he didn't stop after the first verse; he went into the second and the third, and as he played, a warmth and confidence emerged in his expression, like sunlight from behind a cloud. In his groove now, his hands no longer trembled. May's and Joe's expressions were virtually identical and made me think of those daguerreotypes that Mathew Brady took after the Civil War, the dignified, impassive faces of the survivors, staring, haunted, into their unstated loss. Gray looked shyly back and forth between his mother and his brother as though for some clue to what he was supposed to feel. Contented and peripheral, Sumner puffed on his cigar, unaware he was excluded from the deeper loop, or that there was a deeper loop to be excluded from.

The song clearly had a private history for them, one I wasn't privy to, yet as Reed played on, the music slowly cast its spell on me until it seemed to be about my family, too, my mother and father, and my brother Paul, who had carried for us what it seemed to me Reed Madden carried for his family—about Joe now, too, who linked me to this other history as I linked him to mine, each name and face a boxcar on that train that all of us were riding, rushing somewhere, some cars uncoupling, others joining on.

Forewarned by Joe and thus forearmed, by the end of a Christmas Eve as beautiful and catastrophic as only family holidays can be, I'd fallen in love with the whole lot of them.

Twenty

"I guess it's Christmas, isn't it?" Joe said, glancing at the Big Ben on the bedside table, ticking patiently away atop his father's Verne.

"I guess it is."

Reaching behind the chair, he took out a square, flat package wrapped in brown paper and tied with string.

"For me?"

"Open it."

It was the Odysseus print, the one we'd unearthed in the print shop on our Saturday in Ghent.

"Why, you sneak!" I said, surprised and moved. "You dirty little sneak!"

He grinned. "You like it?"

"I love it!"

Doors opened in his face and a shy stranger, happiness, peered out. "I still think it looks like me."

"You're right," I said. "It looks like you. And since we're doing this now, I have something for you, too—two things, actually." I opened my purse and took out number one. "I didn't have a chance to wrap it."

"An airline ticket?" He read it. "Boston . . . There's no return." He looked up with a question.

I beamed. "Will you come?"

"Do you want me to?"

"If you want to. Do you?"

"What do you think?"

Question after question—we were still bad that way. Answers, though, had started to emerge.

"What's number two?" he asked.

I took his hand. "Come here."

In bed, as soon as he'd entered me, he stopped and held extremely still.

I took his face between my hands and lifted it; it was beautiful, like a forest washed dark after rain. "Are you okay?"

"Maybe you should get your diaphragm."

"Don't you have any condoms?"

He dropped his face against my neck and we lay still, our hearts communicating in thumping Morse through our chest walls.

"Okay," he said a moment later. "I'm all right now. I'll go."

"Wait, not yet." It stole upon me by surprise, the trembling in the rails you feel before you hear the whistle of the distant train.

We lay in that moment of delicious languor when the skin feels otter-sleek, glistening to sense, the friction of Joe's chest over mine like the talcumed sliding of two bolts of living silk. That moment was frequently as sweet for me as orgasm itself, like the half-boiled maple sap I tasted once in a backwoods sugar-house in Vermont, light and wild with the greenness of the tree and raw March air and woodsmoke and the mile-long stretch of muddy gravel road I drove to get there, something fresh and rare that doesn't make it through the final alchemy to syrup.

There's a stage in sex that's like that, too, when sensation is generalized throughout the body, not yet focused down so single-mindedly on the result. The curve is still trending upward; magic has begun to strike, yet the deepest and most shattering magic is still to come, and you know you can toy with it and put it off and torture yourself with the delay. You can even deceive yourself, if you're like me, that you can stay there more or less indefinitely, like a tightrope walker trembling on that thread of fragile self-control, while the torrent rushes under you, and not surrender—now, or ever—to the gravity of your own wish, which finally becomes your need to fall.

I'd like to think trust was the reason why—against my principles, training, better judgment—we started sex that night without protection. But maybe it was danger, a way of flirting with my own forbidden wish: the one that had to do with being someone's mother and someone else's wife, entering the old estate of women which I'd seldom seen go right. Once upon a time I'd wanted to escape by being Patti Smith, yet there was a part of me that had grown tired of always being so advanced, that longed to take a slow turn on the dancefloor with that outlived wish like the boy next door you'd grown up thinking you would marry, and maybe that was what it was in bed with Joe that Christmas Eve, or maybe just my sudden, simple love of him. The truth is, I don't know the reason, but when he started to pull out, I locked my wrists around his hips and held.

"Don't go," I whispered. "Not quite yet."

Joe raised up to look at me, his face vivid with the bloodrace. "I'm good for hours now," he said, confident, yet with a hint of question, and then he said something else I didn't catch as the train exploded on me in the roar and clatter of the cars.

It wasn't as if I didn't hear the small voice whispering, *Watch it, babe, it's time to go.* Whispering, *Girl, what are you doing now?* But swept away, I stepped, like Gretel in the fairy tale, into the woods without my loaf of bread, knowing what I needed, what my life required was there.

And the voice kept whispering, *You'll get pregnant;* saying, *It won't be like this tomorrow, you know it won't,* and it was true, I did, but a second orgasm, then a third snagged me like a fish and jerked me into thrashing, mournful, luscious self-forgetfulness. I heard my sobbing cry and Joe said, "Shit, shit, Day?" But I just cupped his neck and whispered, "It's okay, okay, okay," and felt him surrender to it, too, and fuck me harder, each thrust stabbing home like a delicious knife. I stopped listening then, wanting to climb down from the masthead and go all the way for once, and die from it, and see what that was like, to find out what was teeming in the black earth underneath the leafmold on the forest floor, the secret I'd looked for everywhere but there, and maybe knowing it, against all reason, finally, fully live.

My last memory as Christmas Eve turned into Christmas Day was a drifting image of a face I didn't recognize, a girl's. One bright flash, and then she vanished in white light as deep inside I felt the little bulb go off.

PART VI

Twenty-one

What happened to you, Joe? What are you so scared of?

Ray's words still echoing in his ears, Joe stood at the rail and watched the distant lights of Hampton as the *Father's Price,* in full dark now, steamed back past the roads. Ray's question, posed to the querier himself, stood for what Day might have said, probably should have said, but hadn't.

What Day had said, quietly, was "I'm pregnant, Joe."

They were together in the kitchen. It was two weeks after Christmas, the night before the fishing trip was to begin. Joe was opening a bottle of red wine, a good one, bought to celebrate their imminent departure north to Boston, a trip that had triumphal overtones for him, like MacArthur returning to the Philippines, a victorious reentry to the place that for fourteen years had symbolized defeat and bitterness.

"I'm pregnant, Joe," she said.

Happy and a little drunk, Joe Madden, who never laughed at the right time, whose lack of comic timing amounted almost to a tragic flaw, laughed now at the profoundly wrong one. "Good one," he said, turning the metal worm in the soft body of the cork. "You almost had me going."

But when she touched his hand, and he looked up at her somber face, her Delft-blue eyes, he left the corkscrew where it was. "Pregnant . . ." he repeated. "How?"

"The same old way."

"Christmas Eve?"

"Christmas Eve."

"Jesus, Day."

"I know," she said. "Don't tell me."

"What do you want to do?"

"What do you?"

"You aren't considering having it?"

She said nothing.

"What about your residency?"

"It'll be hard," she admitted, "but people deal with harder things."

"You're telling me you want it?"

"You're telling me you don't?" Though it was still a question, her voice had lost its interrogatory note.

"I didn't say that, Day. But Jesus Christ! A baby?"

She approached him and bared her heart. "Look, Joe, I love you. You love me, I think. So you've said. I've been thinking about this nonstop since I found out—"

"When was that?"

"Two days ago. I wanted to be sure before we talked. Believe me, I'm as surprised as you are, but the question I keep coming back to is, Why not? Why shouldn't we? What have we left out?"

His answer was "I can't believe you want this. Are you really ready for a child?"

"Who's ever ready?" she replied. "If you aren't, then whether I am is moot, because the one thing I can tell you is that I'm not going to have a baby by myself."

"But, Day," he said, his expression pleading, "like this? Not like this. It's just like them. Don't you see that?"

Though she answered with a lover's tenderness, the words themselves were hard: "So, what?"

"So what?" Joe remained incredulous. "So what?"

Day turned around and left him at the island with his uncorked wine. As he watched her go, Joe felt as he had in church with Pate and James, wanting to rise, yet unable to, and, in that inability, culpable and demoralized.

That was it, their fight, if fight was what it was. That was what accounted for their melancholy parting at the Little Roanoke docks the cold first morning of Joe's trip. That was why Joe, feeling like an astronaut whose tether to the ship is cut, watched the wedge of geese and asked himself the question he continued asking tonight, in the wake of the chastisement he'd received from Ray, a man he didn't fully trust and wasn't even sure he liked, but whose hard appraisal Joe considered just: *What is the field?*

Day's news called for a decision, but Joe, always Mr. Both-And, metamorphosed in the sequel into Mr. Neither-Nor. A decision was required, but how were they to choose? Based on their decision, a child would live or die. And how could Joe allow its death, knowing the circumstances out of which his own life came? And knowing those same circumstances—the cost his parents' sacrifice entailed not just on them, but on his brothers and, not least, on Joe himself—how could he accept its life? Were he and Day, knowing history, doomed to repeat it anyway, doomed to re-enact what led to such unhappiness before?

A decision was required, but the issue, as Joe had said to Day about the jetty plan, was one on which it was too complicated to take sides. So Joe retreated to his typical mode and asked the questions: Why, and How?

How, knowing what they knew, had he and Day, in 1983, arrived at the same place where May and Jimmy Madden found themselves in 1954? What force in the universe, or in their own flawed hearts, accounted for the repetition? Scientist, professional agnostic, Joe Madden found his not inconsiderable powers of disbelief tested by the magnitude of the coincidence.

Beyond him in the offing, the lights of Hampton had receded, as once upon a time those of Logan and the Mystic Bridge appeared to do from Joey's vantage above the earth on the high floor of the hotel. Everywhere he looked, outside and within, there was pattern, repetition; and as the boat approached Cape Henry, that old fishing trip with Pa and Jimmy drifted through his thoughts once more. Remembering how close he'd come to drowning, Joe presently felt something like a shadow, cold and from above, pass over him, and he shuddered.

That shudder seemed premonitory, and Joe wrote it off, but not without recalling the faces of his shipmates—even Lukey Brame and Jubal, stolid men without a grain of nonsense in them anywhere—the way they quieted down when someone raised the sub-

ject of the signs and omens men receive at sea. The taboo on um-
brellas, whistling, black bags, turning the fish hatch upside down—
the way they hung their mugs in the galley cupboard so that they
faced in, as though, if they opened outboard, toward the ocean,
they might invite a whelming sea. Joe, over the months as he
learned these superstitions one by one, had duly filed them with
the rest of his extensive notes, taking none of it to heart. But as the
boat passed the Cape, plunging back into the dark Atlantic swells,
that sense of premonition dogged him, and in this mood, Joe
could not help asking if this wordless whisper was the voice of
God.

Yet he told himself this trip was all but done. Already they were
heading south, the rising moon was on their left; they were only
ten hours out of Little Roanoke, ten hours to think things over, ten
hours before his decision was required. Then he would be with Day
again. Whatever else remained unclear, his wish to be with her was
sure. And who knew? Maybe, like Odysseus, he would climb down
from the mast and leave the sea for good and plant his oar and
settle down with his Penelope and stake his rows of beans. And
what if . . . For one instant, less than one, Joe allowed himself to
contemplate the possibilities: marriage, fatherhood, a child. Maybe
Day and he, thirty-one and twenty-eight, could handle what had
overwhelmed his parents and succeed where they, eighteen and
twenty-one, had failed. Even if it was a repetition, was it so impossible to think that they might change the outcome? For one instant,
less than one, Joe's mind said, *A son.* And then from someplace
deeper than his mind, a blond-haired little girl with Delft-blue eyes
regarded him with fearless trust and asked him to decide—not both
ways, only one. For one instant, less than one, the question there—
what if?—then gone.

Cold, wet with spray, he turned up his collar and went below,
where, opening his pack for his spare wool shirt, he once more
puzzled over Day's blank Memorex, only this time Joe noticed
what he'd missed before, the thin ribbon of brown tape around the
empty left-hand reel. Punching the cassette back in his Walkman,
Joe heard the gibber of a voice as the song reversed on Play. Day,
it seemed, had recorded something after all, forgetting to rewind
when she was done, or maybe too upset to bother.

Did they tear it out with talons of steel?

The voice was Graham Parker's, who possessed no pop-up label in Joe's dormitory fruit crate, circa 1973, yet whom he vaguely recognized from Day's collection.

> *And give you a shot so that you wouldn't feel,*
> *And wash it away as if it wasn't real?*

In a punkish, urban whine shot through with raw emotion, Parker sang his distinctly modern ballad. If its subject wasn't at first entirely clear to Joe, it became so as he listened in the roaring iron room, and time froze and stopped for him.

> *It's just a mistake I won't have to face*
> *Don't give it a name don't give it a place*
> *Don't give it a chance*
> *It's lucky in a way*

The subject was abortion. Joe got it by the time the song looped into the refrain. And Parker sang:

> *You can't be too strong*
> *You can't be too strong*
> *You decide what's wrong . . .*

So there was a message in the bottle after all, and perhaps no decision would be required of the professor, who had so fervently wished to be excused. Maybe Day, no longer waiting, had made her own. Was that the message? There was no further clue. At the possibility that she'd aborted, though, a siren note of animal grief wailed up within him—the keening of the bear for its lost cub, and in that moment, all the things in which Joe had engaged and, in engaging, called his life receded and became a fatuous and unreal dream. In that siren note, Joe Madden's soul spoke in its true voice, a voice that he had lost along the way, across the years, or maybe never known.

But maybe Day had not yet gone ahead; maybe she was merely contemplating it. They'd only been at sea for seventy-two hours.

Even now, they were less than half an hour from shore. Maybe it wasn't too late.

Yet at that very moment, Joe felt the boat begin to turn. Rushing topside, he stepped out into the spray and wind—and found the rising moon was on their right.

Twenty-two

As he climbed the galley companionway, Joe could see Jubal in the green glow of the instruments. The other men were also there.

"What's going on?" he asked, unconsciously lowering his voice to suit the solemn bristling in the atmosphere.

No one answered. Then Lukey said, "We just got a call from Dolph. Cully's having engine problems. They may need a tow."

"Where are they?"

"Where do you think they are?" Ray snapped. "Same place we left 'em this morning after breakfus'."

Where they'd left them after breakfast, though, was ten hours out, fishing on the hundred-fathom edge. Ten hours out and ten hours back, and the clipper barreling down on them from the northwest out of faraway Alberta, due, at daybreak, to collide with the stationary coastal low that now ruled the weather. The coming storm threatened to be a good deal worse than the Weather Service had predicted.

"What about the storm?"

"I 'spect we'll have to take some dirt, but we took dirt before."

The answer seemed less than forthcoming. What told Joe more was that the captain, in making it, didn't meet his eyes. Trying to learn more, he read the latest transmission curling off the weather fax, noting that the isobars were tightly packed, tighter than Joe had ever seen; they looked like elevation lines on a topographic survey that indicate a steep mountain grade. If Joe knew nothing else, he knew those isobars meant wind, wind unlike any he'd experienced at sea, probably unlike any Ray or Lukey Brame had known. Only Jubal knew what they were in for, and Jubal, staring grimly through the tinted Lexan panels into the roaring dark, said no more.

Joe felt for Cully and his men, but as he peered through the slit window toward the rapidly vanishing Virginia coast, it occurred to him, for a desperate moment, to ask Jubal to drop him back at Hampton or the nearest point of land. They were still only half an hour out; the detour wouldn't set them back that much. A child's life might depend on it—his child and Day's. Yet the lives of Cully and his crew might equally depend upon proceeding, and Joe was under no illusion what the captain's choice would be. Jubal's loyalty was to his people. Joe could hardly blame him—what did Joe want other than to take care of his own? The difference was, it suddenly dawned on Joe—who'd come only to observe and thereby participate vicariously in others' lives—that he had people, too, and who they were.

"I need to call home, Captain," he said.

Jubal nodded. "Make it quick. From here own out, we'll need to keep a open loine."

Engaging the autopilot, Jubal placed a loop of string around a spline of the great wheel and went below. The others followed him.

Their efforts at discretion proved unnecessary.

Joe had the marine operator dial his house, but there was no one home. He next tried Day's, silently rehearsing his message as he awaited her machine, the recording of "Jingle-Bell Rock" she'd put on to celebrate the season. *Don't do it,* he'd say. *If you get this, wait. Please don't do anything till I get home.*

But the voice that answered wasn't Day's: "The number you have dialed is no longer in service. Please consult directory assistance and try again."

Preparing for her move to Boston, she'd apparently had the phone line disconnected. So Joe, who'd received her message on the Memorex, was unable to leave a message of his own.

With a last glance toward Virginia, which had vanished in the offing now, Joe went back down to the galley, where Lukey Brame and Jubal, with their innate good manners, avoided looking at him now, allowing him his privacy. Ray, on the other hand, went out of his way to catch Joe's eye, and when he did, he nodded down to Curtis's *World News,* open on the table.

"Hey, here's one for you." And he read:

WORLD'S MOST BORING MAN

—Collects old tins of floor wax and rubber bands
—Spends his evenings netting and identifying gnats and moths
—Polishes black wingtips up to 17 times a week

Joe watched Ray perform and unwillingly began to hate him, aware that he'd provoked some part of Bristow's malice, but no longer caring if he'd caused it all. He looked at Ray with this in his expression, and Ray looked back as if to say that this was all he'd ever wanted.

The others went back to their duties, and Joe, alone, watched the second hand move on the galley clock, then stop, then move and stop again. Ten hours out and ten hours back and ten hours more to Little Roanoke. Thirty hours. Filling those hours was a task he didn't know if he was equal to. Attempting to begin, he drew a glass of water at the tap. Green-tinted from the algal scum in the tank, it faintly stank of vegetable corruption overlaid with hints of rust and diesel. He forced himself to drink and quelled the urge to retch. Slipping back into his seat, he glanced at Lukey's hand of solitaire, laid out in four neat rows. The left was ruled by the queen of hearts. There was no black king and no more moves. The game was Idiot's Delight.

Joe bowed his head as a nameless desolation welled up from within. Once more a question rose: *What if I have missed my chance?* What if that chance had come through Day and through the pregnancy, and Joe, not recognizing it for what it was, had let it pass him by? But how could he have known? His opportunity— if such it was—had appeared in such a terrible disguise, as what he feared the most. Yet what if the chance on which salvation hung for Joe—who'd zigged each place his father zagged—required his stepping into Jimmy's shoes? And what if final understanding had arrived too late?

You can't be too strong . . .

The words of the song came back, and how was he to know what decision Day had made, or whether she'd made one? One way and one way only. Ten hours out, ten hours back, and ten hours more to Little Roanoke.

He undogged the hatch and stepped outside. Though with dark the temperature had swiftly dropped to twenty-two degrees, beads of perspiration pricked his brow and upper lip. Then, like a trolley rattling down a mineshaft rail, the rumbling erupted, and he lunged for the rail, barely making it before he hurled. A second heave, then a third, left him draped over the side like a dishrag as the bow, ripping through the oncoming seas like a Skil saw down a length of pine, sent volley after drenching volley raining down on his bare head. When the nausea subsided, he stood up, feeling weak and greenly ill, and staggered down the gangway like a drunk.

Below, he took to his bunk, watching as the piss jug scraped across the floor. Rolling away from it, his bare arm touched the wall, which was refrigerator cold and sweating. Beads of condensation formed in patches, streaking down in clammy rills. As they sledded down into a trough, a dull concussion belled the hull, and Joe could hear the faint seltzer rush wash past his ear outside. Just beyond, through three-eighths of an inch of plate, was the cold sea.

For a moment, as he blinked around, the forepeak took on a curious resemblance to his old dormitory room at Exeter—something in the soiled, urine-colored light—and Joe remembered the pain he'd felt in the aftermath of Boston, before that autumn turned to winter and winter turned to spring, and it struck him that he'd conducted his life since with the sole aim of never experiencing a misery like that again. Yet despite his caution, the pain he'd warded off for fourteen years was back. It was as if he'd never left that dormitory room, and time looped back, and there was repetition everywhere.

Against the screen of his closed eyelids, Joe saw a sudden splash of brilliant emerald green, and the fishing trip, that other one, came back from the deep on the in-surge of the cycling tide. At the launch that afternoon, Joey, left to mind the boat, had disobeyed the standing orders of the older men and slipped into the current to cool off. And in the twinkling of an eye, the way his Pa had always warned, he found himself twenty yards from shore, struggling to untie the bow in his right sneaker as he sank. Pushing off the bottom, he broke surface and saw Will stumbling out into the water with his glasses crooked on his nose, crying *Joey! Joey!* As he sank the second time, the water turned a brilliant, jewel-like green, and, mesmerized, Joey lost all sense of peril. He could still recall a shoal of riddled oyster shells whose welts resembled hieroglyphics in a forgotten language he began to fancy he could understand. As he drifted down, two voices warred inside him, the first and stronger shouting, *Hold on, son, keep fighting,* the second, toward the end, whispering, *It's okay, just let go.*

All his life those two voices, the yes and no, had vied in Joe. The first—his Pa's and May's—expressed the wisdom of the world. Theirs was the cause Joe thought he had enlisted in. Yet as he sank into the underlight that other day, it had struck Joey Madden with the pathos of a tolling bell that the second voice—his father's—possessed a wisdom, too, not of this world like Pa and May's, but of some other, imminent, but not yet here. Yes, there beneath the surface in the green precincts of mystery, in the final light of things, his father's words were truer, and Joey on that day, believing, closed his eyes in trust and breathed the water in.

Outside the hull, another wave washed past with a muted seltzer rush. Listening from his bunk, Joe Madden, sick at heart and wanting peace, closed his eyes and fell asleep, beneath the surface once again.

Twenty-three

I ain't gonna cry, I'm gonna rejoice
And laugh myself dry and go see the boys
They'll laugh when I say I left it overseas . . .

"You can't be too strong"—that song ripped my heart to shreds the first time I heard it in a little hole-in-the-wall music store on Bleecker Street, and it did again today, as I was fighting morning traffic on my way to the P.O. And maybe that was what I wanted, to have my heart ripped up, because I listened to it over and over, and maybe I wanted Joe's heart to take a little shredding, too, which was why I'd put it in his pack. Though knowing him, I doubted Joe would hear Graham Parker's passion; he'd only hear the attitude. Then again, knowing Joe, I knew he would. To tell the truth, it probably wasn't very nice to ambush him that way, but I wasn't in the nicest mood, or thinking all that clearly either at four-thirty in the morning when I made the tape. Probably, I wasn't thinking all that clearly on my way to the P.O., because the truth was, in light of Joe's reaction, there was no decision to be made; in light of Joe's reaction, there was really nothing else to do. Yet in spite of Joe's reaction, I could not make up my mind what I was going to do.

Was I angry? Did I blame him? What was there to blame him for, that he had a history he wasn't eager to repeat, and with good reason? Repeating history's never very good—so, at least, they tell us, but then again who makes those rules? And aren't the rules, when you get down to it, just rules of thumb? Isn't each case different, each time new? So, at least, my doppelganger whispered—she was putting her two cents' worth into The Debate Within. There was nothing to be angry at Joe for, but since when had that ever stopped me—or anyone? So, yes, I guess I was—damn straight! Under anger, though, the core of what I felt was disappointment, because I'd made the mistake of hoping otherwise, you see. What maddened me wasn't that Joe had a history, but that he was so ready to capitulate to it, while I, on my side, was thinking, fuck it, why can't we escape? Who says we can't? Then Joe said, "Like this, Day? Not like this." Said it with that pleading, apologetic face, and what was left to say? You can't bring someone along, not over a divide like that. I was so sad, but what else could I do? The choice was crystal clear, yet I could not decide.

Still, when I calmed down some and reason set back in—they'd been at sea for three days now, three days since our fight, if fight was what it was—I had to concede, grudging all the way, that the professor had made a point or two. There was my fellowship to think about—high-risk pregnancy; in light of things, it did seem apropos. Soon I'd be doing eighty-, ninety-hour weeks—I knew what that was like. And moving to Boston was a big step in itself. We'd been together only four months, after all. To make haste slowly is the prudent move. All true, true, true—but the moment I found out, the moment the hCG came back, something soared inside me that made prudence seem beside the point. I thought about that girl in Ghent, little Elsbeth and the edible white trail she'd left, as though for Joe and me to follow her into the dark and find her there, who would be ours and one of us, and finally, if we did our job, herself. Call me crazy, call me irresponsible, but when that lightbulb went off in my head or in my heart—really, that was where—the rest seemed not to matter. But then Joe said, "Like this, Day? Not like this," and suddenly it mattered very much. All those tedious, practical details I didn't want to think about—I had Joe to think about them for me. And Joe, if nothing else, was prudent and attentive to detail. Oh, yes, Joe was careful to a fault.

I couldn't really blame him, but I did. I blamed him very much, because, for once, I wanted to go for it the way we had in bed as

Christmas Eve turned into Christmas morning. Okay, I'm a romantic; I said up front I never had much discipline in love—I never tried pretending otherwise. But I was still expecting miracles, you see, and when that hCG came back, that's exactly what it seemed to me—a miracle—and when it comes to miracles there's no use whining that they're inconvenient. You can't time them—that's another kind of rule, I think, the kind our doppelgangers know and live by there in doppelgangerland on the mirror's other side—and maybe that was where I thought we had arrived.

But what's a girl to do? What choice did he leave me? None, no choice at all. There was only one thing to be done—and the more I thought of doing it, the less able I felt about making up my mind.

At the P.O., I picked up my last batch of mail, closed my box and handed in my key, noting, as I pried it off my ring, that it was stamped "Do not duplicate." Damn good advice.

Back in the car, I absently scanned my final haul—*J.A.M.A., People,* another piece of hate mail from Uncle Sam *re:* my student loan, and my annual solicitation from Planned Parenthood. "As a generous supporter in the past . . ."

Crumpled that one up and gave it the old heave-ho. The season was over, and I was no longer in the Christmas mood. It did seem likely, though, quite likely indeed, that in the new year P. P. would be receiving a sizeable donation check from me. There was also something from Brigham and Womens', which turned out to be my copy of the signed contract.

As I passed the mall, Santa Claus in Ray-Bans and a loud Hawaiian shirt saluted from his perch atop the Cineplex marquee, where he hung ten on an old balsa spear pulled by Rudolph with zinc oxide on his nose. Just beneath him, two boys on extension ladders were taking down the big red plastic letters that had been there ever since I came. *Raiders,* it appeared, had seen its run. Working from both ends, at different speeds, the pair had made a transitory little poem for me:

AIDERS OF THE LOST

Indy Jones was finally coming down, and just when I could have used him to swoop in and make a daring, last-minute rescue. There he was, though, in his great hat, still mugging in the poster box, looking both determined and perplexed. I never saw him without thinking of Joe, though the professor violently disclaimed all association with Jones, filcher of native artifacts. In anthro circles, that's the biggest sort of no-no. But all protests to the contrary notwithstanding, I think Joe did feel a certain brotherhood and pride, and after all, why not? For wasn't he, at heart, a thief as well? My own sweet thief; he'd stolen quite a bit from me, starting with Pate Ames and going right on down the line, and I'd forgiven him for all of it. This time, though, I didn't know if I could let him slide.

And as though to top it off, there they were as I pulled in, the "Pro-Life" picketers from Little Roanoke. Old ladies, mostly, with time on their hands, they'd been there every day since Pate's exposure, a dowdy caravanserai, huddling in their coats with John Calvin in his white Chevy pickup, with the vanity plates: JC 1.

Determined not to let them get to me, I rolled the window down and greeted them, as I had every morning. "Reverend. Cold this morning, isn't it?" I smiled.

Unmoved by my hospitality—which, I confess, was not without a passive-aggressive edge—J.C. frowned and looked down at the Scriptures, picking up where he'd left off. " 'Verily I say unto you, it'll be more tolerable for Sodom and Gomorrer own Judgment Day, than for you and yours . . .' "

"Listen, Reverend," I said, "no offense intended, but why don't you go home? Take the day off; celebrate. After all, you won. I'm leaving—haven't you heard? There won't be any more abortions at Beach Med for a while. What's there to protest anymore?"

My argument, I thought, was eminently reasonable; yet the more reasonably I argued, the more recalcitrant his glare became, and the old ladies, the ones Gray Madden aptly said appeared to be in dire need of a Geritol martini, took their cue from him, as though they not only suspected my motives, but actually hated me for doing what they wanted me to do, namely, packing up and leaving, giving them the victory. And what did they think? That women who get abortions like it? That the providers do? As I parked, it struck me how irrational the whole thing was, as though somewhere along the way it had ceased to be about the point and was just about the pointing.

I was so glad to be getting out of there, out of the land of surfing carpenters with their Vuarnets and their rusty pickup trucks with "Amy" blaring on the tape deck and black Labs in the beds in red bandanas, out of the land of the Rhyses and the Gilliams, F.F.V., and their beamers with the graphites rattling in the trunk. I'd loved the beach and my little dollhouse between the roads, but I had all the shells a girl could ever want or need. Having overstayed, I'd already come to think of Nags Head, North Carolina, the way I guess I always will, as the Last Resort; and Day-O, she was ready to be gone and good to go.

But I do have to admit that it felt like a defeat. Though I'd never meant to stay beyond my year, though I'd always planned to leave at just this time, in just this way, I couldn't shake the feeling that I was leaving Dodge City on a rail, with the posse, or perhaps the Posse Comitatus, on my tail in hot pursuit. The bottom line was that what I'd said to J. C. Teach was true. After my departure, women who'd had to drive a hundred miles and cross state lines before would have to drive a hundred miles and cross state lines again. There'd be no more abortions at Beach Med or for that matter on the Outer Banks. Who was going to do them? Gaither Holman? Not Gaither. Though in training, some years back, he'd done a few, Gaither wasn't going to rock the boat. He'd put all that behind him. Between us, it had come out over a few drinks one night at the Ramada Lounge, in that prehistoric era when he and I had given it a whirl. I wondered, though, as I killed the Ghia's putty little engine and got out, whether that had anything to do with my showing up at Beach Med on this morning, and, wondering, I went inside.

In my office, I threw some books into a box, took down my diploma and briefly pondered it, pondered, too, the patch of darker paint behind it on the wall, a dusky sunflower yellow. Van Gogh at Arles was the design theme I'd been shooting for. The red sofa went along. Standing there in an Arlensian study, not quite brown and not quite not, there was a knock, and my patient, friend and sometime attorney, Lily Mills, peeked in.

"Hey, babe."

"Lil!"

"Are we disturbing you?"

"Girl, get your butt in here!"

And she swept in with the swaddled babe, Priscilla, whom I'd ushered into the mixed blessings of this life the month before.

"You're out!"

"We were feeling brave," she said, already employing the maternal plural. "I was afraid we'd miss you."

"I'm not leaving for a few more days. And you!" I pulled back the pink wrap to peek, and the sleeping infant opened two alarmed and startling blue eyes and took a death grip on my finger.

"I believe we've met," I said, shaking hands with the bambino as I laughed. "Look how big she is!"

"She's gained two pounds." And Lily, whom locals called "the Bulldog"—a tribute to her pugnacity in court as well as a sly wink at her unfortunate resemblance to Sir Winston Churchill—Lily beamed, as though her child's accomplishment deserved a Nobel Prize.

"So how's it going?"

Her luminous brown eyes filmed over. "Basically, it's unbelievable."

"Umm-hmm," I warbled, and sat back on my desk, determined to be happy for her.

One of the few other professional women on the beach, she'd been among my first patients. In her power suit and pearls and the curled, sprayed do that, even now, in the throes of new maternity, she was temperamentally unable to forgo, Lily had given me the impression that she found my feminist ardors a bit over the top. Later, when she let on she was contemplating single motherhood and asked my advice on artificial insemination, you could have knocked me over with a feather. But I hooked her up with a reputable sperm bank in New Haven, and everything went according to the numbers, and now here she was—here they were—doing fine.

"Four weeks old today," she said. Priscilla was awake, her eyes open exactly as they'd been when she slid out, glistening with blood and opalescent vernix, face up, into my hands, and blinked with pupils so profoundly blue that they were almost indigo. It seemed to me I glimpsed in them the transient reflection of the far world from which she'd come, already fading like a dolphin when it comes into the boat, glimmering gold and pink and aqua with the colors of the deep. All we ever know of where we come from, where we're going—so I thought that morning and all the other mornings, noons and nights when I knelt between their mothers' legs and caught them on the slide, and now again today, gazing into Priscilla's new, tiny face with its old, large look of loss and Buddhist calm, its mystical and boundless trust.

"It's just really unbelievable, Day." Lily Mills, the Bulldog, tough as nails and gushing like a schoolgirl.

Even after all the times I'd witnessed it and helped it come to pass, it still amazed me that a biological event, something that had occurred billions of times across the earth to billions of women over millions of years, should stamp and validate in a woman like Lily something that her career had never reached quite deep enough to touch.

"Umm-hmm," I said, as though I knew. I didn't, though. But having professionally guided so many women across a threshold I had yet to cross myself, I thought my turn had come to go find out.

While I was walking them out, we ran into LuAnn at reception.

"Oh, look!" Dropping her clipboard on the counter, she rushed to hold the babe. "Look y'all! Look, Day!" The face she made was tragic, wounded by sheer excess of neonatal preciousness. "Isn't she the most beautiful baby in the world?"

As Lily reached for Priscilla, Lu said, "Can't I keep her?"

"Sorry, sweetie. Feel free to reapply in twelve or thirteen years." She cast a sidelong wink at me.

"Morning, gals!"

Pitching his greeting to provoke a rise, Gaither strolled up the corridor ready to receive it, wearing his bluff, eastern Carolina, old boy, frat house cheer like happy armor.

Knowing him, we all declined to take the bait.

"Y'all look like the three wise women around the infant Christ, or Christabel. Looks like to me this crêche could use a man."

"I guess that rules you out," said Lil, and Lu let out a hoot.

"Ouch, goddamn!" Gaither made a double-handed shield over his parts.

"You asked for it."

"I did? What for?"

Lily tilted her head toward me. "For letting her get away."

"Hell, I tried to make her stay, but after her hitch in Bedrock, Judy Jetson's returning to the future." He gazed at me with a fond twinkle in his confident, attractive, ever-so-slightly piggish eyes.

"If I'm Judy Jetson," I said, fond myself, "then who does that make you?"

Self-set-up, he delivered with a shrug of resignation, accompanied by a sporting grin. "Yabba dabba doo."

"We're outta here," said Lily, giving me a peck.

"Can I see you later?" I asked Gaither.

"You know where I'll be."

Back in my office, I finished packing my books and culled my paperwork, which took a good, long while. Then I went back to the wall and took down Odysseus, who'd been given pride of place, but hadn't hung there long enough to leave a spot. Maybe it was Lily's visit, but as I stared at the etching, I found myself wondering—not for the first time, but for the first time seriously—*What if, Joe or no Joe, I went ahead?*

Excited, I got up and began to pace. And, excited, I climbed into my car and drove to the Thai place at the mall for lunch, the place where Joe liked to joke that you heard plaintive yowlings and meows from the kitchen every time someone pushed through the swinging door. On the way, I punched out Graham Parker and punched in Patti Smith, *Horses*, contemplating drastic moves and ready for a drastic change of mood.

By the time I reached the mall, the ladder boys had done their work. Santa Claus and Indy Jones were gone. Only as I got out in the almost deserted lot, where the wind pushed back my hair and hit my face like I was pulling six or seven G's, did I realize that we were in the middle of a heavy blow. The stoplight at the entrance was jouncing like a hyperactive puppet on its wire, and beyond, where the public access cut the dune, whitecaps, like wood shavings curling off a chisel's face, fretted the whole surface of the sea, now a different, darker shade of midnight blue.

Looking at that ocean, listening to the halyard furiously drumming on the flagpole, where the orange surf advisory flag had been raised, for the second time I felt a premonition lengthen across my mood. But I reasoned with myself. They knew what they were doing. If Joe didn't, certainly Jubal did. He dealt with such conditions all the time, didn't he? I turned my collar up and took my unread mail and went inside. Joe was on my mind.

I sat at a table in the back, poured a cup of steaming tea, clutching it with both hands for warmth, and raised it to my lips. Halfway through a grateful sip, I thought *Caffeine,* and set it down.

Joe or no Joe—was I ready to proceed? What about my job, my contract? I'd have to tell them at Brigham's, wouldn't I? I did hesitate a second—only one. Of course I would! But I could work right up to term, couldn't I? But what about the second year—my contract was for two? Would they work with me? It was a women's hospital, after all. There had to be a way. Lily had pulled it off. But what about Joe? If I went ahead and had the baby, his, without his participation or consent, wouldn't that be taps for him? And if I didn't have the baby, wanting to, would that be taps for me? But I didn't want it to be taps for anyone. I'd had taps enough for one short life, but I still had to choose. I felt anxious and confused, or maybe it was hormones. Jesus, hormones! Me? I was the one who *dealt* with hormones—in my patients, in my women friends. I was the one who talked them down and talked them through. Who was there for me? The only person I really cared to talk to was the professor, and the professor, damn him, was out on that cold sea, and in his absence I'd come down with a major case of his disease, suddenly Ms. Indecisive, Ms. Ambivalence, Ms. Can't-Make-Up-Her-Mind.

And when the waiter brought out my pad thai, so help me, I did hear something in the kitchen, a small meow! Oh, I was getting in a state all right, and when I thought of Lily now, her happiness and bravery had a suspect tinge. What bothered me in her was the same thing that bothered me in Pate. And truth to tell, I saw it in my patients every day. Motherhood made women bloom, but they bloomed one way and one way only. That beginning, precious as it was, was the end of something precious, too. It was as if they passed a threshold and stopped living for themselves, stopped aiming for whatever star it was that had shone on them in childhood. From the moment in my office when they got the news that they were pregnant, the energy of their pursuit was transferred to the child inside them. Focused there for the next twenty years, how hard, I thought, to reclaim that energy again, even when the children left. How hard, I thought, even to remember how to want it back.

I stared out the window at the stoplight jigging on the wire and the sea oats bowing down before the wind, and my excitement turned as cold as the pad thai I couldn't touch. All my hopeful arguments reversed. Why would Brigham's work with me when there were six or seven hundred other applicants angling for my place? And if they wouldn't, could I let it go? Maybe it was time, time to sacrifice my dream like Pate had done. Maybe what to me looked like self-betrayal, like selling out, was simply growing up. And what about Joe's covenant, the old one, self for other? Maybe he was right, and it was a higher one than mine: self no matter what. Suddenly I wasn't sure, and who was there to answer it for me? My doppelganger? She had absconded back to doppelgangerland, leaving me alone at the Thai joint at the mall, staring at whitecaps spreading on the surface of the sea, feeling myself in jeopardy of vanishing. That sort of disappearing act was what I'd fought against my whole grown-up life, and in the end I could not allow myself to lose the fight.

Back at the clinic, I headed straight for Gaither's office.

"Hey," he said, smiling.

"You jammed?"

"Sure, but come on in."

"Listen, Gaither, I need a favor."

His expression sobered at my tone. "Shoot."

"I need you to do a D and C."

He blinked. "A D and C . . . Gee, Day, it's been a while."

"It's simple," I told him. "A, B, C. I'll walk you through."

"Who's the patient?"

I held his eyes, and the answer detonated in the air between us like a bomb.

"I see," he said, professionalism covering his features like a mask, the look I, too, turned on patients, the look we all use. "And when would you want this done?"

"When are you free?"

He glanced at his watch. "It's three o'clock. I should be done by five or five-fifteen."

Then his face opened. There was sympathy, but I didn't want it. "I'll see you then," I said, and bailed.

When I climbed back in the Ghia, there was Patti weighing in. Cranking up the volume, I pulled out, not going anywhere, just needing to kill time and drive. "We had such a maniac amour," she said, wailing off both speakers in that voice like construction paper being torn.

> *We had such a maniac amour,*
> *But no more, no more*

Twenty-four

Joe Madden, who so rarely dreamed, or, having dreamed, seldom remembered, dreamed that afternoon in the forepeak of the *Father's Price*. Alone in the roaring iron room, clutching the sides of his narrow bunk with white-knuckled hands, his teeth gritted as the giant seas roared past and tolled the hull like a brass gong, Joe dreamed he was alone in a large resounding space, like the gym at Killdeer High where Jimmy had sometimes taken him for his weekend pickup games. In the entry there were trophy cases, team pictures on the wall, suggesting some old effort still ongoing in the sound of shouts and charging feet, the echoed dribbling, the skid of sneakers on the varnished floors where amber gleams from the high clerestory windows streaked through a space perpetually cool and shadowed as the deep-sea floor.

Rising in the center of that space was an enormous tree, an evergreen even bigger than the one that May had bought. This tree had never been cut down—Joe knew this in the way you know in dreams. It was alive and grew there, directly from the center of the floor and, deeper down, directly from the center of the earth itself—a mighty tree whose ancient branches had no decorations and needed none except perhaps the summer stars.

The sight filled him with a sense of clarity and order, of rightness in the world. He closed his eyes and inhaled the fir scent, and soon became aware of a rhythmic echo in the gym. When he opened his eyes, he saw a tall, brawny man, in a red-and-black-check shirt, chopping down the tree with an axe whose double edges glistened in the light. The *thwack, thwack, thwack* became confused with the beat of his own heart in the artery beneath his ear. He woke up, sweating profusely, powerfully disturbed, yet aware—in the dim, imperfect way one understands such things awake—that in the tree he'd had a vision of the living power of nature, growing in the ancient place of human effort. The tree grew wild from the heart of life and was connected to his own heart's life. Nothing should have ever harmed it—Joe knew he'd had a right to this, the same right every human being has and must extend to every other: the root of life must never be attacked. And the lumberjack? The lumberjack was Jimmy. When he hacked the great tree down one bad night in Boston, the revolving door spun Joey out and the shattered person who emerged was Joe, his successor, who'd never found his way back into life and, somewhere along the way, had lost even his capacity to dream.

Yet this afternoon, in the *Father's Price,* he dreamed again, the great dream of his life. Joe was granted a vision of the tree of life, which had put out another sprig, his child and Day's. And what did you do when you received the terrible knowledge that the life your parents wanted was different from the life they got, and that the reason why was you? The answer to Joe's question suddenly emerged, and Mr. Yes-and-No for once was clear: you redeemed the sacrifice by paying down to the next generation the ransom that your parents paid for you. His now to save another human life, a child, his own and Day's, and the great tree, felled, might rise and live again, and Joey back from exodus and wandering, Joey, lost forever, back at last.

And Joe thought, *What if I have missed my chance?*

And he closed his eyes and prayed to be delivered.

And the sea outside the hull went *boom!*—the only answer he received. Drained, Joe crawled from his bed and staggered from the roaring iron room.

Lukey Brame was in the engine room, ministering to the diesel, absorbed in something Joe could not begin to fathom, and it was far too loud to ask. Acknowledging him with an upward glance, Lukey went on with his task, and Joe, for a moment, stood and watched.

Fitted into what Joe thought was the fuel line was a clear plastic bowl, about the size of a quart Mason jar, filled with swirling fuel, and something black, like muck dredged from a stagnant pond, was collecting in the bottom. Lukey turned a shunt valve, cutting off the flow of fuel, unscrewed the bowl and dumped the diesel into a bucket on the floor, then reached into the jar and scraped the muck out with his hand. He shook that into the bucket, too. As he wiped his hand on a soiled rag, he met Joe's eye, not even bothering to try to speak above the noise, and formed the message on his lips, a single word Joe didn't catch at first, and then he did.

"Sludge?"

Joe lipped the question back, and Lukey nodded. He raised his hand, his right, and held it horizontally, moving it sinuously to suggest the motion of the boat at sea. Then he raised his left hand, too, and—*smack, smack, smack*—he hit it with the right one, hard, three times. When he pointed to the sludge in the bucket, Joe understood this pantomime to indicate the beating they were taking from the waves, a pounding that was stirring old deposits from the bottom of the tanks, a black cholesterol running through the veins toward the old Caterpillar's heart, and all there was to stop it was the fuel filter—for that was what the clear bowl was.

When Lukey screwed the filter back and turned the valve, clear, greenish diesel jetted foaming down into the bowl. Both men watched, and after a few seconds a black speck appeared, then another, then several more. Frowning, the engineer didn't meet Joe's eyes again.

"Soon's we clean 'er out, she fills roight back."

Crackling across the VHF came Cully Teach's voice. Joe recognized it as he entered the wheelhouse, where Ray curtly glared at him. Jubal didn't seem to notice him at all.

"It's fouling the injectors," Cully said. "We're running own foive cylinders now, and this other one sounds loike she's storting to miss. I don't reckon she'll still go own four."

This was posed in a gray region shy of outright question, but the men understood that it was.

"I don't reckon," Jubal answered. "No."

A beat of silence. "Y'all hold it in the road, Cull. We'll be there by first loight. Gimme your position."

Teach called out the Loran-C coordinates; Jubal put down the handset and wrote them on the cover of the hang log.

"What happens if they lose the engine?" Joe asked cautiously, but Jubal, writing, didn't answer.

"Hord to know," the captain said. "Seas this big, loike as not they'd push her round beam-to and knock 'er down."

"But she'd still float," Joe said, "wouldn't she? If they dog the hatches down?"

"For a whoile she moight." Jubal picked up the handset. "Cully, if you have to, let 'er go. I mean it. It ain't nothing but a boat. You git them boys into the raft and make shore you flip the EPIRB beacon own. We'll foind you one way or t'other. We won't go home until we do."

The captain's face wore the fierce expression Joe remembered on the men in church. He shoved down the throttle, and the old Cat dropped into her bass register. Bearing east-southeast, they plunged straight out to sea, heading for the hundred-fathom edge.

With deceptive languor, the big swells chased the quarter, lifting the boat with a woozy motion as they overtook and ran away ahead.

At lunch—they didn't eat till after three—a wallowing roll pitched a kettle of tomato soup off the range, spattering Joe's cuffs and socks. Warming a second batch, Lukey strapped the handles with a pair of bungee cords. The men ate halfheartedly, boxing in their plates with their arms.

The wind increased all afternoon; the temperature never rose above eighteen. By nightfall it was blowing forty knots, the first time Joe had seen a gale at sea. It began to thrum the stays and vangs—a plunging bass note. Out beyond the boat, it screamed and sobbed, like something sentient cast off in the waves. At intervals, the boat took boarding seas, which roared down the gangways, sweeping tools and piles of fish before them, leaving the decks awash, boiling like scalded milk around the men's boots, but cold, cold as hell, as it swirled above their knees.

Then it became too dangerous to stay on deck, and Jubal called them in. In the wheelhouse, Joe's feet went from cold to pain to numbness, and finally to a tingling, suspect warmth. Sleepless, the men kept vigil in the wheelhouse through the night. Toward five A.M., the wind began to veer in a westerly direction. The temperature dropped five degrees in twenty minutes; it was eleven above zero when Jubal ordered the crew below to catch some sleep.

As Joe climbed in and gripped his bunk, Ray's hand appeared from above, offering his cigarette. "Thanks." Joe, who didn't smoke, took a drag and gave it back, and nothing more was said.

It was impossible to sleep. The boat moved like a seesaw, raising Joe's feet above his head, then almost standing him upright as she rocked back. Gaining the summit of the swells, she sledded down the other side. Striking bottom in the trough, the hull reverberated like a bell, *for whom,* and the backwash streamed away into the wake.

At eight o'clock, unrested, they rose. Gray-faced, with red-rimmed eyes, they marched back through the engine room, where a half-inch of water sloshed back and forth, breaking against the bulkheads in small waves and running back.

A gray light greeted them on deck. The wind had swung into the northwest; over the rail, giant seas began to crest and topple over. They looked like snow-capped ranges seen from a distance. Joe, forlorn and lonely, watched them drive imperiously down toward the southeast, and for the first time in his life he realized that watching has a price. He counted up the sums, while the sad refrain played through his mind: *What if I have missed my chance?*

By the time they went in to breakfast, the wind was gusting up to fifty knots, and they were taking periodic seas—not just over the bows, but over the whole house—roaring down like Rocky Mountain avalanches in the spring. Every time the boat rolled, waterfalls cascaded off the roof to either side. Going through the galley door, Joe held his breath and plunged through the cold curtain to the other side. It was too rough to cook, so Joe opened a can of pork and beans, and the men, standing in squishy socks, passed it hand to hand, sharing the same spoon.

At nine-fifteen they sighted the *Three Brothers* coming toward them, still aimed downwind at Beaufort 9, in defiance of all fishing wisdom. Even Joe, the tenderfoot, knew more. The reason became apparent as the *Father's Price* hove to, passing forty yards to port. The *Brothers'* nets were still out, filled. The weather had become too rough for the crew to take them in, and Cully Teach was loath to use the bolt shears and, with two swift snips at the double drums of the big winch, to send a hundred thousand dollars back into the sea.

"What the hell you doing, boy!" Joe heard his own question posed in Jubal's voice. "Cut them nets away and round up. Round up now!"

"I think we can save 'em, Jubal," Cully answered. "The engine's running better now. Once we git around upwind, I'm gonna troy to haul 'er back. If it don't work, we'll cut away."

"You'll never make it, son."

"I guess we'll see. Y'oll git up there ahead a bit and jog and wait for us," said Teach. "We'll come about and be direc'ly own."

"Cully? Come back, Cully."

No reply.

"You goddamn fool," said Jubal—the first time Joe had ever heard him curse. "You goddamn fool," he said, subdued, without a trace of heat.

Through the streaked aft window then, they watched her fall astern as they jogged in place, rising and falling on the twenty-five-foot swells. As one of these tumbled aft, the *Brothers'* tailbag wallowed up, a porous black grid, out of the collapsing foam. The stack coughed up a blast of smoke, and Cully turned the wheel, racing to bring her bow into the wind before the next sea came. Dragging laden nets, the boat responded sluggishly, her bow turning at a languid pace, like the minute hand on a watch.

As a giant sea washed beneath the *Father's Price,* the *Three Brothers* disappeared behind a gray-green wall.

"Round up, Cully," Jubal said into the handset.

"Come on, baby."

"You can make it."

"Hurry, Jesus."

Like gamblers at a racetrack when the horses come into the stretch, Lukey, Joe and Ray mumbled hopeful exhortations. The *Three Brothers* met the charging swell at forty-five degrees, shooting up the face.

The swell crested, and a curtain closed over the boat, all except her black-tipped mast; it rose and rose, then stopped, suspended in midair like a baton—the instant just before the conductor flashes his live impulse to the orchestra. Then the wave collapsed, carrying the mast over with its weight. The *Three Brothers'* starboard outrigger cartwheeled out of the sea, the stabilizer whiplashing on its chain. For a moment, Joe saw nothing more. The white rubble fumed and boiled. Then, as it sank away, he glimpsed the rusted bottom of the *Brothers'* upturned hull, studded with barnacles, a growth of something vegetable and greenish-black, indelicate, like hair not meant to be exposed.

Everyone began to shout.

"Cully?" Jubal called into the handset. "Come back, Cully. Are you there?"

"She's trying to stand up," said Lukey.

They looked on, horrified and mesmerized, as the outrigger inclined in their direction like a toppling tree, ambivalent at first, then gathering resolve and speed. With a terrific crash, the boat righted on her keel, displacing a great lump of gray-green water. Her superstructure tossed violently side to side like a retriever shaking off the sea. There was no one visible on deck.

"Cully? Cully, this is Jubal. Come back." Jubal looked at his men. "Get set to come around."

A burst of static crackled through the tinny speaker. "Jubal . . ."

"Cully?"

"Jubal, this is James—you read me?"

"I'm here, son. What's your situation?"

"We're dead in the wat— . . . —peat, dead in the water."

"What about the men?"

"Speak up, Cap. Can't hear you. There's a window broke in here."

"The other men!" Jubal shouted.

"All here. All accounted for. Ennis went over the soide, but we got him back. He's in the engine room with Tim and Cully on the manual pumps."

"Your bilge pump's down?"

"Roger. Roger that. Nothing runnin' but the wheelhouse circuit. Ju— wat— come . . ."

"James? James, you're fading own me, son. Come back."

The signal degenerated into disconnected monosyllables, then silence.

"Here comes Cully," Ray said.

Through the window, they saw him in the gangway as he ducked through the galley door—hat gone, the flash of his white head, the first time Joe realized he was bald.

"Tarp this window." His voice came in loud and clear across the VHF. "Jubal? Jubal, this is Cully. Come back."

"Roight here, son."

"There's four foot of water in the engine room, seas breaking off the bulkheads every toime she rolls."

"Can you turn her over?" Jubal asked.

"Negative. She's dead, the whore. Water in the air intake. Reckon you can get a tow loine over here?"

"We can troy."

"Ju—"

"Cully?"

". . . -at- . . . -ded . . . ra- . . ."

"Cully? Say again, Cully. Your signal's bad. Come back."

Dead air greeted this.

"His battery box is prob'ly flooded," Lukey said.

Jubal frowned and spoke into the handset anyway.

"Set toight, boys. We're own our way."

Staring through the windshield, he timed the coming swell. The moment it lifted them, he jammed the throttle lever down and spun the wheel to starboard, bringing them downwind. With the seas behind, they left the *Three Brothers* two hundred yards astern in seconds. Then, attempting the same maneuver that had overturned the other boat, Jubal rounded up and worked back upwind, overtaking her.

"Lukey, take the wheel," he said. "Joe, Ray, come with me."

He spooled fifty fathoms of cable off the starboard drum, sheared it with the bolt cutters and climbed onto the deckhouse roof, where he spliced it around the mast, prying apart the stiff braids of wire with the sharp end of a marlingspike. Ray and Joe prepared a light-gauge heaving line, attaching a float to one end. The other end, Jubal bent onto the cable. As they overtook the other boat and came upwind, Ray dropped the float over the stern and let the current drift it back, where it was fished up with a grappling hook by Timmy Rabb, son of Captain Billy Rabb, who had drowned aboard the *Debra Jean*. Hand over hand, the *Brothers'* crew hauled it in and made it fast. As her stern swung downwind, they cut away the nets. Bobbing up the face of a swell, the severed tailbag wallowed with the languid motion of a drowning swimmer, giving up, then sank away. Huddled beneath the shallow overhang of the *Brothers'* deckhouse roof, James and Ennis Wright gazed forlornly forward from the contracted circles of their green and yellow slicker hoods. Across the transom, Joe and Ray, with heavy hearts, watched the two men drift back and disappear.

By the time they started in for Little Roanoke, it was almost noon. Under the added strain of towing, their speed dropped from over six knots to four. "I 'spect it's going to be a roight long afternoon, boys," Jubal said. "A long afternoon and a long noight. I doubt we'll see the Inlet much before first loight."

As the day declined, the barometer continued falling and the winds increased. The fifty-knot gusts they'd been weathering since dawn had become a steady shrieking Force 10 wind. The air was full of flying spray and spindrift, splatting the windows like soiled meringue. The waves kept building, and the horizon contracted until their world became the interval between succeeding swells. The character of the whole sea changed, from horizontal and expansive to vertical and enclosed. In sunless canyons of gray water, Joe stared up at daylight setting fire to the tops of giant swells that blocked the sky as they formed overhanging crests and broke over the windshield and the house, inundating them for seconds at a time in a wild streaming rush. The boat punched through these like a breaching submarine, exposing a third of her keel to air before she belly-flopped and started luging down the back side, freefalling into an abyss, down and down, with an illusion of appalling leisure that ended with a shuddering brickwall shock. Up and down and down and up, the boat progressed with a fitful-startful rhythm, like a record on a woozy platter.

Talk had ceased. Ended, too, Joe's interior reflections. It was past personal reflection now, in a world of simple, terrifying fact. What Joe saw reflected on the others' faces, what he felt himself wasn't fear so much as awe. The sea had put away its pretense of neutrality and revealed a truer face. Joe could only watch and think of Day and pray to be delivered from the path of its destructive joy.

By dusk, the ocean was completely white. As the light failed, their view of the *Three Brothers* became increasingly compromised. Occasionally they glimpsed her deckhouse bobbing up a swell, then she was lost to view, all except her mast in tossing silhouette, which started to dissolve in the dissolving light, approaching gray from black against the background of a sea approaching gray from white. Joe's last clear view revealed a figure climbing up the mast, clinging there through three or four successive swells. A light came on—Cully's nine-volt, they decided—shining toward them like a small, dim star in the advancing night, the only evidence that the *Brothers* was still there, except the tow wire, slicing deep into the giant seas as they roared back.

With dark, the temperature plummeted. In one hour, it fell nine degrees, to five below. Shortly after eight o'clock they ran into a violent snow squall; the view was whited out. Twenty minutes later, it stopped, leaving three inches of fresh snow on deck, graying as the spray drove into it like a salt rain.

Something about the boat seemed different. Shining from the deckhouse roof, the searchlight had a spectral quality. Jubal reached up and turned the pistol grip to swing the light around.

"Ice," he said. One word. Although Joe had no idea what this portended, he was filled with dread. Then he saw it. On the bow-stem, fifteen feet in front of them, the forestay was encased in a grizzled sheath. The ice had appeared as if by magic and seemed to swell before their eyes, accreting like a terrible disease on every surface.

"Get suited up," said Jubal calmly. "Get the fire axe and the hammers; get the pick out of the hold."

Congregating at the galley door, Lukey, Ray and Joe cinched their oilskin hoods over their watchcaps, eyed one another, nodded readiness, opened the door onto a sheeting waterfall and plunged into the howling dark.

The roar was almost unimaginable, like standing in an airport runway underneath the turbines of a screaming jet. As waves pursued them down the gangway, they raced aft and took shelter in the lee of the deckhouse, where they stood while Lukey looped the safety lines around their waists.

Lukey took a sledge, handed Joe the fire axe and they climbed atop the deckhouse roof; Ray went aft. Standing on either side, they clanged the mast with alternating strokes, like lumberjacks, hacking at the ice, which fell in clumps and shattered on the streaming deck. An intermittent hail pattered their oilclothes and stung their faces, clattering like spilled change at their feet. After several volleys, Joe realized that the spray from the oncoming waves was freezing solid in midair, pelting them like spent birdshot. Pinging off the mast and deckhouse roof, it scattered like handfuls of ball bearings, bouncing away to deck, where brine had turned the snow to a translucent slush. As the seas washed back and forth, each pass of water left onionskin deposits of new ice over the old, like keloid tissue forming over a scar. Stray fish left on deck from the last haul had accumulated against the fishhatch and in the corners of the stern. Frozen solid, they resembled rubble piles of cloudy glass bricks with reproachful croakers staring out of them.

Turning forward, Joe was just in time to see a giant wave loom above them in the dark, spreading and spreading till it was wider than the beam. At the last instant, he and Lukey leaped and scrambled up the mast, where they clung to an icy ladder rung as the wave washed underneath their feet. Choking up on the handle of the axe, Joe continued upward, inch by inch, whaling and framming as he went. The higher he climbed, the more violent the tossing of the mast became. He could feel the difference in the handling of the boat, rolling with a topheavy, lurching motion like drunkenness—the stumbling misstep, the overcompensating adjustment.

In the light of the masthead halogens, the superstructure all around him had begun to incandesce, creating an illusion of mocking festiveness that reminded him of the poles and powerlines on Commerce Street in Killdeer, strung with lights and tinsel every year at Christmastime. Punchy now, exhausted, beginning to veer back toward that interior world there was no time for now, Joe recalled Jimmy lifting him, his big hands in Joey's armpits, to the roof of the Bel Air to see the parade as it went by, the goosestepping drum major leaning backward in his shako, the tubas swaying side to side, the racket of the snares, the bleached, passive faces of the old men from the V.F.W. in the garrison caps of long-concluded wars. In the sobbing wind, Joe heard these sounds again and, losing concentration, almost fell. He clutched the mast with both arms and waited for the dizzy spell to pass. Blinking around as the ice spread like an unsound state of mind, for the first time he realized they were fighting for their lives.

On the hoisting boom and gallows, the mast and its supporting A-frame, all the places that had ladders, the places they could reach, they managed to stay nearly even, though as soon as they turned their backs, the ice re-formed like a terrible secretion exuded from the spars themselves. But there were places they couldn't get to, chiefly the outriggers, and Ray's remark now played back through his mind: *Sissy bars . . . can't use 'em 'cause of ice . . .*

Working from the gangway and the roof, Joe and Lukey hacked out as far as they could reach, but out beyond them to each side were twenty-five more feet of pipe and scaffolding, and they looked on, helpless, as the skeletal arms gestated a cold, deadly flesh.

Under the accumulating weight, the boat rode lower and lower, wallowed more. A breaking sea caught the starboard outrigger, wrenching the boat like a shell when a rower crabs his oar. As the wave passed on, the outrigger came up dripping from the sea, augmented, like a taper dipped in tallow.

At one A.M., they took refuge in the house. Leaning against the walls, barely able to break the snaps, they stripped their jackets and left them where they fell. Between his longjohns and his coat, the back of Joe's wool shirt was frozen stiff. When he bit a fingertip and pulled off his glove, the water that poured out was pink. In the center of both palms, blisters as big as silver dollars had popped and torn away; his aching fingers had contracted into claws.

In the head, his urine was the Day-Glo color of his slicker—for a moment, it occurred to him that he should make a note. The moment after that, the same thought seemed the trumpet blast of madness imminent. He shook it off, and stood with the others at the galley tap, drinking water, glass after glass after glass. Ray opened a quart jar of Jiffy peanut butter and they dug in, eating off crooked fingers as they crumpled slices of Wonder Bread and punched them into their mouths like musket wadding.

Still eating, they filed up the companionway. Jubal's face, in the backwash off the instruments, was drawn and worried. He said nothing. They stood behind him, staring into the pitching dark. Of the eight panels in the windshield, only the central pair remained clear; the others looked like soaped windows in an abandoned store. The heat was going full blast, but the men could see their breath. Exhausted, feeling spasms in his thighs and a twitch in his left cheek, Joe slumped down the counter to the floor.

"I was wondering if we ought to try to raise the outriggers," Lukey said. "They're getting pretty bad."

"Up or down, they're going to make ice either way," Jubal replied. "Worse off having it aloft."

"I doubt they'd come up, anyway," said Ray. "There's ice so thick on the chains, I doubt they'd pass back through the blocks."

"How far out are we?" Joe asked.

"Six moile. Going loike we are, we're looking at another three, four hours. You boys are going to have to go outsoide again."

Joe struggled not to sink into despondency. Sensing what he felt, Lukey put a hand on his shoulder. "You all right?"

"Just tired is all," Joe answered, bracing up. "I can handle it."

The other men regarded him with doubt. There was still sternness on Ray's face, but, through it, something softer appeared.

"Really," Joe said again, composed.

And then Ray asked the question everyone was thinking. "Are we going to cross the bar tonight?"

Jubal pushed out his bottom lip and stared ahead. "I ain't decoided yet. If it won't for Cully, I guess we'd set outsoide and try to roide 'er out. Only I ain't sure they can stay afloat till morning. We may have to make a run."

"What about the Coast Guard?" Joe asked.

"What about 'em?" Jubal said. "I been talking to 'em roight along. There's two draggers grounded in Hatt'ras Inlet, a sailboat capsoized off Ocracoke, distress calls up and down the coast. They'll git to us when they can, but I ain't counting on 'em before morning. By then, God willing, we'll be home taking a hot shower. Now look back there and tell me, can you see Cully's loight?"

The men all stared astern through the slit window.

"It's black as hell on Christmas Eve back there," said Ray.

"There she is." Lukey pointed.

Joe saw it then, a dim star arcing down to the horizon, then going retrograde.

"Keep a eye peeled," Jubal said.

When they went back out, the ice had magically healed itself. In their exhausted state, its vitality was demoralizing. There was nothing else to do but grab the tools and climb aloft again. Too weak to swing the fire axe now, Joe attacked the mast with the six-pound maul, breaking free each ladder rung before climbing up to it. Working near his face, he watched the weblike shatter in the ice explode concentrically around the hammer head. The pattern seemed random, yet fifty times, a hundred, it appeared and reappeared, subtly different, subtly the same, and it occurred to him that this followed immutable equations that eluded human calculation but were subject to the force of law. From a welter of fragmentary thoughts, this one stood out, italicized in the heightened clarity of extreme fatigue. And as he brought the hammer down again, he thought of Day, the pregnancy. From the center where their deep lives touched, a starburst radiated outward, overlayering the former shatter May and Jimmy made, mirroring it subtly, different but the same. That mirroring seemed accidental, but as Joe brought the hammer down again, again, it occurred to him his great mistake was thinking this. It wasn't. That repetition, too, was subject to the law. Everything was. Returning to the beach, his family house, Little Roanoke, the Lighthouse; meeting Ray, Pate and James, Day—Day most of all—all the incidents he'd attributed to luck, mischance and accident linked together in a causal chain that ended there, thirty feet above the deck, where he was hacking ice to save his life. There were no accidents.

Below him, the deck was lit up, brilliant as a stage on which Jubal appeared, running. In the stern he planted his legs wide and peered back into the wake. Ray and Lukey joined him, and, shouting, they conferred. Jubal shook his head. Ray pointed up to Joe and moved to the base of the deckhouse. He cupped his mouth and shouted, "Can you still see her?"

Pushing tall, Joe saw the light, clearer than before. Pointing back, he answered Ray with an exaggerated nod and a thumbs-up. Ray relayed the news to Jubal, who hurried back into the house.

"What's going on?" Joe asked, climbing down.

"Something's wrong," Ray shouted. "She's riding strange. We went backward down the face of that last wave, almost peeled the rudder. You're sure you saw her?"

"There she is." Lukey pointed. The light was brighter still.

"Doesn't it seem closer?"

"How the hell could it be closer?" Ray asked.

"Unless they got the engine started," Lukey answered.

"Then why can't Jubal raise 'em on the VHF?" Ray said.

Joe pointed. "Look how low the cable's cutting in the water."

"She's getting closer," Lukey said.

"No." Ray's tone was dismissive.

"I think she is," Joe said.

Then, like planets moving out of conjunction, three lights emerged from the single light they saw: above her white bowlight, the red and green three-sixties on the mast.

Jubal came running out.

"She's coming, Cap'm! Look! She's got her engine back!"

Without acknowledging the crew's excitement, the captain climbed two rungs up the gallows ladder and peered tensely aft, his gray eyes shelved beneath his hand. And now they caught the first dim glimpse—the lighted pilothouse, the black shape of her hull—looming on a swell. Her horn blew a deep warning blast.

"Lord almoighty God," said Jubal.

"What's the matter, Cap?"

The sinking cable screeched as it scraped along the rail, exposing a bright metal gleam through rust.

"That ain't her!" Jubal shouted, sinking to his hams as he leaped down to deck.

The big boat blew a second blast and veered to starboard, overtaking and passing them at seven knots. A hundred-foot scalloper from New Bedford—*The Northern Lights,* they read across the bow as she shot by.

"She's sunk behoind us own the cable!" Jubal shouted. "Cully's in the water! Get the cutters, boys!"

While Lukey fetched the bolt shears, Jubal jumped onto the port drum of the winch, reaching overhead and scissoring the cable between the cutting faces.

"Stand away!" he roared. Like a retracted slingshot suddenly released, the clipped tow wire whirred as it recoiled, blurring through the air. On the deckhouse roof, the cut antennas dropped like so much grass whacked by a trimmer line. Next, the big exhaust stack fell, missing Jubal by inches as he dove toward the starboard rail. As it crashed to deck, the hot manifold sizzled in the water, releasing a large puff of scalding steam. The retreating cable whanged the net reel, scoring a deep gouge before it slithered over the transom like an angry snake, disappearing in the sea without a splash.

Jubal's knee buckled as he tried to rise. Joe rushed to offer him a shoulder.

"Them boys are in the worter," he said, pulling Joe behind him as he limped up the gangway.

"Can we turn downwind?" Ray asked, following them into the galley.

Letting go of Joe, Jubal took the wheel. "We can turn, but I don't know if we can round back up again. If we cain't, we'll have to run for Ocracoke."

"Can we make it?"

"I don't know, boys, and that's the truth." His glance polled each of them in turn.

"We can't leave them in the water," Lukey said.

"Let's go," said Ray.

What if I have missed my chance? The refrain played through Joe's mind one last time. He nodded, too.

And Jubal spun the wheel.

Twenty-five

Dear God, I thought. *What's this?*

A little after four o'clock, with dark approaching fast, I stopped the Ghia on the hump of Bonner Bridge and stared down at the Inlet and the sea beyond. It was a place where Joe and I had stood one September afternoon not long after we met. There was no traffic coming either way, and he'd stopped the Wagoneer in the middle of the road, climbed out and invited me to follow. "This may be my favorite place on earth," he shouted, hands in pockets, shoulders hunched, way up high there as the wind blew back his hair. "When I die, this is where I hope they scatter me."

"I'll be sure to pass along the message," I replied. I understood, though. It was that time in the relationship when you share such things in bright, first hope, and that was why he took me there, and also why I went.

He pointed to the edge. "Come on." But I smiled and shook my head. He laughed and said, "It's okay; trust me. It's completely safe," and he held out his hand, his green eyes bright and happy then, as he nodded downward toward the drop, and I stepped toward him, but only close enough to glimpse the water, a hundred feet below, running between the massive concrete pilings. The view was something, though, as from the windows of a plane. On that September day, I saw waves breaking on the outer bar, spewing sixty feet into the air, and the dark water where the channel ran, not wide, not wide at all, one way out and one way in, and not a lot of room to either side, no room to make mistakes. "Trust me," Joe said, and I stepped closer, but not all the way. That place was not for me.

Yet there I was, on the afternoon of January 6, in brand-new 1983, the day they call Old Christmas on the islands and up and down the Banks. Old Christmas, Twelfth Night—it goes by many names. So, at least, Joe told me, though, as a cradle Catholic, I wasn't wholly unfamiliar with the date. In RC circles, it's called the Feast of the Epiphany. Not long before he left, the professor, waxing professorial in his uniquely endearing and annoying way, informed me that when the British government switched from the Julian calendar to the Gregorian in 1752, the islanders, long settled here, didn't receive word right away, and when they finally did, felt no compelling need to change their ways. So their descendants still celebrated Christmas in the old style—celebrated Christmas twice, in fact—and on this night, Joe said, Old Buck, a mystical black-and-white steer, came out of Buxton Woods to roam, and the cattle, led perhaps by Buck, at midnight went down on their knees or fetlocks or whatever cattle have and in the surf lowed out the Christ Child's name. Before he left, the professor had been making plans to go to Little Roanoke on this night and had asked me to attend the celebration with him. But I was never much for the villagers and their quaint charms, as I suppose is amply clear by now, and anyway Joe wasn't home, and any steer or cow with sense, I thought, would not be going near that surf tonight, Christ or no.

Today, as four o'clock ran on toward 4:10, I couldn't see the channel there at all, just white, white like swirled frosting on a cake. I looked out at that sea and thought, *Dear God, what's this?* And from somewhere way far back, Stella Maris came to me, Mary, smiling, with her lantern raised, poised there at land's end, for wayward mariners to see. Mary, Stella Maris, Star of the Sea . . . From somewhere that came back to me.

On the way back north, I tuned in WDAR to await the weather, which normally came at twenty past. But there it was, and only 4:15. Today the weather had become the news. *Marine advisory . . . hurricane force winds expected in the night . . . plunging temperatures . . . extensive soundside flooding . . .* Katie Croft, the afternoon DJ, went down the list, reading off the wire.

"A good night to stay at home," she concluded. Wise girl. And sticking to her format, classic rock, she put on some old Rod Stewart, "Buffalo Wind." The professor would have appreciated Katie's segue. Joe was a fan of Katie Croft.

My, but it was getting wild and streamy, though. Where Route 12 passed near Roanoke Sound, there was already standing water on the road. I slowed down and pushed the Ghia through, listening to the lapping rush against the undercarriage. The northeast wind I knew and knew to fear, but this wind, this buffalo wind from the northwest, was new to me. Against the island's western edge, where normally the Roanoke broke in tiny ripplets, honey-colored, over inch-deep shoals where you rolled up your pants and dug for clams, I could now see in the distance great combers roaring in from the direction of the mainland, twelve and fifteen feet, rushing across the flats in Old Nags Head and inundating them from sound to sea. Farther on, where the great dunes are in Nags Head Woods, the waves were storming forty-foot sand cliffs, carving away great slices like greedy children clawing hunks of birthday cake, and the candles, live oaks that had stood there two and three hundred years, toppled down, end over end, and disappeared into the boil.

And the cold. I couldn't remember anything like it, not even in New Haven or New York. The readout at the bank said 2 above as I approached, and, as I passed it, in the rearview it was 1. One above and falling, and in the west-northwest from which that wind howled down, at 4:19, sunset, haunting, vivid, blood-red, there and suddenly extinguished like a match. *Red sky at night,* I thought. *Red sky at night . . .* But wasn't that the good one? Joe would have known. He wasn't there to tell me, though.

Mary, Stella Maris, Star of the Sea . . . As I steered, I rubbed my thumb against my index fingertip, a pill-rolling motion, the motion of an RC girl who used to know her rosary.

And just that quickly, it was night.

When I got back to Beach Med the protesters had disappeared. I checked my watch: 4:35. They never left before we closed at five. Curiouser and curiouser. Had my arguments persuaded them? The idea seemed a stretch. But maybe the cold was just too much for those old blue-hairs; maybe they'd gone home to supper and a fire and that Geritol martini, a stiff one to fortify them in their cause and send them back, refreshed, tomorrow. If not the cold, then what else could it be? Yet it was like the stillness in the forest, where the creatures hear and know before you do and scatter as it comes, and there is only eerie silence, broken by your footsteps and the sound of your own beating heart.

When I went in, there was no one in the waiting room or at the desk. I started down the corridor to Gaither's office, but noticed that my door was open and changed course. Someone was standing by my window, gazing out. Something about her seemed familiar, but I didn't recognize her. Then I did.

"Pate!" I called in, with pleasure that slowly ebbed as she turned and showed her face. There were dark smudges under her eyes, out of place in her young complexion; she appeared drawn, thinner, despite her advancing pregnancy, as though the last traces of adolescent pudginess were melting away, revealing the underlying permanence of bone. She looked five years older. What struck me most, though, what had thrown me off at first, was that her hair, her wild, beautiful red mane, was pulled back off her face in a ponytail, as though her flag had been withdrawn. She looked more than ever like the Scottish lass in one of those old lays, but toward the end of it, after the hammer falls.

Only as I stepped inside to greet her did I see, sitting on my red sofa, her knees primly pressed together, hands clasped in her lap, looking a bit like Mother Hubbard uncomfortable in Arles, Idail, her mom.

"Mrs. Ames," I said, doubly astonished now and none too pleased at all.

Pate, her face composed and frightening, came up and took my hand. "Dr. Shaughnessey, LuAnn said it was okay to wait in here." And the inflected teenage question mark she would once have put on this, the rising intonation, was gone. Her manner had undergone a radical simplification. That other part of her—the playful awareness that winked at you, playing tag above the conversation—that, too, had vanished, replaced by something somber and direct. Someone I didn't know, a woman, took my hand and gazed into my eyes unflinchingly. She frightened me.

"Of course," I said, "but . . ."

"Well, here it is . . ." Claiming the initiative, Idail gave her skirt a formal tug over her knees and started in.

"I'll do it, Mama," Pate said with authority.

Idail frowned. "Then go ahead. Get own with it."

"Dr. Shaughnessey," Pate repeated—and her face was carefully arranged—"we talked to Uncle Dolph a little while ago—at the fishhouse?" The question mark slipped in.

"Yes?"

"Well, the *Three Brothers*—Uncle Cully's boat—they started having engine problems yesterday, and Daddy and them went to help. They started towing her a little before noon today, and now we can't raise them. We can't raise the *Father's Price.*"

"Raise them?"

"She means own the radio," Idail put in.

"Yes, ma'am, the radio."

"What does that mean?"

"It moight not mean a thing." Idail took over. "Or it could mean a lot. Moight be they just lost their antennas; this wind could do it. Or they moight've took a boarding sea."

"But . . ."

"But the truth is we don't know what it means," she said, "and we ain't loike to know before tomorrow anyhow."

"The last we heard," Pate said, "they were due to make the Inlet at first light."

"Tomorrow?"

"Tomorrow," Pate replied. "We didn't want to tell you own the phone."

"No," I said. "No, thank you. I . . . I appreciate you coming all this way."

"Your man is out there, too," said Idail, getting up, as though prepared to end the interview. "Now, come own, Pate, we got work to do."

That, apparently, was it. In Idail there was duty without sympathy, but, then again, what did I expect? In the end, her attitude seemed less a harshness aimed at me than a denial of the darker possibilities she didn't want to face herself. Aimed or not, the abruptness of the shock, and the unbuffered way it came left me reeling.

What the mother lacked, though, Pate offered in abundance, a sympathy deep and rich. She took my hands. "Listen, Dr. Shaugh-nessey, I don't know if you want to, but we're going to the restaurant—Teach's Lair. We'll be there all night, I guess, at least till we hear something. If you'd like to come . . ."

"No," I quickly said. "No, but thank you."

"Are you sure?"

"She answered you," her mother said. "Now let her suit herself."

Pate held my eyes. "You know you're welcome."

"Thank you."

"If there's any word, should I call here?"

I shook my head and scrawled Joe's number on a Post-it.

The minute they walked out, Gaither knocked, took one look at me and said, "Jesus, Day, what's wrong?" And I burst out in tears.

On my red couch in pseudo-Arles, I wept a good long while, and Gaither, Gaither kind and good, sat quietly and held me in his arms.

Then it was done.

It was seven-thirty by the time I finally made it home to Joe's. The windchimes on the porch were going like the bells of chaos, the bells of Christmas Past, Old Christmas, Christmas dead and gone. Inside, I turned to music to distract me, hoping it might soothe the savage breast, as advertised. Sorting through Joe's crate, I put on *Abbey Road,* "the good side," as he, with confident insistence not typical of him and his multifaceted opinions, liked to call side B. But he was right, though, wasn't he? So it seemed to me as Mean Mr. Mustard gave way once again to Polythene Pam who gave way to the Sun King, rolling on, accumulating majesty and power from such small, unlikely fragments, moving ever onward toward the Queen.

And Paul sang, " 'One sweet dream came true today.' "

"No, *'ain't'* true today," Joe had insisted.

"*Came* true today."

"Ain't true."

Laughing and a little drunk, we happily argued it one night.

And which was it? Even listening very carefully, listening as though your life depends on it, the way I did that night, it's so very hard to know.

The Beatles did the job, all right. Listening, I remembered my own Paul again, who turned me on to them in his dark blue Impala headed north on the expressway toward Baltimore, my big brother, who smiled and walked away across the tarmac and forgot to come back home. Oh, Mother Mary, where was he?

Against every reasonable instinct I possessed, I climbed in Joe's Wagoneer and headed out for Little Roanoke, afraid to take the Ghia now. As I turned over the ignition, the big V-8 roared to life, a 360. That winsome fact—referring to the engine's displacement in cubic inches, whatever that may mean—was another the professor had felt it incumbent on himself to share. His instruction generally annoyed me, but tonight it struck me that his habit emerged not from self-display, but from a sweet concern that my lack of info might leave me exposed—beside some lonely highway in the dead of some bad night like this—to the buffetings of fate or circumstance, which had hurt him once upon a time. And Joe, in so far as it lay in his power, was determined to spare the ones he loved, including me, this same experience, and his stiff, tender care expressed itself this way.

Oh, I understood him now. My ethnography, begun in the gazebo that first night and forged in love, was done. What difference if it takes four months or forty years? When the bread is done, you take it out. He gave me his situation, but I got his number on my own. I had him now: my subject. Joe could not escape. But death could take him. What if it had? What if he was gone already? Would I not know it in my heart, the way I knew these other things? I didn't, though. And so I went to Little Roanoke, a place I was unwelcome in and did not wish to go.

The low concrete bridge from the big island was six inches under water by the time I got there. I would have turned back, almost did, but I'd come too far. Driving through the village, I passed the docks, where the boats were six and seven deep now with the influx of strangers seeking port of refuge. Lashed together, they wallowed in the troubled Gut, up and down with a disjointed motion; watching made my stomach churn.

I pulled into the parking lot at Teach's Lair, a place I'd sampled once; hushpuppies and heavily fried seafood lost in a brown crust and coleslaw filled with mayonnaise and sugar were local specialties I could do without.

In a dubious frame of mind, I climbed the rickety external stairs and tentatively pushed open the door. The room was full of milling people, island types, engaged in subdued conversation. The instant I appeared, all conversation stopped, and girl and woman, man and boy, one and all, they scanned me. Not one smile in the whole place. Then they went on talking as though I wasn't there, and I looked around for Pate, embarrassed, at thirty-one, to be in need of social rescue by a girl of seventeen, but looking for her nonetheless. She was nowhere to be seen. The blue-hairs from the protest party, though, were fully represented, out in force, and there was J. C. Teach and, away across the room, Idail Ames. She glanced at me with vindication in her fierce gray eyes, not even pretending not to see me, but making sure I saw her, as though to let me lie and stew in the bed I'd made. And stew I did.

Regrets and second thoughts piled in. But at least no one had attacked me outright or thrown fish blood in my face. Thank God for small favors, right? At that moment, through the kitchen's swinging door, an old lady with a cane and silver hair emerged. Heading for the bar, she caught sight of me and abruptly changed course. Proceeding like a shriveled dreadnought through the crowd, she stopped in front of me, well into my personal perimeter of comfort, about six inches from my face. She didn't bother to introduce herself, obviously assuming that I, or for that matter anyone, including God Himself, would know—and she was absolutely right, at least regarding me: I was perfectly well aware that this was Miss Maude Teach. Tilting her head, she sized me up with chin aggressively outthrust and one eye squinted halfway closed.

"I reckon you're that lady abortion doctor, ain't you?" she said, hailing me in a loud voice, as though I was perched in a tall tree. All conversation again came to a halt, of course. There I was, at center ring.

"Gram!" And now Pate came from the kitchen, and none too soon, rushing to the rescue, while Idail and many more looked on with satisfied impartiality and made no move to save me from my fate.

"Don't Gram me," Maude said. "Well, ain't you, yes or no."

"That would be me," I said. "Day Shaughnessey." And forcing the most brilliant smile I could, I held out a hand the old lady didn't concede to notice; she kept squinting up at me in ferocious indecision.

It was the pin-drop moment, and, in fact, I thought I heard them dropping all around.

"Out here own the oisland," the old lady said, "the midwoife used to do it with a twig . . . ol' Penny Creef. Had one myself. Mama she had two or three. I reckon you best come own in." And without another word, she turned and lumbered back the way she'd come.

It took me a moment to register what had happened. Then it hit me: I'd been the victim of Little Roanoke hospitality.

"Are you okay?" Pate asked, making that apologetic wince.

"Fine," I said, though, in fact you could have knocked me over, feather unrequired. "Have you heard anything?"

She shook her head. "No, ma'am. Not yet. May I take your coat?"

I surrendered it and followed to the entry, where she hung it on a peg.

And when we came back, the whole thing changed. I won't say they took me in with open arms, but the mood passed from cold hostility to cool acceptance, truce, although J.C. and the blue-hairs didn't sign on, nor did Idail and her sister, Inez Bristow. Yet others did. The women gave me food; they made me eat, and it felt curiously familiar, strangely Irish, like a wake, and I began to feel at home, though there was no alcohol—a difference there, and vast— not officially at least.

As I was eating, Dolph Teach, who'd once come to Beach Med— he had a sebaceous cyst on his rear end, and I'd lanced it, to his profound chagrin—walked over. "You'd better come with me," he said.

Alarmed, I followed him into the stairwell, where he looked both ways, reached into his coat and pulled out a plastic flask. He offered it to me with a nod. "You looked loike you could use a snort."

"I could," I said, and I did. I don't know what it was—something strong and sweet and cheap. As I tossed it back, he watched me with dark, angry, knowing eyes. "Thanks," I said and held it out, but he pressed his lips and briefly closed his eyes and shook his head. "You better drink again."

"How worried should I be?"

"It don't look good, but I don't know."

"I'd better not," I said, passing back the flask.

Dolph took a good, long snort himself, and then we went back in.

At the laden table, I cut myself a slice of cake, and as I passed the bar, Miss Maude hooked my elbow with her cane, like a bad act, except instead of yanking me, she pulled me onto stage, where I promptly dropped my paper plate.

"Oh, I'm sorry! Let me get that." I knelt and looked up. "Do you have a broom?"

"A broom!" she shouted. "Lord God, I hope not. Don't you know no better than to sweep at noight? Leave it where it's at! You sweep after sunset, you sweep out a loife . . . Now which one was yours?"

"Which one of what?"

"Which man!"

"Joe Madden," I said, standing up.

"Joe Madden." She narrowed her eyes as though she spied him in the distance, floating in the depths of her own inward crystal ball. "I 'member him—the long-haired boy who wroites. He tol' us he loikes girls and I reckon it was true. It's hord to tell nowdays."

"Yes, ma'am," I said, "I guess sometimes it is."

"Seems to me, he had one M loike me. Won't it, Toxey?"

Behind the bar, a waitress, heavyset and middle-aged, in a pink polyester uniform and a little scalloped paper crown on her gray hair, frowned at me with hard sympathy, a look that conjured an old moll or dame in Chandler, big-hearted, tough as nails. "Yes'm," she said. "Seems to me he did."

"One M?" I said, clueless.

"Here, lemme see your hand."

I held it out, and Maude perused it with a frown.

"What is it, Miss Maude?" a younger waitress asked. "What's she got?"

"Two Ms," Maude said. "One in each. That means you'll live a long and happy married loife."

My eyes filled, and I had to push down, push down hard, in order not to weep.

"There, there," she said, "it ain't no call to get worked up till there's somp'm to git worked up about. They moight be out there eating cake and oice cream, all you know. You gonna croy and weep 'cause Joe's out there eating cake?"

"I guess that wouldn't do," I said, and wiped a bit of overspill beneath my eye.

"Now you're talking sense."

"That's not why she's crying, Gram," Pate said, offering a well-meant but superfluous defense, which reminded me what her other qualities made too easy to forget: that she was only seventeen.

Her grandmother turned on her. "I'm eighty-three years old, girl—you think I don't know whoy? Now, Betty, git out here and git this cake up off the floor, and I don't want to see no brooms, no brooms a'toll till loight breaks through that winder yonder, see?" She pointed with her cane. "Now, dammit, hold it in the road—I mean the lot of you, you hear? Don't make me think of everything! Dolph! Where's Dolph at?"

He raised his hand. "Right here!"

"Go git me a drink of whiskey."

"Whiskey? Where would I git that, Mama?"

"Don't Mama me! How 'bout reaching in your pocket? What, you think I'm bloind?"

"No, ma'am, I don't reckon," he said, and with a wink in my direction, he produced the flask and poured a goodly draught into the glass Toxey pushed across the countertop.

"I wish you wouldn't, Mama," said J.C. "It ain't good for you; you know it's not."

"I want it anyway," she said and tossed it back in one neat shot, then rapped the glass down on the bar. "How's that?"

And the Lion of Judah, after one meek roar, backed down before the wizened lioness, his mom, and roared no more.

He did, however, offer up a prayer, his timing somewhat suspect, but perhaps he felt a need to reassert authority. I wasn't entirely unsympathetic.

"Brothers and sisters," he said, "let's all bow our heads and pray. Lord, remember those brave men out there tonoight own that cold ocean. Make your loight and loving mercy to shoine upon them, let the love we feel be as a beacon to guide them over that rough sea. Bring 'em home, Sweet Jesus . . ."

"Or end it quick."

Everyone looked up, and Dolph, prepared for contradiction, glared around the room with an angry challenge, daring anyone to take him on.

Several women in the blue-haired contingent, including his sisters, muttered shocked and angry disapproval.

"What?" he said. "Goddamn it to hell, I mean it. You think I don't? Where them boys're at, God cain't help 'em. Or won't. If He was worth a good goddamn, He wouldn't put 'em out there in horm's way and bring this shit storm own their heads. What koind of God does that? You tell me, Johnny. Tell me that."

"We cain't always understand the reasons . . ." J.C. began.

"Aw, shit. Not that." Dolph shook his head in scorn and took an open drink. "You tell yourself that horseshit if you have to, but don't sell it to me, 'cause I don't buy it, not one bit."

I have to say, the outburst put a certain crimp in the festivities, if festivities are what they were, though the villagers, for the most part, took it pretty much in stride. Little Roanoke began to make more sense to me, and my insanity in coming, in the end, proved more wise than not. And it was strange, after hating them on principle for so long, in ignorance—as they on ignorant principle had hated me—to finally see them on their native ground, to see them through Joe's eyes and begin to understand the forthright grit he so admired. I think they reminded him of his own people, his Pa and Nanny and other names I didn't know on the lost roll his heart still called. Perhaps, having lost that, losing them, he'd come here seeking among strangers what had vanished from his own first world before I made the scene. So clear to me, at last. And just tonight. Why now? So strange.

Wanting solitude, needing it again, I slipped away, like Dolph, and went out on the deck, where I watched the lashed boats wallowing and groaning in the Gut and heard the ping of metal something drumming on metal something else. Snow was now driving horizontally beneath the nightlight, and the boats, the masts and spars, looked different, exuding a dull glow, like candles illuminated from within. What was that? I didn't know. Some odd optical illusion maybe, almost pretty in a way.

Noting it in passing, I listened to the roll call in the wind and tried to hear his name. I couldn't, though. What if he was gone? And would I know? And a voice inside me whispered, *Lost,* and another said, *Believe,* and I stood there, grieving and believing. In his absence, I stood in Joe's world, seeing through his eyes, seeing double, down with his disease.

Oh, Mother Mary, Stella Maris, bring him home to me . . .

Twenty-six

With the seas behind her now, the *Father's Price* changed her plodding motion to a dizzy glide downwind. From two knots, suddenly she was doing six, nine, eleven, moving down the faces of the waves like an unbalanced luge.

"They won't be far," said Jubal, wiping the Lexan panels with his elbow as he turned the searchlight side to side. "Get up in the bows and look." *How long could you survive*—Joe's question, posed in disinterested curiosity, came back now as Jubal checked his watch. He glanced at the readout overhead. The water temp was thirty-nine degrees.

Sweeping port to starboard, the searchlight, like a polish rag passed over tarnished silver, turned the night-grayed foam a brilliant white. In the bow, his eyes narrowed against the pelting beads of frozen spray, Joe thought how slim the chances were of making out a human face in that.

Two minutes passed; nothing. Then they bumped a dark plank floating on the water, a fishboard. Another minute.

"We must've overshot her," Lukey called.

"Look!" Ray, clinging to the forestay on the deckhouse roof, pointed.

Far ahead, a tiny red light, like a dying ember, blinked atop a swell and fell away into the sea.

As the next wave lifted them, the searchlight beam picked out the black-and-yellow bubble of the raft, bobbing on a crest. Caught by a gust, it ran away, slowing as it sank into the shelter of a trough and allowing them to gain. Like a man running down a hat that blows away each time he leans for it, they chased the raft and finally overtook it.

It bumped the bow, and Joe and Lukey chased it down the gangway. Brame tossed the hook and snagged the painter line, and they hauled it to the rail.

The sealed flap opened from inside, and Ennis Wright appeared. "Have y'all got Cully?"

Lukey's face went grave.

"Shit," said Ray. "He ain't with you?"

"He was in the wheelhouse," said Ennis, blue-lipped and distraught. One foot in a sock, the other bare, he came aboard in nothing but his dripping shirt and pants. "We were waiting own him in the raft. The boat was pulling us down with her. I don't know what happened. The loine just give and off we went."

"Jesus Christ," said Ray.

Timmy Rabb was in worse shape. An arm around James Burrus's neck, he appeared through the flap with the wan, resigned expression of a famine victim. Once on deck, he went down on all fours, arched his back like a dog and heaved and heaved, nothing coming up.

James gripped the rail, but the sea was pulling the raft from under him, stretching him like a man on the rack. Lukey caught his wrist at the last instant, and James flopped in as the raft snapped on the line and instantly swamped as an overtaking sea rushed through its open door.

"Where's Cully at?" Jubal bellowed down the companionway as they helped the injured men inside.

"He went back to get the shears," James said. "We were listing bad to port, and a big sea swept the decks and she just layed right down. She was pulling the raft under."

"The loine just give. I don't know what happened," said Ennis, his teeth chattering. His eyes were like dark wells with two bright sparks of somber, frightened wonder in them. Completely open and defenseless, his face was strangely beautiful, yet the other men, after a glance, avoided looking at him, all except Joe, who found it hard to look away.

"It's meant to give," Jubal said reproachfully. "That's what it's made to do. Did he get out?"

"How in hell are we supposed to know?" James answered, angry, defensive. "We were in the fucking water. I had all I could do, troying to hold Tim in one hand and the painter in the other. Toime we got aboard we was way to hell and gone downwind. We called, but how the hell's he going to hear us and how the hell are we supposed to hear him if he did? We done all we could."

"He must be behind us, don't you figure?" Ennis's question was an appeal.

"Cully's gone," James said with bitter factuality. "Wake up and smell the fucking coffee."

The others looked at Jubal as though for commutation of the sentence, but the captain's face was hard. "Get some blankets own these men."

"Goddamn it, I done all I could." James stripped off his sopping shirt and threw it on the floor. His body, thick and strong but undefined, was still pudgy with baby fat around the waist, shocking in its pallor and its youth.

While Jubal brought them back upwind, the men waited in anxious silence; then the captain's bag was brought from the stateroom and spare clothes distributed.

"Ray or one of y'all, get own the roof and break the raft shell free of oice," the captain said. "Joe, see how many loife preservers you can foind."

Before they could obey, the boat abruptly dipped to port, then violently wallowed back to starboard. There was a terrific crash; rushing out, they found the starboard outrigger trailing in the water like a broken wing. Under the weight of ice, the supporting vang had snapped its fitting on the masthead, allowing it to drop. Acting as a second rudder, it began to steer the boat off course. Groaning against the water's drag like a man whose arm is being bent behind his back, the mangled joint gave way with a sharp crack, and the stressed spar, squealing like a braking locomotive, slid off the deckhouse roof, knocking off gray clumps of ice and striking sparks along the rail. As it scraped aft and sank, several of the men, including Joe, ran after it like frenzied paparazzi, shouting exclamations in a senseless, semi-crazed excitement.

No longer counterweighted, the boat careened to port, unbalanced by the weight of the remaining outrigger. Joe and Ray tumbled backward down the tilting deck and splashed in the cold sea—the port rail was the only thing that stopped their fall. Gasping up in streaming, waist-deep water, they craned their necks to look; the deck reared, steep as a church roof. Lunging for handholds, slipping on the ice, they scrambled up on hands and knees, and then a breaking sea sheeted in across the high side rail and knocked them down again. In fast-flowing, freezing water, Joe gazed up at safety twenty feet away that there was no way to attain. *Is this it?* he wondered. It seemed disappointing and prosaic, yet he realized that he would meet death calmly, and this discovery, which was new, came as a relief. And then he saw Ray beside him, shouting, his face filled with the fierce rage to live, and he felt reproached.

When Lukey dropped the starboard whip to them, Joe, struggling hand over hand, followed Ray up the rope to the high side and, once there, was glad of his reprieve. Yet even as he struggled—effectually and well, without the frantic urgency of fear—the sense of calm remained, and he began to understand that he, and they, were in the middle of a lesson. And Joe, a student to the end, became intent on knowing what it was.

Forward now, the starboard wheelhouse door, tilted toward the horizontal now, strained open like the top valve of an iron clam, then clanged shut under its own weight. At a second mighty heave, Jubal flopped out and, limping, made his way toward them, straddling the V formed by the gangway and the deckhouse wall.

In a trance of concentrated focus, he spoke in a level voice. "Joe, Lukey, see to the raft. Ray, come with me."

While they hacked away at the ice, Joe saw a puff of flame explode below them in the flooded gangway as Ray sparked the captain's torch. The tattered flag of orange fire cast a flickering, infernal light on Ray's and Jubal's upturned faces, dancing on the surface of the thigh-deep water they were standing in, then changed to a blue icepick point as Jubal adjusted the oxygen. Like a swarm of stinging fireflies, white and orange sparks rained about the captain's unprotected face and eyes as he cut the smoking pipe above his head, amputating the great arm of the remaining outrigger.

"Watch it! Here she comes!"

With a sharp crack, the outrigger gave way, and the severed end crashed into the gangway as the outboard end wallowed up out of the sea. Still supported by the masthead vang, it swung aft like the boom of a gigantic crane, and Ray and Jubal, in its path and half submerged, started running in a wading, awkward canter.

"Heads up! Watch it!" Lukey shouted. As the boat rolled upright, the great dead arm swung inboard and smashed the deckhouse wall. There was a lull, then the vang snapped, and the outrigger fell with a ringing crash.

Joe and Lukey leaped to the flooded afterdeck, but there was no sign of Ray or Jubal. Trapped between the rails, water jetted under pressure through the scuppers. As it drained, Jubal emerged, seated in the gangway, his back against the deckhouse wall, eyes closed, as though resting. His right leg was pinned beneath the fallen spar, his white boot unnaturally pronated like a doll's. Behind him, stretched at full length, Ray, face down, lay wedged into the angle of the wall.

Lukey engaged the hoisting winch, while Joe attached the hook. As the mate worked the line, the outrigger slowly creaked off deck. The moment there was clearance, Joe yanked Ray free. The spar swung outboard in a roll, and Jubal, opening his eyes, keeled over and reached out a hand. Joe slid him around the corner of the deckhouse, clear, before the spar clanged back against the wall and fell.

The galley entrance was blocked, so they carried the injured men around the house, where they banged on the starboard door till James and Ennis opened it and pulled Ray in.

Jubal, awaiting his turn, grimly studied his leg. Through a strip of torn oilcloth, Joe glimpsed what resembled the uncooked Christmas tenderloin sealed afloat in its sack of blood. He stripped his belt and cinched the leg above the injury. As he tightened the tourniquet, Jubal's face went gray. His eyes closed, the captain nodded readiness, and Joe and Lukey lifted him through the hatch, his foot flopping like a weight of pennies in a sock.

The situation in the house was equally dire. Timmy Rabb lay on the floor, one foot twitching, his eyes rolling, showing white; Ennis pried his jaws apart, forcing the hang log pen—a clear plastic Bic—across Timmy's rear molars so he wouldn't swallow his tongue.

"How far out are we?" Jubal asked in a weak voice.

"Moile, moile and a quarter." In Jubal's hooded navy sweatshirt, James steered, his jaw square with determination. "You hear that coughing in the engine? That's what ours was doing, too." He announced this angry warning as though there was fault to be assessed.

"I'll go check the filter," Lukey said.

"No, you take the wheel," the captain said.

"I got it, Jubal. Let him go."

"Lukey, take the wheel."

James looked ready to contest the order. "Fuck it then," he said, deciding otherwise, and stepped away.

Observing this, Joe realized who Burrus was: not a bad man, but hotheaded, full of difficult feelings that weren't fully under his control, and it struck him that Day had judged the practical consequences of Pate's sacrifice more clearly. He felt humbled by this recognition and would have liked to tell Day so himself. Suddenly it seemed there were so many things he hadn't owned to her, things he respected and admired. Regret stabbed him, and the clarity that had overcome his mind began to frighten him, as though he were ascending a mountain, and if he kept climbing, there might come a point where he would be unable to turn back—or might no longer want to.

"I'll check the filter," he announced.

"You remember how?"

He answered Lukey with a nod and checked the clock: 4:15. Standing just outside the lazaret, Joe paused a moment as the amputated stump of the exhaust stack coughed up a puff of oily smoke. The vibration in the deckplate had acquired a tic he'd never noticed in all his months at sea, and it became more pronounced when he entered the engine room, where water sloshed across the floor.

The filter was completely clogged, completely black. Silently reciting the steps and checking off each one, items on a to-do list of graver import than any he'd jotted in his steno pad with the Mont Blanc, Joe turned the cock, unscrewed the bowl, emptied it into the bucket, screwed it on and turned the valve again; then he wiped his hands on Lukey's rag. Joe performed this in a heightened state, factual in the extreme, his mind hovering like a camera, objectively recording a scene of which he himself was part, but only part. And in this mood he now recalled the life preservers.

When he undogged the hatch, water spilled over the coaming into the forepeak. The vests were on the bottom portside bunk with all the other gear. Joe had previously counted them, but, on the off chance, counted them again; there were still just five, as there had been before.

Turning, he spied his Walkman on the bunk, the thin ribbon of elapsed tape around the plastic spool reminding him that he'd got only halfway through the song. In the midst of checking off the items on his list, Joe experienced a sudden urge, not clear or factual at all, to listen to the rest. Good soldier that he was, however, he did not indulge himself. On the tide of his missed chances, this would be one more. As he piled the orange jackets in his arms and crossed the engine room, the nature of the lesson he was in the middle of came home with a somber knell. The lesson was death— to find out who he'd be in facing it, and know himself, which Joe did not. So diligent and talented a student of others, he had not applied himself to this, the one lesson that mattered. Wanting something different, seeking among strangers for another, brighter life, he had let his own true life pass by. That life was Day and the child they had conceived, a child who was perhaps already no more than a spot of tissue swimming in a canister of medical-grade waste. Because of him, that child would never have the opportunity to learn what Joe was learning now, to tally up the blessings with the loss and weigh them in the scales and understand what now was clear to Joe: there is no other world than this. And Joe Madden, who'd argued that the movie should have ended at the bridge before the good part started, halfway up the engine room companionway, closed his eyes and petitioned God in silent prayer to give him back his life.

Begun in the forepeak, Joe's brief memorial was complete before he stepped out of the lazaret.

In the house, he dropped the jackets on the floor. "These were all I found."

James Burrus, without hesitation, picked one up and then, on second thought, took two. "Here, Ennis, put this own."

"Shouldn't we give 'em to the injured men?"

"There's enough to go around." James seemed very clear in his entitlement. It was almost admirable, but neither Joe nor Lukey looked at him.

"Hey, Spock," Ray said, "Southern hospitality always gits you in the end, what say?"

Burrus glared, and Joe had to laugh. Lying on his back, exploring gingerly beneath his coat, Ray tried to sit up, but winced and lay back down. "Shit, I think I broke some ribs."

Joe carried over a vest and knelt to help him put it on.

"You keep it. If it's going to happen, I'd ruther it be quick."

"Put it on," Joe said and strapped him in.

The two remaining vests were put on Timmy Rabb and Jubal; the captain sat propped against the cabinets, chin slumped to his chest, eyes closed, frowning as he attended to inward matters from which he appeared unwilling or unable to disengage.

Joe helped James and Ennis move Timmy to the roof to speed evacuation, should it be required. The others inflated the raft and pulled Rabb in; Joe soberly eyed the manifold coughing up black-lunged blasts that vanished in the gallows lights, dispersing like a flock of bats against the moon.

As they neared the Inlet, the seas grew confused, coming not just from the bow but from the sides, at random, as they entered the littoral current driving southward down the beach. From atop a swell, through stinging spray, Joe glimpsed the bridge lights like a solitary constellation in the western sky. Faint and farther off, Gravesend Light swung its sharp beam seaward, like a Siren call, promising safe harbor even as it warned against the shoals. There it was, and gone.

Suddenly, the engine shuddered, started, shuddered.

"She ain't got much more," James said. "What y'all want to do? Me, I say we ain't got a chance in hell to get across that bar tonight."

"Tim ain't gonna make it if we don't," said Ennis.

Joe glanced at Jubal, then at Lukey, who stared straight ahead to steer.

"Nobody's gonna make it if we wreck," James said.

"We've got the raft," Joe pointed out.

"Fuck the raft," James said. "It's blowing seventy knots out there. We'll be halfway to Africa before they find us."

When Lukey finally spoke, everybody listened. "Once we're in the Inlet, the wind should blow us down to the south shore."

"Yeah," James said, "and if we miss the point, still Africa."

Lukey weighed James's point and assessed Jubal, whose chances were not favorable either.

"I think we better cross."

"I vote with Brame," Ray said.

"Me, too," said Joe.

"Then fuck it, that's the plan," James said. "Come on, Ennis, let's go see to Tim."

When Joe started to close the wheelhouse door to preserve heat, Lukey stopped him. "Better leave it open."

The landmass loomed up to north and south, the negative of its remembered self, dark against the pale, roiled sea. Stretching through that whiteness, shore to shore, was what appeared to be a fairy ring, a wall of whiter, still more brilliant fire where the waves met the outer bar. Above the engine noise, above the shriek of wind and sea, Joe could hear the thunder, a deep bass rumble like exploding dynamite.

Leaning toward the chromascope, Brame flipped the switch, converting fathoms back to feet. The reader went from ten to sixty-two to fifty-eight.

"Set the radar to the lowest scale."

They turned to look as Jubal surfaced from his reverie.

"We lost it, Cap," Lukey said. "The tow wire cut the radar mast."

Jubal frowned, remembering with effort. "Keep the red to starboard. You won't see the buoys till you're roight up own 'em."

Lukey glanced at Joe. "Call those numbers out."

"Fifty," Joe said, peering like a sorcerer into the LCD. "Forty-five."

"Where's Number One?" Lukey asked, wiping the windshield with his hand. "Anybody see it?"

Against the starboard bow, a hollow thump.

"Shit!"

Through the door, Joe watched it clatter down the side, a red nun lying over in the streaming current like a swimmer in a riptide, struggling to rise.

"Thirty-five," he shouted. "Twenty-seven, twenty-three, eighteen. It's rising fast!"

In the house-high wall of breakers, a narrow space suddenly appeared where the inrushing tide turned black.

"There's the channel!" Lukey shouted.

"You're dead-on for the buoy," James called down from the roof.

"Ease off on the throttle," Jubal said. "Time it to a swell."

"I'll try, Cap," Lukey said. "The current's running hard as hell in here."

"Sixteen," Joe called. "Thirteen. Nine. Nine. Seven. I think we're on the bar."

Through the door he could see waves breaking fifteen yards away, flying up like geysers, higher than the mast.

"Seven. Seven. Eight. Ten! It's getting deeper—we're across!"

At that, the boat jarred like a locomotive engine coupling with a line of cars. The number changed to five, then six, five, six again.

"Gun it!" James shouted from the roof. "What the hell you waiting for?"

"No," said Jubal in an even tone. "Wait. You'll rip the rudder off."

Sure enough, the next swell lifted them. Like an axehead coming from a block, the keel detached.

"Now," Jubal said. "Now, full ahead."

Lukey shoved the lever forward; the engine hesitated, coughed, and then began to diesel, juddering before it stopped. In an eerie lull, the boat began to drift to port, pushed southward by the shrieking northwest wind. Joe heard the faint hum of the bilge pump running off the batteries.

"Get Ray and Jubal in the raft," Lukey said, cranking the ignition. "Come on." The starter motor whined and stopped, whined and stopped.

Then they hit, not a shock this time, an almost gentle bump, like lovers washing up the dishes after dinner, touching shoulders at the sink. As the boat rolled on her bottom, the floor went vertical beneath their feet, pitching them to port. Square by square, the sea filled the Lexan panels port to starboard, a view as into a dark aquarium. When she stopped, the starboard door was overhead; through it, Joe caught a glimpse of cloudy sky like the last view from the bottom of the grave, and then a breaking sea streamed down like the first spade of earth and buried them.

All along the aft wall, the cabinet doors had fallen open, spilling charts and various debris. Using the cabinet stiles as ladder rungs, Joe clambered up and through the door, then leaned back to help the others. The mate came last. Panting, overcome, the four men lay like wet, exhausted soldiers behind the low redoubt formed by

the starboard rail. Over it, from windward, the sea poured intermittently in thin, cold streams. Occasionally, it broke with force,
threatening to sweep them off. Below, the deckhouse roof sloped
toward the water at forty-five degrees. The raft was gone.

Staring at the space where it had been, no one had the heart to
speak. Joe stood up and gazed to leeward; the shore was two hundred yards away. Against it, the black waves resembled giant saw
teeth, as in a child's crayon drawing.

"What now, boys?" Ray said.

The captain had retreated back into his urgent meditation.

"It's only twelve feet deep," Joe said.

"And thirty-nine degrees," said Ray.

"It's five below out here, and we're all wet."

"Maybe we should wait for help."

"Nobody knows we're here."

The three consulted silently. The truth was, no one knew.

Lukey nodded to Joe. "I'll see to Jubal. You take Ray."

Brame lugged the captain forward, and into a more sheltered situation. Joe turned to Ray. "We stay here, we freeze. We go, and it's
over one way or the other in ten minutes. I say we go."

"You're prob'ly right," Ray said. "Problem is, I ain't in shape to
git much swimming done."

"I'll do the swimming. You just float."

Ray smiled as at the boast of a well-meaning boy. "Listen, Joe,
your chances by yourself ain't great. With me, they're slim to none.
There's no point in us both dying."

"Do you want to go or not?"

Ray's face settled into a defenseless candor, and Joe, answered,
turned his back and headed aft. Using the deck hatchet, he hacked
out a length of the remaining whip and struggled forward again,
head bowed in the frigid wind. Already he felt drugged with the
cold, his hands and feet like stumps. Beyond the rail, whitecaps
were breaking everywhere, lapping the hull with obscene sounds
like something ravening a corpse.

Somewhere along the way, Joe Madden had consciously forgotten the knot Will Tilley taught him as a boy, but in some deeper
place he still remembered—his stiff, cold fingers knew. Lifting Ray,
he looped the line around his chest beneath both arms and
wrapped it round and round itself, then pulled the end back

through and snugged it tight. In the same way, Joe bound himself with the fisherman's knot, which can never be undone, but only cut, as he unwittingly had cut it in himself.

"You don't have to do this, man," Ray said.

"Sure I do," Joe said. "We'll be cracking oysters on the dock before you know it."

"Damn straight," Ray said, moved, with no belief at all.

"We're going to make it, Ray."

"I hope so."

"Have a little faith."

Ray finally smiled. "Good one."

Joe smiled, too, toed off his boots and sat down, testing the water like a man about to climb into a bath. Then he slipped into the sea.

And it was not as if Joe Madden, forensic engineer, had failed to take Ray's point that he was better off alone, but deep into his lesson now, he discovered there was no decision to be made. He had no choice.

Joe, whose heart had craved an act of singular devotion through which he might give himself to something larger, outside himself, had been granted the opportunity with Day and had failed to recognize it when it came. Now God or fate—whatever force had drawn him here like an iron filing in the field of His or Its unfathomable intent—had narrowed down Joe's mortal choices on this earth to one. Ray Bristow was the last chance he had left. There was no choice, and Joe was glad to be absolved of making one. For the first time in his life, Joe Madden submitted to a higher force, and, in submission, for the first time he felt free.

But the sea was gravely unmoved by what Joe felt. The water was strangely warm at first and, in the dead space to leeward, almost calm. Out of the shadow of the hull, however, the racing ebb tide seized Joe hard and swept the two men eastward, lateral to shore. Ray, more buoyant in the vest, swung downcurrent and abreast. The loop around Joe's chest snugged like the harness of an open parachute filled with water and dragged him toward the sea.

He tried to maintain a steady crawl, but his stroke quickly degenerated under the pummeling of the waves, which tossed him like wash in a machine. As seas broke over him, Joe held his breath till they subsided, then lurched up with a scissor kick, gulping foam with insufficient breath, and then the next wave broke. For every yard he gained toward shore, Ray pulled him ten or twenty seaward, and with each stroke, his arms grew heavier with cold.

All too quickly he realized there could be no swimming here. Resting, he allowed himself to sink, hoping to springboard off the bottom. It was only twelve feet deep, yet down and down he went, waiting for his feet to strike. They didn't. It occurred to Joe, in panic, that they'd been swept out past the bar, where the water was ten fathoms deep. He began to claw for handholds in the water, then, out of air, he hit. Rebounding off the bottom, he thrashed upward, blind, through water black as oil.

"Joe!" The thin, distant cry came to him across the waves as he broke through, gasping. *Joey!* Something slammed his shoulder hard. Through streaming eyes, he saw the red channel marker bob overhead like a gigantic broomstick horse, its lit face an inverted caution sign. *Red, right, returning,* he remembered and the cry came back. "Joe!" *Joey!* He reached for the line around his chest, but he had done his job too well; it stayed. As the current swept them onward, the marker fell away into the wash with a deep sigh. The number on the face was 66.

Weighed down by his shoes, Joe bent under to untie them—and found his feet already bare. Somehow he thought he had on his old Converse sneakers, the ones he wore that other time with Pa, who had warned him not to leave the boat. But Joey disobeyed him, and it happened as he said. In the twinkling of an eye the current swept him out from shore, and fighting had exhausted him, hastening the moment of succumbing.

Joe let the current take him, and he sank. As the surface sealed above his head, it shut the wind and wavewash out. The combers' thundercrack, the diesel roar, the urgent shouts—all the strifeful noises ceased. Weightless as a snowflake, Joe drifted down into a dark element of silent peace. As he fell, the voices from the other time came back, one urging, *Hold on, keep fighting, son,* the other whispering, *Let go.* Just beneath the surface of awareness, they'd been there all his life, one louder, now the next. Joe had fought to live according to his Pa's command, yet here beneath the surface, Jimmy's had the truer ring.

Joey, heeding it that other time, had closed his eyes and breathed the water in, and when he opened them, the emerald underlight

flashed on, brilliant as a bank of kliegs. On the beach that afternoon, Jimmy had revived him with the lifeguard's kiss. But as he
sank once more, Joe wondered if perhaps he'd only dreamed his father came. Perhaps he'd only dreamed that he'd been saved,
dreamed that he'd grown up, become a man and lived these other
years. Perhaps he was still there.

It wasn't Jimmy who had failed him. The thought came clearly
now: *The lumberjack is me.* Something in Joe's heart had not con-
sented to come back. For him, the emerald beauty of the underlight
had eclipsed the sunlight of the common world. He'd opened his
hands and let it slip away, the line that bound him to the human
universe, and had never tied himself to anything again. As he
drifted down, no longer sure if he was twelve or twenty-eight, or
whether this was memory, experience or dream, Joe realized that
repetition upon repetition, while he struggled in the vain illusion of
his will, the current had swept him back to this same moment in
the water, to this same choice, whether to turn back to the world
in faith or to proceed, and the man was tempted to make the same
decision the boy had made.

But in the other balance of the scales was Day. He thought about
her clunky shoes, the man's Swiss Army watch, her Delft-blue eyes
that lightened when she laughed. They were the first thing he'd ever
loved in her, yet in reality Day's eyes weren't Delft-blue at all. That
saturated color was achieved by artifice, with tinted contacts, a fact
that she, in vanity and insecurity, had hidden for three months, till
he walked in on her one morning in the bathroom and discovered
it by accident. Somehow it wasn't the public face she kept prepared
for others—with the big laugh and swinging walk that made her
bob toss side to side, the confident smile filled with dazzling white
teeth—but the private, more vulnerable face that Day, in trust, had
shared with him alone, that came back to Joe now.

He understood that at the end of the long trail of bread crumbs
that leads ever deeper into the mystery beyond the world, she
would not be waiting. And where Joey had become exhilarated and
wanted to go on and on into the underlight forever and not come
back to the dull, common pain of life, Joe, the man he had become,
discovered now that his sole wish was to come down from the
mountain he'd ascended in his lesson, to leave the singing jet
stream and the ravishment of spectral black-and-whiteness, to es-

cape the sky's inhuman blue, and descend to an altitude where human life is possible, and there, like Odysseus, plant his oar and stake his rows of beans and love his wife.

If You hear me, if You're there, deliver me. Give me strength to rise.

Having conned the lesson, Joe, with bitter effort, fought off the urge to sleep, realizing his eyes were closed already when he opened them again.

And it seemed that God, or whatever moves the planets in their orbits, had heard Joe Madden's prayer. At just that moment the current shoved him up onto the bar. Struggling to his feet, he staggered forward in the millrace. The water dropped, to his chest, his waist. The beach was fifteen yards away when, all of a sudden, the slack line tightened and pulled back. Losing his footing, he upended in the current and went down, thrashing toward the surface with his final effort as the line around his chest, bent fast and well, pulled him down, to black.

Twenty-seven

"Dr. Shaughnessey?"

Pate, wearing her coat and carrying mine, joined me in my vigil on the deck. "Are you okay?"

"Been better," I confessed. "You?"

"I guess I've been a little better, too."

She held up my coat, and I slipped into it. "Thanks. It's been a good while since we talked."

"Yes, ma'am. I should have called you, Dr. Shaughnessey. I apologize. I thought of it a hundred times, but I didn't know what to say."

"It's okay, Pate. I don't care about that. Tell me how you are."

"I'm all right."

I searched. "Are you?"

She stared into the howling night as the lashed boats creaked and tossed. "The wedding's supposed to be next month. I mean, it is."

"And Chapel Hill?"

A pause. "I don't guess I'm going. Not this year. Maybe later."

"And you're okay with that?"

"Yes, ma'am, I think so."

"Are you, Pate? Because you seemed so set on it before, on college, veterinary school . . ."

"I know. I dreamed of that for a long time, Dr. Shaughnessey.

But I guess you don't always get your dreams. Sometimes you have to take what comes and be as happy as you can with that."

"And are you?" I asked her, whose changing face seemed so profoundly sad. "Happy?"

"I think what James and I are doing is right, maybe not for everyone, but for us. It is for me." She faced me. "No matter what I told you, Dr. Shaughnessey, no matter what I said before, I don't think I could have lived with it the other way. So, yes, I guess I'm happy."

"Do you love him?" No longer her physician, I asked this as her friend.

"No," she said. "No, ma'am, I don't." There was no hesitation; she was clear. "There was a time I felt I did, two years ago. But now I think that was probably something else. Mama says love's overrated, anyway. She says you can't know what it is when you're my age, not till you've been married ten or fifteen years. She says any man who'd stand up for me the way James did has the makings of a good husband and a father, and over time I'll come to recognize his worth, and then respect will grow to something more, and real love, when you finally get to it, sneaks up and takes you by surprise. That's how it was for her and Daddy, and it'll be the same for James and me. That's what Mama thinks."

"What do you think, Pate?"

"I don't know. I hope she's right. I suppose it's possible." That hot, inflected, teenage question mark flashed through her look as she searched my face. "What do you think, Dr. Shaughnessey?"

"God knows, I don't have any answers, Pate. I'm probably the last person you should ask. I guess if you work hard enough, you can improve any marriage. But I think it's also possible for things to stay the same or to worsen over time, no matter how much hard work you put in, especially if the foundation isn't there to start with."

She took my answer in and blinked, then stared away to the north, where a black patch of sky with frosty winter stars had appeared through a tatter in the scudding clouds. "There's the Big Dipper."

"Is it?" I asked. "I've never been too good at the constellations." That was something Joe had tried to teach me, too.

"When I was eleven or twelve, one night at the Lighthouse

after Bible class Uncle Johnny took us out to the parking lot," she said. "He pointed out some constellations—I don't remember what they were—and told us how in olden times the Greeks and Romans looked up in the sky and found them there. The stars were like these little dots, and no one had ever connected them before to make out the pictures. He said how hard they must have had to look, but the effort they made, the names they chose are still the ones we use today." Pate paused, her gaze still fixed on the north star. "Uncle Johnny told us that's how God reveals His purpose in our life. First one thing happens, then another—each thing is a dot. All God gives us is the dots, and it's up to us to make the effort to connect them and, once we see the picture He intends, to abide by it and live a Christian life." She turned to me. "That's all I'm trying to do, Dr. Shaughnessey."

"Then you will," I told her. "I have no doubt at all."

Though it looked five years older, this new face of hers—a woman's now and not a girl's—was just as beautiful, maybe even more, but in the way of someone who's been out to the edge and fought a battle there, a battle she was still engaged in, managing to survive, minute to minute, with no certainty as to outcome. That other part of her—the level of additional awareness that played above the conversation—wasn't really gone. It was no longer on the hilltop, though, above the fray. It had been called into the battle, too, along with everything Pate had.

I still thought she was wrong, however brave. Till then, Pate had seemed an anomaly, a bright-winged bird that arose by miracle or accident from that poor town. But tonight I understood far better who she was, seeing what she'd come from, a heritage of hardship, strength and sacrifice. That heritage didn't make up for the prejudice, the bigotry toward blacks and women, nor did it prevent my subtle heartbreak at the price Pate was about to pay. But looking through Joe's eyes, I began to understand his plea for forbearance in Pate's case. Though my differences with him and with the villagers remained, I saw the question from both sides, and Joe's love of Little Roanoke at last made sense to me. Pate had made her choice, and I respected her, and in the end you have to step aside.

"It's cold," she said. "Should we go in?"

"You know, Pate, I'm going to head back home. He might call there, if they went into port."

"Yes, ma'am," she said, "but if they laid up, I'm sure Daddy would call here."

"I know," I said, "it's probably a long shot, but I wouldn't want to miss it if he did."

"I understand."

"If they do call here, you'll let me know?"

"Yes, ma'am."

"I'll just turn around and drive right back."

She walked me to the Wagoneer, and we hugged before I got in. In the rearview mirror as I pulled away, I saw her standing in the circle of the lamp with her hand raised. Uncertain if I'd ever see Pate Ames again, I thought one last time about those Scottish lasses in the lays, how even if the end was always sad for them, the way they faced it is worth passing on. And perhaps that's why their stories come down through the years in song, to help us remember what's at stake in this, which is so briefly here and quickly gone.

Back at Joe's, I thought of putting on another album, but on second thought I didn't know if I could bear another oldie. It was four-thirty in the morning, too deep for music now. Missing him, wanting something, I took down his picture from the wall and gazed into his clear, troubled stare, searching for him there, and then I opened his closet in the bedroom and touched his denim shirts. I counted them; there were eight, all good, but starting to show wear. I un-buttoned the top collar and slipped my hand inside and read the la-bels, and, still unsatisfied, went into the bathroom and in his brush I found a single glowing silver hair. I crawled into bed and smelled him in the pillow and the sheets. I thought if he was gone, I'd never wash them, all my life; this would be all I'd ever have of him, all I'd have of us.

There is a door in us, a door . . . Joe opened it in me, and I walked through and saw myself in ways that I was never clear about before. And maybe no one ever is; maybe that's why love takes two, so that gazing in the mirror of a lover's eyes, we can be-hold ourselves more deeply than we ever could alone.

As I lay there grieving, waiting for the phone, I had a dream, though, in truth, I never really slept. I thought of growing old with Joe and how his face would age. I saw him somewhere in a study lined with books, poring over one with those scholarly pink glasses he was wearing when he came into Beach Med that first day thinking he had dengue, still handsome, but at a point when the peace he now achieved only in moments had become a settled quality, one that softened and disarmed that penetrating thing in him. I would be older, too, somewhere out beyond the struggle to stay thin and on the edge and twenty-five forever. There was a young girl with me in my dream, a teenager, with braces—maybe she now had the shades and shoes and listened to my old Patti Smith and Chrissie Hynde LPs, or whoever the girls had passed the banner to. In a casual moment, cleaning out a closet in the spring, she'd ask me how we met and fell in love and how I knew he was the one, and I'd tell her, "Your father brought me a fish," and she'd say, "A fish?" and I'd smile, and she would, too, self-consciously, trying not to, covering her mouth to hide the gleam of awkward wire. This would be the story we would tell, and it would give her a grounding and a safety in the world, knowing that there had been a specialness between us and that she'd come out of it.

Lulled by this fantasy or vision, I gazed up at the knots in the old cedar planks, staring down like eyes, and only then did I realize who she was, that girl.

I went out to the big room and sat at the table, facing the bay window, and I grimly waited for the light. When it came, I saw the sea oats, sheathed in ice, like bright swords of glass that broke themselves to pieces as they clashed, and, beyond, the sea whipped white. And then the overhead came on, Pa's light, and quickly fizzled out, and something cold fell over me. I stared at the black phone, praying it would ring and almost wishing that it never would. But then, of course, a little after six, it did.

Twenty-eight

He was on the bottom, deep; he felt the pressure throbbing in his ears. Around him, the water had turned green—not the brilliant emerald he remembered, but a sinister and putrid tint—and something was attacking him. Squatting on Joe's chest, it had him pinned, clicking teeth with him as it sucked the breath from his collapsing lungs. And now he saw it, a black silhouette, void against the silver surface shimmering far above. His bubbles rose like balloons adrift, carrying a silent scream.

Joey!

Stung with the slap, he came to, coughing up a hiccup of salt water that washed over his cheek and burned like acid as it ran into his ear.

"Joe!" The shape drew back, and it was Ray, wiping his hand across his mouth, where Joe, lashing out, had hit him. Blood trickled from Ray's nostril.

Confused, Joe tried to orient himself. Ray had dragged him into the dunes. Over Ray's shoulder, the eastern sky was streaked with vivid red. Against it, black, the sea oats clattered in the wind.

"You all right?"

Joe nodded.

"Brame and Jubal didn't make it. I'm going back to look."

"I'll go with you." As Joe struggled to sit up, fireflies swarmed around his head, stinging ones. He lay back.

"Stay here."

Joe gripped his arm. "Don't go in the water, Ray. You can't help them."

"I'll come back for you," he said.

Joe watched him running toward the beach. The sand was streaming down the wind. Covering his face, Ray turned transparent as he stepped into the cloud; then he disappeared.

When Joe opened his eyes again, it was day. The air was whirring, *whomp, whomp, whomp*. Someone was shaking his shoulder.

"Ray?"

"Roger that. I've got another one up here." The man in the green Park Service uniform spoke into a walkie-talkie. "We're fifty yards west of the point. He's in pretty rough shape. Tell the second ambulance to wait; I'll bring him down.

"Sir, can you tell me your name?"

"Where's Ray?"

"I need to know your name, sir."

"Joe," he said. "Joe Madden."

The ranger repeated it into the walkie-talkie.

Joe sat up. "Did you find Ray?"

"Was he on the raft?"

Joe shook his head.

"We've recovered six men, sir. Three on the raft, two on the boat, and you."

"He went back for Jubal and Lukey," Joe said, as if pleading. "They were in the water."

"Captain Ames stayed on the boat," the man told him. "They just got him up, and they're lifting off the other man right now."

He took off his hat, ducked his head under Joe's shoulder, and stood him on his feet. The Coast Guard helicopter hovered just offshore. *Whomp, whomp, whomp.* Under it, the *Father's Price* lay canted over, gleaming like milk glass, what little of her remained visible—a foot of starboard rail, the angle of the deckhouse roof, the top third of her leaning mast. Standing near the mast's tip, a helmeted guardsman shot a thumb's-up to the winch operator overhead. As the rotor's downwash beat a perfect circle in the water around the boat, he and another man rose skyward, face to face.

"That's not him!" Joe shouted, pulling away from the ranger. "That's Lukey Brame. We have to look for Ray."

"He says there's another one out here," the ranger reported into the walkie-talkie. "Ray?" He looked at Joe.

"Bristow. Ray Bristow."

"Ray Bristow. You better send somebody else up here. Come on, sir, let's get you in the truck. The other team's on the way."

"No," Joe said. "We have to find him first."

"You need medical attention. I have to get you to the paramedics." He opened the passenger door and got Joe into the truck.

"Please. Just look. He can't be far."

The man hesitated. "All right. Wait here."

The radio was blaring, WDAR-AM, the morning show with Rick and Dave. Their hyped, falsely plangent voices were grotesque, like barks of madness. The truck's heater was cranking full blast, but Joe could feel no warmth in the air current blowing past his face. To the east, the life raft was surrounded by a gaggle of flashing lights—patrol cars, an ambulance, a satellite van from the CBS affiliate in Norfolk, imprinted with the seeing eye.

He watched the ranger trotting back. "I'm sorry, sir. There's no sign of him. The other men will be here soon. They'll find him if he's here."

Just offshore, the Coast Guard cutter lay beyond the bar, snow white, dreamlike against the eastern sky, where a few last hints of pink and gold were washing out in pure cerulean blue. The wind had died down considerably, turning the sea black once again. Far out, a few whitecaps were breaking. It looked as though God had pared His fingernails over a table of dark stone. Closer in, the rollers were making up in dress-parade order, magisterial and stern, as they drove across the bar. The ranger turned the truck around; Joe closed his eyes and listened to the waves break with a sound like judgment.

PART VII

Twenty-nine

Ray Bristow was dead. This was Joe's first thought when he came to in the hospital. And his second: Where was Day? Day should have been here; why wasn't she?

Staggering into the bathroom, he blinked into the mirror and a face he didn't recognize blinked back, a face with patches of black frostbite and bruises ripening beneath the skin and eyes like Ennis Wright's that had tunneled too far into molten, secret realms and been sobered by the terrors they beheld. Having asked God for a second chance, Joe, receiving one, had assumed that there would be a happy ending, a reconciliation filled with joy and promises exchanged. The one thing he had not imagined was that the happy ending might turn out to be a dream. The one thing he had not imagined was that his small, poor response may have forced on Day a choice that she could not forgive—or wouldn't.

Why wasn't she here? Joe's battered doppelganger in the mirror posed the question back, reversed: *Why should she be?* Wasn't the reason obvious? After his night sea journey, after his dark night of the soul and the great battle of his life, Joe woke up to find his life as barren after his ordeal as it had been before. All of it had been in vain. Day was gone and Ray was dead and Joe was still alone.

Things turned stranger as Joe limped down the corridor, past the nurse's desk. "Sir?" she said. "Sir, excuse me?" In trance, he walked on, his fixed stare trained on the sign above the door—EXIT, it said, in glowing orange letters—and Joe walked toward it as though that word was the secret summons God Almighty had engraved upon his heart with burning coals.

"Sir? Excuse me, sir?" She caught up to him. "I'm sorry, sir, but you aren't allowed to leave until the doctor checks you out. It's hospital policy. And anyway, that door is only for emergencies."

Joe Madden heard her out respectfully and said, "I think this has to qualify," and went on, undeterred.

And, curiously, as he got closer to the door, sounds of large commotion drifted from the stairwell on the other side. A deep baritone rang out, firing torpedoes of invective in what sounded like blank verse. A bowlegged giant—six-six and three hundred pounds, at least—limped in through the out door pursued by security personnel he threatened with his cane, like a crippled grizzly swatting at a swarm of gnats.

The moment Joe heard that familiar baritone, the moment he heard that shuffling, familiar step, he experienced an overwhelming urge for headlong flight in the opposite direction. It was too late; the way was barred. There's no escaping when the captain rides.

The two men faced off, mutually astonished.

"Dad?"

"Son?"

It appeared that passports might be necessary to confirm ID. Of the two, Jimmy Madden was the swifter to believe.

"Son, are you all right?" he asked, making concern sound like a threat.

"What are you doing here?" Joe asked.

"Reed called. He saw the shipwreck on the news. We didn't know whether you were alive or dead. He said your mother is in Rome."

"Right," Joe said, remembering. "Right, they left last week, she and Sumner."

"Right, she and Sumner." The muscle corded in Jimmy's jaw.

"You came from Key West?"

"I've been on the road for twenty hours. You look like hell, Joey."

Joe decided not to say "You don't look that great yourself." He wouldn't be the one to start it, not this time.

Jimmy now turned on the milling officers with the air of one who's fought the law on more than one occasion and seen the law victorious more frequently than not. "If you're planning to arrest me, come on and pull your guns. Bring on the cuffs and billy clubs, and don't forget to read my rights. Otherwise, I'm going to spend a moment with my son, so you can all back off and take a dough- nut break. Here, have one on me." He reached into his shirt pocket, took out a soiled wad of dollar bills and peeled one off. "Don't consider it a bribe, but a gratuity."

The officers, of course, declined the offer on whatever terms. "Is there a problem here?" one of them asked the nurse.

"Well, I don't guess so," she said, troubled. She looked at Joe. "As long as you don't leave the premises."

"Come on," he said to his father. "We'll go back to my room."

Joe walked slowly while Jimmy, dispensing with his cane, made use of the handrail, dragging his lock-kneed left leg in a limp at- tributable to old sports injuries compounded by unsuccessful Stone Age surgeries. However hard he tried not to watch, Joe couldn't help feeling a pang, and part of it was sympathy. Part of it was anger, though, that the young man who once sank the buzzer shot that brought the state title home for the whole town should be re- duced to this, that life had used him so. Or perhaps it was the reck- less disregard with which this man had used himself.

Joe started to sit on the bed, but switched to the low chair and gave the older man the convalescent's place.

"What's the matter with you?" Jimmy inquired. "You look stunned."

"I wasn't exactly expecting you," Joe said.

"Who were you expecting?"

"The Prince of Darkness, I suppose."

Joe said this with a smile meant to lighten things, but it was not without an edge, and he watched his father scan it with the Geiger counter of his sensitivity, calibrated to detect gradations of offense. Jimmy let it pass.

At closer quarters now, Joe was able to assess the stranger his father had become and compare him with the man he once knew. Though still as thick as fur, Jimmy's dark hair had grayed com- pletely, in contrast to his new coal-black gunslinger mustache. Glasses were another addition, aviator-style, with clear bifocal lenses. Behind them, Jimmy's sea-green eyes were still large and lu-

minous, but the light in them, once sunny, had a covert and smol-
dering quality, like subterranean fire. Battered and aged, he was
not as Joe remembered him, yet, in some essential way, the same.

"I don't have anything to offer you," Joe said, shouldering the
host's burden. "There's probably a Coke machine. Can I get you
one?"

"Don't trouble yourself. I'll go." Gripping the bedrail, Jimmy, to
his son's alarm, began to hoist himself aloft.

"No, no, Dad, really. Sit; stay where you are."

"Here, let me pay at least," said Jimmy, reaching for his wad.

"No, no, I've got it."

"Take the money, Joe! I mean it now!"

And they were into it—hospitality offered, hospitality rejected,
rejection noted, guilt applied—beneath the seemingly innocuous
exchange, several rounds of tense, unsatisfactory diplomacy. Joe,
however, standing there in his blue gown, without his clothes—uncertain whether he still had clothes—belatedly reflected that he had
no money anyway, not one thin dime. "Okay, Dad," he said, "if
you insist."

Licking his thumb, Jimmy peeled five singles off the roll.

"That's too much," Joe said, returning three, and went out to
the hall, only to discover the exact change light aglow on the machine.

"Do you have any quarters?" he said, ducking in.

Jimmy frowned. "How many do you need?"

"They're seventy-five cents."

"Seventy-five cents?" said Jimmy with a wince of protest and
appeal that stung Joe's heart. "Seventy-five cents!" And now Captain Nemo, recovering resolve, dug deep and found his righteous
outrage. "I'll crawl to Vladivostock naked over frozen tundra before I'll pay that for a goddamn Coca-Cola. It's larceny! Come on;
I've got a cooler in the truck."

"I'm not supposed to leave."

"Fuck 'em!" roared the captain. "Fuck 'em, and the horses they
rode in on! Fuck the whole damn cavalry!"

And so, reduced once more to meekness, as he'd been a thousand times in childhood, steamrollered by the churning urn of
burning funk his father was, Joe followed, cringing, as his father
shuffled past the desk.

"Sir! Sir!" The nurse ran after them.

"I'll be right back," Joe said.

"I'm sorry, but you can't leave the premises. I told you that before."

Jimmy turned on her. "Madame! Excuse me, if I may. My son and I—this gentleman—are going to my truck to get a Coke, all right? My truck, I think, is in the parking lot. The parking lot, I think, is on the premises. Is it, or is it not?"

Confounded by the captain's scathing logical display, the nurse said, "Well, I guess it is. But you aren't leaving, right? You're coming back?"

"Barring acts of God and natural disaster," Jimmy said. "Will you be satisfied, Madame? Because if not, bring on the G-men. We won't go down without a fight!"

And with that, Jimmy stormed the castle walls in his habitual manner—attempting not to enter but get out—and Joe, wanting to wake from this bad dream but losing hope, followed to the parking lot.

Jimmy was still driving the truck Gray and Reed sniggeringly referred to as the Batmobile—a Ford F-350 dualie, black, with tinted windows and a camper top. Eight or nine years old, it had rust blisters in the paint around the wheel wells and a major impact crater on the passenger-side door. Mudguards featured six-gun-toting Yosemite Sams. There were two bumper stickers—INSURED BY SMITH & WESSON and LOVE YOUR MOTHER, the latter with a picture of the blue-green earth swimming in a silver filigree of cloud. To Joe, the truck looked like a discount time machine, an impression confirmed when he caught the odometer over Jimmy's shoulder as he leaned into the cab: 387,000 miles and change. The number tugged like a lead sinker at Joe's heart.

"Here, put this on." Jimmy handed Joe a parka as he leaned in for the Igloo Junior on the shotgun side. Joe couldn't resist a quick surveillance of the cluttered cab. A gimbal-mounted compass and a spring-loaded change dispenser, bolted to the dash for expediting tolls, set a theme of exploration underscored by stacks of well-used maps, folded and refolded till the paper was as soft as Kleenex. Like old pirate charts, these were marked with X's indicating favored home-style restaurants. On the gun rack hung a pressed-tin sign, the sort Joe remembered from his boyhood, nailed to the porches of one-pump country stores: MOM'S NOT HERE, BUT THE POP'S ON ICE. On the floorboard was a dog-eared paperback of *Four Quartets* and a Gideon Bible: PROPERTY OF DAYS INN, SPARTANBURG, S.C. PLEASE DO NOT REMOVE. And in the midst of this, somehow out of place and somehow not, the new black Motorola mobile phone Reed had mentioned.

From beneath the seat, Jimmy pulled out a Bowie knife, an AK-47 and a healthy length of black iron pipe, all on the way to reaching what he wanted, a gray cardboard box.

"Open it."

Attending to His Master's Voice, Joe discovered, in two neat phalanxes, dipped in chocolate with white marshmallow hearts, the cookies he remembered from his childhood.

"Moon Pies?"

"Not by bread alone," the captain said. "Take the box."

"Where do you buy Moon Pies by the box?"

"I have a relationship with the distributor."

Joe had to laugh. "The poor son of a bitch. I'll bet he's applied for the witness protection program."

"Huh-huh-huh." Jimmy's ragged laugh was like Reed's, filled with the same rueful self-knowledge.

Joe laughed, too, but not too much. It smacked of fraternizing with the enemy.

Then Jimmy opened the camper top and father and son sat down on the tailgate for a family-style repast.

"I knew something was wrong," said Jimmy, popping a Pabst tallboy, Pa's old brand, as he handed Joe a pony Coke.

"Reed . . ."

Jimmy shook his head. "Before . . . I had this dream. We were playing ball, the two of us, up on the hill by Ruin Creek, and I threw one wild. It went over your head, and you went to get it, and I waited, but you didn't come back. So I went up to the edge and looked, and it just went down and down; there was no bottom to it. You were gone, and I woke up in a sweat. The clock said four-fifteen, and I said, 'It's Joe. My boy's in trouble.' Then Reed called, and I got in the truck and came."

As Joe listened to this tale, intoned by Jimmy in a sonorous voice befitting prophecy, skepticism vied once more with belief, but he'd believed too many times before.

"So you picked up a vibration in the ether, eh?"

Jimmy frowned. "So what happened? Tell me."

Joe thought of Ray and crashed. "I'm sorry, Dad, but I can't talk about that now."

"What can we talk about then, son? What about this girl, this doc Reed tells me you're seeing? Where is she?"

"Good question. I wish I knew."

"You're going to Boston, I understand."

"We made those plans," Joe said. "Now, to be honest, I don't know. All I know is she's not here. I'd tell you more, but that's all I have."

Jimmy frowned and mulled it over. "And your mother," he asked, retreating into ominous politesse, "how is she?"

"She's well."

"And Sumner . . ." It was a clear struggle for this name to pass his lips, yet he manfully performed the task.

"He's well, too."

"Rome . . ." Jimmy sipped his beer as though reproached. "May always wanted to travel. I'm glad she finally got the chance."

The blend of magnanimity and bitterness was hard for Joe to take. Listening, he felt the tug of an old pathos like a rusty fishhook, still embedded long after the line that bound it had been cut.

Glancing surreptitiously across the cluttered bed, Joe noted the debris his father had accumulated—jumper cables, rope, a battered leather suitcase like the one George Bailey never got to use, giant gallon cans of pork and beans, a Coleman stove and lantern: all the accouterments for long survival in the event of nuclear war or winter, everything an old outlaw might require to make life on the lam a little easier the day the revenuers finally came. And looming over everything, in the rear window of the cab, that pressed-tin sign: MOM'S NOT HERE, BUT THE POP'S ON ICE.

As he read the letters in reverse, the question came again: *Why is Day not here?* And a terrible wooziness stole over Joe's mind. He had another premonition, like the one of his death at sea, the one that hadn't come to pass. Or had it? Was this the death he had foreseen?

Here they were, Big Jim and Little Joey, the Madden boys, sitting on the tailgate of the Batmobile, and where was Day? Not here, but the Pop's on ice. He saw his fate now; the future and Joe

Madden came face-to-face: *I am my father,* he thought. And not twenty years from now in some bad future he might still avert. The future had arrived.

This was Joe Madden's dream, the one he'd struggled to wake up from all his life. Day was gone. He'd driven her away as Jimmy once did May, and everything repeating, loop by loop, the old frayed line, the frayed line cut. And some day not far hence, he, too, with his own rusting Batmobile and gimbal-mounted compass and charts worn smooth by an old pirate, scouring the earth in search of that mystic place they say there is, the place you know there has to be and never really find, where they still know how to serve a home-cooked meal like you remember, the closest you'll ever come to tasting what you had and lost.

Joe saw his future and didn't like the view. Not knowing what else to do, he did the only thing he knew.

"Looks like the natives are getting restless," he said with a discreet nod at the security guard frowningly surveilling them.

Jimmy clamped his jaw. "Yeah, I guess this isn't going to go the way I planned."

Joe stood up. "Listen, Dad, you drove a long way. I don't want you to think I don't appreciate it."

"Right," said Jimmy. "Don't try to kid a kidder, son."

Joe considered this. "Right," he said. "Okay, I won't."

As he started to turn, Jimmy stopped him. "Before you go, there's something I want you to have." He reached in his pocket and held out a balled fist.

"What's this?"

"Open your hand."

Into Joe's palm, Jimmy dropped an arrowhead, milky white, made of some translucent stone that looked like quartz. "Remember that?"

As Joe looked at it, something winked and vanished like a trout in a cloudy current. "No."

"You gave it to me," Jimmy said. "Around the time I moved out to the lake to try to write my book."

Joe remembered then. Near a turning in the stream where they used to cross, he'd come on it one day, lying on a bed of gravel in a foot or two of ice-cold water.

"You said it was for luck."

"I guess the magic wasn't all that strong."

"Maybe not," said Jimmy. "Or maybe it was just a different sort of magic than you thought."

Joe felt his heart stir like an old paste and paper kite in a faint breeze from afar. He sat back down and turned the object in his hand.

Jimmy sipped his beer. "You used to find a lot of those on Ruin Creek. The summer we first built—fifty-five, I guess it was—I remember one day your Pa got a call from the excavator. He was out there digging the foundation hole and hadn't been at it fifteen minutes when the backhoe clanged on rock. We drove out, and what he'd hit on was a barrow. There were maybe half a dozen of them out that way—they were the ruins the creek was named for. Some people said they were Indian gravemounds. Others thought they went back to prehistoric times. Your Pa, though, being the original Full Foundation Man, had fairly limited sympathy for the residual rights of Indians and cavemen."

Jimmy smiled and Joe smiled, too, still susceptible to the old showman's charms.

"Mr. Will wanted to dig out in favor of a dry basement with ample headroom," Jimmy continued. "But your mother and I never thought we'd stay in Killdeer, so we overruled your Pa and poured a slab instead. Personally, I always regretted that decision."

"Why?" asked Joe.

"Because we ended living in that house a whole lot longer than we planned."

"So," Joe said with a certain fondness, "a parable on roots from the Gypsy Road King."

Jimmy, though, heard something else. "You aren't going to let me off the hook, are you?"

"I'm sorry, Dad, I didn't realize the hook was where you were."

"I didn't come all this way to fight you, Joey."

"Why did you come?" Joe asked, and looked his father in the eye, his shoulders held more square.

"I was worried," Jimmy said. "I wanted to see how you were. I guess I thought you might need me."

Joe felt the darkness welling up and shoved it down. "I appreciate the thought."

"In other words, you don't . . ."

Joe's first impulse was to neither confirm nor deny this; long practice had made him quite adept at the ambiguous response. But the hour was late, and, things being what they were, there might not be another chance. "Do you want the truth?" he asked.

Jimmy's jaw clamped tight. "Why not? Give me your best shot."

"I did once; I needed you. But you're something I've had to learn to live without. So, the answer to your question would be no, I don't."

"I see," said Jimmy. "Then you're a stronger man than I am, son, because I'm almost fifty and I still need my dad sometimes."

"I'm not you."

"I know that," Jimmy said. "Do you?"

"What's that supposed to mean?"

Jimmy shook his head, his face soft and open in a way Joe had almost forgotten, but not quite. "Maybe I came because I needed you."

And there it was, on the surface, everything Joe ever felt for him, right or wrong, deserved or undeserved.

"So where is Day?" his father asked again.

"I wish I knew."

"Have you considered going after her?"

"I was trying to mobilize when you blew in. The problem is, I'm not sure Day wants me to find her."

"Something happened . . ."

"You could say that. She got pregnant and I freaked. I gave her no support. I thought how inconvenient it would be for my career. I stabbed her in the heart, and then I went away and almost died, and, crazy me, I crawled out of the grave and thought she'd be here waiting with open arms. But she's not—why should she be? That story sound familiar?"

"A bit."

"Come on, Dad," Joe said, "don't kid a kidder, it's the story of your life, and now it's mine."

"Let's be clear on something, Joe, whatever you may think, what you know about my life is fairly limited."

"You're right," Joe said. "You're absolutely right. The problem is, despite my ignorance in this regard, I seem to have an innate talent for repeating it. I mean, come on. You meet the girl and fall in love; things swim right along, and then the girl conceives. She wants to do the right thing, only you can't handle the responsibility, so you fuck it up and the girl leaves. Only the last part, the fucking up that took you fifteen years with May, I managed to accomplish overnight, in a single conversation.

"You want to know why Day's not here? She had an abortion, Dad. She didn't want to, but I didn't give her any choice. I've spent my whole life trying not to be like you, trying to be someone else, and in the process I've repeated what you did, chapter and verse, and here we are, the boys, having a cold one on the tailgate of the Batmobile. And Mom's not here, but the Pop's on ice."

Jimmy's expression had the mild, appraising quality that tended to be typical of Joe, as though in some strange alchemy they were switching places. "I think you may be overthinking it a bit."

"Overthinking it?" Joe laughed aloud. "Come on, Jimmy, even after all these years, you're still packing *Four Quartets*. Don't go groundling on me. You asked me for my truth; well, here it is. The pattern's there; it's real. It's the Rosetta stone engraved inside my brain. It took me twenty-eight years, and cost me everything I had, to finally decipher it. Don't tell me I'm overthinking it."

"Okay," Jimmy said. "Let's say the pattern's there. Even if it is, let me tell you something your Pa used to say. Don't bite your chicken to the bone. Because once you do, it never tastes the same again."

"Meaning what?" Joe said. "That Day's the chicken?"

Jimmy's smile was grim. "Life's the chicken, bud."

"Life's the chicken," Joe repeated. "That's good. I like that, Jim. I'd say that pretty much sums it up."

"You're a bone-biter, Joey, a bad bone-biter."

"That's me," he said. "Bad to the bone."

Behind the impersonal sternness of Jimmy's face were glintings of a father's pity and his love. "You didn't used to be that way. What happened?"

"You don't know what happened? Boston happened, Dad. I guess that's where I bit the chicken to the bone—with your considerable assistance, I might add. Since then, it's never tasted quite the same."

"Boston . . ." Jimmy sighed. "That again. Is that what you want to do, Joe? I came up here for something else, but if that's what you need to do, come on, we'll hack it out once more and rip each other's hearts to shreds, but aren't you tired of it? Don't you know however many times you stage the charge, however many times Pickett sends the troops up Cemetery Ridge, the outcome's always going to be the same? In the end, everybody loses, Joe—not just me; you, too. If Boston's where we have to go, let's get it over with. We'll rehash the same old hash once more."

"Rehash?" Joe repeated evenly, and there was thunder now on his brow, too. "Excuse me, Dad, but when exactly did we ever hash it out before? It's been fifteen years and it's never once been mentioned between us—not one word."

Jimmy's expression drew down. "Haven't we? Because it seems to me we've talked of nothing else. Maybe you're right, though, son. Maybe I've just had that conversation with you in my head so many times I thought we'd spoken it for real."

"I've had it in my head a few times, too."

"And maybe that's where we should leave it," Jimmy said. "My advice to you, not only as your father but your friend, is let it lie. Get over it."

"That's your advice to me?" Joe said, and his voice was even more controlled. "Get over it? You think I haven't tried? What's your suggestion, Dad? Denial? You're talking to the king. I've spent my whole life in flight, but what happened in that room blew my life apart, not to mention what it did to Reed. To you, it may be ancient history, but to me, it's never stopped. Even now, I'm repeating you, willy-nilly, despite myself, and so is Reed, and it just cost me the great love of my life, and it may cost Reed even more. Get over it?" And now Joe's voice was not controlled at all. "You slit me open like a fish, you gutted me and ripped my heart out by the roots and took a giant steaming shit in the place it used to be. You fucked my life. Don't tell me to get over it!"

Jimmy's jaw was going like the telltale heart in tachycardic overload, and it was clearly touch-and-go whether Nemo would fire back, and when the sun comes up tomorrow, let it find a smoking ember where the blue-green planet used to swim through space, or let the sun not rise at all.

But the captain, who once upon a time would almost certainly have sent the *Nautilus* full steam ahead, held back now, measuring this other man, his son, who was not only inflamed with an anger he'd carried and controlled for much of his young life, but was half out of his mind with the shock of the ordeal he'd just endured.

Jimmy stared off across the rooftops where bare January trees clattered in the wind, standing sentinel in some decent residential neighborhood that would be bosky once again for others when he passed on to some other place. Behind his spectacles, his green eyes had taken on a humid shine, a look of loss and sadness that conjured up the photo of that twenty-one-year-old boy on the chapel steps in State Line, South Carolina, in 1954.

"Joe," he said, "sometimes I dream we're still in that hotel room and I can make it stop; it's not too late." He spoke calmly as tears streaked his ravaged cheeks. "I wish it had never happened, son. I wish I'd had the good sense and maturity to have acted better. All I can say is that sometimes when you're as deep into another person's life as May and I were into each other's, it's hard to just shake hands and part as friends. The tendrils go so deep the only way to get them out is to rip them bleeding by the roots. I don't offer that as an excuse. There's no excuse for what I did. It should never have happened. You and Reed should never have witnessed it. For that, I'm more sorry than you'll ever know. But being sorry doesn't change the past. If I had that secret power in my bag of tricks, I'd have used it long ago, but I don't. I'm sorry, son. If I've never said that to your face, then I'm ashamed. I thought I had. I've said it in my heart a thousand times.

"That said, the thing you need to understand about Boston is that it had nothing to do with you or Reed. It was between your mother and myself. That distinction may be hard to make when you're fourteen, but you aren't fourteen anymore, Joe. And what I don't understand is why, however much I let you down, it made you give up on yourself."

The question struck home like a dagger thrust that Joe had not expected on the heels of such a soft approach. "I never gave up on myself."

"I think you did," his father said. "You've said your piece. May I say mine?"

"Go ahead."

"It seems to me you're running scared, and you've been running scared for a long time. Somewhere along the way you stepped out of the game and you've been on the sidelines ever since, or maybe

you decided to become the referee. I don't know why you chose
that role. Maybe because referees don't ever lose, but the other
thing about it is they never get to win. To win you have to play, and
if I taught you nothing else, I taught you that. I'll carry what's mine
to carry, Joe—sins, crimes and misdemeanors. If I can shoulder
some of yours and your brothers' share from time to time, I'll do
it, gladly, but I won't carry that for you. I won't be your excuse for
giving up."

Something hot and rigid lodged in Joe's throat. "You're the one
who gave up," he said, swallowing it.

"Did I?" Jimmy said. "Maybe you're right. Maybe that's what I
did in that hotel room, when I ordered that Scotch I didn't need
and knew I couldn't handle. Apart from that, never. Not for a
minute, not for a quarter of an hour." And his eyes burned with
who he was and knew he was, whatever anybody else might think,
including Joe.

"Neither did I."

"I think you did," he said. "And I think you're giving up again
right now. You say you love this girl? Then why don't you get off
your ass and go tell her how you feel. So she had an abortion—too
damn bad. That's a bitter pill, but if she's what you say, the great
love of your life, you'll have other children. Make up to them what
this one lost. Raise a family. I wish you luck; it's not as easy as you
think. But that's a true dream, the first I've heard out of your lips
in a long time. How many do you think you get in this life, Joe?
You're twenty-eight and you've had, what, one or two? I'm forty-
nine and I've had maybe three or four. I'm here right now because
of one of them: that you and I might be part of each other's lives
again. Maybe you can't extend to me because of what happened in
Boston, but extend somewhere, Joe"—he leaned forward and put
his big paw on Joe's shoulder—"because life doesn't come to you;
you've got to go to it, and if you don't, it passes by and you wake
up one day and realize you weren't even here. You wake up one day
and you're a ghost. I ought to know."

Joe flashed back to the image from the boat—downtown
Killdeer, Christmastime, Jimmy lifting him onto the roof of the Bel
Air, surrendering his place for Joey to get a better view. And it suddenly occurred to Joe that life was the parade, and he'd watched
but never entered it. This was what the ghost of Christmas Past had

come to tell him. Joe, however, wasn't sure he wanted to forgive his father for the news. He was filled with cross currents, angry rejoinders bitten off, amendments, codicils, the same old maybe-yes-but-maybe-no. But it struck him that it came down in that moment to a choice that might never be repeated, whether to forgive his father and step back into the stream of life, or not to, to consecrate himself to grievance as a cause and let his wounds forever chain him to the past.

"You may be right," he said.

"There's no maybe about it, son."

"Don't press your luck."

Jimmy's jaw corded; so did Joe's.

"Life's the chicken," Joe repeated. "I'll have to remember that one." And he accompanied this with a cautious smile.

Jimmy's eyes went light to dark and back to light again. "So does this mean we're friends?"

"Who'd a-thunk it," Joe replied.

Then Jimmy held his hand out, and Joe shook it the way his father taught him to, once upon a time, firm and definite, but not opinionated, holding the other's eye with a clear, open stare, earnest of your good faith and intentions, inviting peaceful commerce and prosperity for all, and keeping in the background, not advertised but not totally concealed, your talent and capacity for war.

"On that," his father said, "I'd better go. Before you change your mind."

"Or you do."

Jimmy smiled. "It won't be me."

"Then it won't happen."

Then, shuffling with interminable slowness on his cane, the old monster, who no longer seemed so monstrous, bearing his disfigurations with a certain dignity and pride, sat down in the driver's seat and rested before pulling in his legs.

"Something else your Pa used to say . . ."

"What's that?" Joe asked.

"He said a dream's a fine thing in its place, but if it doesn't come true and if you hold it past its time, it can poison the real life that's still possible."

"Is that for me?"

Jimmy shook his head. "No, bud, that was mine. The other side of it is that reality without a dream is poison, too. Too much reality without relief is poison to the realist, and that's what worried me about you, Joe. You gave up your dreams too soon, without a fight, because you were afraid of turning into me. If you hurt this girl you love, go tell her you were wrong. If she's the great love of your life, don't let her slip away the way I let your mother go, because that's what she was for me. Whatever else, I loved May and love her still. That's what I wake up to every morning. You want to avoid repeating my mistakes? Start there. Go find her. Build your house and make sure you put a goddamn deep foundation under it. If you have to blast, get dynamite. Don't try to cheap it out the way I did. . . . And since I'm thinking of it . . ." Taking out his wad, he peeled off a fist of ones. "Let me give you a few bucks to tide you over."

"No, no, Dad, I don't need it," Joe, dead broke, protested.

"Damnit, take the money!" said the captain. "If nothing else, apply it to the plastic surgery—you look like Death served cold on a tin plate."

Joe laughed. "All right, Dad. Thanks a lot."

"Don't consider it a bribe . . ."

"I know, I know," said Joe, "it's a gratuity."

As Jimmy pressed the bills into his palm, Joe, reciprocating as he could, tried handing back the arrowhead. "It's yours, Dad. I gave it to you. You should keep it."

"No, no," said Jimmy, "I've had it long enough. Hold on to it, and may it bring you better luck than it brought me."

"Dad, listen," Joe said, "before you go, there's something I want to say. I never understood the sacrifice you and Mom both made for me. I understand it better now."

As his great eyes filled, the captain pressed his lips and shook his head. "No, bud. No child should ever have to thank a parent, not for that. That one's for free."

"To hell with it," Joe said. "Thanks anyway."

Jimmy, with the fierce expression Jubal and the men from Little Roanoke took on when they were moved, held out his hand, but Joe pulled his father into an embrace the way Jimmy had pulled him that day, long ago, on Water Street in Exeter, when everything went wrong. Joe squeezed with every ounce of strength he had, the only safe technique there is to hug a bear and live.

Jimmy, glowering at the guard, flashed Joe a peace sign and cranked the Batmobile—which didn't start, of course, and then it did. As he pulled out to a heavy reggae beat, Joe noted from old habit, which dies hard, the cracked taillight on the left, and "Exodus," thinning on the wind, was "Jamming" suddenly, and he blinked his eyes, and the ghost of Christmas Past vanished in a puff of sulfur-tinted smoke.

As he stared into the distance, Joe remembered that old fishing trip with Pa and Jimmy, how he woke up on the beach with a dark form hovering over him, attacking, the nemesis, and how he fought, except the nemesis was Jimmy, who resuscitated him with the lifeguard's kiss.

And Joe thought, *Is that what I've been fighting? Life?*

And then the nemesis was Ray.

Standing in the parking lot, in his father's parka and his blue hospital gown, Joe bowed his head and pressed his dollar-cladded fists against his eyes, and his wide shoulders shook as he wept for Ray, the man who'd been his subject for nine months, whom Joe had put beneath the lens and never really seen and known at all the way it seemed to him he'd never really seen and known this other man, his father. No longer at home in his first world, Ray had wished to be his friend, and Joe, from fear and intellectual arrogance and a prejudice as mean and narrow-minded as a small-town hick's, a prejudice as mean as that of Jesse Helms, had not allowed this to occur. Yet in the final moment when Joe's fight was lost, it was Ray who pulled him from the water, giving Joe a second chance, though he would have no second chances for himself.

At the rush of wings, Joe looked up. High overhead, a flock of geese went crying down the sky, their voices cracked, unmusical and hoarse, but something in him stirred.

"Sir? Excuse me, sir?"

Lost in contemplation, Joe turned as the worried guard approached.

"I need you to come back, sir. You have to pay your bill."

"You're right," Joe said. "You're absolutely right, I do." And he held out his fists. "Bring on the cuffs. I surrender."

"Handcuffs won't be necessary, sir," the guard said, relieved at his compliance.

"Oh, you never know," Joe said, wiping his eyes. "I wouldn't jump to any large conclusions, sir, if I were you."

Thirty

By the time the ambulance finally got him to the hospital, Joe was in hypothermic shock. His body temp was eighty-nine. The clothes were frozen to his skin. He'd been lying in the dunes exposed for God knows how long, and the temperature overnight had dropped to five below, the wind chill pushing minus forty. A little longer, not much at all, and Joe wouldn't have made it. The margin was that thin.

When Pate called at six-fifteen, the ambulance was already on the way to the hospital. By the time I got there, they had him in water, trying to raise his core temp. The doc was Edward Lane, a friend of Gaither's, madras-clad but no less competent for that, entirely good. In no state to help myself, much less help Joe, I surrendered unconditionally, with gratitude, and let him do his work. Joe was catatonic when they put him in the bath, but the minute he felt water he came to, fighting like a cat, thrashing in the tub as he tried to swim and, choking, cried out, "Ray!" Over and over, "Ray!" As if he was still out there, wherever he'd been, lost and fighting in the waves. Watching made the hair rise on my spine; the nurses, too, were solemn-eyed, and the three orderlies it took to hold him down. When they took him, naked, from the tub, he weighed a hundred and sixty-nine pounds—this strapping six-foot-four-inch man whose normal weight was one eighty-five. He looked like some poor dead sad pathetic wasted little Christ brought down, with no Mary to hold him in her arms, no John, just me. I know, I know the Deposition scene, and surely there was never any sorrier excuse for Jesus Christ than Joe and no sorrier Mary Magdalene than me, but I was in a fit and going totally native, totally RC.

When they finally got him into bed, he was so agitated—thrashing the sheets, still swimming, groaning, grinding his teeth so hard they cracked like tree limbs on a windy night—Edward gave him a sedative, and slowly Joe relaxed, and as he did, his face looked worn and ruined, young and old at once, and overcome with an exhaustion I've never seen in anyone before. Edward tried to comfort me; he said the worst was past, and I knew he was right—medically, he was—but as I sat beside the bed, all through the long afternoon and longer night, I was afraid for him. He looked like a young man in his coffin, a Southern boy who took a wrong turn in the dark and never found his way back home to Ruin Creek and had come looking for it even here. I needed him to open his eyes and tell me that's who he still was so that I could tell him it was me, that he must leave his mother and father now, that I would be his home and family and he could put it down and rest in me, and that I trusted him to do and be the same for me.

Joe was alive, and living's something—living is a lot, don't get me wrong—but living's not enough, and if you don't believe me, ask your doctor, ask any doc you know. They'll tell you; it's the hardest thing you have to learn.

Ed Lane knew it. The second morning when he stopped in on rounds toward ten and found me there in the same place I'd been when he went home the night before, he gently, firmly took my hand and gently, firmly sent me to the cafeteria to eat, and when I said I didn't want to go, he gently, firmly told me he was going to bar me from the room unless I did.

So dutifully I went and dutifully I got my plastic tray and pushed it down the shiny rails, listening, as I sleepwalked toward the cashier, to the happy aliens in line around me blithely chatting on in the happy ET-speak they use on the far side of the wormhole in that alternative universe called Business As Usual. They might have been so many chirping birds—I couldn't understand a word.

When I got back to the room, Joe had risen from the dead and, rising, promptly disappeared. I called his name. I checked the bathroom. I went out in the hall. I tried the desk, but there was no one there. Losing it, I dinged the call bell and dinged and dinged again. Eventually, the nurse came out of another patient's room and told me a visitor had come, some man, and he and Joe had gone out to the parking lot a while ago, and if I saw them, could I please remind them that Dr. Lane would have to check Joe out before he was allowed to leave? She was altogether brisk with me, as though I were responsible for this, whatever incident had clouded her bright day. I took the elevator down and went outside. He wasn't there. Frantic, I took the elevator back, and there was Joe, staring out the window with the crack of his poor little ass partly exposed through the blue tie-on robe and his fists inexplicably filled with crumpled dollar bills.

"Joe?" I said, and when he turned to me, his eyes filled. He didn't say a word, not one, but one look was enough to tell me. And if any further proof was required, the professor, normally so verbal, so discreet and circumspect and shy, in his sudden mute and stricken state attacked me as a starving orphan might attack a crust of bread and wrapped me in his arms and held and held and held, and when I tried to break away, he shook his head and clung some more, until I was forced to protest, with a thin gasp, "I can't breathe, Joe. You're crushing me."

"I'm sorry," he said, gasping, too, like a swimmer taking breath. "I'm sorry, Day. I'm just so glad you're here. I didn't know if you were going to come."

"If I was going to come? I've been here, Joe."

"You have?"

"Are you insane? I've been here since yesterday, right here by the bed, all last night, all morning. A little while ago I went downstairs to get a bagel."

"A bagel?" he said, as though I'd clued him in on unexpected marvels.

"Yes, a bagel; don't get hung up on details now, okay? Follow me. I went to get a bagel, and when I came back, you were gone."

"You were here," he said, "all along?"

"All along."

He sat down on the bed, deflating like an inner tube.

"Where did you go? The nurse said a man came to see you."

"My dad," he said.

"Your *father?* Here?"

"Unless I dreamed it. Am I awake? Pinch me, I can't tell."

"Pinch you? Oh, I'll pinch you. I'll pinch you like a redheaded stepchild if you ever step within a hundred yards of the Atlantic Ocean in your life again. I swear to God I will."

"I'm sorry. I'm sorry." His eyes filled again, Joe, this strong, big man, suddenly like a broken music box, some child's broken little toy.

"It's okay. It's okay, Joe," I told him, forgiving on the outbreath what I'd chastised breathing in. I sat beside him and took his hands. I stroked his face. I smiled.

"It isn't, though," he said. "I'm so sorry, Day, so sorry."

"Sweetheart, Joe," I said, "there's nothing to be sorry for."

"There is," he said. "There is. I misunderstood so much. Ray's dead, and I never understood him and I never understood my father. And us . . . I misunderstood that, too, Day. I'm sorry I was so afraid and small. I'm sorry I was blind. I'm ashamed of what I said, and when I heard that song . . ." He could not go on.

"Joe, listen . . ."

"No," he said, "no, please, let me say this; let me finish. When you told me you were pregnant, I felt here it was, the proof that what I feared the most was true. I was my father, and in the process of becoming him, I'd turned you into May. But when I heard that song, I realized that child's life meant more to me than . . . I realized you'd given me a chance for life, you'd offered it with open arms, and I have no defense for what I did, except that I never expected it to come that way, life, in the form of what I feared the most. I'm so sorry, Day, so sorry, most of all for what I think I made you do. Did you?"

I closed my eyes and shook my head.

"You didn't do it? I didn't miss my chance?"

"You didn't miss it, Joe," I whispered. "Almost. I came so close. I didn't, though. Pate and her mother came and said they couldn't raise your ship . . ."

"Our boat . . ."

He couldn't help himself. It was almost funny, if it hadn't been so sad. "Whatever."

"And you didn't?"

"How could I, Joe? How could I, knowing that if you died, this child was all I'd ever have of you?" I speared him with the blues on that and offered him no succor as he bled impaled on the sword-point of truest love. Oh, yes, I loved the boy, but I drove it to the hilt and gave him no relief. It's hard work, loving them, but you have to train the ones you keep.

"How are we going to do this, Joe?" I said. "I'm starting a fellowship; I'll be doing eighty-hour weeks; we disagree on politics. I don't have the slightest idea how we're going to make it work."

"We can," he said. "We will. We'll make it all up as we go, and we'll be great. Believe it. I do. Day?" And he took my hands. "Marry me."

"I don't accept foxhole proposals," I told him, soaring, as my eyes went awash. "It's this policy I have."

Joe made an earnest blink.

"Right up there alongside not dating patients," I said, giving him another chance.

But he still didn't get it, just blinked those orphaned eyes as if I'd rescinded his voucher for the loaf.

"Don't kid around," he said with a certain dignity.

"Ahhh," I said and wiped my eyes. "You're such an easy target, though."

"I mean it, Day," said Joe. "I've never meant anything more in my whole life. I want to marry you and have this child and build a house. I want to put a full foundation under it . . ."

I laughed. "A full foundation? What, no slab?"

"No," he said. "No slab. A full cellar, with the works. We'll build it on a rock and not on sand. We'll have this baby there, a little girl, I think—don't ask me how I know."

"I dreamed of her," I whispered, happy now and joining in.

"Did you? So did I. It's been so long with us since there were any girls."

"I guess it's up to me to lift the curse."

"You're right," he said, "it is. And you'll do your fellowship and eighty-hour weeks, and I'll hold down the fort at home."

"Tell the truth now," I said. "Have you ever changed a diaper in your life?"

"Actually, no, I don't believe I have," he said, a bit deterred, but only temporarily. "But I'll learn how. I'll read every book on parenting they ever wrote. I'll take notes in my steno pad with the

Mont Blanc and I'll make to-do lists of menial domestic service. I'll leave no stone unturned, and I'll turn every stone with love."

"And you'll wipe her shitty little ass?" I said, enjoying this.

"With love and pride. I'll be the Buddha of house husbandry, and I won't enter Nirvana till every stinky diaper has reached enlightenment, along with every blade of grass I've mown."

I was a little surprised, to tell the truth, at this new side of him.

"Whatever comes," he said, "whatever it will be, I'll be there for you, Day. I'll let you do your work and I'll do mine, though, to be honest, I'm not sure what that'll be. This other thing, ethnography—it's over for me, and what comes next, I don't yet see. But I'll find it; I'm confident."

I held his face between my hands and kissed both eyes. "And maybe that's what I can give you back, the time and space to go find out."

"Thank you, Day," he said. "I think that's what I need right now. I think that's what I need the most."

And who better, then, to give it?

"Sounds like a plan," I said.

"So you'll marry me?"

"Let's get to Boston first and take some time and then decide."

"I don't need time," he said. "I've lost too much already. The decision's made for me. Do you want me to get down on my knees and beg?"

"Well," I said, "if you're really keen on it . . ."

And he did. So help me God, he did. "Ow, ow," he said, "owie," holding the bedrail as he sank like an old charwoman taking to her gams to tell the beads.

"The aching mariner," I said, gazing fondly down.

"Ha-ha," he said. "Don't make me laugh. It hurts too much." And, composing himself and taking a deep, somewhat ragged breath, like Evel Kneivel about to jump a line of twenty cars, he held my hand and asked again. "Please, marry me. Be my wife. Let me be your husband."

"We'll see," I said, and, leaning down, kissed him on the lips and then the cheek.

You have to make them sweat a little, even if you know. That's another policy I've always felt was wise and even honored once or twice, though discipline in love, as stipulated previously, was not my long suit. You don't want to make it too easy on them, though, these ambivalent professor boys, even when they've been at death's door and cracked it open and been a little way inside and come back fully chastened and reformed, ready to toe the line. But I knew my answer.

Oh, yes, indeedy, the loaf was done or done enough for me, and forty years to eat from it, forty years of Sunday mornings in the bed, our fingers smutchy with the *Times,* and soon a blue-eyed bambinette to share the space with us, a contented little sucking animal happy at her work and doing it with an unclouded, flawless sense of self-entitlement to be here in this life, seeing that alone reflected in her parents' eyes, our Welcome-to-the-World-so-Happy-You've-Arrived. And Mommy and Daddy, Joe and I, wondering and waiting with keen interest to find out who she was going to be and to help her reach that place as she supplied the clues, to help her be the one and only one she was, unrepeatable in all of time and all the worlds, the child we made by accident and kept by choice in total love.

That was my dream. I saw it in the distance coming toward us and not slow. And one day she would grow up, too, who was flesh of our flesh, bone of our bone, and pull away, as we had, into her separateness, and make us bleed and pine the way our parents bled and pined for us as she began the search we all inherit and pass on. That was the road it was our job to set her on, the same journey Joe and I were on, and one farther day, he and I would also part and one of us go on.

Considering how close I'd come to losing him, I could not forget that part. I'd found my man and the great love I'd dreamed about. I hadn't settled. Now I could. We didn't have a detailed plan; it wasn't very reasonable, but miracles so rarely are, and that's exactly what it seemed to me, a miracle, the kind that happens all around us every day. But you still have to work at them—never think you don't. You have to let your heart stay open, and if it can't, or won't, you have to open it, no matter how, no matter what. That's another rule, I think, one you violate only at the greatest peril. I learned a lot of it alone, but another part I learned from watching Joe pry his own back open with a shovel and a pick and his bleeding fingernails. It wasn't always pretty, but he'd done the job, and I have to say that, as I held him in my arms, I was proud and happy for him, proud and happy for us both.

Thirty-one

The day of the memorial service, Joe and Day spent the morning closing the house and packing up the Wagoneer, and as they worked, the fine, mild January morning slowly turned into a fine, mild January afternoon. Carrying suitcases and boxes down the steps and climbing, empty-handed, up, and down and up again, Joe recalled that other exodus, in his first world, the day Will Tilley died, when his parents packed the Cadillac, gathering what they could to take away, as the ambulance waited in the drive, the orange light turning and turning unhurriedly as dusk came on; and then they wheeled the loaded gurney down and set out homeward through the night to Ruin Creek.

And another leaving now, this, too, a repetition. *Strange,* Joe thought. Day was pregnant now as May had been. Yet his parents' love and marriage had been over. Starting on their trip, May and Jimmy had been bound and longing to be free, as he and Day, commencing theirs, were free and choosing to be bound. So different, yet lingering within the new the image of the old remained. And in the repetition of the pattern, the pattern had been changed.

While Day was at the U-Haul place, getting the tow bar for her Ghia, Joe showered and dressed, put on his blazer with gold buttons, remembering his father teaching him the four-in-hand as he retied it in the bathroom mirror now.

Standing in the door of the big room, he looked around, rememorizing what he loved and knew. Back in its accustomed place, the clamshell ashtray had been scrubbed and washed by May at Christmas. And perhaps it was May who'd taken another stab at the old sand dollar, broken for as long as Joe remembered, for he saw that it had been reglued, restored to a precarious wholeness whose fragility declared itself in the scar indelibly running through. Gazing down, Joe saw his feet stood in one of the old lay lines scuffed in the grayed floor, a track that he and Day, in following, had deepened, and now other feet to follow theirs. Last, he took a deep, long breath to try to catch the cedar smell, but this eluded him, for it is only on returning after absence that you recover this, the vapor that lingers in the bottle after the perfume is gone.

As he walked into the room, his eye lighted on a folio-sized volume on the bookcase's lowest shelf, a book he hadn't noticed in all his months down here. Kneeling, he took out Gregor Krause's photographs of Bali which once reposed in his grandparents' library in Killdeer, and, sitting at the trestle table, he flipped through it now as he'd done when he was ten years old and it first opened up that other world to him.

Page by page he went, and paused eventually on a bird's-eye view of sarong-draped revelers wending down a dusty road between a portico of royal palms. Shading themselves with paper parasols, they carried the teetering *wadah* in which the ashes of the *raja* lay, paying honor through their service and the effort of the march to their departed king.

When Day came home, she found him there, still studying this, and quietly she joined him, resting her hand on his shoulder, and he looked up and smiled.

"This is *ngirim*," he said, turning the book so she could see. "You know, it's strange. I never thought of it in quite these terms, but the Balinese never really finish burying their dead."

"No?" she said.

He shook his head. "After the first cremation, they collect the bones and bury them. Then at intervals, they dig them up, reassemble the skeletons, dress them in human clothes, take them back home to live for a few days, recremate and rebury, then a few years later dig them up all over. Even when the last bits of bone have been ground to dust in a mortar and thrown into the sea, it doesn't end. They have to make the dead new bodies out of rice or coins. The only way out for the families is to buy a special kind of holy water that's ruinously expensive. And even if you pay, you only get a twenty-five-year reprieve."

"Jeez Louise," said Day. "And I thought psychotherapy was bad."

He smiled. "I remember sitting in the window seat at Pa and Nanny's house after school one day, flipping through this page by page. It was winter, raining out. At five o'clock, May pulled up in the Country Squire and called me from the foyer, but I pretended not to hear."

"Why did you do that?"

He shrugged. "I guess I didn't want to go home." He flipped another page. "Maybe that's what Bali was for me, Day, Bali and all the rest of it . . . not wanting to go home and contriving an elaborate excuse to justify not having to."

"But here you are."

"But here am I," he said. "I guess my twenty-five-year reprieve is up, though, actually, I got twenty-eight."

"Well, if it makes you feel any better, I haven't finished burying mine either," she said. "Maybe we never do."

"That would seem to be the lesson." Joe smiled and closed the book.

"Do you want me to go with you?" she asked, as he got up.

He shook his head. "This one I have to do alone."

The Teach family plot was out at Gravesend Head. Arriving early, Joe found three or four cars pulled off on the shoulder at the end of the state road; one was Lukey Brame's. Inside, his wife and son sat out of the cold, while Lukey stood across the road, his foot propped on the low headwall as he stared across the flat sheet of Croatan Sound.

As Joe came up beside him, Lukey turned. "Hey, Joe."

Joe briefly touched his shoulder. "How are you?"

Lukey held up a newspaper. "See this?" The morning's *Virginian-Pilot* was quarter-folded in his left hand.

WATT DEEP-6S JETTY PLAN

Comparing the Oregon Inlet Stabilization Project to Seward's Folly, Secretary of the Interior, James Watt, in a long-expected move . . .

Joe read no more. They exchanged a look, and in each man's eyes there was still a little of ocean and the lost, wild night. Neither said a word.

Joe repeated his question. "You all right?"

Lukey nodded. "You?"

Out toward the horizon, the low scrawl of the mainland, dusk was creeping up the blue bowl of the sky, while overhead it was still afternoon, just one shade cooler blue with the wet twinkling of the evening star. A mottled band of cirrus clouds white as lamb's wool receded overhead, giving the sky infinite depth.

"Dark soon," said Brame.

A fragment of an old weather jingle teased through Joe's mind, something his Pa had taught him once—mares' tails and mackerel skies . . . That was all he could recall.

"Those clouds," he said. "Tell anything from them?"

Lukey deliberated a while. "Just clouds," he said, delivering his verdict. He looked at Joe. "Coming?"

"I'll be along."

Standing there, Joe heard the bell buoy clanging in the distance, mild as a sheep bell today in the light air, and thought of Ray, what he'd said, how small the channel really is, how much to either side. Joe had heard so many mixed and covert messages in this, but now he understood them to be his, never Ray's. Just clouds. And underneath his small fear and a revulsion smaller still he understood that what Ray had said was true, that intimacy is a door you either open or leave closed, and what matters is the opening, not to whom. Standing on the headwall, gazing out across the sound with chastened heart, Joe saw through Ray's eyes, which were closed, and, seeing, grieved.

Strung between two posts, a strand of rusty tow wire with a red-and-yellow buoy marked the path and warned off parkers tempted late at night. Stepping over it, Joe followed what was little more than a deer track into low scrub woods and came out in a clearing nestled in a hollow in the dunes. There, the cemetery was laid out around a gnarled, lichen-spotted live-oak tree. Closest to the center, the oldest headstones were black with age, no longer legible. The graves rayed out concentrically, like ripples spreading out through time.

In the outmost tier, Joe found the newly mounded grave and

Ray's coffin poised on straps for lowering—the Excelsior, bronze with nickel trim. He recognized it from Midgett's picture window. Inez Bristow had spared no expense for her only child, whose body was recovered in Rodanthe the day after the wreck, carried so far southward on the longshore drift. For Cully Teach, still tumbling somewhere undersea along the hundred-fathom edge, there was no grave, yet each man had a stone. Joe looked down into the pit, where he caught the glint of water, a sheared tangle of thick roots.

On the marker, a rose-tinted granite slab, in an inset panel provided by the funeral home, was a photograph of Ray as a young boy, no more than twelve or thirteen, perhaps the way Inez preferred to remember him. He had shorter, neater hair, falling in a sweep across his forehead, and seemed far less layered and complex, but that teasing risibility was evident in his expression even then; already he looked confident and dangerous. The ocean wind had begun to glaze the plastic sheath with salt, and behind it, the Cheshire cat was vanishing. Kneeling, Joe righted a toppled vase of purple immortelle, then stood and saw Jubal in a wheelchair near the blasted oak, a blanket in his lap, and a reposed expression on his face, turned up to catch a few last rays of sun.

"Captain."

Jubal studied Joe without a smile. "Son."

"How's the leg?"

The captain frowned at the blanket in his lap. "I won't be running races no toime soon, I reckon, but they didn't cut it off. I guess it could be worst."

"Yes, sir," Joe said. "I'm sure it could. I don't think any of us would be here if it weren't for you."

"I don't know," he said doubtfully, with that fierce look. "Cully and Ray ain't here no matter what."

Joe said nothing.

"Lukey told me what you done for Ray."

"It didn't do him any good," Joe said. "He ended saving me."

"You done all roight, Joe. I wish to God it never happened, but all you boys done foine out there."

Joe felt his face flush, touched by this rough compliment as no professor's words had ever touched him.

"I should probably say goodbye," he said. "I'm headed out tonight."

The captain took Joe's offered hand and shook with that soft grip Joe still found surprising, another tribal custom that reminded him that this was not his home.

"Good luck to you, son. You git back this way, come see us if you got the toime."

"Yes, sir, I will."

The crowd had gathered, the immediate family last to come, Inez Bristow on John Calvin's arm, her eyes wet and her face as hard as stone. Behind, Mikey Teach, Cully's twelve-year-old son, brought his tearful mother.

"Brothers and sisters," John Calvin said, looking haggard, "let's gather in and make a circle. I'd loike us to all join hands and bow our heads and just be quiet a couple minutes. Then anybody wants to testifoy about these men, they can."

When the rustling of clothes stopped, Joe became aware of the soft clamor of the waves from out across the dunes. On the far side of the circle Lukey and his wife stood next to Pate and James, James's arm around Pate's shoulder, her head bowed over her clasped hands. They looked, in a way, like May and Jimmy on the chapel steps in State Line, and Joe wondered once again if that was all he'd ever seen, a glimpse as in a magic mirror, whose silvered surface reflected back not Pate and James, but something in his past. That, too, just clouds, and Joe, as they blew by, had gazed and made the pictures up and only seen himself. Yet some force in this world had put him on the path to find just that, and deep inside it came to Joe that this was what he must do now, learn to listen and obey that force, which is not selfish work, but a selfless calling to the self from some place deep and far beyond.

After a moment, Dolph stepped forward with the morning paper, red-faced and furious, his cheeks streaked with tears of loss and bitter rage. "Did y'oll see this?" He slapped the paper against his thigh. "Did you? How many have to doie down here? I want to know. Cully's gone and Ray. How many? I'm going to see this man. I'm gitting in my truck roight now. I'm droiving to Washington, D.C., and if Watt won't see me, by God, I'll knock the door down! Damn James Watt and Ronald Reagan, too—to hell with 'em and God almoighty, too! I mean it! You think I don't? Don't put your hand own me!" He turned on J.C. in a fury when his older brother tried to take his arm and gently lead him away. It was only when

Maude touched her youngest's shoulder that Dolph desisted and, embracing his mother, wept bitterly into her neck. Maude, her old eyes haunted with experience and loss, patted his thick shoulder, and said, "There, there," loving what was left.

James Burrus followed, awkward, cowed and manful, and remembered Cully, his captain. When it came to Ray, there was a shuffling, embarrassed silence that stabbed Joe, though he sensed it came not from meanness or unwillingness, but from confoundment, and, glancing at Inez, hurt and dignified, he cleared his throat and stepped forward.

"I'll say something, Reverend, if I may."

"Go own, son," John Calvin said, "I know you boys was friends."

The pronouncement seared without intent, and Joe, feeling naked and exposed, bowed his head and searched to find what he would say. "I think Ray was my friend," he said after a moment. "I think Ray was a better friend to me than I was to him. I'm not sure I understood him. He was a generous person. He was generous to me when I came here almost a year ago, knowing no one. I mistook that generosity. I think Ray was free inside himself, and large, and that frightened other people—it frightened me. I think he was alone and reached out. When he reached out to me, I didn't know what he wanted, but it was really very simple, the same thing everybody wants—to be seen for who he was and accepted, which was all I wanted, too. It makes me sad that I might have had that with Ray and been a better friend to him, but I was too afraid to ask. Having known him, I intend to be less afraid from now on. The truth is, when I came here last spring, I thought I'd come to study something, but it turned out that I came here to be taught, and Ray Bristow taught me more than anyone. He taught me that belief requires more strength of character than doubt. I thought it was the other way around. The last thing I want to say is this. When we were at the Inlet and we had to swim, I thought I was risking my life to help Ray get ashore. I tied the line around our waists, and it was by that line that Ray pulled me ashore, and the truth is, if I hadn't known Ray Bristow, I would have never found the strength to tie that knot. I wish I'd been a better friend; I won't forget him."

John Calvin met his eye and nodded, and Joe, flushing violently, exposed and unashamed in passion, stepped back, glancing as he did at Inez Bristow, who did not return his look. Suffering, he bowed his head.

"After I left your house last noight, Inez," John Calvin said, "I was walking home, asking myself what I was going to say to y'oll out here today, how I was going to look you in the eye, sister, and you, Lucy, and what comfort I could offer you, and what answer I was going to give to Mikey and his little sister Tina here when they asked me why. Over the years, I've had this sad duty more toimes than I loike to think own, and many's the toime I've laid awake all noight, tossing and fretting in the bed, troying to answer it. This toime was different. Last noight it come to me roight off. Mikey, you come here, and Tina, too."

Dropping on one knee, he put his arms around the childrens' waists as they stepped forward. "This is what I want to tell you and your mama. When the boat foundered, your daddy troied to cut the loine so these other men who risked their loives to help him could go own. If you don't know who Cully was, or if in years to come you're scared you moight forget him, you remember that and he'll come back to you." He kissed their heads and gently shoved them toward their mother and stood up.

"And Inez, all of you, Ray pulled Joe ashore and, thinking two more of his shipmates were in the water, went back to troy to save them. Both these men, whatever faults they had, in the hour of their death took no thought for their own loives or safety, and they perished for the sake of others as Jesus Chroist our Lord and Savior gave His loife and precious blood upon the cross. Ray and Cully doied for what this circle means. Now it's broken here"—he separated Lucy Teach's hand from Dolph's—"and here between Inez and me. Let's bow our heads and feel our loss, the loss of two brave men—husband, father, brother, uncle, son or friend, whoever they were to you. And then remembering them and thinking own the blessed day when Jesus Christ shall come to judge in glory, when it's wrote the tomb shall open and the sea give up her dead, let us go forward from this hour with these men and their example in our heart. Now let's bow our heads and pray and draw the circle toight and close it up again."

When Joe had made his earnest prayer—to what, he still didn't know, but something, of that he felt sure—he looked up as the bell tolled softly off the point. Behind John Calvin and Inez stood Maude, their mother, and near her Captain Ernal, whose lined Apache face expressed in prayer a rare humility and repose. Gazing at the two of them, the oldest there, Joe thought how beautiful and terrible their faces were, weathered almost out of resemblance to human flesh, like geologic chronicles, mute but eloquent. What surprised him as he made his final observation was how soft they seemed in the mild air, their lack of bitterness as they stood at the end of things, facing toward the dark, where Ray and Cully were.

Around them, he could see the legends on the stones—OUR DEAR MOTHER . . . BELOVED HUSBAND . . . BELOVED WIFE . . . NOT LONG WITH US . . . GONE ON AHEAD. Reading, he recalled the Tilley homeplace outside Killdeer, where his Pa's parents had been buried, and theirs before them. How far back it went, he didn't know. But once upon a time his own people had had a place like this, and he realized, with a pang, that he did not know where it was. He'd come here as a student, to observe these people, and did not know his own. And having made his final observation, he posed his final question: What sort of anthropology addresses this?

Before he left, he shook the reverend's hand and said goodbye, and J.C. said, "When it's done now, make sure you send that book, hear? And this toime I'll troy to read it, if it ain't too far above my head or don't put me to sleep."

Joe smiled and took this sportingly, as it was meant.

"Who knows," J.C. went on, "it may help spread the good word and bring another few acrost to the good team. I guess we'll see."

"Yes, sir," said Joe, who swallowed but did not wince. "I guess we will."

Last of all, he stood in line to offer his condolence to the grieving mother. Allowing him her hand, Inez appraised Joe with those same matched pinpoints of surmise, as cold as January stars, giving him exactly what she'd given him the day Ray introduced them at the Lighthouse: absolutely nothing. Yet Joe, if nothing else, understood those stars a little more and what had laid this glittering, hard frost across the mother's heart.

"I'm sorry for your loss, Mrs. Bristow," he said, his face clear and earnest, and, knowing it was time to leave, he turned and walked back down the path he'd traveled in, and left them what was never his.

As the Wagoneer rocked over the segmented roadbed of the bridge for the last time, Reed Madden's home-mixed tape played through its constant loop and brought the question back:

Will the circle be unbroken?

Unbidden now, the answer came to Joe: *Again.* Will what was once unbroken be again?

On the deck now, in a haunted Mississippi voice shot through with loss and strength and sadness, Roebuck Staples sang his hopeful answer, while, behind him, Pervis, Mavis and Cleotha supplied the sweet, high harmony.

By and by, Lord, by and by . . .

ACKNOWLEDGMENTS

The author wishes to thank the following people, who supplied valuable assistance to him in the writing of this book: Dr. Bernie Baker, Steve Brumfield, Dr. Charlie Davidson, Wynn Dough, Roy Enoksen, David Gernert, John Gilbert, Jr., R. Wayne Gray, John Hopkins, Lynn Huntington-Meath, Meghan Huntington-Meath, Tom Hutton, Larry Kessenich, Ned Leavitt, Randy Lombardo, Margaret Long, David Loomis, Phil Moore, Kate Schwob, Cynthia Stuart, Binky Urban, Laurie Wolff, Matthew Wolff, Rosemary Wyche and John Zollicoffer.

Particular thanks are due to Catherine Courtney; to the Reverend David Daniels and the congregation of the Outer Banks Assembly of God; to Professor James L. Peacock, of the University of North Carolina at Chapel Hill, for his tireless and generous assistance; to Billy Carl and Captain Moon Tillett, of the Moon Tillett Fish Company in Wanchese, North Carolina; and to Captain Craig Tillett and the crew of the *Linda Gayle*—Erskine (Boss Hog) Mackey, Bobby (Pop) Barber and James Inness of Poquoson—who took a total stranger fishing on the basis of a fifteen-minute conversation, worked him like a dog and fed him like a king; and to the memory of Early (Uncle John) Gallup, captain of the *Ironsides*, who introduced a green college boy to the rough charms of commercial fishing over twenty years ago.

Lastly, to Steve Rubin and Gerry Howard at Doubleday, who

threw me a timely line to haul myself ashore; to my editorial conscience and nemesis, Frances (Pixie) Apt, who is to copy editors as
Tenzing is to sherpas, Everest to peaks; and to my father, for his
large-hearted co-conspiracy; most of all, as ever, to Stacy, for her
patience and her faith.